PRAISE FOR SAUD ALSANOUSI

The Bamboo Stalk
(translated by Jonathan Wright)

"Absorbing."

—*New Yorker*

"A page-turner with depth."

—*Guardian*

"Alsanousi is a voice of conscience."

—*Independent*

"A force to be reckoned with."

—*Arab Times*

"Ambitious, cultivated and brave."

—*Financial Times*

Mama Hissa's Mice
(translated by Sawad Hussain)

"Imagine the dreadful cultural holocaust which would ensue, were the Mongol ruler Hulagu Khan to step out of the pages of history and set fire to the entire corpus of Kuwaiti fiction. If I were asked to select one book to be saved from destruction—just one book to pass on to future generations—I would choose *Mama Hissa's Mice*."

—Bothayna al-Essa, *Al Sada Magazine*

"I consider that *Mama Hissa's Mice* is no less valuable and significant than *The Bamboo Stalk*, which won the so-called Arabic Booker prize. Indeed, it may be intellectually and artistically deeper. It is a multi-layered, richly allusive novel."

—Mahmoud Abdel Shakour, *El Tahrir*

"With daring frankness and clarity, *Mama Hissa's Mice* reveals the full extent of the crisis of identity in Kuwait and in many Arab countries. It tackles the subject of this impending danger head-on, not hiding its head in the sand."

—Ali Kadhim Dawood, *Al-Quds*

"Perhaps if a dim censor read *Mama Hissa's Mice*, he would catch an early glimpse of what Alsanousi has seen with the clarity of the legendary seer Zarqa' al-Yamama."

—Nedal Mamdouh Hassan, Kotob Wa Kotab

"The novel is a scream of protest to the entire world, that there is no benefit to humanity and no way of saving it unless we are united."

—Ibrahem Adel Zeid, Altagreer

MAMA HISSA'S MICE

ALSO BY SAUD ALSANOUSI

The Bamboo Stalk

MAMA HISSA'S MICE

A Novel

SAUD ALSANOUSI
Translated by SAWAD HUSSAIN

amazon crossing

Text copyright © 2015 by Saud Alsanousi
Translation copyright © 2019 by Sawad Hussain

Previously published as فئران أمي حِصّة by ASP/Difaf in Kuwait in 2015. Translated from Arabic by Sawad Hussain with edits by Mona Kareem. First published in English by AmazonCrossing in 2019.

Published by AmazonCrossing, Seattle

www.apub.com

Amazon, the Amazon logo, and AmazonCrossing are trademarks of Amazon.com, Inc., or its affiliates.

ISBN-13: 9781542042178 (hardcover)
ISBN-10: 1542042178 (hardcover)
ISBN-13: 9781542042161 (paperback)
ISBN-10: 154204216X (paperback)

Cover design by Philip Pascuzzo
Interior illustrations by Meshail Al Faisal

Printed in the United States of America
First edition

MAMA HISSA'S MICE

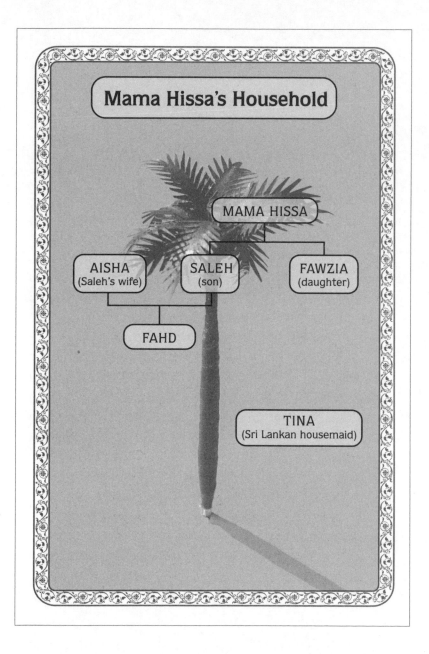

Mama Hissa's Household

MAMA HISSA

AISHA
(Saleh's wife)

SALEH
(son)

FAWZIA
(daughter)

FAHD

TINA
(Sri Lankan housemaid)

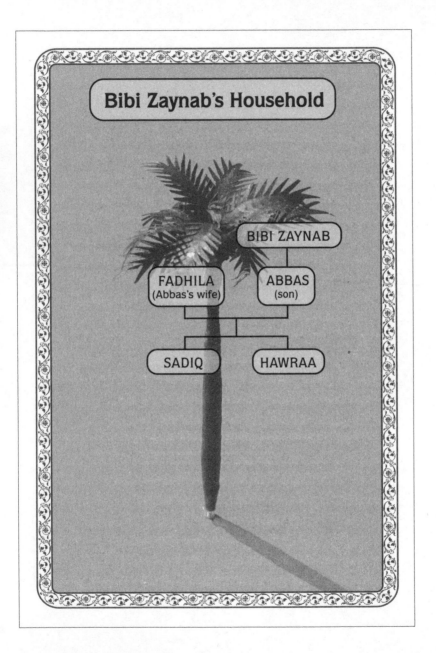

Katkout's Household

KATKOUT'S MOTHER
(Ms. Principal)

KATKOUT'S FATHER

KATKOUT

PROLOGUE

If my mother began her sentence with "By God," that meant it was a divine decree. I was seven years old when Dad gifted me my first bike for good grades. Mom forbid me from riding it in our courtyard during the afternoon. She was worried about the high temperature, which sometimes soared to over 120 degrees. That's what she used to say anyway.

Mom had changed. Dad used to lightheartedly describe her as "the principal at school and at home." But she had become anxious, trembling whenever the wind beat against the courtyard's iron door, its echo sailing down the street. She would yelp if one of the neighborhood boys set off firecrackers to celebrate a soccer victory, or for some other reason, or for no reason at all. She'd be glued to the TV for hours, nervously anticipating what the news would bring. In the course of one day alone, she would call Dad ten times. She would bite her fingernails, mumble, wipe away her tears when no one was looking. This is what my mom was like after the 1985 café bombings, one month before I got that bike. Our elderly neighbor had been among the victims.

"He left his house and never came back," Mom said. She bawled over him for a week. "The poor guy's dead."

That's how Mama Hissa became a widow.

After my father had given me the bike, I would wait for my parents to wake up from their afternoon nap so I could get the house key from

them and go outside for a ride. One afternoon I knocked on their shut
door.

"What?" Mom barked after my repeated knocking.

"When can I ride my bike?"

"When the sun sets," said her voice, heavy, laced with sleep.

I brought my lips closer to the keyhole. I promised her I wouldn't
ride it beyond the courtyard wall. She didn't answer. I went back to my
room and looked out the window at the reason for my house arrest.
The sun was always relentless, beating down on us whenever I wanted
to go out. I looked at its bright face with half-slit eyes—it didn't budge!
I knew the sun was just an excuse, and that Mom was scared about me
going outside while she slept—that I would fall prey to an accident like
our neighbor, never to return, even though the bombed-out café was
far away, toward the sea; even though trying to ride there on my bike
would be a fool's errand.

I turned my back to the window. I sat on the floor, playing with
VHS cases. Nothing held my interest, not the cartoon movies or the
children's series I knew by heart. I ignored Mickey Mouse on the small
TV screen and built towers out of the videotape cases, with tunnels
running in between them. I grabbed my Hulk Hogan action figure and
tucked him inside the makeshift city before swiftly crashing it down on
his head. Whenever I was bored or upset, I built cities simply to knock
them down on the unsuspecting heads of my action figures and plastic
animals. Minutes crawled by like hours. I went back to staring out the
window. Everything was moving in the sky: tufts of clouds, starlings,
pigeons, the tail of the blue kite caught in the neighbor's thorny tree.
But the sun stood still. In our neighbor's yard, I caught sight of Fahd.
He was holding a tennis-sized ball, bent over collecting stones—perhaps preparing for a game of *anbar* with the other kids on our street. In
another part of the courtyard, Sadiq cracked an egg on the metal sewer
cover, watching it slowly fry, sizzling on the sunbaked surface.

I left my room and went back toward my parents' room. I knocked on the door again.

"Hey, Mooom! When can I ride my bike?"

"Uff!" was her muffled response.

I pressed my ear to the door. Her voice slipped through the wood, surging with the hum of the General Electric air conditioner, as if she were stuffed inside a seashell.

"You better watch yourself if you ask me about that bike while I'm sleeping," she threatened. "By God who raised the heavens, if you ask me one more time, you'll never ride it again! Wait till the sun sets!"

Some minutes passed. I stood frozen in front of the door. Gripped with fear, I nearly swallowed my next question. I knew her only too well. When she swore by God, that was it: He'd signed and sealed it, and for her, there was no coming back from that—ever.

But my patience with that unblinking sun had worn thin. I went right back to knocking.

"Now what?" she shouted.

I gulped. "Mom?" I paused a moment. "When does the sun go down?"

My dad's laughter rumbled from behind the door. I heard their bed creaking.

"No chance of sleep. Nope, no sleeping here," I heard her mumble, exasperated.

She yanked open the door and looked at me, her eyes swollen; a tight smile played across her lips in spite of herself. "You sure *are* good at asking questions. Here."

She held out her palm. On it sat the key.

THE FIRST MOUSE: SPARK

Don't make sparks
Don't divulge secrets
For you'll stir up endless storms.
Serenity is in your hands
And glory is yours.
Wisdom is found in silence
And our hope, sought after . . . upon death!

—Ahmad Meshari Al Adwani

Noon

Present Day

I regain consciousness. Sun rays, directly above me, morph into a red infinity behind my shut eyelids. Liquid oozes from where my tousled hair is parted into a pool at the back of my head. I slowly open my eyes, only to tightly close them again to block out the piercing sun. Gravel jabs my back. My throat and lips are bone-dry, and there is a taste of dirt in my mouth. Something returns me to a final scene, a moment suspended between dream and reality. Pain throbs above my left eyebrow. I dab at the pool beneath my head with my fingertips. "Blood?" I bring my palm to my face, casting a shadow against the sun. Carefully, I open my eyes to inspect the color of the liquid on my fingertips, hoping that it's something other than red. I sigh with relief. "Sweat." I shut my eyes again.

The numbness in my shoulder and the tingling in my back speak to just how long I've been here like this. I stretch my arm to grope for the right pocket of my *dishdasha*. My phone and an empty pack of cigarettes. I pat down the left pocket. Relief floods me when I feel my car keys. "The chest has no key"—I hear that song echoing in our childish voices. What reminded me of it?

I struggle to stand, so instead I sit up straight. I nearly swallow something. A pebble, I think. I spit out brown blood, like the color of the betel-nut juice that stained the spit of the Indians who had once lived in our country. I cough. A tooth caught in my throat shoots out. The kids' voices in my head fade in and out. "The key's with the blacksmith."

My legs are outstretched, unmoving, as if they belong to someone else. My dishdasha is bunched above my knees. I look at my feet, one with a sandal, the other without. The image of my lost sandal, flipped over—one of the last things I can remember—is seared in my mind. I draw in a deep breath. Putrid air fills my lungs. I let out a long moan. I shake my head. I survey the dirt square around me to see if my memory still serves me well. I find myself opposite Gamal Abdel Nasser Park. What's left of the McDonald's is in front of me. Well then, I'm in familiar territory, in Rawda. I nod my head, assured of this. The singing voices return. "And the blacksmith wants money."

My car is over there, a pile of scrap on wheels. I barely recognize its new shape, in a spot not too far from Fahd's car, although I can't find Sadiq's. People are going about their business without a care for me, despite the hours that I've been splayed out unconscious on the ground. I vividly remember an old custom that no longer exists—people used to huddle around victims of fights or accidents, spurred on by their curiosity, wanting to help or take photos with their phones. But people don't behave as they used to; with things as they are now, no one wants to get caught up in any incident. "The cowards stay safe," Mom would always say. As for Mama Hissa, she hated cowards. The first woman survived. The second didn't.

I take a look at the state I'm in; afraid, people are looking straight ahead, their heads unturning. Even so, despite their fear, no one in this country is safe. With my hand pushing against the dusty ground, I raise my body up. Once upright, I clap my hands to clean them before swiping my butt to remove the gray dust from my clothes. I squeeze my knee to numb the pain. I hobble toward my car. There's an unbearable pain in my left leg. The children keep singing in my head. "And the money's with the bride."

Kuwait, the so-called Bride of the Gulf. I look around. Nothing resembling a bride here. I'm running away from this old moniker. I'm running away from everything. I look again at my car. "And the bride wants a family." Maybe Fuada's Kids would count, the group I started with my friends. I stop. I wrestle my foot free from its sandal and keep on hobbling. I open the car door. Sparkling glass shards—the remains of my windshield—cover the seat, reflecting the sun. I lurch over to the trunk and open it. I look for something. Anything. Empty except for the spare tire. After prying off the thick leather cover for the spare, I return to the driver's seat. Carefully, I remove the large pieces of glass and spread the leather cover over the remaining shards before sitting down. The windshield is still in one piece, but I can't see through the spiderweb of cracks.

I get out. I look for a rock to knock out the glass. In this country, at this point in time, rocks are the easiest things to find. All that's left after the destruction are rocks that aren't even fit for construction. Big ones and small ones like those we used to collect as kids to play anbar. Or the ones we carefully selected to be the heads of Jews when we'd pretend to be Palestinian children throwing stones; when all Jews, according to Mama Hissa, were Israeli; when according to everyone, Israel was our shared object of hatred.

"And the family wants milk . . . and the cows have the milk." An image forms of Kuwait: a cow in a bridal veil, her udders dry. It seems that the knock to my head is partly to blame for these visions and voices. I bend over. I grab a suitably sized rock from the ashen soil. With both hands I heft it up and smash it down onto the windshield . . . again . . . and again.

"That'll do," I say after the job is done.

Back in the driver's seat, I find windshield fragments strewn atop the leather tire cover. This isn't any better than when the seat was completely covered in glass. Frustration flares up, yet a cackle of laughter escapes at the same time. Gently, I pull off the cover and shake it out. I lay it back on the seat before taking my place behind the wheel and looking at the windshield-free view. There's no escaping this stench, is there? I feel around for my phone in my pocket. Dozens of missed calls and messages from friends. From my parents in London. From strangers asking about our radio broadcast and why one nationalistic song is looping instead of our usual daily show. A text message from my publisher in Beirut: "We're done with the cover design for Inheritance of Fire. You'll need to get rid of four chapters. It's for your own good, and in our best interest, too. I'll wait for your approval before I send it to print." Some of us so afraid of the censors have become censors in our own right. I disregard the text, the calls, myself. I turn a blind eye to everything.

I call Sadiq. "The number you have dialed is not available." I try Fahd. "I'm not here at the moment. Please leave a message." His recorded voice is followed by a clip from an Abdulkareem Abdulqader song: "Between you and me a whole world, long and dark as the night. No longer reminded of where we met, there you go with oblivion and here I go with Canopus, no longer a day left for you in my heart." Every time he uses an Abdulkareem Abdulqader song as part of his voice-mail greeting, I can detect his mood and how things are going with his wife. This song transports me to our old street, to when his grandmother was still alive and to her folktales about the Canopus star. Back to a time when my eyes were transfixed on the faraway, silent sky teeming with secrets, a hideaway for the answers to my Gordian questions. A beep cuts through the song. I leave my message in a voice that I wouldn't know as mine if it hadn't come out of my throat.

"Hi, Fahd . . . please call me."

I make a third call.

"Hey, Ayub, any news of Sadiq or Fahd?"

He answers my question with one of his own, asking about what happened.

"Nothing. I'll speak to you later," I respond.

I find hope in the answer to my fourth call: "Dhari . . ."

"Where are you?" he asks before I can do the same. "Your mom called from London, asking about you. Where are Fahd and Sadiq? They've been MIA since morning!"

"I don't know where they are," I answer, my mouth dry and tongue bitter.

He sighs deeply before reassuring me with his usual refrain: "God will bring the rain. He'll take care of it."

This triggers the lyrics in my head: "And the cows want grass . . . and the grass wants rain." I tilt my head up to the sky, which is empty except for the sun and the corpse-catcher that hovers over me, a grim omen of looming death that seems to follow me more and more, always in my mind's eye. The corpse-catcher spreads out its wings, circling high above, looking for reasons to land on the ground. Its aquiline body is topped by an owl-like head—both crow-black—ready to extract life from the death of others. I look around. People here are like horses with blinders on, pulling carriages. Or cows being driven through irrigation ditches, their peripheral vision blocked. They only look straight ahead. I gun the engine. The radio suddenly roars to life. "God is great! God is great! You're listening to the Lions of Truth," a rugged voice booms, enunciating every letter as if delivering a sermon. My chest tightens. I look at the small digital display on the car radio. The station's frequency reminds me of the songs and different programs it used to play before it transformed into this. I twist the dial. The interrupted whispers of the transmissions, cut off by my flicking through frequencies, become the voices of a large audience intoning, "No way will we be humiliated. No way!"

"Argh!" I thump the radio with my fist and silence it. I stretch out my fingers, failing to shake off the pain. I apply pressure and draw in a deep breath. I turn the radio on again, searching for a station that broadcasts in a low voice, the one based out of the Fuada's Kids headquarters in Jabriya. My palms tremble like those of an addict looking for his next fix. The static from the radio makes me more irritable. Finally, I land on a station that's broadcasting. Despite the garbled noise, my ears prick up at the sound of familiar music. Holding my breath, I close my eyes. The sound becomes clearer. An old song comes to the fore: "This Country Demands Glory." I nod my head slowly, grief-stricken. I let out a long sigh and wearily sing along with the voice on the radio, lamenting how the country races against time. I rest my head on the steering wheel and burst into bitter sobs. And the children's voices keep chiming in my head: "And rain comes from God!"

***

I drive my car, my eyes fixed on what's in front of me, staring straight ahead—like those around me—not just out of fear but also because there's nothing around worthy of our attention. Ubiquitous gray soil has changed the country into a giant ashtray. Smoke rises from fires. I see rubble. Stray dogs. Black feathers. Serpentine lines of asylum seekers in front of the European Commission branch in Rawda. Sandbag barriers border both sides of Damascus Street, accentuated by filth that has piled up since the street cleaners fled the country. It's as if an enormous fist has plowed into Kuwait, leaving it in ruins. I ward off all these images by turning away from them. But my God, the stench! A text message from my mom jolts me back to reality. "Dad and I are worried sick about you. Please call." I leave my phone on the passenger seat. I take the Fourth Ring Road at the roundabout. Rawda is on my left. On the sidewalk between the two streets are withered, leafless buttonwood trees. I take a right toward the Surra area. My heart constricts. Mom's words come back to me: "By God who raised the heavens—you won't go back to Surra as long as I'm here!" Except she isn't.

How time has flown, Surra! You've become a ghost town. With its shattered windows, the deserted McDonald's to my right resembles its brother in Rawda. To my left is a house that was a set for Hayat Al Fahad and Suad Abdullah's popular TV series *Rest in Peace, World*. How can this area stir up such memories even though nothing looks at all like it used to? The old marble monument on the right brings me to a halt. It's close to the now-neglected local pizzeria that fell into the hands of the Pizza Hut conglomerate. The black lettering on the monument has faded, obliterated by the sun. Maybe out of protest, maybe out of pity. Or maybe out of fear that the words would live on in what is now a squalid place. A memory sparks in the dark recesses of my forgetful mind. I retrieve the words that had been inscribed on the polished surface: "O God, have mercy on the martyrs: Jasim Mohammed Al Mutawwa and Abdellatif Abdullah Al Munir." If they had known thirty years ago how things would end up, would they still have sacrificed their lives for our sake? I push away the intricacies of a bygone era; otherwise, it'll swallow me whole, isolating me from everything beyond it. A window to my yesterday cracks open and shows me the child I once was. I feel for that kid, how he was then and how he is now. My eyes fall on a young boy in a threadbare dishdasha with a carelessly wrapped *ghutra* around his head, seated on a chair next to the marble memorial. Spread out on the ground in front of him is a cloth covered with merchandise, like that of the Yemeni vendors of yesteryear. I roll down my passenger-side window. I wave him over with my empty cigarette box. He bounds over to me, carrying different brands. I choose one.

"Eight dollars."

I hand him 400 dinars.

"You don't have dollars?" he asks, irritated.

I shake my head, looking at my now-seemingly-good-for-nothing dinars.

"The dinar isn't worth much anymore."

He takes the money, counting it silently.

I keep driving, passing the roundabout at the junction. On the right is Sabah Al Salim High School, my alma mater. I was proud to be a student there, the first curriculum-based high school in Kuwait. We were the ones racking up excellence points for our school district with our high grades. Here in Surra was the first high school with a college-style curriculum. Here in Surra was the first supermarket to have a parking lot on the roof. Here in Surra was the first pedestrian walkway for those fitness-driven walkers, and the first street ending in a bridge linking our neighborhood to the next one. I look at my high school now; my memory scoffs at its now-unrecognizable shell.

I don't know who you are anymore.

I'm Jaber Al Mubarak High School.

I don't ask how it has become that, why, or when.

I go past my high school, but the memories don't leave me alone. At one of the bends in the road, in Block 3 where I used to live, is a middle school that used to be called Al Najah. Like everything else in this area, the name of my middle school was changed. Its new name, , is emblazoned on the signboard towering above the fence. I joined the middle school's ranks in 1987, thirty-three years ago. I stop the car in front of the school. Why, I don't know. This is where it all happened. With no windshield in front of me, the empty frame seems to hold a screen where scenes from times past are replayed. There, next to the building that houses a generator, I lost a tooth and some buttons from my white school shirt in my first school brawl. I run my finger over my top teeth, counting them. There's a new gap after today's events. I scrutinize the generator building. The vulgar words and crude drawings that I became familiar with as a student are now the residue of letters and words, an *H* and an *F*, masked under neutral-colored spray paint. I manage to make out the beginnings of a

war of words etched into the building's facade in turns by Sunni and
Shia extremists:

AISHA, MOTHER OF THE BELIEVERS,
DESPITE WHAT THE HATERS SAY

DAMN THOSE WHO GO AGAINST THE
PROPHET'S HOUSEHOLD

DEATH TO THOSE WHO REFUSE TO
ACCEPT THE PROPHET'S COMPANIONS

DIE YOU WAHHABIS AND MAGIANS

I can't make out the other words. Scattered all over the generator
building's walls are images of crossed-out mice and warnings that have
proliferated since we started our group:

THE MICE ARE COMING . . . PROTECT
YOURSELVES FROM THE PLAGUE!

Fuada's Kids had done the tagging.

How can simply passing by a place from our history resurrect the
memories buried deep within us? My sense of time is now warped. One
day, during the morning lineup, we were in the school courtyard, shivering from the cold despite our dark-blue coats. Our voices thickened
in unison as we sung to the flag like every other day, "Long live Kuwait.
Long live the emir." Something different happened that morning. A
boy who towered over Sadiq jeered at him as we chanted: "Long live
the Arab nations."

"You guys are *Ajam*!" he said. "Are you even Arab?" he challenged
Sadiq. I didn't understand what he meant. We repeated the chants

together: Fahd, Sadiq, and I, along with our classmates, who included Awad the Yemeni, Abdl Fadhil the Sudanese, Hatim the Egyptian, and Samir and Hazim the Palestinians. I only remember Sadiq's silence and his ears reddening. After the final bell rang, I had my first school fight close to part of the school wall I see right now. It was the winter of 1988, and it was a Tuesday I'll never forget. I heard someone yelling to someone else, "The zoo is in Umairiya, you animal!" Hearing this as I passed the school gate, I turned to the source of the voice. The strapping boy who had jeered at Sadiq that morning was yelling at him again, and Sadiq remained tight-lipped, as he usually did when he was agitated. His red ears betrayed his ruffled inner state. Two other boys had grabbed Fahd, preventing him from helping Sadiq after his tormentor threw him on the ground. Seeing Sadiq being kicked around, I couldn't hold back. I wavered at first, but the sight of blood on Sadiq's shirt drove me to do something. Anything! I shoved my hesitation aside. I charged toward them, fist raised high. I flinched momentarily before bringing it down on my target. I flung my body on the ground across Sadiq's. I shielded him with my arms. I put myself between the kicks and his body. Instead of him, I bore the brunt of one kick after another. I lost my tooth and blacked out.

A day later, I was in the Egyptian counselor's office—at a time when non-Kuwaitis had a place in this country. The only foreigners here now are the blue-helmeted UN Peacekeeping forces stationed around the oil wells and some conflict zones. There are also the Peninsula Shield Forces—drawn from those countries that haven't yet seceded from the Gulf Cooperation Council—that came to settle the conflict between the two warring factions, as well as the extremist groups that arrived from outside after we opened our doors to them. Sadiq's tormentor—let's call him Hercules—gave the excuse that Sadiq had provoked him first by saying, "You don't belong in school. You belong in Umairiya, in a zoo!"

"And that's why you broke his arm and knocked out his friend's tooth?" the school counselor asked incredulously.

Hercules stayed silent.

"Because of the *zoo*?" asked the counselor in a raised voice that scarcely masked his disapproval.

"No," Hercules responded, head bowed.

The counselor looked at him, urging him to go on.

"Mr. Desouky, the zoo is in *Omariya*." Hercules stressed that the name was not how *they* were mockingly pronouncing it—Umairiya.

"Who are *they*?"

The boy didn't answer. Mr. Desouky's voice boomed in Hercules's face as he interrogated him on whether he lived in Omariya or Umairiya, or whatever it was called. The boy shook his head. The counselor's thick lips gaped in surprise. "So, who was it that your classmate was making fun of?" he asked impatiently.

Today, behind my steering wheel, in front of the wall of my former school, an old building with a new name, I still remember. I repeat unconsciously, like an echo, Hercules's answer: "Omar . . . Omar." Back then I didn't know that Hercules's utterance was referring to the second caliph after the Prophet, a Sunni symbol, and that Umair was short for Mus'ab Bin Umair, a Shia symbol. I shake my head now, chasing away memories that I hate returning to. I turn the steering wheel, abandoning those thoughts along with all the other lessons I failed to learn within the school walls. Except for one so difficult to shake. Before driving off, I look to the sign above the school gate for confirmation of where I am. I accept what it says; this is the Humoud Barghash Al Sa'adoun School. This isn't my old school. Not Al Najah. What I was recalling just now didn't happen here. I must be mistaken. I so want to be wrong. I take a look around. Houses have sprouted up on both sides of the street. It looks different from when I used to live here. Years ago, walking to and from school, Sadiq, Fahd, and I used to cross the narrow side streets and dusty, empty plots of land. This overpowering stench sure wasn't here back then. The thin lanes have disappeared between houses that are now competing to touch the clouds. The empty plots and dusty playgrounds for soccer that I knew through and through are now buildings weighing heavily on the area. Buildings that had one or two floors now have three, four, even five; cramped houses with no yards. It was this very sidewalk that I came to after being pummeled by Hercules and his gang; it was from here that we started running away from those hoodlums, looking behind us as we went, afraid they were tailing us. At the scene of the fight, on the cold sidewalk, traces of us left behind . . . a tooth, some blood . . . our dignity.

Had I not left our old neighborhood, I probably would've formed some better memories in it. For years, I didn't dare return to the old stomping grounds. After we left our house, I avoided going by it, anxious that I'd taint the beautiful picture I carried within of my childhood, a beautiful picture set against the abhorrent backdrop of the 1980s. I wish that I'd stayed away from Surra, leaving never to return, like one cut off from his umbilical cord. I had promised myself since my family and I moved to Rawda to never again go back or visit our street out of sadness for the place I'd once loved—a place where I no longer had a home—to avoid feeling jealous of the people who'd bought our house from my dad. I made it a point to never go back. I had Mom make the promise for me because she never went back on her word. On this very corner, the turn leading to our old neighborhood, was the Syrian butcher Adnan and his rented corner shop in the Al Awaidel house that overlooked the street. And over there, in that large run-down building—which back then was the Al Anbaiie Mall—were a number of stores looking out onto the street: the Indian restaurant and its owner, Shakir Al Buhri; the shawarma place, where Jaber the Egyptian would slowly twist his spit around in front of the fire, just how we liked it. One day lamb, one day chicken, or as he used to say with his Egyptian flair, "One day *lahma*, one day *firakh*."

Jaber would make the most delicious macaroni sandwiches with ketchup. He'd blame us if we skipped his restaurant in favor of Shakir's joint: "Just like that you're going to buy from the filthy Indian boy over your Arab brother?" After Jaber's reproach, we boycotted Shakir—not because we thought his Indian restaurant was dirty but rather to stand in solidarity with our fellow Arab. Between the two restaurants, Shakir's and Jaber's, Indian and Arab, was the Iranian grocer Haydar, as well as Salim and Mushtaq, the Pakistani tailor and barber. There was also Al Budur Bookstore, and its old Kuwaiti owner, Uncle Abu Fawaz. The youth in the neighborhood would flock there to buy magazines like *Al Riyadi* and *Al Arabi*, *Famous Five* books, and the banned novels of Ihsan Abdel Quddous. "You shouldn't be selling such trash to our daughters!" some would chastise Abu Fawaz, to which he was content to respond, "The government hasn't banned them." Here, in this other house, was a store to wash and iron clothes—a rented store in an old house. Today, it is a garage at the base of a colossal new house, crowned with tiles. No trace of the traditional handwashing laundry, or the three steps out in front stained with betel-brown spots from the spit of Alameen the Punjabi, as if pockmarked by rusty water. His name was Alameen, even though we discovered some years later that his name was actually Ali Ameen. But in his heavy accent, it came across as Alameen, such an old-world name that it seems he picked it himself. I still remember him: ebony skin, white hair, slim build, and a tatty wraparound. He wouldn't respond to us if we called him by any other name. Alameen, whose letters used to tower above the store on a large signboard:
. He was lucky to keep the name that he chose. Eventually, he left. He left us behind in a country that renames any place as soon as it forms a memory or an identity. Sadly, they have all left. O hapless old street, why are you no longer how you once were?

Here at the head of the street was the house inhabited by the Palestinian men—the *zalamat*, as we used to call them as kids. It's almost normal not to see the house there anymore. Its inhabitants were

the first to disappear during the Iraqi occupation—a time of disappointment. A sad house that, once upon a time, the two brothers Abu Taha
and Abu Naiel used to live in with their wives and brood of children.
A household with enough people to form an entire soccer team. They
used to play with us in the dusty plots of Surra. Sometimes they'd have
the upper hand, and sometimes we'd beat them. They had been around
just as long as we had—a Palestinian family that had come over from
Jenin. Later on we witnessed their departure—or deportation—from
Kuwait. But where is the rest of the mishmash that once colored our old
street? How could Fahd and his family possibly tolerate staying on this
street, when its soul had been stripped bare? I stop at Fahd's door; it's
not how I once knew it. I wouldn't have known to stop here if it hadn't
been for the three palm trees that caught my eye: Ikhlasa, Sa'marana,
and Barhiya, or "the Kayfan girls" as they were affectionately named by
their elderly owner, who, upon moving away from Kayfan, couldn't bear
to leave her palm trees behind. The Kayfan girls stand by a wall outside
of the house, in a small space, planted back when couch grass covered
the entire area. Two of the palms died: Sa'marana in the middle, and
Barhiya to her left, nearest Sadiq's house. Like many other victims, the
drought caught hold of them, drying out their fronds, and their trunks
bent from neglect. Ikhlasa appears dead, but I catch a glimpse of green
at her crown, a new sprouting frond. The green at Ikhlasa's head is a
tender cacophony against the backdrop of yellow clinging to the rest of
the fronds, which droop down. Behind Sa'marana, where the black iron
door is, I see the antique metal placard affixed to the wall, paint peeling
off. Some of its letters are visible despite the rust and dust:
          . Fahd and his family are the only ones who haven't
left their house; it is still standing. The adjoining house on the left also
hasn't changed: dust-colored ancient limestone bricks and the leaning
Christ's thorn jujube tree—home to the supernatural spirits, the jinn—
that pierced through the shared boundary wall. This *sidra*'s roots plunge

deep down into the earth; the jujube tree bends over, casting a bit of shade on Fahd's house and another bit on Sadiq's, which is deserted.

The two houses are an untouched slice of the past, a silent panorama splicing together different eras. Nothing much has changed except for the windows on Fahd's house, which have surrendered to metal bars, and the wall is higher. I used to live here, in a house next to these two, the house of the Al Bin Ya'qub family lying to its left, with the palm tree Ikhlasa nearby. The house is no longer here. By that I mean it is no longer what it used to be. Many years ago, I kicked in the door of this house. I slammed it shut and leaned my back into it, fearing that the boys pursuing us would push against it. I freed my shoulders from the weight of my backpack. I started shouting as loudly as I could: "Mom! Mom!" She had just come back from work. She gawked at what she saw: my dust-encrusted body, my open shirt, my bloody mouth. I wiped my lips with the back of my palm, panting, "Mom, are we Shia or Sunni?"

***

I park my car next to Fahd's house. I get out, barefoot, and make for his rusty door. A corroded door the same age as me. Am I like this decayed door? Here I am now in front of the house. Time deceives me. It's a strange thing—how we stand in the present in a place we left behind long ago, years disappearing between the then and the now, and we are instantly as young as we were then. It's the smell. The past has a scent! On their own, scents are faithful to a place that time itself has forgotten. I wonder if Fahd's mother, Khala Aisha, has washed the courtyard of her house this morning like her mother-in-law used to do. She didn't do anything the way Mama Hissa did. Not a thing. I wonder if she is still combating forgetfulness with her now-outmoded Polaroid camera. She would use it to fend off death. Death stole her father in a car accident in Basra before she was born. There were no pictures left behind except for one in the evidence box, his ID, which depicted a young man she didn't recognize and who would never grow older. I wonder if she still sings that traditional song: "Where has my daddy gone, where has my daddy gone? To Basra he's gone . . . In Basra he was gone!" Is she still bitter, resentful of everything, or has she gotten rid of that prickly attitude after getting what she had been waiting for all those years—the house for her and her alone? Here is that very house, now all hers after Mama Hissa's passing. No smell of the old chicken coop. I remember Khala Aisha saying, "How can I have people over in a house with chickens running around?" I bet that she's not embarrassed anymore, now that the owner and her chickens have disappeared. It's good that she didn't uproot the aged sidra; maybe she believed, just as Mama Hissa did, that "the jinn guard their home." Maybe God heard Mama Hissa's prayer every time she passed the tree. "May they be happy in their home," she would intone. The jinn are more loyal to a place than we are, that's for sure. The smell here is of water choking on dust, damp soil, and ripe buckthorn fruit even though it's five months past its season. How can these smells still be here? I wish I could go past this wall that's blocking what's hidden behind. I take a deep breath. Old beloved smells clash with the resident stench, a thick cloud refusing to leave the place. I can't distinguish between the real smells and those leaked by my memory. I'm almost certain there's fish being fried in the Al Bin Ya'qub family kitchen. That raw fish smell and the herd of cats around the house remind me of Fahd's phone call to his mom just before daybreak today. "Mom, I'm craving your *mutabbaq samak*!"

Behind this wall we had a life full of vim and vigor. Sigh. My childhood is tattooed on the innermost part of me while all other memories are fleeting. In front of the house wall, I feel like a ten-year-old. The wall used to be so much lower; it's more than doubled in height. The top part is a different color, a symbol of how the passing of time changes things. Friday mornings, winter ones specifically, were the best we three could wish for—Sadiq, Fahd, and I. This house and its courtyard belonged to 'Am Saleh, Fahd's dad, and it was our little Eden. I want to push the door, but the dread . . . how I wish I could overcome it. Years ago, I used to crouch down each time, stretch my two small palms inside the horizontal slot below the door, and maneuver the fixed iron bolt cut into the ground out of its place. I would then straighten up and push the door wide open with great ease. Today, I wonder how many bolts, padlocks, and chains are behind this door. With a trembling finger I press the doorbell. I hear an inner door creaking, followed by the sound of footfalls akin to the dragging of a broom across the floor. If Mama Hissa, Fahd's grandma from his dad's side, weren't dead, I would say they were her dragging footsteps behind the wall, but she's passed on, leaving behind her timeworn house, her beloved sidra tree, and . . . us. The footsteps halt. In the horizontal opening below the door is a rest-less shadow, betraying someone's presence. With my palm, I bang on the iron door.

"Who's there?" Auntie Aisha's voice travels to me through the door, fearful and confused by my banging.

I say, in a voice that doesn't sound like the ten-year-old I feel I am again, "Khala? It's me . . ." It's as if I've opened up the jaws of hell by the near-mention of my name.

"You? May your bones become brittle, you spawn of the devil. You've only brought misery and pain to this family." Her hail of curses ends with a question, very much like the one that drove me to her house. "Where's Fahd? Where's my son gone?"

I swallow my question, searching for the very answer that I was expecting from her. She says he was on his way home at four this morn-ing, but he never made it back. "Where's Uncle Saleh?" I ask her. I hear her heavy steps sweep the marble courtyard as they withdraw.

"'Am Saleh? May God never give you good health or increase your wealth." She continues with the string of maledictions. "May He never bless you with children, you sower of evil, blackest of omens." Her voice is raised. There has been no one to rein her in since Mama Hissa's death. Mama Hissa would have said, "Keep it down, Aisha! You're at home, leave your yelling for the girls in school!" Her curses fade out, and her voice disappears with the slamming of the inner door. Silence returns, the old smells and sounds remain. I turn my back to the house, intending to go somewhere else, but I'm not sure where. The inner door screeches again. I listen closely. I can no longer distinguish between the screeching of the door and the shrill wailing of my *khala* Aisha. An octave higher, she yelps, "Saleh, my heart aches!" The sadness in this woman's voice worries me, and here I am standing, idly listening to her wailing. What does time have in store for Fahd? What has pushed his mother to keen like an animal? I remember her in the old days, when, if anything alarmed her, she would tell me that her heart ached, and no matter what was causing it, the next hour a greater calamity would be upon her. Mama Hissa, who always spoke *her* truth, was invariably taken aback by her daughter-in-law's words. Mama Hissa nicknamed her "the soothsayer" because whenever Aisha said these words, a catastrophe would surely happen.

The iron door opens and reveals 'Am Saleh, gaunt, barely recognizable. His plump double chin has deflated, now a leather sack of sorts. With the emaciation of his face, his crooked nose looms larger. He's grown old. He looks older than his seventy years. He has become a spitting image of his Mama Hissa, may God rest her soul. Time has left him no black tufts on his bald head or small beard to remind him of his youth. He stands in front of me, his withered frame clothed in a wide, striped house dishdasha. He doesn't meet my eyes, his gaze fixed on my naked feet. I rush toward him to kiss his forehead. He thrusts out his open palm against my chest. "Stay where you are!" he bellows. He scrutinizes my features. Maybe the sight of my bruises is a harbinger of what fate holds in store for his son. He points his finger at my face, shaking his head and saying, "This is your fruit, you sower of fruitless land. This is all your doing, you and that group of yours, Fuada's Kids." I keep silent. "If Fahd is gone, his blood and his children's loss are on your hands!" he adds, before shutting the door.

THE FIRST MOUSE: SPARK
THE INHERITANCE OF FIRE

THE NOVEL

(Chapters 1 and 2 removed by the publisher)

Chapter 3

At times, ignorance can be a blessing. In our dialect, a child is *jahil*, ignorant, and *jahhal* like us were living in bliss, the sweet bliss of not knowing. Once I had grown up a little, I became preoccupied with forbidden questions. Perhaps it wasn't so much about the answers as much as the need to pronounce the questions and be free of them, or free of the inane feelings when someone finally answered them. When I was in elementary school, I would ask about anything and everything. I annoyed my mother with my barrage of questions: how, why, where, when, and so on. I remember my Syrian teacher Mr. Murhif with his bulging eyes. At Al Najah, my middle school, he advised me not to overdo the questions, especially ones about religion. Irritated with my constant questioning, he said I was like someone who liked to play around with Pandora's box—a box that, once opened, would spare no one from what was inside.

***

"Son, think of the question like a box. Some boxes just swallow up others. Why are you asking such questions?" His *harams* and shame-on-yous cut off my questions. When I persist, mustering up the courage because he called me "son," he interrupts, "Every box has its time." But I don't stop there. I keep on asking.

"Unbelievable!" he shouts. I raise my hand, promising that it is my very last question. He then launches a piece of chalk at me. "Enough! We have work to do!" I wipe the traces of his white bullet off my forehead. He then gives in a little. Patience exhausted, he lets me ask my "final" question. I ask him if humans were originally monkeys or if it was the other way around. Mr. Murhif's eyes pop out even farther than I thought possible.

I try to absolve myself. "Our neighbor Mama Hissa says that the monkey was actually first a man!"

On cue, Fahd gets ticked off because I mention his grandma's name in public.

My teacher pauses uncomfortably, chewing his tongue before roaring in his Syrian drawl, "That's between you and the Islamic education teacher. Damn you, you rotten frog!" The episode ends with me at the back of the classroom, face to the wall, arms outstretched high above my head. I turn to Sadiq, who is busy doodling on his desk in the last row. "Press the button," I urgently whisper, referring to the circle penciled in on his desk. He presses the button, but Mr. Murhif stays put.

***

In elementary school, I was fixated on obscure matters. Having seen sanitary pad ads on TV and in the magazines, I'd run to my mother. "Why do women wear diapers?" I asked, confused. I didn't get a straight answer out of her. The issue didn't bother me much once I'd been liberated, set free, by saying the question aloud. Mom, though, dillydallied in her response, her face reddening. She wouldn't reprimand me the way Mr. Murhif would in the coming years. His doing so only heightened my curiosity about the enormity of the question and the gravity of asking it. I had to get some sort of understanding of at least why it was so dangerous to ask. Soon, all questions pertaining to female matters, especially physical and sexual, died right after I uttered them because of Mom's embarrassment in answering them. *How does a woman get pregnant? Why after marriage and not before? What's a uterus? I heard about it next door. And why didn't Khala Aisha get pregnant after having hers removed? I saw Mama Hissa's rooster doing it with one of the chickens. Where do eggs come out?*

It was only that one question, the one after my schoolyard scuffle, that was impossible to get out of my head, because of the way Mom had quaked, hissing, "By God who raised the heavens, if you weren't already bleeding from your mouth, I would slap you right there." She had let loose as she handed me a glass of salty water to rinse out my mouth and stop the bleeding from the gap where my tooth used to be. We had been in the living room; I was still in my school uniform. I leaned back against the door, my heart still racing after my encounter at school. She went on, this time also wagging her finger at me, "You're Muslim and that's it . . . Isn't that enough?"

She complained about me to Dad. He scolded me and threatened to stop my allowance; all the while I still didn't know why that particular question of mine was so taboo. My father didn't have any hold over me other than threatening to scrap my allowance and not take me to Walid's Toys or Kids and Us at the end of each month. Their bedroom door clicked shut. Burning up with curiosity, I eavesdropped on them.

They were having a serious heart-to-heart; from what I could make out, what I thought I had understood grew murky. "You didn't have to react . . . Ignorant people . . . Kuwait was . . . No longer . . . before . . . after . . . since the Iranian *thawra* . . . then the Iraq war . . ." I backed up to my room, failing to pinpoint an explanation for the intensity of their conversation, unclear on the meanings of their words that sounded like those on the news. What was a *thawra*? I knew *thawr* was a bull, and adding an *a* usually makes things female, so I guessed it must be a female bull. Since that day the whole matter was shrouded in mystery. Only much later on did I find out about the Iranian revolution, their *thawra*. I didn't dare mention the name of any sect again, scared stiff of the swift slap awaiting me. At that age, I concluded that both sects weren't considered a part of Islam. After maturing a bit, I settled on the complete opposite. Fast-forward a few years, with extremists popping up all over the place, I even began to question what I should believe anymore.

Thursday morning, two days after having my tooth knocked out, I went early to 'Am Saleh's house. I saw an Iranian boy—Haydar the grocer's son—in his striped pants, counting cash out by the front door. I greeted him as he assessed the profits from his contraband chocolate sales. Loosening the iron bolt from outside of the door, I barged inside, galloping to the living room. The booming sound from the television clashed with the stolid silence of the courtyard, which could have only meant that 'Am Saleh wasn't at home and that Fawzia, Fahd's aunt, was alone in the living room. I stopped short at the threshold. Shoes and sandals, some of them overturned, were proof that Mama Hissa was also not at home. Though she found it difficult to move, she never stopped bending down, resting her palms on her knees and heaving a sigh whenever she saw overturned sandals in the courtyard or on the doorstep. She would always flip them back over to their natural position.

"Why, Mama Hissa?" I'd ask her.

She'd point to the sky, without actually looking up at it out of reverence. "Heavens above, I ask for God's forgiveness," she'd respond.

Without tilting my head upward, I'd imagine God, on a throne up above. I would bow my head and repeat after her, *"Astaghfurillah."*

"May He forgive you," she would intone as she patted my head.

I began flipping shoes and sandals the right way up. I'd turn the soles to face the devil's abode down below. Though I was scared of him, I insulted him; Mama Hissa's actions made me plucky. Satan's only job was to chase me. "Wicked and crooked," she used to say. If I neglected to cut my nails, there he'd be under them. He'd eat from my plate if I didn't thank God at the table. *Al Shaytan* would walk in step with me if I entered any place with my left foot. He'd steal into my mouth along with the very air I breathed if I yawned without covering it. He'd pee in my ear if I slept through the dawn prayer. I was on guard against him in everything, except the last thing. He must have urinated in my ear countless times! Whenever the sun would wake me, I'd get up and rush to the bathroom disgusted, fingers in my ears, maniacally scrubbing them clean with soap. I'd spend my mornings pleading for forgiveness.

***

I cross the threshold. There to welcome me as usual in the entryway is the Iraqi president, the hero of Al Qadisiya, Abu Uday, or the "Big Man," as 'Am Saleh likes to call him. He dons a black suit in the gilded frame hanging on the wall, right between two large vases of peacock feathers, with creeping plants curling around the four corners. Beneath the frame are newspaper clippings with statements from the ministers of defense and foreign affairs stuck up by the man in charge. An absolute fanatic. I know them inside out, too.

Al Watan: Minister of Foreign Affairs: Kuwait publicly supports Iraq.
Al Rai al Aam: Kuwait refuses foreign military bases.

Al Khaleej: Minister of Defense: To the Americans in Washington:
Stay clear of our skies and seas.
Minister of Defense, confirming all Arab nations' support for Kuwait:
We won't sign any agreement to allow foreign bases or military
facilities.

I move down the hallway to the living room, leaving behind 'Am
Saleh's makeshift shrine. I find Fawzia propped up on a bolster cushion,
watching herself as a child on the TV screen, singing along to a song she
performed in an operetta during the Ministry of Education celebrations
in February 1981. "Listen here, we're telling you, what a story we've got
for you . . . ," she croons softly along with the dancing girls on-screen.
As she reclines in front of me, it becomes clear that Fawzia's beauty as
depicted on-screen hasn't waned a bit in real life. I'll never admit that to
her, though—it's not like she needs any more compliments. In my mind
she is a pink butterfly, enchantingly fluttering around in her gardens of
songs and happiness. Without even turning in my direction, she knows
I am there. She plucks a piece of chocolate, originally hidden under her
pillow, from her lap. I've always been surprised by her secret chocolate
compulsion; she is clearly at risk of dying from too much sugar. If only
Mama Hissa knew the pivotal role that the grocer's son played in fueling Fawzia's addiction.

I approach the wooden TV console. A sturdy one adorned with
photographs. Every time I visit 'Am Saleh's, I come across a new photo
of Fahd stuck on the console's door, next to his old shots. I cast a glance
at the new photo before sitting down next to Fawzia. Because she's
only six years older than me, I address her by her first name, "*Assalamu*
alaikum, Fawzia." She doesn't acknowledge my greeting, as if I'm not
even there. She keeps on singing, with her fingers pointed at her ears,
"Come on you all, come listen to it and you'll never forget it." That's
how she was, pretending I didn't exist unless I put a *khala* in front of
her name. Even if Fahd had duped her into thinking that she was an

auntie, because she was actually his khala, I couldn't wrap my head around having a sixteen-year-old aunt! I stretch my palm in front of her face, coming between her and the TV. She doesn't bat an eyelash. I change tack, pacing in front of her, back and forth, deliberately trying to be a pest. Her eyes remain glued to the screen, as if I am transparent. I cross my eyes, plaster on a goofy, gap-toothed smile, and then shove my face into hers. She tightens her lips, fighting off a smile in spite of herself. Hitching my dishdasha above my knees, I bob my head right and left, imitating the dancing girls on TV. I repeat loudly the song's message about how Kuwait is a small sidra tree, called the mother of goodness and recipient of all God's blessings. She leans back onto the couch, laughing at me as I mirror her dance along with the girls during the National Day celebrations. She pats the sofa, motioning me to sit down so she can talk to me about the operetta. I flop down next to her and, gesturing toward the TV, mock her: "This time, let me tell you about *me* in the operetta!" She beams, watching herself among the twenty girls in fluffy bubblegum dresses. On each of their heads are two roses and ribbons to match their outfits.

"You were nine years old, Fawzia . . ."

"Katkout!" she rebukes me in a loud voice, using her nickname for me, not giving me a chance to finish. She says it without even shifting her eyes from the screen. "I'm not some little girl, you know," she carries on.

"Khala Fawzia," I concede.

She nods her head, confirming her victory.

I continue showing off what she had coached me on time and again: "On the twentieth anniversary of our independence, you were nine years old, you were chosen from—"

"*Bas!* You've memorized the lesson well enough, boy."

I stick out my tongue and resume my ludicrous dance moves.

She looks at me intensely. "All Kuwaitis know who I am, the sweet girl on-screen. But you? Who knows about you, Katkout?"

"You're only considered sweet because your blood is hopped up on sugar," I shoot back while dancing.

She doesn't answer. Seeing the impact of my callous joke on her face, I stop abruptly and sit down beside her, staring into her face, regret washing over me. This face of hers looks just like it did the day she was on television as a kid—except that now she is a woman with a childlike way of being that has never left her.

***

I remember her wide eyes, brown skin, and jet-black hair covering her entire back—"reaching past her butt" as Mama Hissa would put it, which irritated Fawzia. "Say down past my back, Mom!" she'd retort. I remember her sharp nose, which her mother used to describe as a fencing foil. I never passed up the chance, a plastic sword in hand, to sidle up to her and say, "Wanna parry?"

The only thing Fawzia would talk about was her being on TV, dancing with other girls who'd been chosen from Ishbiliya Elementary School, on the street of the same name. It happened at the time when the Al Bin Ya'qub family lived in an old house facing the mosque, which became widely known as the Bin Abidan Mosque after its imam. This was before her family had moved from Kayfan to Surra. In the words of the pink butterfly, as I had secretly named her—Seville Street cut through verdant lawns in bloom, fruit-laden trees, and ponds floating on green carpets. "Kayfan is definitely more beautiful than Surra!" Fawzia would always insist. She would get lost in her words as she retrieved the memories of her old hometown: Andalus Park, Ishbiliya School, Al Mas'ud Theater, and opposite it, Bin Abidan the imam reciting the Quran. Not a day of her chatter passed without me seeing how our areas were reflections of each other in everything, except in name. Whenever Fawzia waxed a bit too lyrical about Kayfan, Mama Hissa would respond with the well-known saying, "Everyone thinks his own country is an Egypt!"

Despite Fawzia's good fortune of having appeared on famous TV shows such as *Mama Anisa and Kids*, *The Young Artist*, and *With the Students*, her appearance on the national operetta, representing her old school, was a world apart. She was proud of it in a different way, because the emir of the nation had been in attendance, seated in the front row. She would become even more tied to these memories of hers when her brother Saleh, years later, opposed her enrollment in college after she had finished high school. He did not want her to mix with men at college. We all knew that he bore an intense sense of honor for the women in his household. His sister's dream was to graduate from college with a praiseworthy GPA so that she could one day shake the emir's hand at the annual graduation ceremony organized under his auspices. Her dreams went up in smoke because of 'Am Saleh's stubbornness about what he deemed to be permissible for her, and because of what would happen to her later. Mama Hissa couldn't get on board with her son's decisive stance that Fawzia's place was in the home, even though 'Am Saleh didn't stop his wife, Khala Aisha, from teaching—justifying it to himself that her work was in a girls-only school. In her brother's absence, Fawzia would say, "Always a lion with me and a chicken with his wife." Mama Hissa would in turn fawn over Fawzia to others: "Oh, she's unlucky . . . fatherless . . . pulled down by her illness."

Right after the song on the TV finishes, I ask Fawzia about Fahd's whereabouts. "The ever-faithful guard is still fast asleep." 'Am Saleh; his wife, Aisha; and Mama Hissa are all on their farm in Wafra. Fawzia doesn't like going to the farm; there is nothing there except cucumbers, onions, lettuce, and tomatoes. "There's no pool, no pets . . . It's a vegetable market, not a farm," she whines. She goes on, grumbling about the time wasted on the farm instead of just buying produce from the market in Al Shuwaikh.

Her nephew, under strict orders from his father, has to keep an eye on her while the rest are away so that Fawzia won't be alone. She goes back to being distracted by the TV. With my postponed question still stuck in my head, I jolt her from her reverie.

"Fawzia." She looks at me sharply. I slap my palm against my forehead, correcting myself.

"I mean, Khala Fawzia."

"Yes?"

I feel my lips mouthing the words of my mother's threat. What if I ask Fawzia which sect she belongs to? Would she also slap my big trap shut? I cloak my question in such a way that it spares me from getting into trouble. "The zoo . . . which area is it in?"

"Omariya, why are you asking?"

Aha! I've cunningly discovered which sect 'Am Saleh's household belongs to.

"Omariya or Umairiya?"

"What's the difference?" she snaps.

"I'm asking you what the difference is."

She thinks aloud, "Maybe on the billboards it's written as Omariya in formal Arabic, but in everyday language it's Umairiya." She says that she isn't sure but that, in any case, it is said both ways.

I feel her answer is unsatisfactory. I wait for Fahd for a long time in the living room, but he doesn't wake up. Fawzia fidgets in her seat after the national songs end on TV. She starts singing, *Shalluh Mallouh, illi dil baiteh yaruh.* He who knows the way home, off he goes. Of course, she's trying to get rid of me, but I ignore her. She asks me outright if I am going to stay much longer. She seems disconcerted. I tell her I'm not going anywhere until Fahd wakes up. She lets out a sigh, scarcely masking her impatience. She then pulls a pillow out from under her elbow, beneath which she has concealed the contraband that Haydar's son had delivered. Looking at me, she smiles tenderly. She fishes out a book along with two chocolate bars: an Aero and a Nestlé Lion. "You're not going to tell my mother anything," she orders as she offers me a piece. Insistently, she waves the piece of chocolate at me, but still I don't bite. Finally, she pointedly looks at me. I nod my head in acquiescence. She splits her bar with me as I glance at the book in her hands.

I don't even have to guess. "Ihsan Daqqus, right?"

"Abdel Quddous," she corrects me. "Don't mention his name to Saleh."

I nod once more, completely understanding the gravity of the matter, namely her brother's opinion about romance novels—they corrupt the mind and morals, and encourage forbidden acts. Fawzia leaves me, as she climbs the stairs to her room, singing absentmindedly, "And we're the children of this pioneering Kuwait . . . onward and upward, onward and upward on our way to glory."

***

12:36 p.m.

Present Day

"If Fahd is gone, his blood and his children's loss are on your hands!"
'Am Saleh's words still echo in my head. I shut the car door. I don't
turn on the engine. I lean back against the seat. I try again to call Sadiq
and Fahd; Sadiq's phone is still off and Fahd's has a demanding automated voice that orders me to leave a message. It's too late now to leave
a message, and what would I say anyway? My vision wanders, and I
survey our old street. Sadiq's house is pretty much a relic. Deserted for
sixteen years since its inhabitants left for a new house in Rumaithiya.
A mixture of dust and rainfall has coated the ground, the wall, and the
three steps in front of the door with a film of clayish mud. Below the
carport are rusty chains and the words   that I can still
make out on the wall. It's said that Uncle Abbas wrote it on the wall
of his house during the second day of the funeral, which took place in
the Al Bin Ya'qub household when the elderly master of the house died
during the café bombings. 'Am Abbas had been fed up with the hordes

of mourners at his neighbor's. He cordoned off the area in front of his house with chains and wrote: .

I stay in my car in the middle of our old block. I nudge the radio dial. Maybe something about what happened today will be mentioned. The state radio station broadcasts the song "O God, Where Have the Days Gone?" by Abdulkareem. I remember Fahd being enamored of the singer as a child and then being obsessed with him as a teen. "Why him out of all singers?" I'd ask my friend. He'd answer that he felt Abdulkareem sang for him alone. Fahd would describe each song in a way I couldn't understand. He'd see in each song its own color, season, smell, and taste. He'd ask me what I saw when we listened. I never saw anything. "This one's a cerulean blue; that's cotton white, and another is the color of a sandy sky, or crimson like Sadiq's ears. This is the color of wintertime and that one is springtime, or another is scorching like July . . . salty, sweet, bitter, sour like my grandma's achar, or aromatic like Arabic coffee," he'd say. I'd bait him. If he didn't end his chatter once and for all, I'd insult his idol.

"You animal!" he'd grunt, ending our conversation and shaking his head at me.

Today, I recall Fahd's words in front of his old house. I find they sit with me even better than before, even though I still can't find the colors in the music, not with this ashen scenery around me, a misshapen and ambiguous season, a vile taste, and an unbearable smell.

Abdulkareem sings to me now, just me: "The house . . . that house . . . and its easy road . . . I'd die if I pass by . . . from my longing for its people inside." As usual, the media doesn't report the reality of what we are living through; it's as if we are in a different country altogether. But I must admit this time the broadcast is a welcome distraction. It takes me far away from myself. It takes me to a place far from my memory. I'm overcome by a sudden yearning. We're not in a time that allows us the luxury of reminiscing over our long-gone childhoods, but it is nostalgia for an era, in spite of its flaws, in which we lived life to the fullest. I take in the surrounding area. I remember the children's rhymes, poetic songs, jubilant ululation, flags and decorations.

I look at 'Am Saleh's house and its now-run-down appearance. The radio snaps the final thread that was holding me together; Abdulkareem's voice lashes me and stirs up more memories that are best forgotten. I find myself as absentminded as Fawzia was, watching herself all those years ago. Abdulkareem is lovingly disciplining me: "This house, how beautiful it is. What years of wonder we had here. We were under its roof . . . staying up late and not falling asleep. Our spirits are pure and our hearts are even more so."

What if the children buried within us awoke once more, and if their past was all simply a hoax, vanished with a magician's flick of the wrist? What if I were to draw back the curtain to reveal the truth today? Were our spirits really pure? Our hearts? How do I stop these questions, which have never been of any use? My phone rings.

"Hello?"

"Where's Sadiq?"

"'Am Abbas?"

"Damn you! I hope you go blind. I'm not your uncle!" he roars. "Damn your fathers and your stupid Fuada's Kids group, you sons of bitches."

He hangs up. Khala Aisha was more forgiving in her litany of curses.

That phone call spares me the danger of the road I am planning on crossing to the Rumaithiya area. So Sadiq isn't at home, then. In the car, I open the compartment below my elbow. I take out a cologne bottle and dab some onto my palm. With a deep breath, I inhale the scent to clear my nose and lungs of the putrid air. I turn the radio dial to another station, a Shia one this time: "In an unannounced move, the forces known as the Infidel Peninsula Shield have pulled out the last of their troops from Kuwait on this blessed day, early this morning, as an immediate response to a new revolution that our brothers are reviving in our neighbor's backyard, to complete the Muharram Intifada of 1979."

I try a Sunni station. "This is what the source responsible for stabilizing internal security has confirmed, contrary to what the Iranian supporters are spreading abroad . . ." I surf between stations, unsure of whom to trust. What I do know is that I miss Mama Hissa talking back to her transistor radio. "Don't look for truth on the lips of liars!" she'd declare.

THE FIRST MOUSE: SPARK
THE INHERITANCE OF FIRE

THE NOVEL

Chapter 4

Like any other Friday, I set off early for the courtyard at 'Am Saleh's with the hope of having enough time to go to the mosque afterward. Once at the mosque, I would sit in my favorite spot, leaning against a column while listening to the *khutbah* or reading the Quran before the sermon got underway. When I returned to the house that day, 'Am Saleh's car stood in the shade of the three Kayfan girls. The car was laden with different types of vegetables, meaning they had just come back from Wafra. Yesterday morning, I had waited for what seemed a lifetime for Fahd to get up after Fawzia retired to her room, but I ended up going home without getting to see him.

I crouched down by the door. Inside the courtyard, a hose extended from the spigot and slithered under the door as a python would, gushing water into the bed that held the three trees. After having freed the bolt at the bottom, I pushed open the iron door. As usual, Mama Hissa was seated on a wooden chair below a roofed shelter made of palm branches stripped of their fronds, its canopy pierced by the sidra's trunk. To my right there were some plants in a rectangular terra-cotta basin, the size of a medium swimming pool. Some blades of grass were also spread here and there throughout the basin. The courtyard was a collection of white tiles inlaid with chunks of stone: black, brown, gray, all different shapes and sizes. On the left side of the courtyard was an annex where the kitchen, *diwaniya*, and a bathroom for the lounge were. Usually on Fridays the diwaniya would be concealed behind sheets and white pillowcases flapping on the drying line. The sheets sweated out a comforting fragrance that consoled me as the dread of going back to school sank in.

That day, I saw Mama Hissa, in her black *thawb* and thick wool stockings, sitting beneath the sidra tree on her short-legged wooden chair; her black *milfah* thrown across her shoulders, revealing her graying henna-dyed hair. She had her round brass dish balanced on her knees, her eyes narrowed, sifting through the rice grains and picking out insects. In her run-down voice she sang along with the starlings, chirping, "O sidra tree of lovers, O magnificent leaves . . ." Winter and spring were the only seasons she'd go out into the courtyard below the palm shelter; both short-lived before the arrival of drawn-out summer. In the summer, she rarely went out, except to water her beloved tree now and again. She wouldn't stay for long under the palm shelter; she was content, as she would say, with a few minutes leaning over the soil instead of the lifeless, tiresome cold concrete of the house.

I paid attention to the chicken coop, anxious that a mouse might scurry by and ruin my morning, despite Mama Hissa assuring me that mice wouldn't dare approach the chicken coop unless one of the eggs was broken, and a hen would never abandon her eggs to a mouse unless she could see the insides spilling out. I interrupted her song by pecking her forehead. "*Sabbahich Allah bil khair,* Mama Hissa," I greeted her before sitting on the ground next to her.

Her henna-tattooed hand combed through the rice. "Morning to you, too," she responded. "How's Ms. Principal doing?" She didn't wait long for my response, picking up where she had left off in her song for her husband. "How could I not miss him, O sidra tree of lovers?" I didn't know if Mama Hissa was taunting her or praising her profession when she called my mom "Ms. Principal."

What I do know is that I'd always respond, "Mom is good." Mama Hissa had been upset with my mom going on a year because one time she'd publicly chastised Aisha, who was teaching at the same school. Mama Hissa said that when Ms. Principal saw Aisha laughing with one of the other teachers in the hallway, my mom barked at her, "You! What are you laughing at?" Pointing to the teachers' lounge, she'd ordered, "Get back to work!"

Mama Hissa considered what my mom had done to her daughter-in-law as a betrayal of their friendship. Once she started about my mom, I couldn't stop her no matter how hard I tried. Mom had boycotted the Al Bin Ya'qub family house since Mama Hissa had yelled at her, pillorying her for being so strict with Aisha in school. "Ms. Principal didn't like what I had to say and still holds it against me, even though I've gone to and come back from God's house. She can't even be bothered to visit me and greet me like the rest of the neighbors!"

My imagination drifted, picturing a plane heading for God's house. "You went to God's house?"

She removed her hand from the rice. She wiggled three fingers in front of my face. "Three times," she replied.

"And you saw *God*?" My voice rose.

She left the brass dish on her lap and raised her arms to rest them on her head. "What a fool you are! You're going to bring the sky down on our heads."

I hugged the leg of her wooden chair. I shielded myself with my arms, scared of the sky falling. I quickly washed my hands of my question. "But you're the one who said you've been to God's house."

"God's house meaning the Kaaba, you idiot! *Istaghfir!*" She yanked my ear until I thought it would fall off. I mumbled prayers of forgiveness and clasped my earlobes to show just how sorry I was.

From the neighbor's courtyard, the voice of Nazem Al Ghazali blared. The brass dish still rested in Mama Hissa's lap. She interlaced her fingers and cracked them Iraqi-style. Raising her voice, she inquired, "Playing music on a Friday, Old Lady Shatt?"

"God has more than enough space, you troublemaker!" Mama Zaynab chortled. "All morning, I've heard you singing, 'O sidra of lovers'—it's halal for you but haram for me?"

The two grannies doubled up in unison. The question my mom and Fawzia hadn't answered roiled around in my head.

"Mama Hissa!"

She fished out a beetle from the rice and threw it to the wind. "What?"

I hesitated before posing my question about the zoo. She looked intently at my face. The gap between her eyes and her eyebrows grew. She pursed her lips, forming a straight line as she swatted away the question. A gray pigeon landed on the boundary wall. Mama Hissa got up and made her way toward the pigeon. She scattered some rice grains on the grass, urging it to come closer. *"Ta'! Ta'!"* The pigeon responded by alighting on the ground. "Now, don't scare it off," she warned me.

I whispered my question to her again. "You didn't give me your answer. Where is the zoo?" She turned away to look at her chickens crowded around the plastic water bowl, sipping the water before craning their necks, beaks to the sky, gargling, eyes closed.

Mama Hissa nodded her head, her eyes crinkling at the corners as she beamed. "Praise be to God." She extended her outstretched finger in the direction of the coop. "Look!" She urged me to look at the chickens acknowledging their God above, praising Him for their drink. Her face suddenly clouded over. "Even the chickens know God . . . if only Abu Sami's wife could see the same."

I ignored her words. "The zoo, Mama Hissa. Where is it?"

She looked suspiciously at me. "Why do you want to know?"

I grew embarrassed. A familiar voice shot out, interrupting us. A croaky voice that was synonymous with Friday mornings. *"Khaaam! Khaaam!"* The pigeon flitted off, leaving behind the rice grains on the soil. It was the Yemeni fabric salesman, as usual. His voice would ring out from the top of the street, reaching a crescendo as he approached our homes. Three sounds struck terror in my heart when I was a boy: the cries of the Yemeni fabric salesman, the clamor of the trial warning sirens that became commonplace during the first Gulf War, and Abu Sami's unleashed saluki yapping in his courtyard. Abu Sami's house, or "the house with the American wife" as the neighborhood women had dubbed it, was across from Sadiq's. On the other hand, there was only one voice that would melt away all the nerve-racking sounds of our street, a voice equally loved by all the neighborhood children: that of Abu Sameh, the middle-aged Palestinian ice-cream seller. Every afternoon, he'd pass by with his trusty cart and red umbrella, calling out, "Ice cream! Ice cream!" Sometimes he'd park his cart at the end of our street, rest his chin on his palm, and repeat his favorite Palestinian ditty in a weary voice: "Fill the Jug Up for Me." He'd stay there, serenading his beloved cart that had allowed him to enroll all three of his sons in college.

Mama Hissa's ears pricked up at the sound of the fabric seller's calls. Grinning, she shared that Tina had been waiting for him for a week. She handed the brass dish to me and instructed, "Hold this." She suggested I try doing what housewives do. She stood up, short in stature, dusting off the remnants of unclean rice from her thawb. The fabric seller drew near. "Khaaam! Khaaam!" I sat on her chair, balancing the brass dish on my knees. Mama Hissa quickened her pace, making her way into the house as she called out for Tina.

She disappeared behind the sheets on the drying line. A few seconds later, Tina, the *hindiyya* of 'Am Saleh's house, came out trailing her.

"The Indian" was actually Sri Lankan, wearing a loose house *dara'a*. Most of the house help in our country was from India, so the word *Indian*—male or female—in our shared consciousness could only mean a servant, whether the Filipino hindiyya from Abu Sami's household or the Bengali *hindiy* from the Al Awaidel household. Out of jealousy for her mother-in-law's exaggerated good treatment of Tina, a mere servant, an illiterate Sri Lankan girl who had fled her country's civil war between the Sinhalese and the Tamils, Khala Aisha bitingly referred to her as "Mama Hissa's daughter." I wouldn't have known that Tina couldn't read if it hadn't been for her holing herself up in her room at the end of each month to record voice messages for her family on tape rather than writing to them. She spent many years in 'Am Saleh's house like she was one of the family. She'd eat with them on the floor every day, and she took however much time she wanted to watch the Bollywood films shown every Friday afternoon. "Tina, come quick! It's an Amitabh Bachchan movie," Mama Hissa's voice would loudly summon her whenever it was time. We'd sit alongside Tina, all of us engrossed, despite the over-the-top scenes that were the hallmark of his sensational films. No one would dare give Tina something to do during a movie. That in itself was uncommon, something I wouldn't have witnessed if it hadn't been for the matriarch of the household, Mama Hissa.

Mama Hissa wrapped her milfah around her head and fastened it before Tina opened the iron door for the fabric seller, inviting him in. The man positioned himself on the ground near the iron door, undoing the ties on his blue bundle, patched up with fabrics of different colors. He rolled his bundle out on the tiles as Tina walked toward where I sat under the sidra, her hair slicked with coconut oil. She scolded me, ordering me to give her "Big Mama's" chair. "Right away, Khala!" I replied as I gave it up for her, nodding my head obediently. There was no harm in her being an aunt because she was just about at the right age, in any case. She carried the chair hastily over to the seller for Mama Hissa. I sat on the dusty ground. I was about to rest my back against the sidra's trunk. I hesitated. I tilted my head back, looking up at the branches through the gaps in the palm roof. Mama Hissa noticed and reassured me, "Don't be scared now. The jinn live higher up, there, in the branches." I let my back sink into the trunk while I undertook the role of a housewife for the first time in my life. Torn between needing to be on the lookout for any movement from the jinn, my fear of the sharp-voiced and sullen-faced fabric vendor, and my worry over the probable appearance of a hungry mouse, I kept turning to the chicken coop. I breathed cautiously—a semblance of an inhalation, exhaling before it filled my lungs, in fear of the plague that Mom had warned me about, the one that could transfer from mice to humans. Mama Hissa had also told me what it was like before, about ten years before that day, when there were television public service announcements about the danger mice posed and the importance of eradicating them. "I saw with my own two eyes some mice taking on a couple of cats!" she claimed.

Mama Hissa installed herself on her chair, holding out a fold of her milfah, screening herself from the seller's gaze, who out of respect hadn't even raised his head from his bundle of fabrics. She rested her other palm on her hip whenever she bent over to examine the swathes of cloth before Tina settled on what she wanted. I was trying to avoid looking at the man's face, but I failed. I stole a glance at him as I over-turned rice grains in my small palm; he was a short man who, if I didn't dislike him so much, I would have said looked like one of Snow White's beloved seven dwarves. A Yemeni turban circled his head. Deep crevices were etched across his surly olive face. His spiky beard sprouted white, but then lower down bled into red henna. Under his heavy coat, he had wrapped an *izar*, its colors crisscrossing around his lower half. I cor-ralled a bunch of beetles from the rotten rice grains into my palm and squeezed the life out of them. I waited for Mama Hissa to turn my way so I could remind her of my question. She chatted away with the man while she inspected his wares. She grabbed a piece of cloth and asked him the price. Before he even managed to string his words together, she said, "Too much!"

The man laughed. She asked him to lower the price. He gently refused. She started to flatter him, praising his country. "Yemen is the cradle for all Arabs," and for that he should be more forgiving with his pricing. Chuckling, he eventually gave in to her demands. He folded up his bundle after Mama Hissa had paid him for the fabrics that Tina had chosen for her saris, to be sewn by Salim the tailor in Al Anbaiie Mall. He turned in my direction and flashed me a winning smile that I never imagined could have graced his face. He left, resuming his call, "Khaaam! Khaaam!" until it fell out of earshot as he made his way to the end of the street. I made room for Tina to put the wooden chair back in its place. After dropping her milfah to her shoulders, Mama Hissa sat down with her hands outstretched toward me so that I'd hand back the dish of rice.

She looked up at the tree branches above her through the cracks in the palm shelter. "Assalamu alaikum." The jinn didn't return her greeting. "May you be happy in your home," she added. I gulped as I handed over the dish. I unfolded my fist to show her the outcome of the role that I'd played. She looked at the bloodbath in my palm. She shook her head, reprimanding me. "Aren't you scared of God?"

What Mama Hissa didn't know is that I actually was scared of Al Shaytan, with his two horns, pointed tail, and trident. At a time when God represented goodness for me in all His ways, I had a whole spectrum of feelings toward Him, but fear wasn't one of them. She slipped her fingers in, sifting through the grains. "This is a life," she murmured as she clutched between her fingers a beetle plucked out from among the grains. She intentionally set it down on the earth to roam free.

"He's as good as dead anyways," I said confidently.

"God doesn't forget His creatures."

I looked over at the mousetraps, emblazoned with the health ministry logo, scattered around the chicken coop. I asked her about the mice: "Don't they have a god?" She casually draped her milfah on her head before she stood with her brass dish. Dragging her feet to the kitchen overlooking the courtyard, she wasn't the slightest bit interested in my question. She slipped through the sheets on the drying line. "Kids today, such big mouths," I heard her fume. I trailed behind her to the kitchen, where a scrawny brown cat crouched by the door, wagging what was left of its stump tail. I looked at it. "Hey, look, it's Fahd waiting for his lunch!" She laughed at the cat that somewhat resembled her grandson before shooing him away. *"Tet! Tet!"* I got to the kitchen door before her, insisting, "Mama Hissa! Mama Hissa!"

"What?" came her irate response. She did not turn around once she'd gone past.

"You never answered. The zoo—"

"Like they say, the idiot keeps on with the same story," she cut me off, chortling. That she called me an idiot irked me because at that time, according to my mom, I was the brightest kid on the block. I stood at the threshold of the kitchen. Tina was scaling three frozen fish. A swarm of flies clustered around them. *"Kish! Kish!"* Mama Hissa chased them away. She handed Tina the brass dish as if I wasn't even there. She said that I wanted a story and that she didn't have time for stories. She knew I was impatient, waiting for the answer. As usual, my inquisitiveness amused her. "You answer me first. Why are you asking?"

"I'll only tell you if you answer me first!" I said in the hope of getting her to answer quicker by piquing her curiosity.

"Am I your playmate now?"

Frustrated, I answered, "So I can go to the zoo."

She nodded her head, feigning interest.

"And why are you going there?" she queried after focusing her gaze directly on me.

I felt that this whole thing was already going on for longer than it should, and my need to hear her answer got the better of me. I ached to hear the name of the area, one way or the other, from her lips. In order for the question to die as soon as the answer was born, I responded, stifling my irritation, "So I can see the monkeys."

Her wrinkled face smirked. "Ah . . . I see . . . family obligation calls!"

***

12:43 p.m.

Present Day

I turn on the engine, leaving our old neighborhood. 'Am Saleh's house recedes behind me. I head for our headquarters in Jabriya; maybe I'll find Fahd and Sadiq there. I take Ali Bin Abi Talib Street toward the Jabriya Bridge. It was the only street in Kuwait named after him until other streets with the same name cropped up. Ali Bin Abi Talib Street, the one over in Surra, has his name on the street sign itself, followed by a   .   It's   not   an   entirely   different   story in other areas: Rumaithiya, Dasma, Al Qurain—but the same name on each   of   those   signs   is   followed   by   a   .   Each   phrase distinctive to each sect, claiming this companion of the Prophet. We no longer know the names for a bunch of neighborhoods since they've been renamed by their residents, as if the names were exclusively for them. It didn't stop at Ali. Some started renaming streets, taking turns at ticking off others: Yazid Bin Mu'awiya Street, Ibn Taymiyyah Street, and Abu Lu'luah Street.

I take the bridge between Surra and Jabriya. It runs over the Bayn River, which is actually a road that runs under the bridge and was so named after it started overflowing with a deluge of sewage a few years ago. *Bayn*—between two places. Filth has collected in it, floating to the surface and emanating a nauseating stench that clogs the nose. The corpse-catcher lands on its bank and drinks from its flow. It's said that since the outbreak of our civil war, all those who have disappeared or been swept away have settled at the bottom of the Bayn River. Noticing traffic at the head of the bridge, I slow down. It must be an accident or a security checkpoint—that's what they call it, even though it makes you feel apprehensive rather than safe. As I get closer, I realize that there hasn't been an accident. My stomach churns. Have they reinstated the ban on crossing the bridge? What about the two-day-old cease-fire? Closer now, I see the black flag raised among masked men brandishing rifles, confirming my suspicions. They lean on sandbags, their rifles merging into an iron barricade obstructing the street. On either side are two tire fires, spewing black smoke. The stench becomes more pronounced the closer I get to the bridge. It's weird that whenever I complain about the fetid water smell, my friends respond, "What smell?" From Fuada's Kids, only Ayub finds it as off-putting as I do. I muzzle my nose and mouth with my palm as I continue driving. From under the seat, I take out a piece of paper tied with a string that I save for moments like this. The image of a red heart with the name of Aisha, one of the Prophet's wives, is emblazoned in the middle of it. Beneath the heart is an inscription: "Mother of the believers, despite what the haters say." I lift the string up, planning to hang it from the rearview mirror before I remember that I smashed out the entire windshield with a rock earlier. I stuff the paper back under my seat and take out a bundle of prayer pamphlets, which have written on them,

"Abu Bakr is in heaven, and Umar is in heaven
Uthman is in heaven, and 'Ali is in heaven
Talha is . . ."

I turn my radio dial to the Lions of Truth station. It's the only way
I can avoid getting into trouble given the neutrality of my name, which
is difficult to pin to the sect that I should belong to. I roll down the
car window, handing my ID over to a mask-less man holding a rifle.
"Good afternoon."

He examines my details. "May the peace, mercy, and blessings of
God be upon you," he responds.

He examines my features as he strokes his thick beard with a frown.
He gestures with his weapon to my hand, asking why I am covering
up my nose and mouth. I explain that the stench is overwhelming. He
turns away as if looking for something. He looks at the burning tires.
He points to my missing windshield and asks what happened. I shake
my head, feigning disgust. "Those good-for-nothing Shias." His interest aroused by what I just said, he proceeds to search the inside of my
car. His eyes fall on the bundle of papers. He asks whom I work for. I
wish I could answer that I'm part of Fuada's Kids . . . but instead I look
toward the sunroof. I gesture toward the heavens. He nods his head,
pleased by my answer. He struts around my car, examining it. I seize
this moment of his temporary absence and pump up the radio volume.
He comes back and hands me my license, smiling a smile that doesn't
shift an inch of his features. "I don't recommend that you enter Jabriya
at this time," he warns. I look back at him questioningly.

"*Rafida* are lying in wait for us."

That's one of the monikers they use to describe their enemies,
Rafida, the refuseniks, those who refuse to invoke God's blessings on the
Prophet's companions—Abu Bakr, Omar, and Uthman—and his wife,
Aisha, because they see 'Ali as the only rightful caliph. Their opponents
see things differently.

I tip my head in the man's direction and point to the sky. "God doesn't forget His creatures." To myself I say, looking at him all the while, *If only you were Mama Hissa and I one of those measly rice bugs!*

"You armed?"

I shake my head. *"Alhafiz Allah."* God is the almighty protector.

He pulls at his lips before he turns around and bellows to one of his comrades, "Open, open it up!" I make my way across the bridge until I reach midway. I like this middle ground despite the putrescent smells wafting up from the rancid water below. A *barzakh*, a no-man's-land between two hells, the lonely place I find myself after Surra and Jabriya have declared each other enemy territory. I slow down my car again. I turn to the left, toward the pedestrian lane on the side of the bridge. I remember being here as a child, basking in the sun, spending time with Fahd while crossing over to Jabriya on an exhausting trip, all for the sake of the Al Hashash video store. Right over there used to be large billboards reading,   . They became widespread in 1991, twenty-nine years ago, and stayed on for some years afterward. It seems that there are quite a few things that weren't forgotten, so many of the memories that we produce today, we create for tomorrow—if there is a tomorrow—and we don't think that we'll forget them. My catchall memory is wearing me out. I turn the steering wheel, running away from the inside of my head. I look to the right. I park my car just as I hear a young girl shouting below the bridge. She kneels on the bank of the Bayn River, staring intently into it. She clasps her palms together. "Dad! Dad, for God's sake, I beg you, please answer me . . . Dad, can you hear me?" Gunshots ring out. The girl sprints away, tripping over her black thawb, her unruly hair and backpack trailing her as she goes.

From the middle of the bridge, I see a second security checkpoint before the end of the bridge, green flags billowing in the wind this time. I stash my bundle of papers under the seat. I squeeze my finger through a Shia-approved agate ring that I always keep in the glove compartment and turn the radio dial to another station. Voices burst

forth on a rhythm regulated by the beating of chests, songs for Imam
Hussein, the son of 'Ali. I step on the gas pedal, pushing it as far as it
will go before I intentionally slam on the brakes, my tires screeching
on the asphalt. Three young men hem me in. Ghutras wrapped around
their faces leave only their eyes showing; they aim their weapons at me.
"Get out! Get out!" they shout. I oblige hastily, looking behind me in
fake panic. "Those rogues almost caught me on the other side of the
bridge!" They lower their weapons. Their leader is the first to talk. "God
damn those filthy *Nawasib*; it's okay now, you can calm down." He
turns to his comrade. "Get him some water!" he orders. He tells me to
get back in the driver's seat. I am struck by the word he used: *Nawasib*,
those who cheated 'Ali of his rightful caliphate. I recall the radio station
repeating the word in reference to those who are hostile to the Prophet's
cousin, Ali Bin Abi Talib. He hands me a bottle of water. I tilt my head
back, guzzling greedily without faking the dizziness that seizes me. I
feel the cold water go deep down into my belly. I tilt my head down.
Everything is spinning. The young man asks me if everything is okay.
I blame my condition on the noxious stench of this place. He removes
his mask and sniffs the air. Surprised, he asks, "What smell?" I ignore
his question and make up an excuse about needing to see a sick relative
at Mubarak Hospital in Jabriya. I request that he let me pass. He makes
way for me on the side. He waves goodbye. "Allah and Muhammad and
'Ali be with you."

I cross the rest of the bridge alone.

THE FIRST MOUSE: SPARK
THE INHERITANCE OF FIRE

THE NOVEL

Chapter 5

I trailed Mama Hissa into the house; she was still tittering at me and my alleged wish to visit the monkeys. I should have chosen a different animal. Mama Hissa didn't like monkeys at all. She saw them as deformed humans cursed by God. She once told me a story about a woman who wiped her son's butt with a loaf of bread after he had done his business. God then punished the woman by turning her into a monkey. In Mama Hissa's eyes, all monkeys were actually humans who'd fallen from grace. Because she so blindly believed this, I remember always having my heart in my mouth, whereas it only made Mama Hissa more humble in her daily life.

I went through the small hallway facing the front door, passing by the "Big Man" on the wall. Fawzia was preoccupied with her mother. She kissed Mama Hissa's forehead, then hugged her tight, closing her eyes and drawing in a deep breath to take in her mother's heady, woody scent of *oud*.

"Have you taken your meds?" Fawzia asked.

Mama Hissa smiled, nodding her head. "And you?"

"Me too," Fawzia reassured her.

Mama Hissa didn't seem at ease with Fawzia's answer. "All that chocolate . . . Be responsible . . . Don't go and break your poor mother's heart now."

Fawzia kept on hugging her in silence.

I stood in front of the TV, hunting for the latest photo that Khala Aisha had taken of Fahd. My hunch proved right when I found yet another photo where Fahd was compelled to smile for his mother's camera. Like every other Friday, Abdulkareem Abdulqader was on TV, with his lopsided *egal* and famous hand gestures on display as he sang "Sparrow and Flower." Like every weekend morning, 'Am Saleh was in his striped house dishdasha and white skullcap. Though there was no shortage of sofas around him in the living room, he would sit cross-legged on the cerulean Persian carpet under the crystal chandelier, a monolithic ornament. His tea was always with milk. He'd justify sitting on the hard floor by saying it was better than those too-soft sofas that hurt his back. His grumbling about aches and pains would inevitably set off Mama Hissa. "You're only thirty-eight! May God heal you!" She'd pester him, saying that the real reason behind his back pain was what preceded his late-night showering in the wee hours. I didn't get why he'd laugh and chide her at the same time, saying, "Mo-ther!" And I didn't understand why Khala Aisha would flush red, seemingly disapproving of the old woman's comments. I didn't get a lot of things back then, like the neglected newspapers on the ground beside 'Am Saleh, who never bothered reading them. There was nothing worthwhile in the papers, he'd say, and that since the government had enforced its censorship policy they were better used as place mats. I'd commit to memory what he said; I wasn't like Fahd or Sadiq. They actually understood the ins and outs of censorship and the dissolved parliament. I knew that 'Am Saleh would eagerly anticipate Mondays, just like Mama Hissa. She would fast while he went out with a bunch of men carrying placards, but I didn't understand what they wanted. I learned that the Monday diwaniyas—as they were called—were collective demonstrations for protesting the government's censorship and dissolution of parliament.

Fahd sat in his white dishdasha behind his father on the couch in the corner, holding scissors, lost in his reverie—a cat playing with a ball of yarn—while paging through a copy of *Al Riyadi* magazine. I didn't need to ask him what he was up to. I knew he was looking through the sports magazine for shots of his favorite player, Muayyad Al Haddad, to add to his ever-growing collection on his bedroom wall. I can see his face now: olive skin, wide black eyes, sunken cheeks, coal-black hair. Maybe those were his happiest moments: gazing at Haddad's photos in a magazine, listening to Abdulkareem's voice on TV in the background crooning, "Glory to You and thanks to You, O God." Fahd put down his magazine. He looked at the screen and, squinting, emulated his music idol by playing the invisible strings of an air oud. The song came to an end, and the living room fell silent, except for the hum of the AC and the intro music for the opening credits, announcing Sheikh Mutwali Al Sha'rawi's weekly *halaqa*. Fahd's dad would always make sure to catch this recurring religious discussion before going to the mosque for Friday prayers.

At that time my understanding of religion was far removed from what we were taught at school. Instead, it was what I picked up from the religious TV serials: images and sounds that left an indelible impression on me before any words were even uttered. The simplicity of Sheikh Al Sha'rawi, sitting cross-legged on his wide, engraved wooden seat; the serenity of Sheikh Khalid Al Mazkoor on his show *With Islam*; Sheikh Ali Al Jassar's quavering throat on *Weekly Khutbah*; and the sound of Ahmad Al Tarabulsi reciting the Quran whenever you turned on the TV in the morning on any given day. The time would come when I'd dwell on these images, but I wouldn't be able to identify with them any longer.

I approached 'Am Saleh to kiss his head. His protruding, hooked nose almost beat his lips to his teacup. I salivated at the aroma of cardamom, freshly baked flatbread, and *nakhi*. He turned to me with his full double chin jiggling, and asked maliciously, "The boys knocked out your tooth, huh?" I bit my tongue, turning to Fahd for some sort of sign of what to say or not to say. He retracted his head between his shoulders as a turtle would, without breathing a word or glancing in my direction. "If I were them, I would've cracked your skull open!" 'Am Saleh jeered. Mama Hissa, who was sitting next to her son and the tea tray, didn't like that one bit. She shot him a withering look. She reminded 'Am Saleh about what they had spoken of at the farm. "What did we say just yesterday?"

He wasn't bothered in the least.

"Fear God, Saleh! Children don't know any better and you do. Stop stirring up trouble."

"They should know who's on their team and who isn't, Mother."

I'll never forget the sharpness of her face as she looked at him head-on.

"The only thing you'll get from fire is ashes." It then clicked, at that very moment, why she had been eluding my question about the zoo. Fahd had already told them about the fight at school. 'Am Saleh became a different man after the tragedy of losing his father three years before, when those cafés had been bombed. Years later, I would come to hear the speculations about the bombers' identities. It was said that they were part of a plan hatched by groups loyal to Iran, exacting their revenge on Kuwait for its staunch support of Iraq during the first Gulf War. Iraq stood for a sect. Iran stood for the opposing sect. Looking grave, 'Am Saleh responded, "*They're* the ones who started it, Mother." He referred to "them" just like Hercules had done two days ago. Them. My curiosity around "them" grew. Mama Hissa poured a little bit of tea in her saucer as she usually did to cool it down, before she drank it with a loud slurp.

"You're all idiots!" she exclaimed. "They're tearing each other to pieces over there, and here you're all just being copycats." She started to talk about the Iran-Iraq War. I remember her falling silent, staring at the tea saucer in her hand, pensive. She spoke of Sri Lanka's and Lebanon's civil wars: "Next it'll be us, you watch! God will destroy us like the other fools." Mama Hissa looked at her son. "Before you know it, your wife will be working as a servant in someone else's house!" Her son snorted at this prophecy of hers while she remained quiet. For many years to come, my ears rang with her words about the civil wars started by the "idiots" as she called them: the Sinhalese and Tamils in Sri Lanka, the Muslims and Christians in Lebanon. 'Am Saleh pestered his mother, saying that if she kept listening to Tina's stories about back home, that she'd soon be speaking fluent Tamil. She ignored his wisecrack. "Tina's brainwashed you." Fahd finished cutting out pictures of Al Haddad from the magazine. He started to play around with the scissors, opening its jaws wide and snapping them shut. Mama Hissa yelled at him, ordering him to stop that very minute, to stop bringing misfortune and discord into her home. Fahd furrowed his eyebrows, not catching on to what his grandmother had said. She started telling him about the invisible strings that bind members of a house to one another. By his horsing around with the scissors, he could cut these ties without realizing it. Her grandson laughed. She upbraided him. She got up and pointed to what was between his lazily splayed thighs with her fingers moving like scissors. "Keep it up and I'll cut off your balls!"

He hastily slammed his thighs shut. He drew his knees to his chest. "*Tawba! Tawba!*" he chanted in repentance, begging her to have mercy. She lowered her voice, insulting him the only way she knew how: "Jew!"

Mama Hissa looked at the wall clock with its pendulum. She turned back to Fahd in his corner and urged him to take me out to play in the courtyard. We still had ample time before Friday prayers. Fahd pulled at his lips in disappointment, and badgered her, "Do we really have to go pray?"

"Don't go, then . . . let the sky fall on our heads!" she baited him as she wagged a finger. I asked her why the sky would fall down on us if he didn't pray. She bowed her head, meditative, and thought aloud. "We all die, and when we do, we'll go to heaven, but he'll go to hell." Turning to Fahd again, she barked, "*Yallah*, out." Turning to 'Am Saleh, she observed, "Question after question!" Before we left she reminded Fahd, "Don't be late, lunch is mutabbaq samak, you stray cat!" Fahd's face lit up at the mention of his favorite fish dish. He spread his fingers out, clawlike, and meowed in delight. He'd never leave the house when his nose picked up on fish fat frying in Tina's kitchen. Mama Hissa looked at my face, feigning apology. "Oh, I'm sorry, my dear boy. It looks like we're fresh out of bananas!" She read the expression on my face like an open book, it seemed, because immediately after her quip, she opened her arms wide. "Come here." She hugged me to her bosom and whispered in my ear, "Don't get upset and cut us off like your mother . . . I'm laughing with you, not at you, my boy."

In the courtyard, near Mama Hissa's sidra, Fahd told me that everyone in the house already knew about our schoolyard scuffle, going on three days now. Like mine, his head was pulsing with questions. "Such things won't do you any good," his grandmother had warned him, urging him to drop this talk that would only breed resentment and headaches. "Soon we'll all die and leave you, Fahd," she had told him, "and your friends are the only ones who'll stand by you." Fahd gestured to Barhiya, Sa'marana, and Ikhlasa, the three palm trees behind the courtyard wall. "Mama Hissa told me to be like them, the Kayfan gals." I looked to where he was pointing. I listened to Mama Hissa's advice from his lips about these palm trees that had moved together from the old Kayfan house to the new Surra one, outlasting their owner, Mama Hissa's husband. "You promise you'll stick together?" his grandmother had asked him. "*Wallah,*" he solemnly swore.

"If you swear to God and lie, know that the sky will crash down on us!"

'Am Saleh never said the same things that Mama Hissa did. The relationship between him and 'Am Abbas didn't match the one between their two mothers. But 'Am Saleh did respect Mama Zaynab, the mother of his nemesis. He ascribed his respect for her, as Fahd told me, to Mama Zaynab's mother—whom we knew nothing about, except for her name, Hasiba—because she wasn't one of "them."

Fahd's dad blamed his son for getting himself caught up with Sadiq. He advised Fahd to keep away from him. He had no qualms telling Fahd about what the *ulema* thought of Sadiq and his family. "They call them infidels!" I imagined Sadiq's father and mother, Uncle Abbas and Auntie Fadhila, in black clothes with scowling faces, throwing thorns in the path of the Prophet—in accordance with how unbelievers were scornfully portrayed in TV shows and films. I warned Fahd not to tell Sadiq about what his dad had said. "Whatever, it's normal. I mean, Sadiq said that his dad was going on about how that family damns us," he responded straightaway.

"Wait, you mean 'Am Abbas's family?" I asked incredulously.

"No, moron, the Prophet's family—Ahl al-Bayt—that 'Am Abbas, Khala Fadhila, Mama Zaynab, Sadiq, and Hawraa idolize," he responded with a chuckle.

I was left to think about what he had said.

"Remind me of Sadiq's grandpa's name," he said.

"Abdul Nabi."

"Abdul Nabi . . . Slave to the Prophet." He nodded his head in confirmation. "Get it now? They don't worship God; 'they' worship the Prophet and his family."

***

1:08 p.m.

Present Day

I park my car in the basement garage of a building in Jabriya. Tranquility—something that was inconceivable only a little while ago when I was passing through the bridge checkpoints—clutches me in its embrace. I get out of my car and drag my lame leg toward the elevator. I press the buttons for the fourth, fifth, and eighth floors as a cover before I finally press the button for the tenth floor—where Fuada's Kids is headquartered. I'm used to all this cloak-and-dagger stuff, especially given the recent threats we've received to disclose our tucked-away location. I pleaded with Fuada's Kids to move our HQ to a neutral location, far away from Surra and Jabriya, but . . . oh well! I transfer all my weight to one leg to give my injured knee some relief. I catch my reflection in the elevator mirror; I'm a walking corpse. A cripple with dusty hair, a missing tooth, and dried-up blood crusted on my lower lip. If only this elevator were a coffin, going past the final floor in this building and ascending into the sky, it would take me to . . . and like a reflex, I utter, "God forgive me." Is it true what Mama Hissa used to say way back then, that the sky was closer than we thought? The elevator stops at the final floor. My steps are heavy, as if the tacky hallway floor leading to the apartment is covered in glue. The door is open. There's a paper stuck on the wall next to it: I examine the paper. It's stamped with the slogan of the Atheist Network, as they've started calling themselves lately, getting rid of their old name to make it easier for people to know exactly what they stand for. Their activities are no longer restricted to the Internet. They've started roaming around residential and public areas, handing out their leaflets, though we've actually never come across them making their rounds. Whenever we tear up one of their flyers, another one appears as if it has sprouted spontaneously out of the wall. I grab the flyer and rip it up. I make my way inside, aware of the difference in pace between my heartbeat and my steps. "Hey, guys!" I move through the apartment, opening one door after another. "Anyone here?" But it's just me, the computer, photo printers, and a transmitter connected to the Internet, still playing on repeat the song we dedicated to listeners at the end of our radio broadcast after midnight last night. "This Country Demands Glory." How long will we insist on something that will never change? We ripen like dates: soft and pliable flesh on the outside, with an inflexible, hard seed inside. We go on trying to hide what's within us—after having failed to repair it—with songs that have faded away. It's as if we gathered here in this apartment to exact revenge on a deceitful past by tricking an idiotic present, by replaying and broadcasting out-of-date music. We're trying to pull one over on the next generation so that we don't feel that we were the only ones who were hoodwinked into believing these idealistic songs.

The sudden ringing of my phone startles me. Ayub's name flashes on the screen. "Hello!" I hear when I answer.

"Any news?"

He hesitates before responding. "You're not going to like what I know."

After throwing my weight down on a nearby chair, I ask, "Sadiq or Fahd?" He calms me down only to raise my blood pressure once more.

"Neither of them, actually . . . Forget about the cease-fire. Clashes in Mansuriya have forced the internal security forces to step in and break things up"—I feel reassured that the internal security forces still have enough numbers to get a grip on the situation in the country, but the reassurance doesn't last long when he finishes his sentence—"using lethal force."

I don't say a thing.

"There's word about men dying both from the security forces and the warring factions."

The song on the transmitter is still playing: "Thank God for His abundant grace . . . that has shielded us from the darkness of ignorance."

"The Tahrir detention center is packed with men who are suspected of being involved in the whole fiasco. The interior ministry has set aside a sum of $10,000 for whoever fingers the killers. Over 3,000 Kuwaiti dinars—now that's not to be sniffed at!" Ignoring my silence, he asks me about Sadiq and Fahd. I tell him that we were up until dawn this morning. I keep quiet about how things ended up in the dirt square in Rawda. His voice takes on a grave tone, urging me to continue. I promise that I will fill him in later. I'm still unable to disclose and relive what happened at dawn.

He guesses that Fahd and Sadiq argued as usual, so I respond, "Pretty much."

Spurred on by my near silence on the line, he starts to reassure me despite his own anxiety. "Don't worry. You know Sadiq. Whenever he gets pissed off, he turns off his phone and makes himself scarce."

"And what about Fahd?" I know that Ayub's worry drains him, but he remains calm and collected, making light of the situation to make it bearable.

He forces a brittle laugh that pricks me. "He's like a cat with nine lives, remember? What's going to hurt him? You'll see. You'll find him in a café carping about his marriage."

I think of Fahd, the "stray cat" as Mama Hissa would say, with his childish face. I explode, swearing at them all. I curse myself. I curse Sadiq and Fahd, our miserable situation, and this godforsaken country.

Ayub lets out a long sigh. "Take it easy."

"O God, give our Ayub here patience like the Prophet he's named after."

"Don't you worry about my patience. It seems like you're the one who needs it!" Ayub finishes the call by ordering me to resume our broadcast and announce that today after sunset prayers there'll be a sit-in in front of Al Arabi club in Mansuriya. "For the imminent civil war, to condemn today's events. We've got to band together!" he says.

He's still calling it the imminent civil war, as if it hasn't already been around for the past few years. My show airs at nine tonight, and I can't stay here until then. I know: what I'll do instead is air Fahd's piece because now's the time for it anyway. I've started to hate this broadcasting business of mine. The listeners hate my voice, too. I've become like the corpse-catcher cawing over the rubble, my name linked to death and destruction.

I pull my chair in close to the board. I adjust the headphones on my ears, bringing my face close to the microphone after confirming that what's being transmitted is reaching our website. I lower the volume of the patriotic song already playing, creating a musical backdrop for my voice. I close my eyes, thinking of Fahd's face when he was still a boy. "Dear listeners, we apologize for the earlier disruption—we'll now resume broadcasting, starting with the *What's New Today* segment before the news bulletin at three o'clock." I jump to the program's theme song for a minute, tops. During that time, I prepare one of the poems that Fahd has recorded in his own voice, accompanied by himself playing the oud to one of Abdulkareem Abdulqader's most famous songs.

"Our friend apologizes for his absence from the show today," I resume, "so on his behalf we'll start it off with a poem that he prerecorded. A poem by Khalifa Al Waqayan." I switch back to the theme song again. A text comes through from Ayub in the meantime: "Your voice is wavering, get a grip!" Fahd's emotive voice comes to life, reciting the poem:

> "Glory to darkness
> To thieves stealing from the mouths of babes
> Stealing their power to speak
> Stealing away from their mother's eyelids
> The appetite to dream."

I catch the flash of my phone. Ayub's calling me again. I ignore it. Fahd's voice cracks with emotion as he continues with his most exquisite recitation:

> "Pride is for arrows
> For burning bloodthirsty spears
> Wandering on paths
> Its yearning mirrored by
> Doves of peace."

My phone is blowing up with calls from Ayub that start to worry me. He follows up his call with a text: "Stop broadcasting the poem, NOW!" Fahd's voice gets louder:

> "Victory is for the cadavers
> For those exiting the excavations of eras
> Their only lines, written on tombstones
> Their faces, features of stone."

Ayub stops calling. The screen doesn't stay dark for long, though. It lights up. "Thank God, your father and I are now hearing your voice online." Mom's words are followed by a plea for me to stop being so obstinate. To come and do my work from London, and later return to Kuwait. Who are you kidding, Mom? Yourself or me? You know too well that when I leave a place I love, I never return. Another message from Ayub: "I'll keep on calling. Put on a song and answer me!"

> "Victory is for nothingness
> For those walking in the spring funeral procession
> They are asleep when the world wakes up
> As if they were sheep."

After Ayub's last message, Fahd approaches the end of the poem. I decide to pick up his call.

His voice thunders through, accompanying Fahd's emitting from the radio next to him. "Have you completely lost it? 'Glory to Darkness'?"

"Who should we be glorifying, then?" I respond with an iciness that surpasses even what Ayub is capable of. He asks me to stop the madness. My mental state, he stresses, should never dictate what I broadcast to listeners. I tell him it's not my mental state but the state of the country on its last legs. He sarcastically hums a melancholy melody. "Can you hear me playing my violin for you right now?" he says, before continuing in thinly veiled anger. "Sadiq is right about you. You're such a drama queen." Fahd's voice fades out on the transmitter as he sums up:

> "Death to the pen
> To every quill and mouth
> When the springs of pain explode."

I go for a music break. On Ayub's call I listen to Fahd's voice, delayed by a few seconds from the playback in front of me. "The poem's finished. That's it," I reassure him.

His voice grows soft. "Now wasn't the time to play it."

"And now's not the time for the country to demand glory, like that song's lyrics claim," I say, my voice rising.

He reminds me that the location of our headquarters is no longer a secret.

"The government can't protect us. We're being watched. You can't ignore the threats from the religious groups."

"Don't forget the religious communities who *do* support us," I remind him.

"The loudest voice always wins," he answers.

I respond, upset, by asking how he knows that they're coming to burn the Fuada's Kids HQ.

He repeats the name, stressing each letter, "*F* . . . *u* . . . *a* . . . *d* . . . *a*. Just a little while ago, someone from one of those religious groups commented online on our name. 'How can a nation prosper with a woman in charge?' They think we're women!" He bursts out laughing.

"This isn't something to laugh about!" I yell.

He ignores my rebuke and proceeds to ask what's new with the manuscript for my novel, *Inheritance of Fire*.

"Nothing."

"Use an alias. Just think about it," he suggests for the umpteenth time.

If only he knew that contrary to my usual practice of changing all my characters' names, his name was actually one of the ones mentioned in the novel. *Oh, Ayub, if only you knew that you feature as yourself in my novel, would you still advise me to use a pen name?*

Ignoring my silence, he asks me not to forget the three o'clock news bulletin. He's going to prepare a brief report for the *Al Rai* newspaper about today's clashes, all in line with the censorship regulations. He's then going to email me the whole thing to broadcast. He'll come back later to prep a report on the probable Mansuriya demonstration to post on our website.

"Ayub, do you still believe that what we're doing is worthwhile?"

"More than ever. The name Fuada's Kids, which we used to make fun of a few years ago, is now a slogan that people use in the streets. But frankly, someone else should be asking such a question. I'm asking you to leave the microphone and make use of the national songs if you're in a bad mood. Stay away from the provocative poetry. You know exactly what I mean. Even if we were free from the government censors cracking down on us, we'd still have the rest of the country to answer to."

National songs. One listens to those damned national songs and wonders, *What nation are they singing about?* I hang up. I continue with the *What's New Today* segment, sometimes in my voice, and sometimes with voice recordings prepared earlier by Fahd. I text Dhari, asking him to come and finish what's left of today's show. I need to leave as soon as possible.

Dhari calls me. "Hey, ma-man!" he responds with a stutter. "I was listening to *What's New Today*. You sounded emotional." He hesitates. "But g-good for you; it was a good episode."

I wonder what he thought of the poetry, knowing full well that he's conservative when it comes to that type of stuff. "Could be taken a-any which way," he always says. Surfacing from my internal dialogue, I pay attention to his warning at the end of the call. He asks me to take the stairs if I'm planning to leave the station after the sunset prayer because, according to him, the government is going to resume rolling blackouts in some areas this evening to force people to stay at home. The government is afraid that the situation will escalate. Poor Dhari. Blackouts have always plagued him. Many years have passed since his father's death, and he still hasn't been able to conquer his fear of the dark. I've seen him humbly praying, "Dear God, please ease the darkness of the grave for us." I reassure him that I won't stay here until sunset anyway. "You, sheikh, are going to come now to finish broadcasting the show."

From the lilt in his voice, it seems he's smiling. He's the one always insisting that his flowing beard doesn't mean that he's a religious elder. "I'm ready. Just let me get changed."

"Take a route other than the bridge between Surra and Jabriya," I alert him. He thinks I'm warning him about the sour odor of the Bayn River.

"Oh, m-man, no one can smell that except for you and A-Ayub—you guys are de-delusional!"

It wasn't the smell that made me ask Dhari to avoid taking the bridge, but rather his name as printed on his ID and his thick beard, which will guarantee him safe passage through the first checkpoint but will inevitably get him in trouble at the second one. If I tell him this, he'll take the bridge just to make a point. Ever since I pleaded with him to get a fake ID, one without his tribal affiliation, he's been able to keep out of trouble at the checkpoints on some occasions. But he's always justified when he says, "My dad did it before and no fake name helped him." He confirms that even with the best of names it doesn't always work. I think of my novel that's in the process of being published, Ayub's advice that has me stuck somewhere between my name and a pen name, and the calls from the Lebanese publisher, who suggests I cut out four chapters to avoid the book being banned. I drive away my thoughts.

"Don't forget to bring a flashlight and some candles," I remind him.

"Why?" he asks as if he has forgotten what he just told me.

"M-man, the government is going to flip the switch!" I mimic his stutter jokingly.

"Glory to da-darkness!" he says and ends the call with a laugh.

***

Just as the resonant afternoon call to prayer rises up, giving me peace, the boom of a nearby explosion pierces my eardrums—the apartment floor shakes, my ears are ringing, and there are cracks in the window facing me. The rat-a-tat of gunshots follows. I find myself on all fours. How is the sky falling down even though a cease-fire has been announced? God have mercy. I crawl toward the wall. Leaning against it, I crane my neck to the window that overlooks the street. Even through the web of cracks, I can clearly see a thick dark cloud of smoke rising and the corpse-catcher excitedly fidgeting.

Dhari calls me, scared to death. He's just left his house. "Did you hear the explosion?"

I tell him I did and that I see now what it's left behind: smoke and dust rising behind one of the towering buildings.

"Good Lord! Unbelievable. It was s-so loud, I thought it happened here in Al Faiha."

I beg him not to go any farther than Al Faiha, to turn around, go home, and lock himself in. Things have gotten a whole lot more complicated. He insists on coming, saying that he's already taken the Fourth Ring Road and is about to enter Jabriya. Tunisia Street is just a stone's throw away. More gunshots. I don't hang up until he gives in.

"Okay, okay, I'm on my way back home now. Don't you dare leave HQ!"

I call Sadiq and Fahd again. Nothing new: still no response. I dial Ayub's number; the lack of a response doubles my worry. The wailing sirens of fire trucks and ambulances break through the continuous gunfire. My phone lights up with a call from an unknown number. The +44 code tells me it's from London. I don't pick up. I wander through the apartment, pacing back and forth like someone in a hospital corridor waiting for news on a relative in the ICU. If only it were like that instead, it'd be easier to handle. With every catastrophe that's heaped upon our heads, we hope that it'll be the worst and last one.

But disasters are funny things: they come charging at us one after the other, eating our hopes alive. They rub their middle finger in the face of this alleged cease-fire.

THE FIRST MOUSE: SPARK
THE INHERITANCE OF FIRE

THE NOVEL

(Chapter 6 removed by the publisher)

Chapter 7

Khala Aisha sits in a corner of the living room, correcting her students' notebooks with her red pen. Her face is taut, tight as a rubber band. I don't know how her students survive her class; the woman never laughs or cries. Sadiq, Fahd, and I are lying stretched out on the floor, with our hands cradling our heads and our feet resting on the small wooden cupboard under the TV. Fawzia is on the couch, half-reclined, while Tina sits in her usual spot on the first step of the staircase. We are watching an episode of *Rest in Peace, World*, which Fawzia recorded earlier. We love this TV series more than any other, our chests swelling with pride because it was shot in Surra, where we live. The three of us delight in pointing to different spots whenever we stroll on Tariq Bin Ziyad Road, which cuts through the dusty, sprawling plots: why, there were Hayat Al Fahad and Suad Abdullah, the two heroines of the show, in a scene from the last episode, running away from the mice, seeking refuge in the asylum! Fahd suggests a new name for the street: instead of Tariq Bin Ziyad Road, he proposes Tariq Uthman Street, after the show's producer.

"Tariq Uthman is Palestinian, not Kuwaiti!" Fawzia tells her nephew.

"As if Tariq Bin Ziyad *is*?"

She doesn't respond.

***

We would sit for hours, our backs up against the Abdulmohsen Al Bahar elementary school wall, across from Tariq Bin Ziyad Road, facing the red building used as the psychiatric ward in the show—waiting in vain for one of the characters, Mahzouza or Mabrouka, to come out. One day, we sped to where their house was, as depicted on the show. For hours on end, we waited there, but no one came out except the people who actually lived there. They snickered at us, as if they were used to seeing kids eagerly waiting for the two actresses. We turned our backs then, heading for Hippocrates Hospital on Ibn Ziyad Road. We patrolled the gate, hoping one of them would appear. No one did. We split up the posts—with Fahd at the front door of their house, Sadiq at the psychiatric ward, and me at the Hippocrates Hospital gate. At the time, we didn't know that the show had been filmed months before, that the red building portrayed as the psychiatric ward was in fact a police station under construction, that Suad Abdullah and Hayat Al Fahad's home was no more than a house just like any other in Surra, and that Hippocrates Hospital turned out to be the Sheikhan Al Farsi wedding hall. They'd only used the facades of places in Surra. And yet, we still felt elated anytime we saw a scene shot in our area, *our* Surra.

While watching, we never got over suddenly shrieking, "Look! Look!" and pointing to something as mundane as the dirt plot in front of our school.

"Put a lid on it!" Fawzia demanded that we pipe down so she could watch in peace. We ignored her and carried on with our running commentary.

"Enough!" Khala Aisha intervened because Mama Hissa wasn't there. We kept quiet, eagerly awaiting the events at the psychiatric ward. Despite how infuriated Khala Aisha was, we weren't able to muffle our howling at the patients: how they looked and their wildly exaggerated comical gestures. The sight of Mahzouza and Mabrouka being chained to the bed, screaming and flailing about like rag dolls during their electroshock-therapy sessions had us in stitches. Tina fought back her laughter, too. Khala Aisha had a go at her as well. "You! What are you laughing at?" She pointed to the door leading to the kitchen outside. "Go on!" Tina slowly got up from her corner on the step while we continued guffawing over the show's lunacy. One of the characters was Fuada Abdul Aziz, a former history teacher who always wore a bloodred dress and a light-blue bow in her hair. Among all the patients, she was the one who'd ruin the show for me when her croaky voice erupted before she actually graced the screen. She would be hugging an orange mousetrap, roaming the corridors warning, "The mice are coming . . . protect yourselves from the plague!" The other patients were unsettled by her sudden appearance and the nurses' ensuing panic, all the while confusing Dr. Sharqan; the hospital director, Abu Aqeel; and me. Her voice qualified as the fourth sound that scared the living daylights out of me. My fear of Fuada was founded in what I'd heard in the old TV public service announcements warning us about the dangers posed by rodents. Both Fuada and the announcements fueled my childhood fear of mice. Mickey Mouse was no longer one of my favorite cartoon characters. I began to understand the reasons behind Tom's hostility. I'd lost my compassion for Jerry. I tried to bury my fear of Fuada, but nothing stayed hidden from Fawzia, who knew exactly how to put me in my place if I annoyed her. She'd pretend to be Fuada with the hoarse voice; staring directly at me with glassy eyes, she'd wag a finger and croak, "Katkouuuut! I'm history in its entirety! And I'm warning you all: the mice are coming . . . protect yourselves from the plague!" She knew exactly how to push my buttons, and there was nothing I could do about it.

Mama Hissa came out of her room, swept past us, and made her way toward the kitchen in the courtyard. "Where's Tina?" she asked. We all turned to Khala Aisha, expecting her to respond. Mama Hissa halted right before the hallway leading outside and turned to face us. "Focusing on your studies is better than watching this garbage." Again, we didn't engage. "I'm making dinner for you, *labneh* with olive oil and za'atar." She continued on her way to the kitchen, advising all of us to eat copious amounts of za'atar so we'd be as smart as the Palestinians and get "bravo" grades. At that time, this myth of hers about the mystical properties of za'atar was one we wholeheartedly believed. I mean, we never found any other plausible reason for the academic prowess of the Palestinian students in our school, so we drew a correlation between their high grades and their daily za'atar consumption. We would eat a lot of it, until our stomachs were past being full—without any benefit. Back when my father bought me that bike, I was first in my class at school without any za'atar, ahead of all the other students, except for the two Palestinian brothers, of course—Samir and Hazim. First among us Kuwaiti students, at least, because we blindly subscribed to the belief that the actual top-of-the-class spot could only be held by a Palestinian kid who'd consumed an abundance of za'atar.

We hadn't yet finished watching the show when 'Am Saleh trundled in, carrying a white cardboard box emblazoned with in red letters, and placed it on the ground in the middle of the living room. "A Japanese camcorder," he announced cheerfully. From that moment on, the camcorder was a member of the Al Bin Ya'qub household, standing upright at all times in the living room corner on its metal stand, with an old abaya draped over it to protect it from collecting dust. Never leaving its corner, like a little old lady wearing a robe full of holes, it used to startle us from time to time before we got used to it. We named it "Mama Hissa's twin," despite how ticked off she got by the comparison. "I'm short, all right, but I'm not a midget!" she'd protest.

Khala Aisha's face beamed with joy in a way I'd never seen before at the prospect of this new device, where memories were immortalized in living form rather than the frozen slivers of time gleaned from her Polaroid camera. We made a ring around the camcorder, much like Mama Hissa's mice crowding around a broken egg in her chicken coop. It was a hefty thing that fastened onto your shoulder or the metal tripod, and linkable to a VCR or charger. Drawn in by our excited quacking, Mama Hissa let her curiosity get the better of her; she drew close with Tina not far behind, carrying her legendary fish dish.

That evening I didn't leave 'Am Saleh's house until after he had finished setting up our new friend. In the hallway, we stood in one line between the flower vases of peacock feathers with "Big Man's" photo behind us. Fahd, Sadiq, and I faced the camcorder, buzzing with anticipation. We straightened up in front of the lens. It was a chance to show off our acting chops. The red light on the video camera started flashing. From behind the camera, Khala Aisha, with an expression that was far removed from its usual dourness, started singing her go-to song; "Where has my daddy gone? Where has he gone?" Mama Hissa's eyes shone as she looked on sadly at her daughter-in-law. "God rest his soul," she remarked wistfully. Our voices unified with Khala Aisha's melodic singing as we all stood in front of the lens. "To Basra he's gone . . . In Basra he was gone." She went on crooning, "What will he bring me? What will he bring me? *Sharaq waraq, sharaq waraq.*" She smiled, her mouth widening as she sang, "Where do I put it? Where do I put it?"

"In the chest, in the chest," came our reply.

Our voices rose higher still with the slow tune as we completed the song, "The chest doesn't have a key . . . the key's with the blacksmith." Even though there was no link whatsoever between Al Haddad, the blacksmith in the song, and Muayyad Al Haddad the soccer player, Fahd was left with a dreamy look on his face nonetheless. The song ended with "And rain comes from God." Mama Hissa bobbed her head in agreement. "There's no God but God." Fawzia nearly interrupted her, but she hesitated. She asked her brother if he'd allow her to sing. He almost refused her when Mama Hissa stepped in to encourage her. "Sing, Fawzia, sing." 'Am Saleh nodded, a tight smile plastered on his face. Mama Hissa started to clap.

When the video camera's blinking light resumed, Fawzia started mimicking her Kuwaiti idol Sana'a Al Kharaz, who sang to the emir. "The sweetest days of our lives these are, living with him, our hearts beat with joy . . . Jaber's been our father for such a long time," Fawzia sang as Mama Hissa ululated. 'Am Saleh pointed the lens toward Mama Hissa to get a better shot. She hastily pulled her milfah over her face to conceal it.

"Why so camera-shy, Mother?" her son asked with a chuckle from behind the device. She turned into stone—no sound, no movement. Still laughing, he turned the lens to "Big Man's" photo on the wall. Mama Hissa came back to life.

Fawzia kept on singing, "Long live the emir! We'll sacrifice ourselves for him. All of us will!"

"Enough!" 'Am Saleh interrupted, cutting her off. "If only the parliament were still around," he mumbled resentfully. He left his sentence open to interpretation. Fahd straightened his body, puffing out his chest like a rooster about to crow, and executed a salute, imitating the soldiers from the front line broadcast on Iraqi television at a time when whichever Iraqi channels the antennae picked up were garbled. Fahd spurted out in the Iraqi dialect we had picked up as children, "I'm Attiya Khadheer, soldier in the Eighth Regiment . . . I salute my leader from the Erbil base camp. I'm letting him know of our imminent victory." I caught Sadiq's ears reddening as he started to move away from the camera, frustration written over his face. Mama Hissa gaped broadly at her grandson's performance. Giggling, she held her milfah, poised to cover her face at any moment lest the lens happen to fall on her. 'Am Saleh covered his mouth from behind the camera. Caught up in the moment, I also spouted in Iraqi dialect as Fahd did, "I'm Hamza Abu Al Ma'ali, soldier from the Third Regiment, the Takrit armored corps, greetings to my family and my clan."

"The president must come first!" spluttered 'Am Saleh, correcting me.

I set myself straight. "I . . . I . . . Greetings to the hero of Al Qadisiya, president of the Republic . . ." The scene didn't last long; we finished it with a salute up high, our palms facing outward in the middle of our foreheads. We stomped both our feet with fervor, in the Iraqi *hosa* fashion: alternating, then both at once rhythmically as we chanted, "We're all your soldiers, Mr. President, all of us are your soldiers." I think that evening was perhaps the first time I saw Khala Aisha smiling. She joyfully looked on at the new camera. She believed in an immortal life for those you love. 'Am Saleh noticed Sadiq edging his way to the end of the hall to make a sharp exit.

"Come back here, boy!" he shouted. Sadiq disappeared. He didn't respond to 'Am Saleh's mocking, "Come say hi to Khomeini!"

In my memory, the scene ends with the iron courtyard door slamming.

***

3:10 p.m.

Present Day

After broadcasting the three o'clock news, I call Dhari, wanting to ensure he has arrived home safely. He doesn't answer my calls. I can't keep up with whom I should be worrying about. I'll never forgive myself if he's been injured; after all, I'm the one who told him to come. I can't just sit around and wait any longer. I squeeze my feet into some sandals, fearful of leaving the headquarters to go to Al Faiha to check if he got there or not. I wait for the elevator in the hallway. Ayub's call comes first. From his unusually restless voice, I sense something horrible has happened. The explosion that was heard a short while ago in several areas was a response to the fire set to the Sunni Abdul Wahab Al Faris Mosque in Kayfan last week. I ask him for clarification. He responds, disbelieving what he himself is saying. "There've been news reports, or maybe they're just rumors, about one of the buildings in Jabriya being blown up."

"Blown up?" I repeat uncomprehendingly. I sense his hesitation before he resumes.

"Some people say that it's the *hussainiya* that was blown up."

I lean back against the wall. The elevator door opens. Seconds later it closes. My feet are unable to move. "Man, you all are some sons of bitches!" he adds bitterly. His words sting me; we—Fuada's Kids—were meant to be a group that did not choose sides.

"Ayub!" I yell, hoping to jolt him out of his newfound bias.

He seeks refuge in his silence.

"Not you too!" I beg him. Right now I don't know who he is. I plead with him, as the sights and sounds of what happened this morning are still etched in my mind. "Let's not have a repeat of what happened at dawn today, please!"

"Astaghfurillah," he says as he lets out a tormented sigh that so often follows a plea for forgiveness. He prods me, aware of my skirting his earlier question. "You still haven't told me what happened this morning."

"Later."

"Is it something I should worry about?"

"No, no need." I end the call.

I cross the hallway, returning to the station, which also serves as our headquarters, not concerned with anything except making my way to the site of the bombing. I decided to make use of the equipment in the closet to justify my presence at the crime scene. Among the items I stumble across are a small camera, a pair of shoes I can't use because they're the wrong size, and a tank top with the *Al Rai* newspaper's tagline on the back. How crazy is this? I was just using Fahd's microphone, and now I'm wearing Ayub's clothes. I go back to the board, apologize to the listeners for the hiatus, and let them know that we'll be back on air soon. In the meantime, I put on some songs that I don't believe in anymore.

I enter the hallway again. As soon as I jab the button, the elevator doors open to reveal Dhari's smiling face, a cloud of his *oud* cologne preceding him. He's carrying a flashlight, a pack of candles, a pot of

food, and some dates in a box. I try to forget my earlier insistence about
him staying at home. As he is about to walk out, I step forward to hug
him. The elevator doors collide with his shoulders. "Take it e-easy!"
he says, trying to unload what he is carrying. I ask him about the pot.

"It's Thursday," he says.

That is enough for me to get it: he fasts on Mondays and Thursdays.
He asks me about Fahd and Sadiq.

I shake my head. "No news."

He stares intently into my face, then looks at his watch. "A-Are you
hiding something?"

I don't answer. I'm not sure.

He grins. "God will bring the r-rain." His phone dings, alerting
him to a new text. He reads it, his face draining of color. He extends
his hand toward my face to show me the phone's screen. "By joining
Fuada's Kids, a suspicious group, one that isn't yours, you're no longer
Muslim." I ask him to elaborate.

"This is because of the A-Atheist Network's support."

"Who are the atheists supporting?"

"Not for you to worry about," he reassures me.

He masks his frustration with a smile as he taps away on his phone.
I peer again at the screen cradled in his hands to read his response.
"Islam isn't your father's house, so you can't throw me out whenever you
damn please." I grab his phone before he sends his text.

I don't hide what I'm thinking. "Hold on, take a minute to think
about it."

He laughs, dragging me along as he makes his way inside. "Whoever
wears Ayub's clothes must have the same p-patience and nerves of steel,"
he declares. If only he heard Ayub on the phone just a little while ago.

THE FIRST MOUSE: SPARK
THE INHERITANCE OF FIRE

THE NOVEL

Chapter 8

Sadiq refrained from visiting 'Am Saleh's courtyard for a few months. Sure, I was young, but that doesn't mean that I didn't feel confused about 'Am Saleh's harassing Sadiq and the veiled messages that he would want Sadiq to pass on to 'Am Abbas. Maybe I didn't understand it all, but I knew it was upsetting for Sadiq. We'd only see each other in class from then on, in the last row where we always sat. As usual, he'd be pre-occupied with doodling on the desk: faces, eyes, fighter jets, and a circle the size of a coin with *Press here, teacher goes poof!* scrawled underneath. The magic button quickly spread to each of the desks and walls of the classroom, in the hope that the teacher would actually disappear, when in reality we'd only be rid of him when the bell rang.

I started keeping an eye out for Sadiq at sunset, as he would stand outside his house laden with notebooks, waiting for 'Am Abbas to transport him somewhere. I later learned that he'd been going to the hussainiya, where religious lessons were taught, as 'Am Saleh would say, according to Shia beliefs not covered by the standard curriculum at school. As a result, 'Am Saleh wasted no time in enrolling Fahd in a similar religious establishment of the opposite sect. My dad altogether refused to allow me to join any religious club or center. "You already have a *sajjada* you can pray on in your room or, if you want, Al Ghanem Mosque is only two streets away from here." I grew closer to Sadiq. He was reserved, with little to say. I couldn't desert him; it was as if 'Am Saleh's courtyard was missing something, or more like someone. It wasn't complete without all three of us there.

It was a few days before the end of Ramadan, in April 1988, when the Kuwaiti plane—named *Jabriya*—was hijacked, an event that made the headlines. Without hesitation, the newspapers pointed the finger at Hezbollah elements loyal to Iran. The TV blared Kuwaiti national songs around the clock, which kept an enthralled Fawzia glued to the screen, recording the songs on the VCR.

I decided that day to visit 'Am Abbas's house. My mom didn't usually let me go out during the week, especially during such tense periods, but I seized the opportunity when she joined in with the neighborhood women after evening prayers to visit our neighbor Abu Sami to congratulate his American wife on her conversion to Islam. Mama Hissa's joy was matchless when she heard the news. "God guided her," she gushed about the woman, who she had always said was *bint halal*, a good girl, even if she was not Muslim. Just three minutes after Mom had set off, I heard Abu Sami's saluki yelping away, welcoming strangers in his own way. I knew now was the time to make a run for it. I arrived and rang the doorbell. It chirped. For a few seconds I waited on the three front steps, my back against 'Am Abbas's boat, opposite the plaque above the bell that announced: .

Sadiq's twin sister, Hawraa, caught me off guard when she opened the door. It was the first time I saw her wearing a hijab and an abaya, shrouding her from head to toe. I was sorry I would never see her thick brown hair again. How can a child become a woman by simply donning a hijab? I consoled myself with her rosy cheeks and kohl eyes—all that were left of the girl I once knew. I almost asked her about her hijab or congratulated her or said something about her new look, but my mom's list of what-not-to-dos thrummed in my head. I wondered if Fahd already knew about this whole hijab development. He'd get wound up whenever I brought up Hawraa. He thought I was alluding to whatever his khala Fawzia went on about whenever she'd speak about Hawraa. One day Mama Hissa had sent him to Sadiq's house with some food, and from then on he'd insist on always delivering food to Sadiq's house. Whenever Fawzia saw him lingering in front of the window facing Hawraa's house, she would start teasing him, singing "Return the Visit," his favorite artist's song. Fahd's face would flush beet-red.

"Come in. Sadiq's around," Hawraa said, interrupting my extended silence. I found Sadiq in the living room, clasping an Atari joystick with a red button, dodging fighter jets on the screen. He was completely obsessed with fighter jets. Under the stairs 'Am Abbas sat cross-legged in front of a woven basket, his glasses on the tip of his nose, untangling fishing lines and recoiling them around wooden spools. A melodious Nazem Al Ghazali song came wafting from one of the rooms. No doubt it was Mama Zaynab's room. It was my first time in Sadiq's house. With its prayer rugs, furniture, and chandeliers hanging from elaborately engraved plaster ceilings, the house wasn't any different from the Al Bin Ya'qub house or ours. What did stand out, though, were some of the paintings on the wall behind the TV: highly detailed images of horses, lions, swords, and handsome men with finely crafted features who were more attractive than the man I'd seen crucified in the picture hanging in Tina's small bedroom. I remembered what Fahd said that morning about how 'Am Abbas, Khala Fadhila, and Mama Zaynab worshipped the Prophet's family. That evening, my tightly wound mind was released, new understandings blossoming: the paintings, the images of tearful eyes drawn by Sadiq, and a photograph on one of the shelves in the TV console. The photo was nestled between two early childhood pictures of Sadiq and Hawraa: a man in a black turban with a thick white   beard;   written   below   it,   in   florid   script,   was   . Neither the name nor the photo was new to me. I'd known each of them before, but as separate entities.

What was new for me that evening was the two together, matching the name to the face. He was the leader of the opposing side in the war, and I barely knew anything about him. My head was bursting with questions, the kind that could leave me with swollen lips, given Mom's perpetual threats to slap me for asking such things. I swallowed my questions and gave the standard greeting, "Assalamu alaikum."

'Am Abbas responded accordingly, then asked, "Is it just you?"

I nodded.

"Where's that son of the devil, Fahd? Or did the devil himself forbid him from entering my house?" demanded 'Am Abbas when he finally pulled himself away from the fishing lines. I was used to hearing Fahd likened to a cat, *bazzun* in Mama Zaynab's tongue and *qatu* in Mama Hissa's, but "son of the devil" was a new one. For a few months already I had had the sense that 'Am Abbas's household was no different from 'Am Saleh's, that each one was a reflection of the other. It had dawned on me the night I'd gone with Sadiq and his dad for *al qumbar* at low tide. 'Am Saleh wouldn't let Fahd join the fishing expedition. His ban on his son entering his neighbor's house also extended to the neighbor's car, and even being in his company. We walked barefoot in the darkness. With the tide as low as it was, we were able to make our way farther from shore than we normally could. Flashlights in hand, Sadiq and his dad combed the salty seabed below, leaning on two spears they'd use to collect the fish trapped in misplaced *taroof* nets or shallow depressions covered by just enough water. I stood to the side, carrying the *zabeel*, placing the fish they collected inside the woven basket. Their disinterest in the crabs, there by the dozens, surprised me, but that didn't stop me from yelling and pointing at one of them whenever I saw them scuttle, leaving in their wake a dotted line in the wet sand. "'Am Abbas, look!

Look! A crab!" He was indifferent; they didn't eat crabs because such creatures consumed sea refuse, making them haram. When I told him that we did eat them, he responded offhandedly, "As if *you all* really know what haram means." "You all" was what he spat out as a response to the "them" that 'Am Saleh was always going on about. He didn't appreciate my pensive silence, it seemed. "You let good ol' Saleh know that I don't eat such dirty things like *you all*," he sneered.

That night when I first entered 'Am Abbas's house, I didn't say anything in response to his question about the absent "son of the devil." And before that, I didn't inform 'Am Saleh of what Sadiq's dad had said about his neighbor the night we went on our al qumbar expedition. I twisted my body to face Sadiq in front of the TV screen. He turned toward me, holding out the joystick. "C'mon, play." As soon as I sat down beside him on the ground, Khala Fadhila appeared, clad in her abaya and with Hawraa in tow, carrying something wrapped up that looked like a gift. Al Ghazali's song fell silent. Mama Zaynab emerged from her room. They were all on their way out.

"Where to?" 'Am Abbas asked.

Clutching her abaya under her chin, Khala Fadhila turned to him. "To Abu Sami's house. Florence converted to Islam."

His hands, busy again with fishing wire, relaxed. 'Am Abbas adjusted his glasses. "Which sect?" he asked her, intrigued.

"Her husband's sect, of course," Mama Zaynab chirruped, smiling.

'Am Abbas swatted the air in front of his face in a gesture of disappointment. "She would have been better off if she had just stayed whatever she was before."

***

3:50 p.m.

Present Day

"*Allahu akbar* . . . God is great . . . death to the enemy!" shouts the Shia mob crowded around the hussainiya. It's not going to be easy for me to limp to the crime scene, despite its close proximity to our headquarters. I drive my car instead and park it nearby. Policemen have cordoned off the explosion site. In front of the building, there's a deep crater stretching over four yards. Ayub's shirt is my ticket past the ring of security.

Fires are burning in different places. Ash covers everything. Among gray pieces of masonry are corpses, most of them right outside the hussainiya building, which was empty after midday. The injured, now gray, appear as living, breathing ashen statues. Some of them moan and others crawl away from the rubble, signaling their existence with their hands. A filthy black dog scampers away, its jaws clamped around an amputated arm. While emergency personnel run around, I can smell burning flesh and hear crackling fires, women wailing, and others cursing, insulting, and praising God all at once. The firefighters yell out to one another. The policemen conduct searches of the scattered bodies,

yelling for ambulances. "Stretcher . . . Here, here . . . He's breathing
. . . He's moving . . . We've got a live one!" They open fire on the wildly
excited corpse-catcher that has landed beside an armless, now-lifeless
man, blood freely spurting out from the shoulder to which his now-lost
arm had been attached. We used to think a corpse-catcher wouldn't
approach a dead body until it started to decompose. Today, it's less
patient and more bloodthirsty than we'd imagined. I hobble on the
now-slippery ground, dragging my injured leg. Water from the firemen's
hoses transforms the soil into a mixture of blood, dirt, ash, and rubble.
The scenes and sounds of death I've gotten used to seeing on TV from
other countries in the region are now live in front of our eyes, without a
remote control beside me and no special button like the one on Sadiq's
desk to make it all disappear. The targeted building belonged to one
sect. The victims around it are from both. *Your nerves of steel put me to
shame, Ayub. If you were here, you'd be snapping photos. I know you'd do
what I can't.* I can't even take a single picture. I hate what I see. I fail to
steady my trembling fingers. What's the point of preserving an image
that I can't bear to look at? I imagine a similar fate for Fahd and Sadiq.
My tears choke me. I call Ayub.

"Hi, is there any news?"

"You're where it's all at. You tell me," he says.

Turning around to examine my surroundings, I'm left dumb-
founded by the unfamiliarity of it all. "Nothing new except the number
of dead bodies" is all I can muster as I fail to hold back my tears.

"Listen to what I have to say. The shit's hit the fan."

I don't breathe a word, ready for his bad news.

"A fatwa, or something that looks like it, more extreme than anything before, prohibiting people from listening to Fuada's Kids on the
radio, visiting our website, or following any of our accounts on social
media. 'Fuada's Kids are misguided' is what it says."

A lump in my throat turns to bitterness under my tongue. My eyes
settle on the crater in front of the hussainiya building.

"Who issued it?"

He lets out a sigh laced with the ghost of a laugh. "Both of them. Can you believe it? It was first issued by the Lions of Truth and then backed by the religious elders in the other sect. It then spread like wildfire on social media and by text."

Both of them! Both of them, who can never agree on which day the new moon appears to mark the beginning of Ramadan so that fasting can commence. Both of them, who never wish the other a happy first day of Eid because they each have different first days of Eid. Neither of them can agree on prayer timings, or the percentage of *zakat*, or burying their dead in one cemetery. Both of them can't agree on anything except shunning the other. In a bid to shut us down—us, whose throats have grown hoarse from continually calling for equality and peace —both of them have now agreed on something for the first time.

Ayub then makes things worse, making me feel like I'm drowning in quicksand. "Some of the extremists on both sides consider killing us as halal."

I focus on the dog that had scampered off with the amputated arm; it is now returning, without the arm. It sniffs the ground. Given my silence, Ayub simply charges on.

"I don't want to scare you even more, but one of the religious elders issued a fatwa calling for government intervention to stop you after what happened today on the *What's New Today* segment. Apparently if we don't stop, hell is where Fuada's Kids is headed. Burned to a crisp will be our fate."

"What government?" My sarcastic question is out of place, aimless.

"That's what the religious elder said."

"I see that you're calling them elders now. Ayub, it's been less than an hour since the show aired. How can a fatwa be issued that quickly?"

"Fine, it's not an official one per se. It's not a literal fatwa as much as it's an immediate response in the face of the Atheist Network's declaration."

At the sound of their name, my insides shrivel up. An ambulance siren goes off, as the vehicle makes it way from the bomb site. "And what do we have to do with them?"

Ayub waits for the siren to die down. "On their website, the Atheist Network praised the *What's New Today* segment and the 'Glory to Darkness' poem. They say that it's a call to wake up from the blindness of religion."

"But we—"

"They're just using the poem to advance their own interests. You know how it goes. Since they came into being, they twist everything for their own benefit." Ayub tells me that the fundamentalists claim that Fuada's Kids or the Atheist Network is the spawn of the other. In a voice tinged with regret, Ayub's final words are about the poem I defiantly broadcast earlier on: "Didn't I tell you now wasn't the time?"

THE FIRST MOUSE: SPARK
THE INHERITANCE OF FIRE

THE NOVEL

Chapter 9

As if nothing had changed, the three of us were back together, whiling away the time in the courtyard of the Al Bin Ya'qub household. With Sadiq back in the fold, I was walking on air. It was the tenth day of Ramadan, or the ninth if you went by 'Am Abbas's calendar. Mom only let me out after I had promised her that I wouldn't leave the neighbor's courtyard or go anywhere with the family if they invited me along. *Charged* was how I would describe the atmosphere in the country. The eight-year war was coming to an end: the first Gulf War, or the Iran-Iraq War, or Saddam's Qadisiya, as it was known in 'Am Saleh's house—harkening back to the seventh-century Arab conquest of the Persians—or the Holy Defense as it was dubbed in 'Am Abbas's house. Just the day before, a bomb had exploded at the Saudi Arabian Airlines office, less than twenty-four hours after the Saudi government had announced the severing of diplomatic ties with the Islamic Republic of Iran.

Every single time my dad and I hoped that Mom would return to her normal self, news of another bombing pulled her deeper into her vortex of distress. She would fall straight back into her state of trepidation, as if we were still in July 1985. Transfixed by the television screen, calling up her brothers and all our relatives, making sure they were safe and sound. Three years since the café bombings and Mom was still unable to get the better of her nerves. With every new bombing, she grieved anew the murder of our elderly neighbor, 'Am Saleh's dad. She remembered Abu Saleh for doing what he did best: watering the three palm trees outside his house every morning, without fail. Like my mother, my dad was also consumed with worry, but it was a different, fluctuating kind of anxiety: he followed the stock markets after every bomb blast, fearful of a collapse like the Souk Al Manakh crash in 1982. He had high hopes for stocks he bought during that economic crisis at dirt-cheap prices. As for Khala Aisha and Fadhila, they lived in a suspended state of fear, whereas Mama Hissa was unique in that, despite the great loss that rendered her a widow ("He's in heaven now") and despite her daughter's disease brought on by the shock of her father's death ("God is the mighty healer"), the old lady never seemed worried, fortifying her faith with the mantra that "God is the almighty protector."

There we were under the sidra, on a mild day in the middle of spring 1988. Everyone was caught up in a flood of joy after the hostages on the hijacked plane were released, despite the bomb blast days before, which had roused waves of worry once more.

After the muezzin's call to the afternoon prayer, we set off in search of unripe lotus fruit. Once found, we collected our harvest in a basket that Mama Hissa had commissioned us to fill. She used the lotus fruit to prepare achar, which was wildly popular on our street. Mama Hissa's achar, which only she could bring to perfection, and which Fahd the stray cat confirmed the mutabbaq samak was no good without. She would pickle everything and anything to make achar: Assyrian plums, mangoes, lemons, garlic, cucumbers, tomatoes, eggplants, cauliflower. That year she wanted to try her hand at something new: lotus fruit.

"Mama Hissa! How will you make achar from *kinar*?" Fahd asked, his nose crinkled in disgust.

As if she had anticipated his question before he even posed it, she quipped back with the popular saying, "Eat what pleases you, and wear what pleases others."

"But—"

She cut him off, shooing him away to quietly collect more lotus fruit; otherwise, she'd make achar out of him. "Your mother's achar doesn't stand a chance!" she declared. Mama Hissa said, as she pointed to her chest with a tremulous finger, that the secret to *her* delicious achar—what really set it apart from that of others—was using her homemade vinegar instead of the bottled kind from the market.

"Does Ms. Principal know how to make vinegar?" she'd tease me. The mystical ambience surrounding Mama Hissa never ceased to enthrall me whenever I found her seated on her braided palm frond mat, courtesy of the Kayfan girls, a mat that might as well have been a magic carpet from a faraway time that bore no resemblance to our present. Cross-legged, she would sit in front of ceramic vessels full of vinegar, preparing them in the corner of the courtyard behind the kitchen, her head bobbing side to side, eyes closed, breathing bismillah and Quranic verses over them.

"Mama Hissa! Why are you reciting Quranic verses to the vinegar?" I once asked.

She stopped bobbing her head and, with her eyes still closed, responded, full of devotion, "So that the vinegar doesn't turn into wine."

The sidra branches were bowed with ripe lotus fruit and others still unripe, green and yellow. Fruit was strewn all over the ground and there was undoubtedly more on the roof of the palm tree shed. Mama Hissa ordered me to climb the tree to pick some of the fruit suitable for her achar. "Get the green kinar; they aren't fully ripe." I countered that Fahd was better at climbing than me. Her eyebrows danced. "Fahd is just a cat, but you're a monkey!" How I hated the day I'd asked her where the zoo was! Hesitant, I removed my flip-flops at the base of the tree, looking up at its branches through the large gap in the ceiling.

She read my mind and reassured me. "God locks up the jinn and demons during Ramadan . . . Get up there, you chicken!" I clung to the tree trunk, inching upward as she sat on her stool on the marble courtyard floor. "Fahd!" she suddenly yelled.

She gestured to my footwear on the ground. I looked down through the gap in the shed roof at my flip-flops. One of them was overturned. Fahd chortled as he flipped it right side up while I fearfully chanted to myself, "Astaghfurillah."

Mama Hissa looked up at me. "May He forgive you."

Instead of scolding Fahd, she insulted him in her own way. "Are you laughing, you Jew? We'll see who's laughing when the sky falls on us!"

Imagining the sky falling, I felt my grip slacken momentarily. I clung to the branches of the sidra. "How can the sky fall on us if God is . . . ," I wondered aloud. "God forgive me!"

Fahd kept laughing.

His grandma looked at him with pity. "Boy, I warned you," she said as she shook her head. "Can't teach an old cat new tricks either, it seems!"

Only years later did I finally grasp the true meaning of what she had said. How I wish that everyone could learn to change.

We scraped together a small amount of fruit, some not yet ripe and some on the verge of ripening. I tossed some fruit into the basket on the ground. My mouth watered and my stomach growled as the aroma of Tina's food wafted from the kitchen that opened out to the courtyard, reminding the three of us of the emptiness inside us. This was the first Ramadan where we actually fasted. From behind the courtyard wall, we could hear the crunch-crunch on the asphalt of the wheels from the shopping cart brought all the way from the central supermarket.

"Old Lady Shatt's train has arrived." Mama Hissa snorted about Mama Zaynab, our neighbor, or Bibi Zaynab in Iraqi dialect, as her twin grandchildren called her. She looked just like any other grandmother on the block, but stood apart because she could read—the Quran, her cookbooks, and the telephone book—without having to go through the state-sponsored literacy program that Mama Hissa had failed, despite claiming, "The Miss told me I was bravo!" Mama Zaynab was educated in Iraq up to elementary school level before she ended up marrying Sadiq's grandfather, Abdul Nabi, and leaving her country behind. It was a source of pride for her grandchildren that not only could she read and write but she also descended from a noble Iraqi bloodline. Mama Zaynab's pastime, for which she was known in our neighborhood, was going to the supermarket with her shopping cart—a cart from the store itself. The market manager would often blame her for what the asphalt had done to the shopping-cart wheels. "The cart's for using *inside* the store, not outside!" he'd shout.

"Shame on you that I have to keep reminding you! My son, Abbas, paid good money to establish this supermarket. Withdraw however much it takes to put things right from his fund, number 364," she'd respond. Not once was the manager satisfied with her response or able to convince her to do otherwise. She'd always have to jog his memory of how much we in the neighborhood put in when the Surra Cooperative Supermarket was being established in the mid-1980s.

"Open the door for Old Lady Shatt," Mama Hissa commanded Sadiq in a voice louder than the crunching of wheels on asphalt. From high up in the tree, I watched Mama Zaynab behind the wall. She was sporting a wide grin that doubled the wrinkles on her face, all the while pushing her cart brimming over with fruit and vegetables. On the way to her house, she stopped at the Al Bin Ya'qub residence. "I heard you, troublemaker!"

"God spare us the hellfire," teased Mama Hissa.

Mama Zaynab's guffaws echoed hers from beyond the wall.

"Come on in, come on." Fahd's grandma insisted that Sadiq come in despite the short amount of time left before the sunset call to prayer and the setting of the table for iftar, when they would break their fasts. Between the two households there was a difference in timing for when fasts would be broken. "Your sun sets ten minutes after ours . . . Why the rush?" joked Mama Hissa. From behind the iron door to the court-yard, Mama Zaynab peered in with her deeply lined face, her abaya tightly drawn across her forehead and chin in a fashion that was a stark contrast to Mama Hissa's hijab. She passed through the door, greeting Fahd in her usual way: "How are you, my bazzun?"

"Meeeeow!" he chimed in accordingly as he clawed at the air.

Mama Hissa dragged her feet toward the door to welcome Mama Zaynab and kissed her forehead, not thinking anything of it. This level of respect between the neighbors left us bewildered. Mama Hissa turned to us, justifying her reverence. "We've got to respect our elders!"

Mama Zaynab shuddered, vowing in her Iraqi dialect, "I swear to God and on my mother's milk, you're older than me."

"Are you off your rocker?" Mama Hissa asked incredulously as she beat her chest with her open palm while staring at her neighbor.

The two old ladies spent some time in the courtyard debating who was younger while the three of us looked on, deriving more enjoy-ment from their scene than that of the patients leaving the psychiatric ward on our TV show. Their feigned squabble turned to kitchen talk, then to tea sit-downs in the Gamal Abdel Nasser Park in Rawda after the evening prayer, then to news of the bomb blast outside the Saudi Arabian Airlines office that had shaken the city yesterday, before finally ending with the war.

Mama Zaynab was talking about Iran with the same sort of com-passion that she had for Iraq. After having thrown down the last of the lotus fruit into the basket, I found myself unable to contain my ques-tion any longer and I cut her off. "Bibi Zaynab! Who do you support? Iran or Iraq?" Both grandmothers turned to me.

"This is a war we're talking about here, may God protect us, not a soccer match, you fool!"

I didn't pay Mama Hissa any mind, and kept my eyes locked with Mama Zaynab's. She shook her head indecisively, pulling at her lips. She finally settled on the common saying: "In my back and in my stomach, I feel pain. Both hurt just the same."

***

4:20 p.m.

Present Day

I sit in my car and close the door. I'm holding Ayub's camera, empty, free from the images in my head that are clamoring for attention. My attempts to get in touch with Sadiq and Fahd have been fruitless. What Ayub said shortly before spurred me to log into our email account. No messages, except for one from Ayub with the six o'clock news brief attached. I move to the Fuada's Kids Twitter account, even though I had entrusted its management to some members of the group, exempting myself a while back from this responsibility in particular. I had long ago discovered my threshold for tolerating attacks from Twitter trolls: some were extremist religious groups, while others didn't recognize any religion. They meted out their accusations to us, cursed and threatened our families so that they would be forced to get involved, and put pressure on us to end our "bullshit," as they called it. Many demanded that we reveal our identities. "If you're real men!" I type in *@FuadasKids* on my phone's app. The profile picture for the page pops up: Fuada in her bloodred dress, sky-blue bow in her hair, her eyes as wide as possible and mouth agape, carrying the orange mousetrap, wagging her finger as she warns whoever will listen. I cast my gaze over the words below the photo. *I'm history in its entirety! I'm warning you all, the mice are coming . . . protect yourselves from the plague!* I hear this repeated within me, in Fawzia's dry and hoarse voice, which used to scare me as a child. The most recent tweet on the page is a few minutes old. "God is one," it says. It looks like Dhari tweeted it. I don't think Ayub is behind it, seeing as he limited his involvement with the account to only tweeting news items. It has four likes and eight responses bashing us, and more than fifty comments from different tweeters going at one another:

"What crap, we know that God is one, but you guys are nonbelievers!"

"You're scum, all you Shi'as who don't revere the Prophet's companions."

"God damn you all!"

"Nawasib."

"Damn you!"

"I hope your faces get smashed up!"

"Umar, Umar, Umar!"

"#Shi'aswontbehumiliated."

I can't take it. I don't have it in me to delete tweets that aren't mine. Nonetheless, I still click on the upper-right-hand corner of the tweet "God is one" and delete it. My phone rings, showing a number I learned by heart as a child and still know; it covers up the Twitter page. It's 'Am Saleh's house line; the first few digits match those of 'Am Abbas's and our old house. They were the first phone numbers I ever memorized, back when there were only seven digits in a number, easy enough to learn before they increased and became . . . How many now? I press my phone to my ear.

Apprehensively, I let out a "Hello, Fahd!"

The voice from the other end comes through: "It's me, Um Hassan."

I breathe in sharply. "Hawraa!" The name rolls off my tongue like it used to many years ago. So much has happened since I last said her name. Perhaps the phone number on the screen is what took me back in time, to a time when, if she came up in conversation with Sadiq, she was "Hawraa." After she put on the hijab, you could only call her "sister," ensuring there was a respectful distance between you. Then she got married and was only known as a mother, "Um Hassan." Even now, whenever Fahd does mention her briefly, she's swallowed up by the blanket term *family*, her name never to be uttered again. "I went out with the 'family' . . . Hold on, phone call from the 'family' . . . I told the 'family' . . ." It got to the point where I found myself having to sign off all our calls with "Say hi to the fam."

I take another look at the screen to confirm the number. Maybe it's 'Am Abbas's house in Rumaithiya. I find the number is the same as the first time I saw it. It's the Al Bin Ya'qub's house. Despite their ups and downs, I expect good things from Um Hassan's call, seeing as she's calling from her husband's house after their rift. I ask how her two boys are doing. She responds that they're playing outside. She asks me about her husband and her brother. Other than the stock "It'll be fine," I don't have a response for her. To me, who knows her so well, her demeanor speaks loud and clear as to how pained she is over their disappearance. It reminds me of what her grandmother had said long ago: "In my back and in my stomach, I feel pain. Both hurt just the same."

"Khala Aisha is broken. She's worried sick about Fahd," she says, sounding worn-out.

Both of us knew what this woman's worry would end in; the Soothsayer, as we used to jokingly call her, because everything she worried about came to pass. She would lie in wait for earthquakes before they happened.

I hear myself nosily prying into her and Fahd's marriage. "So, Um Hassan, you've gone back to . . ."

She doesn't give me any wiggle room. "'Am Saleh's been in Mubarak Hospital for the past hour. He was whisked away in an ambulance with Khala Aisha at his side."

I'm hoping that whatever has happened to Fahd's dad was the only source of pain for Khala Aisha when I saw her earlier this afternoon. I hope it wasn't more than that. Hawraa keeps silent before going on to say that she can't make head or tail of anything; Fahd's mother came back from the hospital after two hours, picked up a pot of food from the kitchen, and left again without so much as a word. I barely hear what Hawraa is saying. I'm not interested in Fahd's mom's obscure quirks. If only Fahd could come back now to see his wife, who has returned to their home. As if she read my mind, she explains why she is back in her husband's house in Surra. "I couldn't leave Fawzia alone."

Something indescribable washes over me every time I hear the name of Fahd's aunt. I ask how Fawzia is. "She'll be fine, God willing," Hawraa says before abruptly hanging up on me. I look down at my phone; the Fuada's Kids Twitter page is showing again after my call with Um Hassan. People are unleashing profanity at Fuada's Kids—ruin, downfall, and other horrible things. I nearly sign out. A tweet with an image of our slogan *God is one* has popped up; it says: "Fuada's Kids have deleted their tweet "God is one" for their friends the Atheist Network. Pens down, ink dried. Too little, too late."

Dozens of people have retweeted it. Whereas others have responded by hurling accusations at us, calling us everything from Sunni to Shia to atheist extremists, from being loyal to the government to conspiring against it; the Atheist Network is content with one tweet that adds fuel to the fire: "Religion is a blindfold." My trembling fingers type our group's name in the Twitter search bar, waiting for the results. Some hashtags pop up: "#TheMiceAreComing" and another seemingly recent one, "#StopFuadasKids."

The final hashtag leads me to a tweet of Dhari's ID, with his picture and personal details: "Well, look what we have here: one of Fuada's mice."

THE FIRST MOUSE: SPARK
THE INHERITANCE OF FIRE

THE NOVEL

Chapter 10

Hardly had Mama Zaynab set off on her way home, pushing her shopping cart, when she came back to the Al Bin Ya'qub family courtyard, her face grim. She had forgotten to buy some tomato paste.

"Tiiinaaa . . . Tiiiiiinaaa!" Mama Hissa called out.

"Really, there's no need, Um Saleh. Let one of these boys go to Haydar before he closes the store."

We would fall over ourselves to go to the grocery store or the supermarket whenever either of the grandmothers needed something; those errands were an invaluable opportunity to make an escape. Oh, the joy whenever Mama Hissa needed samosa flour; we'd race to Shakir's Indian restaurant to surreptitiously buy it so that Jaber, his Egyptian competitor, wouldn't be any wiser. We'd come back and ask her, "Don't you want liver or kidneys? How about some kebab?" She knew us, that we'd only be satisfied if we could go to the end of the street, toward the Al Awaidel house, where Adnan the Syrian had his butcher shop. We'd

draw out what should have taken minutes into hours before returning. Mama Hissa would go out now and again to meet her friends in
Gamal Abdel Nasser Park or to the fresh produce market, accompanied
by Khala Aisha whenever Tina's kitchen was running low on fruits or
vegetables. She'd pass by us, wearing her abaya. We'd stand in front of
her, blocking the courtyard door. "Mama Hissa, take us! Take us!"

She'd ask us, "Now who do you love more . . . God or me?"

Our faces drained of color. She'd insist on hearing the answer that
pleased her. "God, of course," we'd all dejectedly chime.

"Excellent! Let God keep you with Him then, and I'll be free of
you." Time and again she cunningly extricated herself from our pester-
ing. She'd hide behind the door, stifling her laughter at our downcast
faces. At these times, I would wonder how I could love God as much as
I said I did but not want Him to keep me to Himself. Since my question wavered between *ayb* and haram, what was shameful and what was
forbidden, I swallowed it.

We huddled around Mama Zaynab that day, grabbing at her abaya.
Our voices grew louder, begging her to send us to Haydar's to buy
tomato paste. "Bibi Zaynab, pick me! Pick me!" She stuck her varicose-
veined hand into her black leather handbag, giving Sadiq enough for
the tomato paste, then gifting each of us a quarter dinar to buy whatever
our little hearts desired. "Instead of buying gum and sweets, you should
. . ." On one such occasion, just as Mama Hissa started to counsel us,
Fahd interrupted her; his back bent over, lower lip jutting out, and
mimicking her, he finished her sentence with the usual refrain, "Donate
to Palestine." She looked hard at him, her eyes so wide it seemed her
eyeballs would fall out. She freed her foot from one of her sandals. She
bent down to pick it up as she yelled, "You're making fun of me, eh,
you Jew?" Fahd set off running with Mama Hissa's sandal flying behind
him, before it careened into the iron door and then fell to the floor. The
loyal bloodhound that I was, I ran to the door and flipped the sandal
over to its rightful position.

At the front door stood Samir and Hazim carrying a dish of roasted sumac chicken and *awwameh* for dessert. Like every other Ramadan, their mother had sent them. Mama Hissa's face lit up as she called Tina to collect the food. She sent the two boys on their way, carrying her greetings to Um Taha as well as her update that "the Nablus soap has almost run out." After the two boys left, Mama Hissa spoke to Bibi Zaynab about how fair Um Taha's forearms were, thanks to her magical soap. "You'd have to wash yours with Clorox to get that white!" Bibi Zaynab joked.

Both Fahd and Sadiq had inherited a trait from their respective fathers, which I started to observe in the way each of them spoke. A few days earlier, we were on our way to see Hassan the optician at the main supermarket overlooking Tariq Bin Ziyad Road, which stretches to the bridge that leads to Jabriya—Mahzouza and Mabrouka's street, as we used to call it. We were running on that very street, but not in the direction of the psychiatric ward; instead, we were running away from the mice, as Mahzouza and Mabrouka had done. Fawzia had sent us to buy contact lens solution; she'd been suffering from deteriorating vision brought on by her worsening sickness. Outside Hassan the optician's, Fahd whispered to me, "Why this place? Why not Omar's?" 'Am Saleh had exaggerated his hatred for his neighbor to the point that Fahd thought he automatically had to hate what his neighbor liked. When I pushed Fahd on what the harm was with Hassan, he responded, "It's a name that doesn't belong to our sect."

"But my uncle's name is Hassan!" I retorted. My uncle's serene face and long black beard came to mind. "Also, didn't we learn in Islamic education class that 'God's peace be upon the Prophet's grandsons Hassan and Hussain, which are Ali Bin Abi Talib's sons—May God be pleased with him'?"

Fahd's eyebrows shot up. "You swear those were their names?"

Sadiq, taciturn as always, responded on my behalf after his ears had reddened. "By God the Almighty," he swore in affirmation, before he asked, "Why do you like Omar?"

Fahd contented himself by saying, "God was pleased with him."

"Why shouldn't we like him?" I rashly responded to Sadiq's question with one of my own. I reached for my lips as Mom's voice reverberated in my ear: "If your mouth wasn't already covered in blood, I'd slap you!" I didn't say anything more.

"Because he's damned," Sadiq uncharacteristically slipped in, referring to a childhood lesson.

Fahd mulled this over before reminding Sadiq, "*You* told me that your father says that the Prophet's family damns us."

Before stepping into Hassan the optician's, Sadiq shot back, "And *your* dad says that our kind hijacked the *Jabriya* plane and that we're infidels—that's what you told me!"

I became more reserved. More cautious. More anxious that any stray word from my mouth could end up with me facedown on the sidewalk, maybe with a bloody lip and missing another tooth. The grocery store was behind our houses, three streets away, parallel to Ali Bin Abi Talib Street, where we lived. I wonder if Fahd had, as a kid, ever asked about the name of our street: "Why Khalifa Ali Bin Abi Talib? Why not Khalifa Umar Bin Al Khattab?"

Back in the courtyard, we hitched up our spring dishdashas, folded the hems, and wrapped them around our waists, making it easy for us to run toward Haydar the Iranian's store to buy the tomato paste. What had happened at Hassan the optician's a couple of days before was a harbinger of what was to come at the grocer's. Fahd didn't like Haydar because his son conspired with Fawzia to sell her sweets, and because he favored Sadiq. Only Sadiq would enjoy a free piece of candy or gum every time we frequented the store. "It's because he's one of *them*," Fahd said.

We passed under the balloons and the rainbow rubber balls hanging above the door. Haydar smiled widely, revealing his gold tooth and raising his unibrow—a long, stretched-out caterpillar perched above his eyes. As usual, he asked how Sadiq was in his Farsi-tinged Arabic, "*Shlonak*, Sadiq?"

I don't know what prompted Fahd to comment. "Sadiq, like all of your kind, isn't as truthful as his name suggests." We all wheeled around to him for clarification. I knew he wanted to say more. He went on unabashedly, "Just like Khomeini!" The passage of time has worn away many things in my life, but Haydar's face that day isn't one of them. His protruding eyes mirrored his alarm. His lower lip trembled. He preoccupied himself with adjusting the woolen hat that he wore in summer and winter alike. He turned around and came out from behind the sweets and mixed-nuts counter. He yanked Fahd by the collar of his dishdasha, dragged him to the door, and pushed him outside. Haydar stayed inside, the threshold dividing them.

He raised his hand, warning, "You better not say that again!" I was shaking. Fahd glared straight back at him. "Say what you want about my mother, my father, but you better not say anything about . . . ," Haydar threatened.

After performing our prayers in Maryam Al Ghanem Mosque in Block 2, we were partaking in iftar. Mom let me stay behind at the neighbor's so that I could go to the mosque with 'Am Saleh for the *Maghreb* and *Isha* prayers. 'Am Saleh's hand crept among Mama Hissa's and Um Taha's dishes, skipping Bibi Zaynab's culinary delights as usual, not going anywhere near them. Crabs and what 'Am Abbas had said the night we had gone for al qumbar popped into my head.

"'Am Saleh, is eating crabs haram?"

"Who said that?"

"'Am Abbas," I replied meekly.

"He's not your uncle, you blind bat," he corrected. "They don't even know halal from haram."

I remember Fahd then, pale, silent since before the sunset prayer when we came back from the grocery store. He held a spoon in his right hand and a glass of *laban* in his left.

"Don't drink with your left hand. Al Shaytan drinks with you then," Mama Hissa scolded him. I looked at her, and then reminded her of how she said that all demons are bound up in the month of Ramadan. "But here you are with us!" she snapped without looking at me. She cackled. I giggled. 'Am Saleh, Khala Aisha, and Fawzia all joined in fits.

Fahd sliced through our lighthearted moment. "Why doesn't Saddam just butcher all the Iranians?"

***

4:34 p.m.

Present Day

A cloud of misery hovers over me after Hawraa's call and the disaster of Dhari's personal ID being passed around through social media. My fingers mindlessly press against the air-conditioner control. The air coming through its vents melts away, mixing with the air blowing in through the glassless windshield. I'm worried. I try calling Dhari again. No answer. My fingers move, playing with the radio. Fuada's Kids broadcasts Dhari's voice speaking to his listeners. "The Prophet, p-peace be upon him, used to seek the protection of God from tempta-tations a lot, as quoted in Zayd Bin Thabit's hadith about the P-Prophet. He said, 'Seek refuge from God for the o-obvious temptations and the hidden ones.'"

I find myself whispering, "The Prophet himself, peace be upon him, if anything aggrieved him, said, 'O giver of life, O Guardian, by your mercy I ask for your help.'" I look up at the sky through the sunroof. Is now the time for the sky to fall on our heads? I text Dhari: "Time's up, sheikh. Go home now!" I follow up my message with some other ones, telling him what Ayub shared with me: "A fatwa or something like it, both groups issued it, forcing people to boycott us, saying it's okay to kill us. They're saying that we've gone astray, that we've gotten mixed up with the Atheist Network."

The broadcast shifts to Islamic hymns. Dhari finds refuge in them during the breaks, avoiding music, which he doesn't listen to at all. He calls me, laughing, reassuring as always. He says that he received a call from Ayub, who told him everything. He blames me, just like he blamed Ayub before me, for believing the hype. "Do you believe that the religious sch-scholars would a-actually say something like that?"

Silence is my response.

He goes on making light of it. "A-All that's been said is just c-crazy-people talk and excitable t-teenagers babbling."

His response only compounds my worry. "Right now, there's nothing more dangerous than those teenagers," I say. He reassures me that there are a lot of moderate religious groups that support Fuada's Kids.

I borrow Ayub's words. "The loudest voice has the majority!"

Dhari stays silent. I waver on how to break the news to him. I finally tell him about the image of his ID card making the rounds. I beg him to stop his show and go back to Al Faiha as quick as possible. "M-My ID card? W-Where?" he asks me, his interest piqued. "The break's over, g-gotta get back to the b-broadcast!" he says.

His voice, accompanied by faint songs in the background, pulls his listeners back to attention. He picks up where he left off before the break. "M-My loved ones who f-follow God . . . and Ibn Abbas, may God b-be pleased with him, the Prophet, peace be upon him, s-said, 'God brought me night, the most blessed and most high in the best of f-forms.' The hadith goes on to say that God said, 'O Muhammad, when you p-pray say: 'O God, I ask You to help me to do good, to help me stop committing reprehensible acts, to love the poor, to p-pardon me, to have mercy on me, to forgive me and, if Your creation is about to be tempted, then p-pull me close to You before I am.'" The final clause that emerges from his tongue possesses a timorous quality. Dhari repeats it thrice. As if I can see him before me with his eyes closed, submitting to God. "P-Pull me close to You before I am, p-pull me close to You before I am, p-pull me close to You . . . before I am." I feel bad for him whenever he stutters, certain words resisting him.

I scour the rest of the radio stations, searching for more news.

THE FIRST MOUSE: SPARK
THE INHERITANCE OF FIRE

THE NOVEL

Chapter 11

In the mornings at 'Am Saleh's house, we would crowd around the *Al Watan* newspaper. We'd devour its pages. We would pore over the news about the first Peace and Friendship tournament. With a feverish eagerness not expected at our ages, spurred on by Fawzia, we'd read anything linked to the preparations: the statements by the head of the Olympic committee Sheikh Fahad Al Ahmad Al Jabir Al Sabah, the meetings between officials, pictures of the field equipment, students' rehearsals for the opening ceremony, and news of the selected teams participating.

It was a Friday—September 22, 1989, to be precise. I didn't waste the opportunity to rib Fawzia when her song, "Kuwait and the Arabs . . . Family and Kinship," came on TV. Groups of students who'd participated in the famous national operetta that took place ten months prior parroted the lines. I left everyone scrutinizing the newspaper on the ground and stood up almost reflexively. My silly moves harmonized with the rhythm of the song I was singing along to: "They are to

Kuwait, the eyes and lashes." I bent over and shoved my face in Fawzia's, my eyebrows wiggling above my crossed eyes.

"May God strike you blind," she said without cracking so much as a smile. I sat on the ground once more in the corner of the living room, next to Mama Hissa's twin, between Sadiq, Fahd, and Fawzia. There was nothing of note in the news except for something that suddenly altered Sadiq's mood. He snatched the newspaper and intently read the first few pages. The reddening of his ears pushed me to read what was on the front page: *Charged for the bombings in Mecca, the Holy City.* Below it, in bold font: *Saudi Arabia executes 16 Kuwaitis and acquits 9.* "Th-they've been wr-wronged! That's not fair!" Sadiq stammered, directing his words at no one in particular. He left for home immediately, leaving me wondering, *Who are they?* I forgot all about it until forty days later when they were commemorated, and I realized that they belonged to the same sect as 'Am Abbas's household, just as 'Am Saleh had said. Sadiq became wary when I asked him about it. I was frustrated with his answer. I felt that both of them, Sadiq and Fahd, understood more than me because of their fathers. They would mock me for my ignorance and endless questions, telling me to go back to playing with my wrestling dolls and collecting pictures of Hulk Hogan.

The recent report in the newspaper reminded me of Sadiq's outright resentment when he had asked me how 'Am Saleh viewed him and his family after the Great Mosque of Mecca had been stormed by armed men from our sect ten years before. And when I asked my mom about the Juhayman group that Sadiq had told me about, she responded, wagging her finger, "By God Almighty, I forbid you from hanging out with those two!" She swore at Sadiq and Fahd. I didn't ask the question again. I remained a prisoner to my burgeoning jealousy. Why? Because my two friends seemed to know it all.

Forty days after the death penalty had been carried out, 'Am Saleh preoccupied himself with taking out both of his cars and his wife's car from the carport and parking them in front of his house. I couldn't figure out why until Fahd explained his father's reasoning, based on some news that one of the neighbors had relayed to 'Am Saleh that morning. 'Am Abbas was going to hold a commemoration, an *Arba'eeniya*, for those Kuwaitis executed in Saudi Arabia forty days ago: acquitted by one, and accused by another. It was the first time I'd heard the word *Arba'eeniya*.

'Am Saleh called my dad and the rest of the neighbors, asking them to also park their cars on the street so that 'Am Abbas's guests, the mourners, wouldn't crowd up the street by parking in the empty spaces in front of our houses. 'Am Saleh held an old grudge against his nemesis of a neighbor from back when 'Am Abbas had cordoned off the empty plot in front of his house with chains during 'Am Saleh's father's funeral. But, I mused, if 'Am Abbas hadn't done that back then, would 'Am Saleh's position really have been any different?

A couple of the neighbors complied with 'Am Saleh's request; in fact, most of them didn't. Our informant neighbor called Fahd's father back to correct the information he had passed on earlier that day. "Abbas is going to attend a memorial service at the Imam Hussein Mosque. What I told you in the morning was fake news."

The few cars by the sidewalk promptly went back under their canopies.

***

4:42 p.m.

Present Day

I'm in traffic, trapped in my car—unable to get out of the area, hemmed in by the security forces. Kuwait National Radio broadcasts news of flights in and out of the international airport being suspended, without explanation. The BBC confirms in its news brief that the UN Security Council has agreed to double the number of peacekeeping forces stationed in Kuwait. One of the radio station guests responds to the news with disconcerting levity. "Two security officers are more than enough for Kuwait, instead of these peacekeeping forces!" he says before bursting out in laughter. Something within me lets out a howl of despair. For months now we've heard about the peacekeeping forces being sent, but so far there has been nothing to show for it, except for the forces surrounding the oil wells.

A beep from my phone alerts me to a long text message from the publisher: "What's happening? I've been following the news on TV . . . Tell me you're okay . . ." I ignore the message. Pictures of the old Lebanon run through my mind, accompanied by a Mama Hissa voice-over, barking the epithet "Idiots!"—which she'd repeat whenever the newscaster alluded to one of the Lebanese warring factions during their first civil war. Ayub calls me, cutting short my reverie.

"Things are getting worse. Clashes have increased on both the Yemeni and the Iraqi sides of the Saudi border. Unconfirmed reports I've heard say that Saudi authorities have decided to temporarily close down the border crossings between their country and Kuwait. Meaning that . . . we're all stuck here."

I think of my parents, and then I answer him, "Whoever wanted to leave, left when the war broke out."

"Hundreds of cars are lined up bumper to bumper, unable to pass," he confirms.

"The northern borders are open for whoever wants to leave! Only a lunatic would flee this Kuwaiti fire, which has scarcely started burning, to the Iraqi cinders whose smoke we've been inhaling for years," I comment dryly.

"In which part of Iraq are they trying to seek refuge?"

"Idiots." The word slips out of my lips.

He lets out a forced laugh. "I swear to God, there's no safe place to hide or run to anymore." His words remind me of Dhari.

"Apparently, it's still all unofficial," Ayub reassures me. Before hanging up, he asks, "Aren't you ever going to tell me what happened at dawn today?"

"Later." I end the call. I call Dhari repeatedly. No answer. I tune the radio to our station. I don't get what's happening! Dhari's reading a poem—yes, a poem—he who doesn't recite poetry. He who thinks poetry is inherently open to misinterpretation. What led him to do this now? And why did he backtrack on his original stance? His voice comes across as angry, which is unlike him; it is angry at everything: his state of being, our situation, and his stutter.

"Explode
O you banished anger from w-within, now
        outside
O you f-fading brilliance
In the s-strangled extent
In the dust-sprinkled horizon."

He's just recited "A Charm in the Time of Dying," another Khalifa
Al Waqayan poem. Does Ayub know? Does Dhari know what he's reciting? Is now the best time for this? Or will it be better when we're dead?
His voice grows faint, quiet, as if he's surrendered. The Islamic songs
play quietly in the background as he goes on:

"Explode
If the earthworm c-creeps
And the rabid baby locust
Harvests your verdant field."

Why am I shedding tears for you, Dhari? You were the one who
was reassuring me that it was going to be okay. What's become of you
now? The calmness with which you're reciting the poem doesn't dispel
the state of confusion that I'm in. I search for a side street to turn down
to escape the congestion and make my way to headquarters. Dhari's
voice flays me as it continues the recital with a delivery that doesn't
sound like his:

"Explode
If night is a m-murderer
Folding up its expanse
Grabbing the napes of the stars . . . and the full
        moon
Giving a drink to the blade of the d-dagger

It comes . . . it looks out
In the so-called name of G-God
God Almighty
It advances to the pulpit."

"God is great!"

THE FIRST MOUSE: SPARK
THE INHERITANCE OF FIRE

THE NOVEL

Chapter 12

October 30, 1989: it was the evening that we had all been eagerly awaiting. With his skinny frame, Fahd squeezed himself behind the wooden television console, fiddling with the antennae, clearing up the snowy image on the screen. Fawzia fed the VCR a tape. Before returning to the sofa, she pressed the button to record. It was a day of celebration, the opening day of the first Peace and Friendship Cup; unbeknownst to anyone at the time, it would also be the last. The household's members, Mama Hissa's twin, Sadiq, and I sat gripped by the TV in the living room of the Al Bin Ya'qub household. Even Tina had taken up her usual seat nearby to observe our antics as we watched. We waited for the operetta marking the opening of the games to start. The atmosphere was electric. The TV volume was as high as it would go, as the air conditioner grumbled in the background, fighting off the last heat waves that marked the end of summer. Enthusiastic whooping from the audience on-screen; the aroma of saffron tea; milk with ginger; the sound of nuts being shelled, cracking between fingers and mouths around me; copious dollops of ice cream that we'd bought especially for this occasion from Abu Sameh the Palestinian before he went into hibernation during the winter months.

Each of us had something that we were looking forward to before the games began. I wasn't interested in any sport except for freestyle wrestling, and I definitely wasn't concerned with the sportsmen who had come from forty-four Arab and Muslim nations to vie for victory. All that concerned me was two countries meeting for the first time after such a lengthy hiatus: Iraq and Iran. I was impatient for November 5, just a few days later, when their two soccer teams would go head-to-head. And meet they did. There was a roar from the stadium when both team captains shook hands and Sheikh Fahad Al Ahmad gifted both captains a copy of the Quran before the match. *If only Sheikh Fahad would come to our street and gift both 'Am Saleh and 'Am Abbas a copy,* I thought to myself. That idea quickly evaporated when the referee's whistle signaled the beginning of the match and roused the commentator Khalid Al Harban into action, despite the eventual unsatisfying draw.

On the opening day of the games, we were exchanging whispered words when Mama Hissa silenced us with a shush. Immediately, the announcer's voice came to the fore. "We have been kindly obliged by His Excellency Sheikh Fahad Al Ahmad Al Jabir Al Sabah, the chairman of the Kuwait Olympic Committee, member of the International Olympic Committee . . ." Mama Hissa was delighted to see "the Man," as she fawningly called him. After all, he was the prince, the man who had fought for years in the Palestine Liberation Organization's ranks, among the resistance fighters against those "Jews" inside the occupied territories. She was a bit fuzzy on the details, as she didn't know much about what had gone on out there. The man had fought against the Jews, and that was more than enough for a woman like her. Making his way up to the stage at that moment was the man himself, Abu Ahmad, to give a speech minutes before the opening of the games, whose soundtrack included his lyrics. The audience stirred—as did we—their enthusiasm stoked, in response to what Abu Ahmad said to his brother, the emir of Kuwait. "O Jaber Al Khair, the meeting point is here; all Muslim brothers are gathered here. This is my cousin, here is my brother, and this is our religion of forgiveness—Islam," intoned Abu Ahmad. Spellbound, we watched. The emir officially opened the tournament. Groups of students erupted forth to the rhythm of national songs, wearing the traditional costumes of the participating countries, leading a parade of all the teams across the soccer field. I remember, as if I can hear it now, the brouhaha of the crowd—clapping, yelling, singing. Each of us in the Al Bin Ya'qub family household on that evening sang late into the night, enjoying the jamboree.

Khala Aisha kept giving Tina something or other to do. Anything, just so she wouldn't stay sitting with us in the living room, not working. Without peeling her eyes away from the screen, Mama Hissa commanded, "Sit down, Tina!" Blood boiling, Khala Aisha withdrew to her room. Fahd and Sadiq watched her depart in silence. They then started commenting on every sentence the Olympic Committee chairman uttered during his speech, as if they were in competition to show off who knew more. They listened closely to him. "There are people in some countries, starving, fearful of destruction," the chairman said.

Fahd and Sadiq fought to answer him. "Somalia and Palestine!" Images of metal donation boxes I had seen, seemingly ubiquitous, sprang to mind: in the stores, the mosques, the schools, and even in Fahd's bedroom. One box that had the picture of the Dome of the Rock on it and another that had an African boy, a tear running down his cheek, with the following phrase emblazoned above him: *Will you wipe away the tears of this poor boy?*

"Let us call out in the name of peace . . . and make amends between one neighbor and the other." Jostling each other, each boy responded to the chairman, giving priority to the country they were raised to respect—"Iraq and Iran" or "Iran and Iraq"—and I, who wanted to build bridges between my neighbors, wished I could've jumped in before the both of them saying, "'Am Abbas and 'Am Saleh!" or "'Am Saleh and 'Am Abbas!"

Sometimes I found myself, like the others, following what was happening on the TV. Other times, I found myself like Tina, watching the faces around me, each pulled in by some different aspect of the opening festivities. Fawzia watched with a smile weighed down by a sadness I didn't understand. Maybe she was craving some of the frozen contraband that was in our hands, or maybe she was wishing that she could be one of the dancers on-screen, reliving her heyday. I sensed her cursing her days now, as a seventeen-year-old woman, a woman bound by her elder brother's authority, who saw some shortcoming or other in everything she did. Fahd, as if hypnotized, sat on the floor, his legs folded under him, watching eagerly, mouth agape, his scarcely blinking eyes unmoving from the screen lest a single scene pass him by. I knew that the soccer games themselves didn't mean much to him. After all, Muayyad Al Haddad hadn't been called up to the national team; it was rather Abdulkareem Abdulqader's singing in the opening ceremony that drew him in. He listened with a delight incongruous with his young age. Maybe he wasn't as interested in the song's lyrics as he was in his favorite singer's voice, and his presence at the heart of the throngs of students belting out his songs. Mama Hissa wavered between nodding her head while smiling and being on the verge of soundless tears—perhaps no one saw her but me—during the Palestinian musical performance led by Abdulkareem in harmony with the voices of the groups around him. "And when a voice calls out, when will my country return?" they sang. She blew her nose into her tissue. She then wiped her face before exploding, "Jewish bastards!" All the while the dancing groups repeatedly sang, "We've drawn the red line under this: Here, we may only be children, but on the battlefield we're adults," fueling our zeal.

These songs would inspire Fahd, Sadiq, and me, propelling us into action, to the point where we became obsessed with gathering rocks from houses under construction in Surra, we who had never previously gathered such things unless it was for a good old game of anbar. Our dishdashas would be folded up into pouches to be filled with stones. For such occasions we adopted new names: Sabhi, Mazin, and Mustafa. One day, hidden behind the sand heaps and cement bags, we pelted some construction workers on a scaffolding frame. A worker carrying a large electric drill caught our attention. We turned and aimed at him, unleashing our loads like rain, repeating breathlessly before taking off with the wind: "If you have a cannon, I have a stone . . . Here, we may only be children, but on the battlefield we're adults!" I remember Fahd catching his breath, kneeling down in the courtyard after our reenacted resistance to the imaginary occupation. "Man, if only we were Palestinian," he said wistfully.

"So Abdulkareem would sing for us, 'O time, look at them, our children—who is like them?'" Sadiq concurred, completely on the same page.

"How I wish we were Palestinian!" Fahd gushed. He would try to get close to the children in the house where the Palestinians resided, interested in befriending Samir and Hazim, our classmates. He parroted a garbled version of one of Abu Sameh's favorites, written after 1967 for the displaced Palestinians who'd traversed across Jordan and Iraq to settle in Kuwait: "Fill the jug for me, fill the jug for me, O Mother. Kuwait is far, and the desert will make me thirsty." Whenever we expressed our admiration for Mahzouza and Mabrouka, Fahd would remind us who wrote the series, the Palestinian scriptwriter Tariq Uthman. Fahd would share with Samir and Hazim Mama Hissa's lessons and tales, forever impressed in his mind, of the glorious oranges she had seen during her visit to Palestine as a girl. She swore that she had been able to put her hand out the car window and pluck the oranges straight off the trees; she'd raise her hand up high to reenact the scene, collecting imaginary oranges in her lap. "Like this! Just like this!" Mama Hissa would crow as she recounted her adventure.

Such idealistic national sporting events brought everyone together. All household members, at least, in one house, at the same time, in front of the TV, consumed by being Arab. We genuinely believed what the national songs said. We'd be joyous or angry, or we'd cry, struck with emotion. After the Palestinian team's segment, Abdulkareem chanted, "Lebanon's for Arabs, not for wars . . . blood of the innocents covers the roads!" Mama Hissa pursed her lips, incensed. She couldn't believe how the sons of one country could ignite a civil war. "Idiots!" she'd spout. If only she could have lived to see the idiots that we ourselves would become.

In February 1990, the exact same scene took place in the living room on the opening day of the tenth Gulf Cup championship, hosted by Kuwait. At that time, despite the competition, we became more *Khaleeji*, prouder of our Gulf roots than at any other time. The television kept on broadcasting the famous song "Our Gulf Is One and Our People Are One." The song was featured during both the Gulf Cup and at the GCC summit, only to sink away into the background—except it had a lasting effect on our collective psyche. It had been about a month since Fawzia had holed herself up in her room after the death of Ihsan Abdel Quddous. The Gulf Cup pulled her out of her self-imposed seclusion. She fed the VCR a tape to record the opening festivities. The members of the household, plus Tina and I, were all assembled; the only one missing was Sadiq, who had crossed over into the realm of puberty early. Seemingly out of nowhere, his mustache had appeared. Pimples cropped up across his cheeks, and his voice broke. He knocked on 'Am Saleh's door that day, carrying dishes that Mama Zaynab was famous for: fatty *dolma* and *damlooj*, which we found even more delicious when additional powdered sugar and cinnamon paste were sprinkled on top. Tina took the food-laden plates in. Sadiq made for the inside of the Al Bin Ya'qub household, but was stopped by 'Am Saleh declaring, "You've become a man . . . You can't be with the women any longer."

Before, I had been restlessly waiting for the outline of my mustache to make an appearance. When it did eventually emerge, I would remove the fine fuzz with a razor blade in the opposite direction of the growth. I would then rub the shaven stubble with castor oil, hoping that the hair would grow back more coarsely, like that of Hulk Hogan. Every day I would raise my arms up in front of the bathroom mirror, scrutinizing my armpits. I would feel my smooth pubic area, eagerly awaiting the imminent hordes of hair to colonize my body. I yearned for that world that Sadiq had beaten me to: the magical, miraculous world of adults. The dreams that he'd narrate to us were our only source of thrills. Every morning we'd listen hungrily to the infinitesimal details as well as his exaggerated embellishments, as he recounted dreams where voluptuous movie stars, TV actresses, and news anchors all came together. Fahd started stealing women's fashion catalogs from Fawzia's room. After he was done with them, he'd lend them to me and I'd page through the lingerie sections, pawing at the images, imagining what was under the blacked-out lines covering the forbidden parts on the model's bodies, paving the way for my own dreams, champing at the bit for puberty. But at the same time, I dreaded it ever since Sadiq had been banned from entering 'Am Saleh's house. I longed to be a child for the rest of my life, lest I also be forbidden.

We observed the festivities in silence. Mama Hissa stretched out her legs and rested her wool-clad feet on the radiator. Aisha was turning over the chestnuts above the *duwa*, releasing the smell of burning and cracked peels from above the embers. She left the brazier and headed toward Mama Hissa's twin, to ensure that we all appeared in the video being recorded. Fahd was buoyant, as Muayyad Al Haddad had made the team and Abdulkareem was taking part in the opening ceremony. His voice completely whisked Fahd away to another world. Fawzia's eyes flickered, looking at the clock, anxiously waiting for the beginning of the Kuwaiti team's display in the parade.

'Am Saleh was another matter. I had never seen him as radiant and ecstatic as he was at that hour. How could he not be? The opening performance had started by praising the picture of the man in his hallway. A section of the audience raised colored boards, which once combined formed the slogan of the Iraqi Republic. An enormous hot-air balloon floated skyward with the Iraqi president's picture, the very same one framed in the nearby hallway. The duet by Abdulkareem and Abdullah Al Rowaished started to the beat of the *kasour* drum:

> "Hail the Arab sword, in my right hand I hold
>   you
> Come on, he whose origins history praises
> Come on, he who planted his palm tree
> And watered it from the Shatt River."

The lyrics themselves didn't mean much to me, except for the Shatt Al Arab. I linked these words to Mama Zaynab, who came from there, something Mama Hissa reminded us of every time she warmly greeted her friend, "Hi to you, Old Lady Shatt!"

"Hi, back at you, troublemaker!" Bibi Zaynab would retort.

Mama Hissa would always tremble reverently and then reply, "May God spare us from hellfire!"

'Am Saleh raised his fist up high, as was customary for Sheikh Fahad Al Ahmad. "O God, O God, Abu Uday!" exulted 'Am Saleh, who was enraptured by the lyrics dedicated to Saddam. The dancing troupes repeated a welcome to the Iraqi national team, *"Halla bilha-jaiie."* "What's the big deal with Abu Uday? It's Abdulkareem who's singing!" Fahd wondered aloud, his voice betraying his exasperation. 'Am Saleh didn't pay any heed to his son's observation; he ignored Fahd and continued listening to the rest of the duet:

> "Baghdad, you're on a long road

The eye and the caretaker
O heavy-footed thoroughbred horse
Saddam is your rider."

He was still pumping his fist in the air, repeating the rhyming ends to the song's lines: "The caretaker . . . your rider . . ."

Fawzia, who appeared to be frowning the whole time, waiting for the other nations' displays to end, left the couch to check that the tape was still recording before the Kuwaiti team began at the very end.

The opening ceremony ended in a song for Kuwait. The hijacked plane loomed in my mind. Fawzia was on cloud nine, and so were we. I remember her wide smile, which lasted until the end of the ceremony. Afterward, the sound of the vacuum dragging across the floor grew louder. Fawzia, Fahd, and I set the living room back into shape. We helped Tina pick up the husks of long-eaten nuts from the carpet, singing as we worked, "I'm Kuwaiti. My word is . . ." The annoying thrum of Tina's vacuum silenced us, while 'Am Saleh and Khala Aisha returned to their room, singing softly as they went, *Halla bilhajaiie*, welcome to you."

THE SECOND MOUSE: BLAZE

In my mouth a drop of water grows
It grows
And on both sides the flame yells
Is there more?
Us and the rocks, we were the fuel
Us and the rocks, we remain the fuel

—Khalifa Al Waqayan

THE SECOND MOUSE: BLAZE
THE INHERITANCE OF FIRE

THE NOVEL

Chapter 1

The final week of July 1990: your parents traveled to spend the rest of their summer in London. Summering in London wasn't exactly a penchant of yours; you'd be alone without any friends like every other year, the same humdrum most of the time, trailing your mom on Oxford Street, bent over, laden with her shopping bags while you anticipated manhood. You pressed Mama Hissa to do something, begged her, kissed her forehead, but she cut off your pleading. "Don't put me in an awkward spot with Ms. Principal."

When you stopped going over to the Al Bin Ya'qub house to protest her giving up on you so easily, she sent Fahd your way with a message. "Mama Hissa says, 'We've beaten up the dog that bit you.'" So she had decided to deal with the issue and put an end to your boycott. You smiled at Fahd, urging him to go on. "She'll call your dad." You flew as happy as a free bird when she, your elderly neighbor, succeeded in convincing your dad to let you stay behind in Kuwait. Your mom, on the other hand, got all worked up about it. She refused outright. She raised her finger to the sky, and would have sworn an oath if you hadn't hugged her, covering her mouth with your hand.

"No, Mom, please don't!" You were lucky, or maybe not, when she just glared at your father instead.

She tried to sway him. "The old woman says the boy will be well taken care of," came his frank response. She was still determined to have the last word. He placated her. "Think of it as a honeymoon!" Begrudgingly she left you behind, for the sake of the so-called honeymoon.

You shifted to the Al Bin Ya'qub household after your parents left without you (only after an endless list of promises had been made to your mom). At night, the neighborhood was quiet, like every summer. Silent except for the beating wings of the night *suweer* and the occasional sound of a car passing through. Most of the house lights were off, and the cars were wrapped up in dusty fabric covers under canopies, their owners on holiday. Your joy at being in your neighbor's home turned into heavy regret only one day after your parents' departure when 'Am Saleh decided to keep Abu Sami's dog in his courtyard while its owners were in America. At first, Mama Hissa refused. "A dog? In *my* house?" she asked defiantly, as she beat her chest with her palms, before explaining that a dog in the house would chase away the angels. 'Am Saleh tried to change her mind. "Our street is so much darker now. Too many people are away. The saluki will be good for security. It's just for a few days, and then he'll go back home." She didn't budge.

"Abu Sami is our *neighbor*," he reminded her. He didn't need to elaborate that the Prophet entreated one to respect their neighbor, even those seven doors down. She reluctantly assented. You never imagined that the day would come when both you and the dog would be brought together in one place, with you trembling at the saluki's faintest bark. During playtime, you divided the courtyard up between the both of you: the dog in the corner, his zone dictated by how much leeway the leash would allow; for you, your zone started from the building adjoining the house and overlooking the courtyard—where the kitchen and diwaniya were—and ended with the chicken coop near the sidra. You hated how scared you were. You were afraid that others would smell your fear. Now and then, the round-the-clock news on TV would mention of the Iraqi-Kuwaiti fracas, whose every detail 'Am Saleh was intently following.

You were sitting inside the house with Fahd's dad, pretending to be watching TV, rooted to the spot. News about Crown Prince Sheikh Saad Abdullah Al Sabah's visit to Saudi Arabia to partake in what the media came to dub "the Jeddah Dialogue," corralling together Iraqi and Kuwaiti delegates for the sake of resolving their lingering issues. You asked Fahd's dad why. He answered and you still didn't get it. He simplified his answer further and again you didn't grasp it. He broke it down even further.

"Kuwait is stealing Iraq's oil . . . That's what they're saying."

"Who are 'they'?"

"The Iraqis."

And when you asked him what he thought, he kept silent, preoccupying himself with what was on TV. Five months before that day, Iraq had put forth an official request to lease two Kuwaiti islands, Warba and Bubiyan; such matters were things that you would come to know about when you grew up. You hadn't the faintest idea what was going on around you except for how perturbed people were over what was on the news and their unsatisfactory answers to your big questions. The one thing you do remember vividly was what 'Am Saleh told your dad that day as they stood on the sidewalk opposite Maryam Al Ghanem Mosque in Surra: "If I were in power, not only would I agree to lease out those two islands to Iraq, but I'd throw in Miskan Island, too, as a cherry on top!" In 'Am Saleh, your father saw an unhinged man captivated by the Iraqi president's personality, blindly believing all his allegations, a man biased against those in power in Kuwait since the

dissolution of the parliament, brainwashed by the opposition who organized the Monday protests, the diwaniyas. Your neighbor 'Am Saleh saw
in your father an opportunist who was only interested in money; the
"crisis trader" as he called him, exploiting the collapse of the Al Manakh
stock market by buying shares at unbelievably low prices; a man who
approved of parliament's dissolution as a solution, as unconstitutional
as that was; a man who voted in the national assembly elections—an
illegal substitute for the Kuwaiti parliament—justifying his involvement by saying that it was for the sake of stabilizing the country and
helping it recover from its economic crisis.

You remember your father in front of the mosque, in heated discussion with 'Am Saleh, making no effort to mask his concern over the
fraught relationship between the two countries and what could happen in the future. He abruptly brought up how the Iraqi government
postponed its efforts to resolve the simmering border issues, despite
agreeing to draw its Iraqi borders with Saudi Arabia and Jordan. Your
mind wandered, drifting to the maps drawn on wax paper in your
geography classes.

"You have an explanation?" your father asked your neighbor. Your
eyes darted between them, listening as the images of school maps
swirled around in your head, Kuwait appearing small and barely visible.

'Am Saleh raised his voice. "Iraq isn't overstepping its boundaries.
Enough with the rumors, *akhi*!"

Not a word from your father.

'Am Saleh wasted no time in reminding him of the emir's trip
to Iraq—a couple of months before that day—and how Saddam had
warmly received him before conferring on him the Order of the Two
Rivers, *Wisam Al Rafidain*. "I think you get what I'm saying," 'Am
Saleh concluded. You remember your father not responding, shaking his
head, making his way to his car, frowning. You remember the questions
you threw at him during the ride home, though he didn't pay you any
mind. You asked him why all parties couldn't just agree on redrawing

the borders. The space between his eyebrows grew, his astonishment not hiding his crack of a smile.

"Re-demarcation? And what does a ten-year-old boy know of such things?"

His mistake exasperated you. "Twelve!"

He didn't react. He busied himself, listening raptly to the radio. You repeated your questions. "*Uff!* You never stop asking questions!" You didn't understand why your questions made everyone clam up. You didn't understand your father or 'Am Saleh. Not only did Fahd's dad believe that the Iraqi president was the "Guardian of the Eastern Gate," but apparently he was also convinced that since the emir had dissolved the parliament, obstructed the constitution, and imposed in 1986 a mandatory governmental review of all newspapers before they went to print, parliament wouldn't be resurrected in Kuwait except through Iraqi means or pressure from Saddam.

This fascination with Saddam infected Mama Hissa, too. She wasn't concerned in the least by the photo on her hallway wall until Saddam made his statement four months earlier, that he would burn down half of Israel. You remember your question to her about how she was the one who'd said the only thing you'll get from fire is ashes. Pleased, she responded that fire was good if it left behind Jewish ashes. 'Am Saleh intervened, trying to explain the difference between Jews and Israelis. She cut him off. "They're all the same!"

Two days after Abu Sami and his family had left, or maybe three days after, a rumor circulated through the neighborhood about why they had to travel, even though they did it every summer. It was said that his wife had received a call from her country's embassy, urging her to make haste and leave Kuwait. It was also said that a number of other embassies had relayed the same to their citizens in Kuwait. "Rumors . . . just rumors," 'Am Saleh kept insisting. He reassured the women in his household, relying on the foreign minister Sheikh Sabah Al Ahmad's statement: "The Iraqi-Kuwaiti problem is a passing summer cloud."

And you, beside him, seated in front of the TV, kept on asking questions that—according to him—weren't suitable for a child to ask. He would answer unwillingly and you'd ask more. He'd fall silent. You'd ask again. He finally raised his voice, bellowing for the first time in your face. "Who do you think you are, asking such questions?" He asked why you didn't just go on out with Fahd to the courtyard. You retracted your head between your shoulders, not saying a word. He left the living room in the direction of the hallway leading to the courtyard. He came back after a few minutes, understanding why you were still there, and in a soft voice said, "I've tied up the saluki."

THE SECOND MOUSE: BLAZE
THE INHERITANCE OF FIRE

THE NOVEL

Chapter 2

You were now their *amana*, someone they had to take care of properly, and so, the old lady didn't let you sleep in Fahd's room, far from her reach. Instead, she made space for you in a small corner of her room on a foam mattress on the ground below her bed, on top of a carpet, bright red like Fuada's dress.

Next to her bed was a small side table, on which rested heart, blood pressure, and diabetes pills; an alarm clock; and a glass of water with dentures plunged in. Nothing intrigued a boy of your age as much as staying in a room like hers, where everything was out of the ordinary for you: antique carpets; a brass bed and a tiger-patterned woolen blanket; a wooden comb; henna powder; lote tree soap; Nablus soap; a honey jar; dried figs; and three bags of dates from Barhiya, Sa'marana, and Ikhlasa. Expired saltine crackers and glass bottles filled with scents—you could make out cardamom pods, saffron, sticks of incense, and ripened aloe-wood fragrance. Other things you didn't recognize, such as black stones and some tools that looked like they could possibly be for scraping dead skin from your heels. The air was heavy with a pervasive smell, most likely Vicks or Tiger Balm that Tina brought from Sri Lanka. There were other strong odors, pleasant ones, hovering like a cloud. Mama Hissa went to bed early and this annoyed you.

On the second day, she allowed Fahd to share your mattress after much imploring from the both of you. But staying up late was still out of the question. She liked to split you up by placing a long pillow between you both. "Don't remove it!" Her insistence took you by surprise.

"You're drawing boundaries now?" you pestered her.

"Shut your mouth and go to bed!" she said in exasperation, as she lay down on the bed.

You both stifled your laughter at her elephantine snoring that started up as soon as her head hit the pillow. In the dark you observed her movements. She would wake up sporadically, raise her head from the pillow, and then glance down at both of you before she slipped into sleep again. You didn't understand the need for her over-the-top surveillance until the following night. You woke up in the middle of the night to the sound of her scolding her grandson: "Go to sleep, Fahd!" At once, he pretended to snore. She warned him that even in the dark she could see him. "Haram!" she upbraided him. He didn't respond. For good measure, she reminded him that his hand would get pregnant if he kept on doing what he was doing.

Since that night, you went back to sleeping solo and without the long pillow. The whole incident opened your eyes. Endless dreams disturbed you. You were afraid to shove your hand into the "secret" place, to discover an unexpected newness to your body and release wetness, as Sadiq had told you, that looked like egg whites. You feared that you'd be exposed, someone would catch you red-handed, exploring yourself, and that you'd be thrown out of the house—a man with a pregnant hand.

***

The old lady's snoring no longer makes you giggle. You toss and turn on your mattress, trying to steal a few minutes' sleep whenever the snoring eases up. Mama Hissa's words come back to you: "Even in the dark, I can see you." You imagine her as a witch. An image of the glass with her dentures chattering away floats through your mind. Sleep refuses to settle on your eyes. You squeeze your pillow. You groan.

"Go to sleep, for God's sake!"

You complain to her about how bored you are, how you can't sleep.

"Tomorrow I'll tell you a story," she promises.

"I already know them all," you say, certain that you had already memorized all the sidra jinn stories.

She lowers her voice as you attentively listen to her air of mystery. "Tomorrow I'll tell you about the four mice."

"Why tomorrow? Why not now?" Your fear of mice doesn't deter your curiosity. She says it's a long one. You get up, sitting on your haunches. You look straight at her in the dark and ask about the four mice. "What are their names?"

"One mouse is called Jamr."

Embers. "And the others?"

"Ramad," she grumbles, naming one more.

Ashes. "There are still two left!" you hiss impatiently.

Her snoring resumes again—she is fast asleep. You try guessing the remaining names. Mickey Mouse? Or maybe Jerry? Can't be. You try to sleep. You count sheep. No good. You count mice. Sleep still evades you. The light coming in from under the bedroom door flickers. It catches your attention. Someone must be out there.

"Mama Hissa!" I said.

"Hmm?" she responds softly, her voice barely making it out of her throat.

"There's someone outside the door!"

She turns to her side, her bed creaking from the weight of her movement. "You're dreaming."

You scrutinize the door. The shadow in the light under the door is still dancing. "Wallah, there's someone behind the door," you confirm.

"The saluki wouldn't have let anyone past the courtyard door," she reassures you. "Go to sleep, you scaredy-cat."

"There's a shadow under the door. Look, look!"

She lets out an impatient sigh. "It's just Fawzia reminding me to take my medicine."

Since Fawzia doesn't say anything from behind the door, you insist, "No, it's not her." You leave your mattress, making your way to the light switch. The old woman gets up, raising the blanket midway over her face. "Don't! Go back to your bed." She shrinks away from the light so that you don't see her without her dentures, while she keeps repeating in a garbled fashion, "Over my dead body you'll see me without my teeth!"

You sit on the mattress, folding your legs under you, taking in the moving shadow under the door. You confirm that whoever is behind it, it definitely isn't Fawzia or a thief.

"Maybe it's the mice," Mama Hissa mumbles.

You curl into a ball behind your blanket. You're drowning in a sea of sweat. You curse the day you asked her to convince your dad to let you stay in Kuwait. You grasp at the fringes of sleep. You poke a leg out from under the blanket. You wiggle your sweaty toes, making space between them, to feel the air-conditioned air. You suddenly remember the mice and sharply retract your leg back under the blanket. Fuada's voice explodes in your head, rising to a crescendo as she warns, "They're coming; they're coming!" Her voice disappears as soon as Fahd says from behind the door, in a voice just barely louder than a whisper, "*Fajr* prayers."

***

'Am Saleh, Fahd, and you sat in a circle around the low dining table on the floor after your return from the mosque. Mama Hissa came in, holding a jug of milk, with Khala Aisha behind her, balancing the tray of food. Tina never got up at dawn. "Because she doesn't pray like us!" Mama Hissa quipped to her daughter-in-law. You'd asked her a few years earlier, when both Tina and Florence were Christians, "Why do you like Tina and hate Florence?"

"Tina's a servant, and Florence is a Muslim man's wife who doesn't fear God! What if his children become Christians? You're such a chatterbox, always asking such heavy questions," Mama Hissa complained.

The light before sunrise bathed the living room windows in a gray-blue hue. The place smelled of bread, broad beans, nakhi, and cardamom milk. The phone rang. "Let all be well, God," Mama Hissa prayed before sitting down, harboring a bad feeling about the phone ringing at dawn. Fahd jumped to pick up the receiver.

His mother turned to him, her face ashen. "My heart is aching; there's nothing but disaster behind this call."

"Only God knows the future, you sham soothsayer," Mama Hissa countered. 'Am Saleh put back some broad beans he had just taken out of the pot. All of you looked at Fahd expectantly. He returned the greeting. He nodded his head. He stretched out his hand with the receiver to his mother. "Uncle is asking about you."

Khala Aisha took the receiver, her eyebrows restless. Her lips trembled before she put the phone down, confirming, "Disaster!" She paused. "Kuwait's gone!"

You didn't understand how Kuwait could be gone just like that: poof. And if so, where to?

"The Iraqi army"— with her eyes trained on her husband in particular, she completed the news she'd just received—"has entered Kuwait!" *Dukhool* . . . entry—it was the only word you could come up with that day, while trying to digest the news; days passed before the word changed, growing and hardening into the bitter truth. Their "entry" became a "crisis," the "crisis" an "invasion," and the "invasion" an eventual "occupation."

Mama Hissa rambled on somewhat in denial about what the Iraqi president had done. "A change is going to come." She rushed to take her medication. "Where's the man who said he would burn down half of Israel?"

You don't remember anything that Khala Aisha said, or the stricken faces of everyone around you, asking what was to come. You don't remember anything except for 'Am Saleh yelling at his wife, "Rumors! It's just a rumor." You wished you could seek refuge with Fawzia, who had withdrawn to her room, heartbroken by her brother's decision after her high school graduation a few weeks ago. "No college for you," he had determined.

"The Iraqi army has entered Kuwait!" you yelled up to Fawzia. You looked over at 'Am Saleh, the word *enter* taking you back to half a year ago when he was humming *Halla bilhajaiie,* we welcome you. You looked at his wife, wondering just how she had predicted that the phone call would be bad news.

After the sun rose, it didn't take long for the news that Fahd's father had so wished was hearsay to become a reality. Baghdad radio broadcasted statements, one after the other, as well as people ululating, joyful over Kuwait being freed. You all wondered: being freed from whom, though? On Kuwait National Radio, before the frequency was jammed, the voice of Yusuf Mustafa, the broadcaster, was unusually tremulous. "Here is Kuwait, you free Kuwaiti citizens, you Arabs in every place. Treason has bared its fangs, and tyranny has shown its claws." The hours dragged on. The phone didn't stop ringing. Your mother called from abroad, completely broken. She could barely string together the following words: "BBC news . . . Iraq . . . Kuwait . . . war . . . your *khal* Hassan will come get you and take you to Al Faiha. You have to stay at home with him, understood?"

'Am Saleh was fixated on the TV, as still as stone, his eyes blinking the only movement. The scene in front of you was at the base of the three Kuwait Towers downtown. There were men—their dishdashas were Kuwaiti, but their faces weren't—yelling and performing the Iraqi hosa dance, just like you had for the Hitachi camcorder. They were there, welcoming the valiant soldiers that stood up to help those who had rebelled and demanded that they be freed from the brutal, tyrannical emir, or the Korah of Kuwait, as the Iraqi media would call him, after one of Pharaoh's sinister ministers of yore. *The Kuwaiti rebels welcome the most glorious Iraqi soldiers,* read the yellow chyron at the bottom of the screen.

You didn't understand a thing. You just felt, and that was it. You felt something, but you weren't sure what it was. The questions that were fizzing in your head died on your lips. You weren't able to lock yourself away in a room like Fawzia, or plunge into prayer like Mama Hissa, or distract yourself by answering phone calls like Fahd, or remain stonelike and expressionless like Khala Aisha, or close your eyes and rave like Tina recalling images of bloodshed in the Tamil Tigers' clashes with the Sinhalese government. You were just like 'Am Saleh: frowning while watching it all unfold on TV. You took in the faces around you. Thrumming of choppers loomed within earshot. You hoped that they were Kuwaiti helicopters, but they weren't.

A slight sense of reassurance filled you after you received somewhat confirmed news: the emir and the crown prince had left the Dasman Palace. They had reached Saudi Arabia. Your childlike memory recalled Fawzia's grand dreams: graduating from university and shaking hands with the emir. What if their time away lasted longer than planned and was even further drawn out? What if the emir . . . ? You shook your head, dismissing the thought. No sooner had you all sighed with relief at the head of state safely reaching Saudi Arabia than a phone call came in and confirmed, "Sheikh Fahad Al Ahmad has been martyred at the Dasman Palace gates." How was he murdered? Each story contradicted the next. What was corroborated is that he didn't know his brother the emir had already fled. He had made his way to Dasman Palace for his brother's sake. He had come to blows with the Iraqi Republican Guard outside of the gates before three bullets struck him down. Mama Hissa burst out sobbing. "The man's gone!" She slapped her thighs in grief. Aisha wept for him. Fawzia wept for him. You recalled the last time you saw him on TV, the day of the Peace and Friendship Cup. The opening song about brotherhood echoed in your ears. Your head swam with questions. The weakness that overcame you and Fahd made you both look to 'Am Saleh for some kernel of strength, but he was running his thumb under his eyes, revealing the redness of his eyeballs, pretending to be fine. He shook his head defiantly at the news. "Maybe . . . maybe it's all just a rumor."

THE SECOND MOUSE: BLAZE
THE INHERITANCE OF FIRE

THE NOVEL

Chapter 3

Your country, which you had always known as Kuwait, transformed in a matter of days to the nineteenth province of the "glorious" Iraqi Republic. A Kuwaiti citizen you were no longer. As the TV and radio declared, since the first week of the occupation, you had become an Iraqi citizen of "the reclaimed" Al Nida province. A province that had been wrongly cut off by the colonizers and had now rightfully returned to the bosom of the larger nation, thanks to God and the determination of the diligent soldiers now in power. "God is great," Mama Hissa would utter when faced with the claims on the radio. Kuwait had been in the midst of a revolution; that's how the Iraqi media painted it in the first few days, using to their advantage the Monday demonstrations protesting the emir's dissolution of parliament. Apparently, the leaders of the revolution had asked their brotherly Republic of Iraq for help. In less than a week, the revolution became the young Republic of Kuwait, its government headed by a Kuwaiti citizen on TV cloaked in a *bisht*, shaking hands with the Iraqi president. Mama Hissa cradled her head. "O God, land him in trouble!" she prayed. At the end of the first week, the alleged revolutionists announced the accession of the young republic to the mother republic.

'Am Saleh, on the evening of the first day, Thursday, August 2, 1990, came out of his isolation after spending hours in his room, boosting his morale, giving himself hope: things would go back to normal in a couple of days. Perhaps it wasn't so strange that you had no idea what was going on. 'Am Saleh himself didn't understand anything. On the second day of the occupation, the new regime blocked all international communication, leaving only domestic lines active. On the third day, Tina refused Mama Hissa's offer to accompany her to the Sri Lankan embassy, preferring to stay with "Big Mama." "Bint halal, what a good woman, better than the rest," the old lady would say of Tina, while she grumbled, "Strangers are not respected in a strange land." She ridiculed those in a rush to leave Kuwait. "Chickens," she called them. Her words took you back to another time, to two years before, sitting under the sidra, hearing about how chickens gave up on their broken eggs, leaving them to mice that didn't dare to approach the cage unless the egg yolk or egg white was visible. On the fourth day, your khal Hassan called up to let you know that he was making arrangements to get his family across to Saudi Arabia by land. You being his sister's son, he was responsible for you.

"Pack a small bag," he ordered. "Tomorrow at dawn." Sudden sorrow wore you out. How were you going to leave Surra? What if returning became impossible? Fahd simply asked one bewildered question swathed in sadness: "You're leaving us?" You winked at him, indicating for him to follow you to your house. Mama Hissa had no control over something like this. No interventions in such exceptional circumstances. You had made up your mind.

You and Fahd reached your house. It looked mournful as it always did. You bent down in front of your parents' room.

"Why?" Fahd wondered.

"The key!" You pulled back a corner of the carpet by their door. You found a cluster of keys. Fahd looked at you, not questioning what their room had to do with you packing. He was humming softly, veiling his sadness. That's what he always did when he wanted to cover up how he felt. "The key's with the blacksmith," Fahd sang. You tried one key after the other. You opened the bedroom door. You turned to your friend and replied, "The key's with me." He jumped on to the last words of the song, "And rain comes from God." You rifled through the drawers. You searched for your passport among your father's certificates, shares, and banknotes.

Looking at Fahd, you asked him where to hide it. His wide smile preceded your suggestion. Right after you both arrived back at Mama Hissa's, Fahd crouched down below the sidra, like a cat shitting, and dug a hole two hands wide. You were worried about the easily provoked saluki in his corner, his yapping getting louder. Fahd dropped the plastic bag containing your passport. He then filled the hole back up with his feet. After completing his mission, he dusted off his palms. He wiggled his butt at the angry dog, and let out a *"Meeeeow!"* Despite your worry, you both roared with laughter, not fully grasping the danger of what was going on. Slowly, you both walked the length of the hallway to the living room. You nudged Fahd, indicating with your chin the now-empty wall—hanging plants framing the bare square between the two vases with peacock feathers. "The president is gone!" you declared.

"And the newspaper clippings," he added. Khal Hassan, who had come with his son, Dhari, in tow, searched your house high and low. He decided to travel on ahead without you. He wrapped you in his arms and squeezed tight. His thick beard grazed your cheek. "I'll get the family across and then come back to Kuwait."

You exchanged looks with Fahd, suppressing your smiles. Your uncle left, entrusting you to the care of your old neighbor until he returned. You and Fahd sprinted back to the bottom of the sidra to extract your passport. You couldn't agree on exactly where it was buried. Neither of you could find it. You raised your head and peered up at the branches, clapping your palms together and murmuring, "May you be happy in your home."

The jinn of the sidra tree must have seized your passport. After five days, you found out that your uncle had made his way to his house, thanks to another Kuwaiti family, after his van had been seized at the Al Nuwaiseeb Iron Gate. He invited you over to his place. You refused. He then left you to your own devices in the care of the old lady, and said that he would drop by at some point. Fahd's uncles decided to leave Kuwait and called up their sister, saying, "Aisha! Come with us to Saudi Arabia." 'Am Saleh refused. "No one's leaving," he insisted. Mama Hissa rejoiced at his response. 'Am Saleh's wife pressured him, asking why. He responded that the borders weren't safe. The old lady swatted the air in front of her face and pulled at her lips, dispirited. On the sixth day, the crisis was still all around you. You clung to Mama Hissa. She was carrying her transistor radio. There was statement after statement about the Iraqi leadership. The news indicated Iraq's intention to pull out after stabilizing the situation and handing over the reins to those who had cooperated with the Iraqi army; the Iraqi media dubbed them "Kuwaiti rebels." The old lady shook her head in disbelief. "Don't look for truth on the lips of liars!" The seventh day: 'Am Saleh acted in accordance with information he received through phone calls; the occupying soldiers were storming houses, and they would go as far as entering bedrooms to search for contraband or whomever they were looking for. Based on this intel, he had a word with Khala Aisha and Fawzia. The man of the house decided that the women must remain in their hijab and dara'a, even when asleep.

He made no effort to hide his anxiety. "I'm worried about the women, Mother." You remember how both his wife and his sister had to wear their wide long-sleeved dara'a even when they were going into their rooms to go to bed. Khala Aisha was in a hijab all the time, while Fawzia kept her hair in a tight braid. Neither one wore perfume, makeup, or any sort of adornment.

You remember how concerned Mama Hissa was. "Whoever wants to"—she began, then abruptly stopped and continued, skipping over the forbidden word—"a long thawb or hijab won't hold them back."

The eighth day: Fahd and you made your way out to see who was outside. A man, a distressed Kuwaiti, stood in front of you. He looked like he was in his thirties, with a bushy mustache and a short coal-black beard. He wore a tatty ghutra on his head. His face was familiar; maybe he was from the neighborhood. He extended his hand out to Fahd, handing him a plastic bag from the central Surra co-op supermarket. "What's this?" Fahd asked him.

"Bread." The man smiled. "Bread and cheese, so you don't have to go out." He then turned on his heel before Fahd queried, "Who are you?"

"Jasim," he answered on his way back to his car. He opened the trunk and took out another bag, making his way toward your house. He turned to both of you and clarified, "Jasim Al Mutawwa." He pressed the doorbell. You let him know that your house was empty. "They're traveling." He gave your house the once-over, before making his way to 'Am Abbas's home. You both went back inside. 'Am Saleh scolded you both. "Don't ever take anything from a stranger!"

"He's not a stranger," Fahd protested. He said that he'd seen his face somewhere, maybe at the supermarket, or at the mosque, or on the dusty plots where we played soccer.

***

Fawzia fishes out a leaflet from between the loaves. Her brother snatches it and then reads it. "Can we go?" she asks him, hopeful. The leaflet calls for people to come join a demonstration. "To your room!" he yells at Fawzia, his finger pointed. She scrambles to her room, sobbing. He crumples up the leaflet in his palm and rushes to the censer to burn it.

***

"Jahhal," he called them. Children who didn't know or understand the serious implications of their actions. He turned to his mother after the paper had burned to ash and said, "What good will it do to pick a fight with the occupying forces?" Mama Hissa was seated cross-legged on the ground behind her sewing machine, on her lap a Mackintosh's sweets tin in which she kept her spools, needles, pins, and thumbtacks. While sewing up a tear in her prayer thawb, she smiled a mysterious smile that meant something or other to her son. His face flushed. He reminded her, as if justifying himself, of the young photographer who had been slaughtered at the Rumaithiya protest the day before. The old woman stopped spinning her sewing machine.

Without looking at him, she asserted, "God is our protection." 'Am Saleh's face twisted in a mixture of anger and embarrassment. He made his way to the staircase, intending to make amends with Fawzia. He was certain, though, that she wouldn't open her bedroom door for him.

He turned to you. "Come with me." Once outside her room upstairs, he whispered, "Go on, knock on the door." You were just about to do so, when 'Am Saleh grabbed your hand. He pressed his ear against the door and listened. Fawzia was reciting the Quran softly with a heartrending timbre to her voice. 'Am Saleh sighed as he smiled. He told you she was reciting the Quran the same way Sheikh Bin Abidan, the imam of their old mosque, used to. Her recitations stopped. She didn't say anything else. He prodded you to call out, "Fawzia!" She didn't respond. You pressed your lips to the gap between the door and its frame. "Aunt Fawzia . . . open up." She opened the door. She looked at you, irritated by your deception. 'Am Saleh strode forth, his face peaceful. You were right behind him until he put his hand on your chest . and ordered, "Enough, run along now!" He shut the door. You were almost halfway down the stairs when you heard his bellows from above. Mama Hissa left her sewing machine, making her way to Fawzia's room.

She leaned her weight against the banister as she mounted the first steps. Her son appeared at the top of the staircase, waving some folded papers. "This girl is ridiculous!" The old woman didn't say a word. "She's stuck Kuwaiti flags on her closet! Pictures of the emir! And the crown prince!"

He found some matches in the drawers of the TV console in the living room and took them into the courtyard.

***

On the ninth day, London and Monte Carlo radio are the only two reliable news sources, as the occupying forces have taken over the TV stations. We are on tenterhooks while listening to the Arab nations' stances during the emergency summit in Cairo. Waiting for them to condemn or stand beside the Kuwaitis, all in limbo between gratitude and pain. Countries that vote for. Countries that vote against. Countries that did neither.

***

The following morning, the two brothers Abu Taha and Abu Naiel dropped by. "Dad! The zalamat are here to see you," Fahd called out. 'Am Saleh looked at his son quizzically. Fahd shed some light by sharing that they were the Palestinians who owned the house at the end of the road. Baffled, 'Am Saleh asked what they wanted.

Fahd pulled at his lips and shrugged his shoulders. "How should I know?"

The two of you followed 'Am Saleh to the courtyard entrance, where he met the two visitors. He appeared fearful. "What?"

"Here? At the door, you want us to spill the beans?" Abu Naiel reproached.

'Am Saleh stayed quiet. Abu Taha intervened. "There's no problem with that; you're right to keep us out here. We've just come to tell you . . . we've gone to all the neighborhood houses—"

"The other houses in the neighborhood aren't my business," 'Am Saleh interrupted. "What now?"

A car drove up and stopped by their sidewalk. Fahd recognized the driver and said, "Dad, that's Jasim Al Mutawwa."

'Am Saleh got wound up about the arrival of the man who had brought the bread, the cheese, and the pamphlet. He pretended to ignore what Fahd had said. He turned to Abu Taha. "What else? Are we done? Spit it out!"

Abu Taha nodded sympathetically. "What you've heard on the news about Palestinians doesn't apply to us. You know how long we've been living here. What's happening to you is exactly what we're going through."

"I don't know anything. Is that all?"

Abu Naiel chimed in, "Okay, we're done here; we get it." He signaled to his brother that they should get a move on. "C'mon, let's go."

Abu Taha gripped his brother's arm. "Hold on." He looked at 'Am Saleh. "No one from the neighborhood has stopped us being here. Our children are like yours; they don't know any other home. They'd actually die if—"

"It's got nothing to do with me," 'Am Saleh cut him off again. He turned his back on them and firmly shut the black courtyard door behind him. He opened it once more when the bell rang. It was Jasim Al Mutawwa with a bag of bread. "We don't need your food!" he barked gruffly before the man could get a word in.

Jasim held out the plastic bag to Fahd's dad, letting him know that between the loaves of bread was a sum of money supplied by the Kuwaiti government now in exile.

THE SECOND MOUSE: BLAZE
THE INHERITANCE OF FIRE

THE NOVEL

Chapter 4

Swarms of flies invaded your neighborhoods—a result of the garbage bags piled up on the sidewalks. The flies stole into the houses. Shiny, big, sticky blue flies whose buzzing could be heard from a distance. Stubborn flies that didn't pay any mind to Mama Hissa's "Kish! Kish!" The number of stray cats also multiplied even though fish wasn't being cooked anymore. We all began to get used to the seemingly ubiquitous kittens and stopped chasing them away. Pungent smells became the hallmark of our area. After the foreign sanitation workers had fled, we waited for the young men from the neighborhood, volunteers, to remove the garbage and burn it at a faraway location.

Water was no longer abundantly available as it once was. It was cut off, always at a different time. We all economized when drinking or washing up. You cleaned your body every few days with moist towels. You, Sadiq, and Fahd teased one another about how smelly you were. Your necks and knees became black with grime. "Filthy is what we are now, and so is the country," Mama Hissa commented as she pinched her nose whenever any of you passed by her. The times when water did flow in the bathroom, she would call the three of you to remove your clothes, but keep your underwear on. She rubbed your bodies with red soap or Nablus soap, grumbling as the black water coming off you ran over the white marble tiles. "You boys are dripping in oil!" She had filled up all the large kitchen pots and pans, as well as the bathtubs, with drinking water in anticipation of the long periods of time with no water at all. The old lady didn't seem troubled about the water shortages, except when it came to Ikhlasa, Sa'marana, and Barhiya, the three Kayfan girls. "I'm worried that the palms are thirsty." You didn't understand how her brain worked: strict faith and rigidity toward the occupied nation, and a continual worry about the palm trees being thirsty.

The mice no longer only hovered around the chicken coop beneath the sidra; they had snuck into the house as well. Whenever you reclined on the living room sofas, you smelled a sour soil smell, unsure of where it came from. Even though you never saw a single mouse indoors, Mama Hissa confirmed that whenever she removed the couch cushions, she found small dark-brown pellets the size of rice grains. She'd say it was the mice; she didn't have to see them in the flesh to know they were among us. You remembered her promise and reminded her, "When are you going to tell me the story of the four mice?"

She pretended to be busy cleaning. "Tonight."

Night fell like any other night. She removed her dentures. In the darkness of her room, she started the story as she did every story, "Zur Ibn Al Zarzur, *illi 'umro ma kadhab wa la halaf zur.*" Zur the sparrow's son, who never lied or bore false witness. Her snoring preceded the rest of the story.

The unfamiliar circumstances brought you closer than ever to one another.

***

The doorbell never seems to stop ringing. A number of youth volunteers from the Surra co-op walk up and down the streets, asking what families need, and accordingly hand out bread, baby formula, diapers, and whatever else they can to keep families from having to leave their homes.

"Every day bread, bread, and more bread. Isn't there any fish?" Fahd complains.

"No, you spoiled brat," Mama Hissa answers. She laments how things are now: barbed wire and trenches running parallel to the Gulf for the length of Kuwait's coastline. She gestures toward the neighbor's house and speaks of how 'Am Abbas's boat hasn't budged since this disaster befell you.

***

One day, Fahd and you stood under the sidra, scattering seeds to entice the pigeons and starlings. "Ta'! Ta'!" you both beckoned. The birds didn't budge. You didn't understand why the pigeons felt at ease with Mama Hissa but not with you two.

"Mama Hissa's voice is different," Fahd offered. The doorbell rang. Both of you raced toward it. There was a huge garbage truck being driven by a masked man with dark sunglasses. Another brown young man, who looked like he was in his mid- to late twenties, stood close to your door, his ghutra carelessly wrapped around his head. "You guys have any trash?"

Fahd rushed inside to ask Tina to take out the garbage, while you stayed outside with the young man. He was looking at your house. He went and stood between the cloth-covered cars, examining the house like a potential buyer would. His wide black eyes were striking, piercing whatever his gaze landed on. He had a delicate black mustache and carefully sculpted eyebrows. Fahd returned, Tina trailing him, carrying bags of garbage. "Who rang the bell?" came 'Am Saleh's raised voice as he exited the diwaniya.

"The garbage truck, 'Am."

He approached the young man. He recognized him. "Abdellatif?" He pumped his hand, greeting him. "God bless your efforts!"

Tina and Fahd threw the garbage bags in the back of the truck as 'Am Saleh said, "We don't see you at Al Ghanem Mosque anymore."

The young man appeared in a rush. "I've been praying at Al Rubayan Mosque." He was looking at your house while he answered.

"There's no trash over there . . . They're lucky to have left the country before"—Fahd's dad paused to look around, then lowered his voice— "before those people came in!" The young man nodded his head, his gaze piercing through the now-empty house, its inhabitants gone. He hopped onto the back of the garbage truck and clung to a metal handle as the masked man revved the engine and moved on to the next house. "Dad, do you know him?" Fahd asked his father.

"That's Abdellatif, Abdullah Al Munir's son."

The third week: Iraqi voices on Kuwait National Radio called for the citizens of the nineteenth province to practice their professions and return to their workplaces in the ministries and other establishments. "Whoever fails to do so will find himself on the wrong side of the law," the voices averred. A month had passed since the second of August, and we were all in the living room. 'Am Saleh had just come back from the Surra co-op supermarket, his face red with frustration. He described the panic on the faces of the shoppers who were trying to verify the accuracy of this news amid myriad rumors. It was said that some Palestinians living in Kuwait were joining the ranks of the Iraqi national army. Mama Hissa interrupted, "People say many things." 'Am Saleh disregarded his mother's comment and carried on as she scowled, describing what he saw in the co-op—shopping carts bursting with food items, their owners seemingly preparing for extended hibernation, years long. Cans, sacks of rice, bread, sugar, and bottles of mineral water. There were posters on the electronic gate to the co-op urging inhabitants of the nineteenth province to replace their license plates.

They were obliged to drive with the new Iraqi-Kuwaiti license plates or be barred from refueling. The TV made it clear that the final deadline to replace the plates was September 26. Whoever failed to do so would have their car confiscated if they were lucky; otherwise, they themselves would be taken in.

Hours passed by. An unflagging 'Am Saleh went out now and again to the sidewalk to investigate his neighbors' cars, examining their plates. If one of them had replaced his license plate, then it would relieve him of the awkwardness when he removed his own. "I'm not the first to do so," he could then say. But the Kuwaiti plates were all still in place. The cloud of worry that surrounded Fahd's dad floated to you. Because you didn't understand much and because your questions were too annoying to everyone, you tried to gauge from adults' eyes how you should be feeling at any given time. Their eyes held only heavy anticipation for the unknown, the yet to come.

What was odd was that you didn't miss your parents. You only missed the peace you had felt at the Al Bin Ya'qub household and the freedom it had given you. Maybe what did kindle your yearning one day was when Mama Hissa called out to you. "Come here, listen to this." It was your mother's voice on the *Kuwaiti Calls* program being broadcast in Saudi Arabia, where your parents resided at the time. It was a radio show set up to help the Kuwaitis abroad send messages to those inside the country.

Your mother's voice came through, broken. "Your father and I are okay," she said. She urged you to leave Kuwait with whomever was making their way out to Saudi Arabia. She could barely catch her breath, making the most of the few seconds allocated to each caller. "My son is in your care, Um Saleh; my son is in your care." She burst out sobbing before another Kuwaiti caller started, searching for another someone who couldn't answer. You were all scattered, somewhere between being refugees and cut off from the world. This Saudi radio program made you all realize just how helpless you were. On the show *Kuwaiti Letters*, the broadcaster implored Saudi citizens to donate to their "Kuwaiti guests" residing in Saudi Arabia. They referred to the increasing number of families as "refugees." Families living in the classrooms of Saudi schools. The radio broadcasters' calls reminded you of the donation boxes that used to have the Dome of the Rock or the image of an African boy on them. Now they had a picture of a child draped in the colors of the Kuwaiti flag. Fahd read your mind. "A donation box for Kuwaitis. Who will wipe the tears of this poor boy?" he said. You took pity on those who had left. You loved the Al Bin Ya'qub house. You loved Surra even more.

Since you had been entrusted to Mama Hissa's care, she ordered, "Don't go outside!" And whenever you countered that Fahd whiled away most of his time in 'Am Abbas's courtyard, she'd cut you off, saying, "His father is in charge of him." Your uncle Hassan called you, letting you know of his plan to take you along to Basra to make some international phone calls to your relatives abroad. You were afraid that you'd never return. You offered your missing passport as an excuse for not being able to go, not knowing that there was no need for a travel document between the provinces of what was now effectively one country. "The boy is in my care, Abu Dhari," Mama Hissa cut in.

You were rooted to the spot in front of the windows, the sole source of news you understood, unlike the radio bulletins, which only the adults could wrap their heads around. You would keep an eye on the occupying soldiers whenever their jeeps rolled by, hoping that they wouldn't stop in front of the house to storm it. You noticed Fahd and Sadiq, along with Samir and Hazim, in the small garden of the courtyard next door, under the shade cast over 'Am Abbas's house by the sidra tree. They were bent over, collecting things from the dry grass. You didn't have to guess that they were . . . rocks! They had a small mound of them. That was more than enough of a good reason for Fahd to stay away for long periods of time at Sadiq's house, far from his father's gaze. Your concern for them, or perhaps it was actually your jealousy over their meeting without you, pushed you to snitch on them to 'Am Saleh. "Fahd is collecting rocks . . ."

"Maybe they are for anbar," he responded, unconcerned, until you finished with "At 'Am Abbas's house." He whirled around and asked angrily, "At Abbas's house?" You nodded your head meekly. You told him that both Fahd and Sadiq were collecting a lot of rocks. Anbar, the popular child's game, only needed seven.

You sank your head between your shoulders, embarrassed at the sound of 'Am Saleh yelling from the middle of the courtyard. "Fahd!" No one answered. He looked at you and ordered, "Go get him!" The idea did not appeal to you. You didn't find him in the courtyard next door. Instead, he was under Sadiq's staircase in the living room; both of them were playing around with rubber bands and pieces of tape, trying to fashion slingshots.

"Your dad wants you," you told him, while you cast a cursory glance around the place. The walls in Sadiq's house weren't as they were the first time you saw them. You surveyed the living room more thoroughly: no family photos, no white horses, lions, or swords—the walls were completely bare. You glanced at the shelves in the TV console: there were only two photos—one each of Sadiq and Hawraa. The picture of the imam was no longer in the middle.

As soon as Fahd opened the iron door to his courtyard, his father gave him a thunderous whack that rang in your ears. "Stones, you son of a bitch? And in Abbas's house?" You didn't understand why the man was cursing. What you did understand was that you were the reason behind that slap. He ranted, swearing at the rocks and those who owned them. He explained to his son that the occupiers didn't know anything about the land they were occupying. The people who were known for throwing rocks in their own country, who "you're imitating," had been in cahoots with the occupier, being their eyes and ears, guiding them to the houses of wanted individuals. Just like you, Fahd didn't believe what his father was saying. "Are you going to follow their lead?" 'Am

Saleh screamed. You thought of Abu Taha and Abu Naiel. Is the zalamat house actually a danger to your street? You hated yourself for what you'd brought upon your friend by telling on him. You hated yourself even more when Mama Hissa called you out for what you did by naming you "fire starter." She was known for giving nicknames so apt that they stuck forever: Ms. Principal, stray cat, soothsayer, the American's hubby. You put up with her insinuations and comparing you to a monkey, even if they were made in jest, but you weren't ready to accept this new nickname and the blame associated with it. After all, you had hated fire ever since she said the only thing you get from it is ashes.

Fahd stood in front of his grandmother, telling her what his father had said about all Palestinians being traitors. "All your fingers aren't the same, are they?" she answered as she thrust her palm in front of his face with her fingers outstretched.

'Am Saleh heard her and countered, "Yes, they are!" She reminded him of the Kuwaiti man the occupying forces called the president of the interim Kuwaiti government. "Are you and him the same?" she asked him.

You secluded yourself, far away. You blamed yourself endlessly until 'Am Saleh made up with Fahd that night. Usually, he would have bought him a toy from Walid's Toys or Kids and Us. In those circumstances, at that time, the only gift he could offer was "Tell Sadiq he can come over here whenever he wants."

"Or I can go to his place?" Fahd suggested.

"No!" his father barked decisively.

THE SECOND MOUSE: BLAZE
THE INHERITANCE OF FIRE

THE NOVEL

Chapter 5

Brimming with curiosity, you would usually make a run for the phone whenever it started ringing. You were crazy about ringing bells: the phone, the doorbell, the school bell when it rang out announcing the end of a boring class. In these new exceptional circumstances, though, you hated nothing more than ringing bells. The doorbell most likely meant an inspection to see if all the family members were home or, at best, it meant Jasim or Abdellatif: the first distributing resistance pamphlets nestled in bread or money given by the exiled Kuwaiti government; the other asking for trash. The ringing of the phone would dictate 'Am Saleh's next move, based on the news he received.

He put down the phone and burned all photos of himself in military fatigues from the time he was conscripted. He put down the phone and made his way through the courtyard to the kitchen where, with Tina, he worked to fill up plastic containers with gallons of drinking water. He put down the phone and buried his hunting rifle close to the sidra in the garden. He put down the phone and hid the three cars inside the courtyard so that no occupying soldier would catch sight of the license plates that still said .

We remained in this state of fear after every phone call that brought news or a rumor that could very well be true, from the occupier's intention to cut off the water supply to the death penalty for anyone in possession of a weapon, even a hunting rifle, or being arrested for having any military affiliation—the mere possession of a photo from one's former days of service would suffice. Fawzia was in her room most of the time and didn't open up for anyone. She'd make an exception for you, though, whenever you knocked on her door with news that might interest her. Since you knew that Kayfan meant the world to her, you would bring her news about the exceptional resistance activity in that area, and how people were now calling it Kayfan Al Samud, perseverance personified.

"Kayfan's something else," she said, beaming.

"Surra too."

She poked your *surra*, your belly button, making fun of Surra's name. You don't know what came over you the moment her finger made contact with your body. An army of electrified ants scuttled up your spine to your head. You looked at her face, your lips slack.

Her eyebrows knitted. "What's wrong with you?"

You ran from her room without a word.

In September, the heat of the summer finally broke with the appearance of Shail, the Canopus star in the sky. Sleep rarely visited any of you. When the electricity was cut off, so there was no air conditioner, the nightly routine was to go out into the courtyard and sleep on the floor. The street was quiet, except for the chirping of the night suweer. Your only entertainment was the courtyard. The moon was full, giving you reasonable visibility in the dark. The old lady carried a cane with a spear-like knife fixed to its head in one hand and a flashlight in the other. As she made her way to the chicken coop, her milfah wrapped haphazardly around her head, looking like a ghutra, Fahd and you asked, "What are you up to?"

"Al qumbar," she responded without even turning around. 'Am Saleh guffawed at her joke. The suweer stopped chirping as she walked between the grasses by the coop. Mama Hissa faltered, afraid that she had trampled on it by mistake. She stopped for a few seconds until the chirping started up again. She smiled when it did, then leaned over the grasses, speaking to the insect of the night. She urged it to keep on singing so that its female partner could respond. She turned her back to deal with the traps, clearing them of the dead mice, using her spear. "Can't you smell it?" You all shook your heads. "Clearly, you're all still very smelly." You and Fahd preoccupied yourselves stroking the stray kittens you'd all gotten used to. Mama Hissa welcomed their presence, no longer telling them to scat by saying "Tet! Tet!" and hoping they would keep the mice away from her chicken coop. If it hadn't been for the surge of mice, she wouldn't have been content with the cats, she explained, before contradicting herself, saying, "What a difficult time! Mice, cats, and dogs in my house!"

She finished collecting the dead mice. You and Fahd left the kittens to their own devices. You followed Mama Hissa to the courtyard door. She sent you both outside to dispose of the sack of mice, on a dusty plot next to Abu Sami's house. She stood examining the three palm trees, a smile of reassurance written on her face. "Hey, Mama Hissa, do you love the palm trees that much?" She appeared distracted as she responded, "And how I love their soul mate." Her ability to humanize Ikhlasa, Sa'marana, and Barhiya surprised you. How Abu Saleh, God rest his soul, brought them here as sprouts from different places: Al Qaseem, Basra, and Al Ahwaz. He chose them from among dozens of palm trees to live next to him instead of planting them with the others on their farm in Wafra. He would travel a lot, and whenever he tasted delicious dates at his hosts' houses, he would ask where they came from and pay everything he had to get his hands on a sapling from the mother tree.

Then he'd carry it back home and plant it in his garden or at his farm. Mama Hissa told you two about her first meeting in the Kayfan house and how the fledgling trees got to know one another, each bearing its history on the nodules of its trunk. How fast they grew, one outdoing the other, offering the tastiest fruits out of love for their owners. She locked the outer door, returning inside the courtyard, praying for her husband's soul and wishing her three Kayfan daughters a long life.

You all circled around the radio on the rough blue-and-red-striped rug in the middle of the courtyard. The adults drank tea, the air tinged with a hint of moisture, listening closely to the news, as if it were different from listening in the living room. The chirping of the suweer stopped again. "It found its beloved," Mama Hissa surmised. Resting your heads on the old lady's thighs, the two of you gazed at the guest star in the sky, a sky whose blackness had been transformed into a dark blue by the full moon. Mama Hissa turned off the radio. "How beautiful the moon is." She looked up at the sky, pulled in by nostalgia for a bygone era when the sky was closer, as she used to say, when she was in Al Murqab living in an old mud hut, whose rooms opened out into a courtyard roofed only by the sky. "We used to know the sky better . . . and it used to know us." She exhaled. "It was a time of blistering heat before ACs, and we'd sleep on the roof . . . The floor was our mattress and the sky our blanket."

You looked at her face. She was staring at the full moon.

"Mama Hissa, how old are you?" you asked.

She bowed her head. "By God, I don't know, my son. I'm ancient!" She looked out into the expanse as if she were chanting hidden words. "My mother, Sharifa—God rest her soul—told me, 'You came into the world, Hissa, in the year of the storm, or two years after it . . . when the boats sank in the pearl-diving hubs of the Gulf.'" She stopped all of a sudden and continued just as abruptly. "Yes, that was a time and this is another time." She said that she would tell you all a story as long as Shail—Canopus—remained a guest of your sky.

"The story of the four mice?" you turned to her and asked expectantly.

"No," she said, clapping you on the forehead, "it's too long."

"But we're bored with the jinn stories!"

"May they find peace in their home," she murmured, casting your words aside and looking intently at the sidra in the dark. She stared out into the sky once more. She started recounting the legend of Shail the star. Shail, which brought the good news of winter or rain. If only it would give us the good news of the occupiers leaving our country as summer leaves us, the old lady wished aloud. Her eyes remained trained on the sky. "This story was told to me by the sweetest of women, my mother, Sharifa—may God have mercy on her soul—back when I was a young girl." She closed her eyes and took a deep breath, starting the story in the usual way: "Zur Ibn Al Zarzur, illi 'umro ma kadhab wa la halaf zur . . ." Stroking our heads, she began to tell the story: "The mice came among Shail and his friend—"

"Where did they come from?" you asked her impatiently.

"Why would I tell you?" She fought back her laughter and tugged at your hair. Moments later, she carried on telling us the story that happened a long, long time ago in a place somewhere between the desert and the coast. "Many, many years ago, when there was no oil, no electricity, and no concrete—"

"But where did the story take place, Mama Hissa?"

"If you interrupt me one more time, I'm not going to continue!"

But then she did, telling the tale of Shail and his friend, bound together by their love for a girl called Aaqiba, and the land they had inherited from their ancestors many years ago. They cultivated it and lived off the fruits of their labor, not knowing any other shelter but the land. During the day, they would tend to the land. At night, they would take turns guarding it. Since they didn't budge from the land for even a single day, or ever neglect it, or hand it over to strangers to till it, the mice were unable to steal their rice, wheat, corn, and barley crops.

The mice starved. If a mouse starves, it will risk its very life to satiate its appetite, even if it comes at the cost of destroying homes. The wicked creatures realized that they wouldn't control the land as long as Shail and his friend remained two peas in a pod. They didn't want to get rid of both of them, though. For the mice to survive, one of the friends would need to remain. He would have to till the earth so that it could continue to produce crops one season after another. The mice knew that both friends were madly in love with Aaqiba, each seeing himself as more worthy of her love. They saw this as their sole opportunity to gain a foothold on the land and drive a wedge between Shail and his friend. The mice attacked Aaqiba in her faraway tent. She screamed for help. Shail and his friend rose up, each trying to outdo the other to rescue her. They charged into the darkness, following her voice and the light from her lamp streaming out of her tent. Jealousy crept in between them. Each one yearned to save the damsel in distress and win her love.

Shail and his friend quarreled by the tent, each claiming that Aaqiba had called out his name. Shail picked up a sizable rock and fractured his friend's skull with it. His friend fell to the ground, blood pouring out from where his hair parted. At the sight of his friend's blood, Shail was inconsolable. He fell to his knees, shaking his friend's shoulders. Shail thought he was dead. He yelled, cursing himself. He fled, running away from the sin that now stained him. The only way to atone for his sin was to shut himself away from the world, running away to the southern sky, far, far away. Alone, without any stars nearby. The sky cried out in anguish over the two friends' predicament, its tears pouring down all over the earth. As the mice ran to the friends' land, the injured young man regained consciousness. Upon waking up and not finding Shail nearby, he wanted to search for him. Aaqiba gave him her lamp. Not finding Shail on the land that the mice had left in ruins, he kept wandering in the wilderness, carrying the lamp, calling out to Shail, who had disappeared into the sky, no longer to be seen.

Every year, on the same day that Aaqiba had called out for help, Shail reappears when the sky remembers the misfortune of the two friends and cries for them. Shail would look out at the land and survey what had happened to it, searching for his friend, who carried Aaqiba's lamp and faded into the desert. That's how Shail became a star. As for his friend, he simply vanished. He was forgotten and the legend didn't remember his name, though some people started calling him Shuhab, the shooting star, claiming to have set eyes on him fleetingly one night carrying his lamp, darting across the sky. The mice died on the land, useless without its owners. And as for Aaqiba, she remained all alone without a lamp.

"I wish I could die and become a star," Fahd said to his grandmother. She shuddered. "That's God's choice and not yours." She feared an angel may have just been passing by and heard his wish, carrying it to God.

"It's only so that I could see you all from up above if I missed you," he added sadly, looking at her face.

"May my day come before yours," she said, swatting his forehead.

"And the story about the four mice?" you asked her. You shielded your forehead with your palms, fearing a similar whack. She ignored you, so you made clear to her that you weren't all that interested in Shail's story, which couldn't possibly be true.

"Ibn Al Zarzur never lied or bore false witness in his life!" she countered. "The sky will crash down on us!" You were reminded of the fate awaiting those who lied. The sky had to fall down, with Shail, so that he could meet his friend, you thought before you asked God for forgiveness. The saluki started yipping. You glued yourself even closer to Mama Hissa. The old woman grumbled that she hadn't kept track of the dog's upkeep during his time at her house.

"Me neither," 'Am Saleh said, and went on to convince himself how important it was to keep a dog to protect the house. The dog kept barking. 'Am Saleh turned to Fahd and ordered him to untie the saluki and take him to the patch of dirt nearby in case he had to respond to the call of nature. He looked over at you, ribbing you by revealing your secret: "Scared of the dog, are you, boy?"

The old woman responded without looking at you, "Others fear dogs dressed in clothes!" 'Am Saleh's face drained of color. She looked at you and ordered you to untie the dog. You were paralyzed.

You swallowed your spit. "Me?"

She patted your back and urged, "Come on now, you lion!"

Fahd beat you to the corner of the courtyard and yelled, "Come on!"

His grandmother stopped him from going any farther. "Sit down, you!" Your sweat poured out despite the moderate temperature. In your heart you started cursing Shail, who had pushed you all out into the courtyard to chat late into the night. No sooner had you gotten up from the ground, dragging your steps to the saluki's corner, nearly halfway there, when shouts and chants of "God is great" rang out from the roofs of the surrounding houses in condemnation of the occupation troops. At first only the dog was scared; then you were too. A long fusillade of gunshots rang out, burning red, filling the sky like rain. The saluki's barking imitated the staccato sounds. You all shook with fear, scurrying inside.

The last to reach the living room was Mama Hissa, her footsteps sweeping the ground, carrying her radio, terrified by the hail of gunshots. "As the saying goes, if you see Shail, then you know it's going to rain," she quipped. You all burst out laughing at the height of your panic, even though it was raining bullets. The phone rang, silencing the squawking in the living room. You exchanged nervous looks as you did every time the phone rang. 'Am Saleh cradled the receiver, his face transforming into that of someone who had just received tragic news. His mother murmured, "Protect us, O God." He didn't speak much. He was looking at the top of the stairs. From his trembling hands we could tell how dangerous a call it was.

Aisha whispered, "Nothing bad, I hope?" He signaled to her with his hand to be quiet.

He stammered into the phone, "There is no power or strength save in . . ." He set down the receiver and let out a long sigh, staring at the ground. He couldn't get his words out.

"Is everything okay? What's wrong?" Aisha yelled at him.

Mama Hissa's voice rose, warning Aisha: "Your volume!" 'Am Saleh disappeared into his room, his wife trailing him. Your curiosity, like Fahd's, was at its height. You both asked Mama Hissa what was going on.

"Wait for Aisha: maybe she will have some news," she advised.

Her daughter-in-law came back, her face drained. In a hushed tone she informed you all, "They're rounding up and sending off girls to the detention centers."

"Why?"

Aisha lingered, hesitating to answer Mama Hissa's question, looking at both of you out of the corner of her eye, still regarding you as children. "Why do you think?" Wordlessly, the old lady beat her chest with her palms. Fahd's mother shook her head. "May God keep our girls safe," she breathed.

'Am Saleh didn't stay in his room for long. He came out gripping an electric razor, like the ones Mushtaq the Pakistani barber used when shaving our heads. With light, quick steps he climbed the stairs. The old woman was speechless, staring at him wide-eyed. She yelled out to him while trying to stand, ever so slowly stretching her arms out to Fahd so that he could support her. "Where's he going? Wait, Saleh, fear God!" She then egged her daughter-in-law on. "Go on, Aisha, catch him!"

Fahd and you were frozen in your place while Mama Hissa dragged her feet toward the stairs, leaning against the wall, calling out to her only son. All we could hear from upstairs were violent knocks, desperate knocks on Fawzia's door and Aisha pleading, "Open the door, Saleh! For God's sake, no!"

THE SECOND MOUSE: BLAZE
THE INHERITANCE OF FIRE

THE NOVEL

Chapter 6

Staying in the old woman's room at night drew you together, closer than ever before. Slowly, your annoyance with her dissipated. Her nightly chatter in the bedroom was nothing like her daytime words. It was as if when she removed her dentures, under the cover of darkness, she bloomed into a different woman. You started to believe that these dentures stood between you and the stories that you ached to hear. Such stories were only freed from the old woman when she took out her dentures. After dinner you went to her bedroom straightaway while she would go to the bathroom to wash up and do her ablutions before going to bed. You were surprised that she did *wudu'* even though she was just going to bed and not praying. She'd always respond, "It's so that even if God comes to take my soul while I'm asleep, I can die pure."

She would always enter the room, drying her forearms with a perfumed towel. You would fold your arms over your chest, leaning against the wall next to the door as you waited for her to finish preparing your

designated area to sleep. "I'm not an old lady!" she'd rebuke you whenever you approached her, trying to help. She would finish arranging
your mattress beside her bed on the floor, despite her difficulty bending
over. You would lovingly look on at her effort, breathing in her refresh-
ing nightly scent: Lifebuoy soap, or the red soap as she would call it. She
would brace her hands on her knees as she bent over, saying, "O God,
on You alone I lean and no one else." You would press your lips tightly
together so that no laughter would escape; her already ample backside
grew larger whenever she bent over. She would then proceed to her
wardrobe and open its wooden door, the scent of white naphthalene
balls quickly flooding the room. Next, she would remove her milfah and
deposit her bracelets in the wardrobe. Picking up the Pompeia cologne
bottle, she would finally pour out a sizable volume of golden liquid into
her palms before returning to her bed. She would sit down and request,
or sometimes order, "Turn off the lights."

"Not yet, Mama Hissa," you'd say, pulling a sad face.

"Turn it off," she would repeat, shaking her head. "We won't sleep
without story time—don't you worry." Your smile widened. You flicked
the switch without shifting from your spot next to the door. You didn't
wait long to turn the light back on. You found her ready, poised, smiling just as widely, flaunting that her dentures were still in place. She
was onto your game. Clasping the bottle of solution for her teeth, she
looked at you and said, "Turn off the light and come to bed, you Jew!"

You tried to get on her good side, coming across as wounded. "But
I want to see you take out your teeth, please."

"Over my dead body."

You turned off the light. You groped your way through the dark.
Every night her utter devotion silenced you. You listened to her whispers as she spoke to God, intoning praises to Him before sleeping. Only
with her did you feel that God was close, as if He was soaring up, high
in the sky above. The old woman would read verses for protection. She'd
then blow into her hands. She would mumble some words, but you

could only make out the ones with *s*'s. "Ss*subhan* . . . prai*ss*e be to . . . O God of the *ss*even *ss*skies . . . God, I a*ss*k You . . . You who fed u*ss*, gave u*ss* drink, and gave u*ss* enough . . . There i*ss* nothing before You . . . *biss*s*muka*, O God . . . in Your name . . . I entru*ss*t myself to You." So she hadn't taken out her dentures yet.

As soon as her praises to God petered out, you'd start with your questions. She would then begin telling the stories you loved, the *sss* of her prayers replaced by different hissing sounds. She answered your every question, telling you all kinds of stories, but not the one about the four mice that she had promised. She always postponed it to the next night. She spoke about whatever *she* wanted to speak about. You understood some of what she said. There was a lot you didn't know. She would speak, propelled by the need to speak, with your questions or without them. At nighttime, Mama Hissa became something else entirely. In these nightly story sessions, you learned what you didn't before, such as why Mama Hissa came down hard on Saleh—it was because he himself was so strict with Fawzia. Saleh was in charge at—and only at—home, a man lording his misfortune over his sick, fatherless sister. Why was Fawzia ill? It was a trial from God. Why did God put her to the test? He was testing her. Why was He testing her? Because He loved her. "Doesn't God love me? I'm healthy and don't have any sicknesses." "Shut up and ask God for forgiveness." "God, forgive me." "May He forgive you, my boy." "If she passed the test, would God forgive her?" "The real test is with your mother, Ms. Principal, you fool." "When has God ever given her a test?" "I've never seen a jahil like you who asks so many questions." "I'm not a child. When did God try her?" "When her father died in those coffee-shop bombings five years ago. How she cried, but even when faced with her crying, I wasn't able to cry. I didn't cry for Saleh's father, but I cried for Fawzia. 'Daddy's girl' is what he used to call her, God rest his soul. I cried for her when we had to take her to the hospital completely in pieces. She'd fainted. Saleh, who I wanted to be a man in his father's absence, became a child. Aisha, since the beginning, was Aisha. I didn't detect any sadness in her at Saleh's dad's departure. Maybe she still considers him alive in those photos that she keeps, silly woman."

The old lady fell silent.

"Mama Hissa, did you fall asleep?"

"Where would sleep come from, my son? God please heal her and strengthen her . . ."

She spoke to you about her love for Fawzia, Daddy's girl, the apple of her eye, and how God had granted her life in her womb after the death of nine boys between Saleh's birth and that of his sister. She started repeating what her daughter's doctor had said after losing Saleh's dad: a sudden high spike in blood sugar, a symptom of a psychological crisis. The doctor didn't disguise his concern about the possibility of the momentary crisis becoming a lasting sickness due to Fawzia's genetic predisposition, her neglect of treatment, and a lax approach to eating what was off-limits.

"Then what happened, Mama Hissa?"

"It wasn't a matter of two days as the doctor had said. Other than illness, what else have I passed on to my daughter? She used to remind me when to take my medication. Now we remind each other. Does 'Am Saleh hate Fawzia? Saleh hates his weakness, poor man; he feels helpless, but he loves his sister and worries about her. In spite of what he did to her yesterday, Fawzia didn't challenge him. She understands that he loves her and what he did was only out of worry for her. You were in the courtyard when he came down to the living room, the electric razor in hand, crying like a jahil, his mother's dearest soul."

"Mama Hissa, did you see Fawzia? Did she open her door for you?"

"I saw her, apple of her mother's eye, like a pigeon whose feathers had been plucked."

"Did 'Am Saleh remove all of her hair? Huh? Mama Hissa, are you asleep?"

Mama Hissa sobbed. You wished you could see her face, but it was too dark. The old lady stopped crying and asked her God for forgiveness. Without you even prompting her, she carried on speaking about Saleh.

"Saleh, God help him, is my son and isn't my son. I have never understood him, even when he was a child. If only he were more like his son, named after his grandfather Fahd, may God pardon him, his son who inherited his grandfather's features and nature . . ." She let out a sigh that sounded like a laugh. She advised you to be good to her grandson. She took it even further with what she said to Sadiq later: "You three are like the Kayfan girls. Your friends are your support and help." She fell silent before she focused on Fahd, her chatter laced with great love. He was his parents' only child since Aisha had had the operation. The matter of the womb no longer provoked questions in you; neither did the link between the removal of it and how that meant no more sons after Fahd. You were listening to the old woman like someone getting to know a woman that no one else knew, a complete stranger.

She went on. "Fahd has become a man; he resembles his grandfather, even in how much he loves mutabbaq samak . . . the stray cat that he is." The old lady fell silent. A smile filled her face at the thought of her husband. "Saleh is a darling, but he listens too much. One word takes him far away, and another brings him right back to where he was. He listens to Aisha . . . to his friends in the diwaniya and the mosque gatherings . . . to the TV, news on the radio and in the papers . . . and the Monday demonstrations," she added.

You don't know why, as of late, the old woman slipped into talking about her son, who you didn't care about as much as Fawzia. You remember how 'Am Saleh behaved according to the phone calls he had received since the first day of the occupation. Mama Hissa continued, "He completed his college degree in Cairo. The pictures of Gamal Abdel Nasser that Saleh's dad had put up on the walls of the house multiplied when his son came back from Egypt." She was quiet for a moment and then asked you, "Do you know the leader Gamal Abdel Nasser?" You didn't respond. "Shame on you! How can you not know such men?" Her voice went up. "Abdel Nasser who fought the Jews!" She made fun of you and your friends, and how you parroted "Greetings to the Arab nations" every morning at school without understanding what you were chanting.

She didn't notice your silence and went on. "Saleh's father, may God have mercy on his soul, was a man who loved Gamal, recording his speeches. He was always either listening to them or to Umm Kulthum. As for Saleh, may God set him straight, every day was something different: with them, against them, with them, against them. Once, he shortened his dishdasha; another time he wore Western. He liked to put up photos: sometimes Abdel Nasser and other times the resistance fighter, the one with the plucked-out beard." Even though she wasn't happy with her son, she talked about him fondly. She remembered when he came back during the break after his first semester in Cairo, in a brown suit with parted glossy hair and a fine mustache. He stood in front of his bedroom mirror, dressed like an Egyptian, listening to Abdel Halim Hafez and holding his hairbrush close to his lips as he sang along.

She interrupted herself, as if she had remembered something important. She spoke to you about the time when the Iranians revolted against their shah. Saleh carried a picture of Al Khomeini, telling his parents about the man who had come back from exile for the sake of the Islamic revolution. "And his father and I, God help us, didn't understand what he was saying, except about the Islamic revolution itself. By God, long live the revolution; anything Islamic must be good, right?" She groped around in the dark for some water. She said bismillah. She took a gulp before she went on. "They had carried out their revolution. Saleh then took down all his photos from the walls during the Iran-Iraq War. He hung up Saddam Hussein's photo instead. I don't know what came over our children, for from that day on, each one thought God was only on his side, and against the other. We didn't know anything about this, wallah . . . Such strife . . . such strife . . . God, You alone are enough for us. Such fighting is filthier than a mouse's tail!"

She confided in God, asking Him for spiritual guidance for Saleh and Abbas and to have mercy on her and her neighbor Zaynab. She let out a heavy sigh. "Just like how maggots crawl out from a man's own stomach to eat him, this foolishness of theirs will only bring bad things. Boy! Do you hear me? O, boy . . . Are you asleep?"

THE SECOND MOUSE: BLAZE
THE INHERITANCE OF FIRE

THE NOVEL

Chapter 7

Bordering on its second month, the occupation soldiered on. The situation had deteriorated. The occupier's grip on everything grew ever tighter. The nearby gunshots at dawn made your blood run cold. 'Am Saleh came back from *Fajr* prayers at Maryam Al Ghanem Mosque, carrying bread; it was said that a youth had shot at military vehicles on their way to the Jabriya area. Imagine if the occupying forces heard him saying that forbidden name for the area! All of the areas had taken on the new names imposed by the occupying forces; your Jabriya became Al Ahrar, liberation neighborhood. Your Kuwaiti dinar after some days became Iraqi. Your residential areas—Al Salmiya, Salwa, Al Khaldiya, and Al Shuwaikh—had new names: Al Nasr, Al Khansa, Al Jumhoriya, and Al Rasheed. If it went on like this, you soon might not recognize yourselves either. You rubbed 'Am Saleh the wrong way when you asked him, "Why all the name changing?"

"You don't let up, do you?" he said, his voice raised.

Only Mama Hissa responded. "So that Kuwait is no longer Kuwaiti." Her answer left you on edge. You hoped that a new name wouldn't take hold of Surra, too.

That day, your mom's brother Hassan called to confirm that the soldiers were carrying out random searches of homes, looking for those involved in the attack on the military convoy next to the Jabriya Bridge. Your uncle cautioned Fahd's father that none of you should go near or inside his sister's house, under any circumstances. And if any of you were asked about the house and its owners, you should claim that you didn't know anything except that the family was traveling. 'Am Saleh started pacing the living room. "Hassan's up to something!" he yelled at both of you, seized by the fear of a surprise visit. "You and Fahd, follow me." You both trailed him to Fawzia's room. He ordered you to search her room thoroughly; maybe the crazy girl had kept some contraband that would cost you your lives. He opened the cupboard and started rummaging through the clothes and shelves with his son. He looked at you and gestured to the drawers of the small desk. "Look there!" Fawzia, her face swollen either from sleeping or crying, her hijab stuck to her naked scalp, understood the reason for your intermittent glances at her. She didn't object. She gestured toward her desk drawers, urging you to investigate. You approached the desk; in your head fluttered the image of her as a pink butterfly. Long black hair reaching past her butt, as her mother would say, or past her back, as she herself would say. No sooner had you opened the first drawer than you closed it, quickly moving to the drawer below. Without meaning to, you'd attracted 'Am Saleh's attention. He charged at you and ordered, "Open it!" You opened the bottom drawer. "The first," he demanded. You looked in Fawzia's direction. She nodded. You slowly opened it, revealing many chocolate Mackintosh's bars atop a plastic bag with "Al Budur Bookstore" written on it. You held your breath in anticipation. Fahd's dad opened the plastic bag and investigated the contents: three Ihsan Abdel Quddous novels. He let out a sigh of relief. He returned the bag. Picking up the bars of chocolate, he left one behind. "This is bad for your health," he said, closing the drawer. He didn't say anything else. *What about what is muddying her mind and morals?* you asked yourself. As you made to leave her room, 'Am Saleh turned and looked kindly at Fawzia. "If Kuwait comes back"—he allowed himself a smile before going on—"you'll go to college."

That afternoon you all gathered in the living room to listen to the Monte Carlo radio station, following the details of the much-anticipated Jeddah conference, a conference that brought together the government in exile and different groups of Kuwaitis, among them politicians, businessmen, and voices of the opposition that had arisen since the dissolution of parliament. The emir's voice as he read his speech wrung the hearts of the women in the Al Bin Ya'qub household. Fawzia shed tears. Mama Hissa, as if she were talking to someone, kept on nodding her head, repeating "Yes . . . yes" after each phrase from the 1960s head of parliament, Abdul Aziz Al Saqr, as he delivered his speech, championing the Kuwaiti cause. 'Am Saleh listened, his eyes narrowing. You didn't understand why he suddenly flared up in anger, kicking the radio. "Shut him up!" The radio crashed to the ground after Al Saqr's insistence that "the stance of some Palestinian leaders won't affect our staunch solidarity with the Palestinian people in their just struggle to free their country."

Mama Hissa picked up and cradled the radio like a baby. She looked at her son. "Have you gone mad?" You didn't know the reason for her reaction, whether she supported what had just been said in the official statement or was only worrying about her radio.

She turned it back on. Al Saqr's voice rattled through. "We want to announce that despite our pain and injuries, despite the calamities and disasters that the hostile, sinful Iraqi regime has visited upon our people, we don't harbor any ill will or hatred toward the Iraqi people." The old woman shut off her radio, silent, distracted.

A voice rang out from the street. "Ice cream! Ice cream!" Abu Sameh, the Palestinian ice-cream seller, at the worst time possible.

At the prospect of ice cream, your heart beat fast, but your joy was cut short as 'Am Saleh shot up from his seat, his eyes wide, something clearly on his mind. "That bastard! How dare he!" His words shocked you. He usually didn't speak like that in front of the other members of the household. The seller's hawking didn't last long when faced with a louder voice that overshadowed his. Fahd's father clambered outside in his house dishdasha to see what was happening. You and Fahd followed him. You found your neighbor 'Am Abbas yelling at the man standing behind his cart and broken red umbrella. "There's no good in any of you people, you're all sons of . . ." 'Am Abbas lifted the lid of the ice-cream cart while Abu Sameh tried to hold him back in vain. 'Am Abbas then bent over the ground in front of his house and scooped up a handful of earth.

Weakly, in a dialect that took you all back to school, Abu Sameh pleaded, "What have I done?" 'Am Abbas threw the dirt on the ice cream in the cart. Abu Sameh cradled his head in his hands in disbelief. "Ayb! Shame on you . . . Haram!" The two words were strung together in a different way than when you asked your questions: *ayb, haram*; shame on you, forbidden.

'Am Saleh's anger boiled over. "Do you guys even know what haram is? Damn you and your liberation movement, you bastards!" You two cried, or nearly did—you and Fahd—at the sight of the man pushing his cart far away from your houses. You thought of what Abu Sameh had said about the cart that had put his three sons through college. Neither of you had anything to do with the liberation organization. Neither of you had anything to do with what you didn't grasp. Neither of you had anything to do with anything except for the man whose name on your tongues was synonymous with vanilla, chocolate, and caramel. He left with his middle-aged face, his beard sprouting white fuzz, and skin roasted by the sun. The calls of "Ice cream! Ice cream!"

disappeared. Abu Sameh left along with his song: "Fill the Jug Up for Me." For so long, you had wanted your two neighbors to get along. Their unlikely agreement finally came over something you didn't actually want.

Immediately after you all returned inside, you found the old lady waiting silently. Fahd asked his father, "Dad, was 'Am Abbas right?"

"Of course!" he asserted. You and Fahd looked at each other in confusion that 'Am Saleh picked up on. He patted his son's back and clarified, "Me and my brother against my cousin . . . and me and my cousin against the stranger." But the only strange things about that day were first, how 'Am Saleh had described his sworn enemy of a neighbor as his cousin, and second, how he had labeled Abu Sameh a stranger.

Involuntarily, your eyes flitted to Mama Hissa, believing that she would say something about the novelty of the description.

But . . . she didn't.

THE SECOND MOUSE: BLAZE THE INHERITANCE OF FIRE

THE NOVEL

Chapter 8

Just before sunset, the three of you were in the courtyard, in front of the Hitachi camera fixed atop its metal tripod. Fahd wore a yellow Qadsia club jersey, pretending to be Muayyad Al Haddad, the top scorer in the Emir Cup of 1990, while Sadiq was in a green Al Arabi jersey. They kicked the ball back and forth between them near the sidra, pretending all was well for the camera. While they did so, you spoke to the camera, making a video to send with whomever made it to Saudi Arabia in the hope that it would reach your father.

A few days ago, you had received an audiocassette with voice messages from your parents. It was delivered by someone who had snuck in illegally over the closed Kuwaiti-Saudi border. You didn't have to fake your smile in front of the camera while speaking to your parents. You truly were happy with everything, except the danger of what was going on outside of the house: news of arrests, and stories of inmates in the occupying forces' makeshift prisons tortured to extract confessions.

You waxed lyrical for the camera. You grinned as you said, "Mom, we're well."

***

Your eyes glisten when saying, "Mom." You choke back a sob. The word lands painfully at a time when she can't hear you. The horn of the garbage truck blares. You rush before Abdellatif's likely visit interrupts you. "Don't worry about me—I don't ever go out . . ."

"Start again . . . from the top!" Fahd and Sadiq interject, gesturing toward the sky where a reconnaissance chopper is flying over your heads, its whirring dispelling the safe haven you had all played a part in fabricating. You stop filming, waiting for the chopper to pass over and the sound of its rotor to fade away. You then resume your roles. Your two friends assume their places in the background, kicking the ball back and forth, stuck in their repetitive, silent roles. You address the camera, saying, "I don't go outside the house, Mom . . . I sleep in Mama Hissa's room on the floor . . . I still haven't seen an Iraqi soldier. Don't worry . . . Actually, there aren't any soldiers in Surra!"

Gunshots at the end of the street cut you off. In desperation Fahd yells out, "Ohhhh!"

"We're pooped," Sadiq says as he falls to his knees.

You try to get them back on track. You smile hopefully. "Again . . . just one more time," you urge them. You start rolling again, repeating your words, not leaving anything out except your smile, which had been there just a few moments before. Beads of sweat drip down from the hair behind your ears, sticking to your back. Behind you are your friends, beyond exhausted, their collars blackened with sweat from kicking the ball around; their faces worn-out, eyebrows furrowed and ears finely attuned, on guard for any sound that might bring the idyllic scene you have set up crashing down.

***

You barely managed to complete your video. You replaced the video cassette with a new one, all of you collectively creating a "fun" atmosphere, exhausting all possible game options inside the courtyard: football, anbar, hide-and-seek, and tug-of-war. You detested the last game. Every time you switched sides, sometimes pulling with Sadiq and other times with Fahd. You hated being in that position, between the two, with no choice but to join one against the other in a game solely based on strength. You abandoned those games and decided to kill time with some improvised acting. In front of the camera Fahd pretended to be Abdulkareem Abdulqader, imitating his hand gestures and his voice as he emphatically sang, "Patience is for someone else . . . Enough, the heart has let go of you."

You and Sadiq begged him to stop imitating Abdulkareem. "We've had enough of him!"

"Last song, wallah, I swear," he promised. Reluctantly, you both gave him time to choose a new song.

He stood still, his arms wide open in front of the camera. He drew in a deep breath. He shut his eyes tightly. He opened his mouth. He started singing in a voice that, while not exactly like Abdulkareem's, matched its cadence to an astonishing degree: "A voice calls out . . . When will my country return?"

Sadiq warned Fahd once he finished his song, "That Abdulkareem song is about Palestine." Fahd bobbed his head, but said nothing. You and Sadiq stood, acting out different personalities, exchanging fatuous, improvised dialogues. Fahd and Sadiq eventually went back to soccer. Sadiq moaned about not being able to go out and play in the Gamal Abdel Nasser Park. You stood behind the camera, following their game. You commented as Khalid Al Harban would: "Fahd Al Bin Ya'qub . . . He's got the ball . . . He crosses it . . . Goooooooal!"

The urgent chirp of the doorbell jolted you. We exchanged horri-
fied looks. The unknown finger continued pressing the doorbell. You
hoped that it might be Abdellatif, despite not having seen him since he
last accompanied the garbage truck, whose driver was content to simply
honk his horn whenever he was on your street. Fahd made for the door.
"Don't open it!" Sadiq hissed, warning him. The ringing stopped, giving
way to forceful knocking on the iron door.

We almost ran inside, but a loud voice commanded, "Open the
door!"

Sadiq's face turned sheet-white. "Bibi Zaynab!" He dashed to the
door to see why she had come. Her appearance unnerved you all; she
was wheezing, barefoot, without her abaya, looking somewhat thin-
ner, her milfah loosely wrapped, leaving strands of her graying hair
flying in all directions. She scurried inside, yelling, "Abbas . . . Abbas!"
You followed after her, faces blanched. She stumbled at the doorstep.
Sadiq propped her up. Everyone raced to the hallway, prompted by the
wailing of your elderly neighbor. As soon as she saw 'Am Saleh, she
clutched his hands and cried, "Abbas . . . They've taken Abbas!" Her
knees betrayed her. She fell to the ground. 'Am Saleh stood dumb-
founded. The reddening of Sadiq's ears spread to his face.

"Dad!" he sobbed.

He raced out of the house. Khala Aisha and Fawzia rushed to
support Bibi Zaynab while you stared at Mama Hissa's face, examining it. She remained standing, looking at her son. Confused, he was
unable to meet his mother's gaze. His lips exploded angrily, "It's all that
Palestinian's doing!" Abu Sameh came to mind. Mama Hissa stayed
silent, looking at him with eyes that asked, *What now?* There was nothing left for him to do as the sole man among all the women, except to
go to his room to fetch the car key. Khala Aisha followed him.

Mama Hissa raged at her, yelling, "Aisha! Stay here!"

'Am Saleh came out of his room, a red ghutra hurriedly wrapped
around his head. He padded outside, head bent, in his house dishdasha.

His wife yelled at him, demanding to know where he was going. "Surra police station," he stammered as he kept walking.

She followed him, pleading, "For God's sake, don't go . . . My heart is aching!" 'Am Saleh looked to his mother's eyes. She was still staring at him. He kept on walking. Aisha persisted, hanging on to the excuse: "But the license plate . . . it's Kuwaiti!"

'Am Saleh halted in his tracks at the edge of the hallway, deep in thought. He glanced at his mother. She was still staring intently into his eyes. He bowed his head, frowning. You'd never seen him as weak and confused as at that moment. He caught you off guard when he called you over. You looked at him, your stomach in knots. "Where's your bike?" he asked you.

THE SECOND MOUSE: BLAZE
THE INHERITANCE OF FIRE

THE NOVEL

Chapter 9

Someone had trod a path in the accumulated layers of dust in the court-yard of your house; the footprints started from the gate and disappeared behind the inner door leading to the living room. You then also spotted a separate trail returning from the inside out. It troubled you. They certainly weren't yours or Fahd's from the day you had searched for your passport, which was now over two months ago. You almost entered your own house, crossing the courtyard, but failed to—fearful that a stranger was lying in wait for you, coupled with your obedience to Khal Hassan's warning not to go in.

'Am Saleh waited in his house for you to return with the bike. You handed it over to him, your head swimming with questions about the footprints you had just seen. 'Am Saleh took off on your bike in search of 'Am Abbas at the Surra police station, where the occupying forces were camped out, and was yet to return. The last image you had of him was of his head down, avoiding his mother's looks, with the edges of his dishdasha wrapped around his waist as he rode off, teetering like a child. The last sound from him had been the words "Where's your bike?"

***

Everyone in the house questions, talks, invokes God's name, and prays except for the old woman who is silent, unlike herself. Ghostly pale. Khala Aisha sent you to 'Am Abbas's house.

There is nothing new about the women wailing, except for Bibi Zaynab beating her thighs as she cries out, "We don't know any Ibrahim, wallah; we don't know any Ibrahim!"

***

She echoed this refrain to any soldiers who stormed her house, asking for the owner of that name. She would beg them to leave her alone. "My boy, may God be pleased with you. Don't you have any mercy in your heart? Our fate is in your hands. Please help us." She thought that her accent would suffice as her intercessor, softening their hearts, but her Iraqi tongue didn't do the trick. Her beloved dialect was now only fit for barking military orders.

One day passed, then a second. No news of 'Am Saleh or 'Am Abbas. Their relatives rushed to search for them. In vain. You called Khal Hassan to let him know what had happened. He promised to do something. He knocked on the house door after having been to the police station and a number of schools that had been converted by the Iraqi leadership into internment camps. "No news; they don't know anything," Khal Hassan shared.

***

You and Tina discover the old lady is on a hunger strike. Only a few sips of tea dribble down her throat each day. You lie beside her brass bed at night. The room is lit up until a late hour. The old lady recites what she has memorized of Quranic verses in an audible voice, twice as humble. After exhausting the storehouse of her memory, she orders you to go do your ablutions before asking you to grab the Quran to read more verses. "I don't know where I put my glasses," she claims. You know she can't read. She doesn't even own glasses. She came out of the literacy classes only knowing her numbers, which helped her use the phone and know the price of goods at the central market. You know very well that she doesn't like to come across to you as needy.

Understanding her situation, you stride to her wooden cupboard, where the Quran is. "I'll read for you whatever you want, Mama Hissa." The smell of naphthalene assaults your nostrils upon opening the cupboard. You squat on your mattress on the ground.

The old lady mumbles, "Yunus who returned from the whale's stomach—read that one, recite it well."

You open the Quran in your hands and begin to read.

Fawzia's knock on the door interrupts you. "Mama, don't forget your meds."

Mama Hissa follows your reading for some more minutes before you stop to remind her, "The meds." You resume reading and keep an eye on her. She clutches a blister pack of medicine. In her left hand, she gathers five pills. In the same hand she grasps a glass of water. She clasps her right hand over her mouth, swallowing nothing but air before transferring the glass to her right hand and bringing it to her lips. Your eyes stay on her left hand, your face betraying your incredulity. The old woman sets her glass down after sipping a little bit of water. She stealthily gathers up her unconsumed pills with a tissue and tosses them into the garbage basket under her medicine table. You spend the whole night wondering without daring to ask the question. You are half-asleep when a voice that seems like a dream comes to you.

"You, fire starter!" She warns you not to divulge what you had seen. And because you hate the name she brands you with, you give in.

It is the third day since the disappearance of both 'Am Abbas and 'Am Saleh. Khala Aisha is as composed as you have always known her to be, or maybe she is just pretending to be calm. She makes one phone call after another. She cracks her knuckles. She gnaws at her fingernails. She disappears into her room. When she comes out, her eyes are swollen and her nose red. She raises her voice, yelling at Fahd while his grandmother listens, "Your father is gone!" She clenches her jaws, cursing no one in particular. She glances at Mama Hissa out of the corner of her eye and says, "May God hold accountable the person who caused this."

The old lady doesn't make a sound in Khala Aisha's presence, her color drained. Her face is a pale yellow. You alone know why she is wilting, whereas everyone else attributes it to her missing son. You're caught between the rock of being the fire starter and the hard place of being her secret keeper.

You stare at her face while she shakes her head in what resembles a prayer. Mama Zaynab, Khala Fadhila, and Hawraa all take turns visiting the Al Bin Ya'qub household, exhaustion etched deep in their faces, each asking, "Any news?" No news. Mama Hissa shrivels up, the dryness of her lips worrying you, her fingers trembling.

Fawzia approaches and hugs her. She strokes her back and says, "You're as dear to me as my eyesight." She asks her mother, "Have you taken your medicine?"

The old lady bobs her head yes. You run toward her room. The mountain of pills in her garbage basket takes your breath away. You wish you could just tell everyone, but you aren't a fire starter. It would probably be better if you were dead . . . Oh, if only you really *were* a fire starter . . . if only!

***

Khala Aisha called your uncle to accompany her to the Surra police station. You and Fahd went along. Khal Hassan's license plate caught your attention when he arrived: it said. One point for 'Am Saleh. Khal Hassan's obedience irked you. You had barely made it down the street, passing by the zalamat house, when your uncle stopped his car to see why the women of the house were banshee wailing. Abu Taha was spread out like a blanket, carried by his brothers and his sons to the car. A heart attack. You learned later on that the man had collapsed on the spot after the Iraqi authorities issued a decree making the Kuwaiti dinar equal to the Iraqi one, giving a deadline of twelve days after which anyone still dealing in Kuwaiti dinars would be held responsible. The man couldn't fathom let alone stomach the idea that his 100,000 dinars, the fruits of his life's toil, converted in one day into a mere 6,000.

Khal Hassan and Khala Aisha got out of the car while you and Fahd stayed inside. You were parked in front of the police station that you had for so long imagined to be the psychiatric ward from your favorite TV show. There was a stark difference between the humorous scenes of the batty women and the sad ones of the soldiers inside the red building. You imagined the leading actors of your beloved show—Mahzouza, Mabrouka, Dr. Sharqan, and Abu Aqeel, the director of the hospital—all in handcuffs and blindfolded, with Fuada specifically muzzled, unable to yell, "Protect yourselves from the plague!" Barely a few minutes had passed when Khala Aisha came out accompanied by Khal Hassan, stroking his beard, frustration evident on his face. You didn't ask him anything. You had barely pulled out of the parking lot when Fahd yelled, "Mom, look there . . . the bike!" Your bike was chained to one of the posts.

Aisha raised her voice. "God damn that bike and whoever owns it!" You sank into the car seat, Fahd squeezing your knee to comfort you.

For nine days, Khal Hassan searched for the two missing neighbors in every possible place: the former garden nurseries, now torture chambers, the interrogation centers spread out in the districts, and the hospital morgues.

Nothing.

Mama Hissa kept quiet. Not a peep from her except for some faint chanting; you couldn't tell whether it was a song or a recitation from the Quran. She sat down on the short-legged wooden chair beneath her sidra. She plucked morsels of bread and scattered them on the ground, calling out, "Ta'! Ta'!"

Fawzia, with her hijab clinging to the skin of her scalp, could not conceal her worry about the unknown malady that had befallen her mother.

You were in the living room. It was the tenth day since 'Am Saleh had left with your bike. Mama Hissa was crouched in her corner, seemingly focused on sewing Tina's sari. Aisha erupted suddenly, yelling, "May God judge you, I've never seen a woman with a heart as hard as yours!" Your bones trembled at the volume of her voice in the old lady's presence. Mama Hissa was operating her machine, staring at the position of the needle without any reaction to her daughter-in-law's revolt. Aisha went on, "The man left because of your stubbornness. No one else in this house gets you the way I do. I've put up with you for years for Saleh's sake, and I won't do it anymore now that he's not here!" The old lady sped up the spinning of her sewing machine, distracting herself from her daughter-in-law's verbal stabs. Aisha advanced toward her. She leaned over the machine and grabbed its wheel, stopping its humming. She put her face close to Mama Hissa's and hissed, "I'm not going to end up like you." The sudden rise in her voice jolted you as she screamed, "Look at me!" The old woman wasn't strong enough to meet Aisha's eyes. She kept her head down and withdrew further into herself, her loose brown robe slack like a neglected sack of rice. Aisha went on, her jaws clenched. "Do you want me to end up like you? A martyr's widow?" Mama Hissa's eyes didn't falter from the needle. Aisha's eyes remained on the old lady's face. "You long to see Fahd like

your daughter, sickly and fatherless, so that your heart will be at ease."
She snapped again, "Look at me!"

The old woman raised her head and looked into Aisha's eyes.
You stared at Mama Hissa's face. Her red eyes were glistening, on the
verge of tears. Her lower lip trembled. The doorbell rang. The old lady
emerged from her silence, gasping as she did, as if she'd been electrocuted. Rivulets of tears streamed down her smiling face, her mouth as
wide as it could go. "Saleh . . . my boy?" she exclaimed expectantly.

THE SECOND MOUSE: BLAZE
THE INHERITANCE OF FIRE

THE NOVEL

Chapter 10

Abbas was arrested because of the empty bullet cartridges that the occupying soldiers had found in the yard in front of his residence. This happened during the raid carried out after an unknown young man was shot as a military convoy crossed the Ali Bin Abi Talib Street, on its way to the bridge connecting Surra and Jabriya. We wouldn't have known these details if Abu Sameh hadn't informed us when he rang the doorbell that day. He came without his ice-cream cart. He held out his hand, passed a piece of paper to Aisha, and said that both Abbas and Saleh were there. Fahd's mother read what was scribbled on the paper: *Basra security station.* She beat her chest with her hands. "Basra?" You looked at Fahd. You remembered his mother's song, "Where has my daddy gone? To Basra he's gone . . . In Basra he was gone!" Abu Sameh turned to leave, but Aisha stopped him when she belted out his usual refrain: "Ice cream!"

A laugh that didn't resemble a laugh slipped out. Abu Sameh responded, "We're out of business."

"Now hold on, don't go . . . for God's sake," she urged him. She invited him to enter the diwaniya that overlooked the courtyard.

He looked around before he said, "Okay, but quickly." Khal Hassan had arrived as well, responding to Aisha's phone call. He spoke with Abu Sameh to glean more details. There was not much else to tell except that the charge against Saleh was that he had asked about Abbas's where-abouts. Abu Sameh said Abbas had nothing to do with the cartridges; they most likely had come from Ibrahim Mansour or Al Munir.

"Abdellatif Al Munir?" your uncle Hassan asked. Abu Sameh assented, but said he could not remember the person's first name. He said that he'd seen him in the Surra co-op market, and he'd often pass by Al Munir's house with his ice-cream cart, and that he had recently started seeing him roaming around the Surra streets in a garbage truck before disappearing from sight altogether. It was said that both Ibrahim Mansour and Al Munir were working with Jasim Al Mutawwa's armed group. Both of them were wanted by the Iraqi security agencies after Jasim had been arrested. You and Fahd exchanged looks. You both remembered the name well. The bread, cheese, and pamphlet-supplying Jasim. You stopped at the phrase "had been arrested." Abu Sameh said that a man had ratted out Jasim. After Jasim had been arrested and tortured, he was released but put under surveillance with the aim of discovering the remaining members of the group, and was then arrested once more.

Khal Hassan's face blanched. "How do *you* know all of this? Who told you these names?"

Abu Sameh's voice got louder. He responded as if he had just been insulted. "I've buried three of my brothers in this country . . . I'm more Kuwaiti than you!" He got ahold of himself and went on. "I've been roaming the streets of Surra for more than sixteen years, Abu Dhari. I know Jasim well, and I know Abdellatif by face; only Ibrahim

Mansour doesn't seem like he's from around here, from Surra." Khal Hassan undid the button of his dishdasha. He looked intently into Abu Sameh's eyes and then asked, his eyes harboring an accusation, "So, who told on Al Mutawwa, then?"

"A man in the army got close to him and discovered his secret."

Khal Hassan stroked his beard. "The Iraqi army?"

Abu Sameh shook his head and said, "The Kuwaiti army."

Khal Hassan got agitated. "That can't be right."

"Well, it's the truth," Abu Sameh insisted. Aisha fidgeted in her seat. She let out a half sigh that Khal Hassan picked up on. "Who told you about Saleh's and Abbas's whereabouts?"

Abu Sameh stood up, his hands raised. "Please don't get me involved. I beg you, they'll destroy my house if . . ."

Khal Hassan shook his head, disappointed, narrowing his eyes. "Are you working with them, Abu Sameh?"

The man shook with fear. "God forbid! If I were, shame on me!" He drew a breath before he bent his head down and added, "If I gave you an answer, then you'd put all of us Palestinians in danger."

THE SECOND MOUSE: BLAZE
THE INHERITANCE OF FIRE

THE NOVEL

Chapter 11

It was your first time in Iraq. Khal Hassan crossed the Safwan Road on his way to Basra. He was behind the wheel. His son Dhari was stuck to the door; you were sharing the front seat with him. Aisha, Fadhila, Hawraa, and Fahd were all in the back seat. You all were piled up in the car just as Abu Sameh had instructed Khal Hassan: "Take the women and children with you to make it easier to see the prisoners." You had left Mama Hissa at home in the care of Bibi Zaynab, Fawzia, and Tina. Her poor health after receiving Abu Sameh's news had left her house-bound. The road, though short, felt long. The beat-up AC spewed out air that barely cooled the temperature inside the car. Despite the moderate weather outside, the car was suffocating with nervous breathing. Agricultural reserves peppered either side of the road. You saw scattered tamarisk trees nearby. The unfamiliar sights enthralled you: farmers' faces, their white ghutras speckled with black; pipes for artesian wells; small clay houses dotting the vast, empty spaces. Silence united all of you, listening to the radio—the small peephole through which world news came. You all were afraid the news bulletin would terminate without a single mention of Kuwait, that your situation would be forgotten. The female and male broadcasters took turns reading the news. The Yemeni tribesmen stood with Saudi Arabia, against their Yemeni president, who supported Iraq. You recalled the hawking calls of the fabric seller: "Khaaam! Khaaam!" Iran said it supported the GCC countries in their efforts to find a peaceful solution to the crisis. Haydar the grocer's face, with his gold-toothed smile, came to mind. Just like that, faces and voices emerged in the wake of every country alluded to in the news. Tina. Mr. Desouky your teacher and Jaber the Egyptian. Shakir Al Buhri and Alameen the Punjabi. Mushtaq the Pakistani barber. Adnan the Syrian butcher and Mr. Murhif the teacher. Your Sudanese classmate Abdl Fadhil. Unintentionally, you were assembling them into a cast of characters. You sorted them into boxes based on their governments' positions. During the sports bulletin, you felt like someone who had achieved a long-awaited victory, someone who wasn't used to winning: Beijing had thrown Iraq out of the Asian Games. The word *expulsion* came as a compensation for what you couldn't achieve against the occupation forces in your own country.

Khal Hassan knew the way well, having visited the telephone exchange in Basra from the initial days of the occupation to phone his relatives living abroad. As we made our way up a street leading to the Zubayr District, Fadhila motioned to Khal Hassan to take a left. She pointed to a mosque that seemed far away, which stood out, distinguished by its antique minaret. She asked to get off there. "Just five minutes, I won't take long." Khal Hassan understood what she was after. He stopped the car near the Imam 'Ali Mosque in Zubayr. Fadhila got out of the car with Hawraa and Sadiq in tow.

Fahd stretched out his arm from the seat behind you. He pinched your ear. You ignored him. He asked, "What are they doing?" No one answered him. Fadhila remained out there with the twins for about ten minutes, begging and praying to the imam to bring back her missing loved one. She came back, her face much calmer. Khal Hassan turned the car in the direction of downtown Basra.

You remember well how pale your khal looked at the Basra telephone exchange. He stretched out his hand to the telephone exchange employee, in it a paper with different phone numbers. The man gestured toward one of the booths. Time flew by. You only remember your mother's voice on the line, her sobs punctuated by fragmented sentences. The phone call finished quickly only to be followed by other hastily made calls. Khal Hassan closed his trembling hand around the phone receiver. You recall the sadness that engulfed his voice as if he were reciting poetry. "He's gone. Two days ago, he and Fayez Kan'an in front of the last house in Al Faiha . . . I wasn't home. My son, Dhari, saw everything."

Khal Hassan stopped the car in front of the security headquarters. He got out and accompanied Aisha, Fadhila, and the twins, while you and Dhari stayed behind in the car. The courtyard in front of the headquarters was overrun with cars, on them new Iraq-Kuwait license plates. Many families were asking about their sons, trying to confirm their whereabouts. A long time passed. Dhari bit his fingernails as he stared at the entrance to the building. "My d-d-dad is late!" You asked him why he was worried, not understanding his speech pattern, unfamiliar with it. His eyes were fixed on the door. His breath condensed on the passenger window. "I'm scared they're going to take him." Some of his worry washed over you. His lips quivered before they opened to say, "They murdered Abdellatif. Fayez Kan'an too. And shot someone else." He started to describe the scene on the pavement in front of his house. Once again his stuttering caught your attention as he tried to express himself. For many years you hadn't understood what had happened to his tongue. How had Dhari become D-D-Dhari?

You asked him about the third person. It could be the Ibrahim Mansour that the ice-cream seller mentioned. He shook his head and went back to chomping on his nails as if he were going to wolf down all his fingers. You felt a moist warmth spread under your right thigh, soaked up by your shared seat. While gazing out the window he added, "I saw them from my b-bedroom two days ago, the old brown blood-stains s-s-still there, bloodstains and a p-piece of the skinned scalp on the sidewalk, hair and blood and . . ."

He clammed up. You needed some time to piece together that it was Abdellatif Al Munir who had disappeared. The garbage truck was now being driven by a masked man who just honked while making his rounds in the area, after Al Munir had gotten involved in armed resistance. Dhari's face lit up when, after nearly two hours of waiting, the door to the security headquarters opened to reveal his father.

Khal Hassan returned with disheartened faces in tow. You looked at Aisha and Fadhila, followed by their kids. One could mistake them for sisters, all with the same shiny reddish faces. In such trying times, all faces looked the same. They all piled into the car. Prompted by the lingering smell, Khal Hassan looked at his son. He opened the windows. He was about to drive off, but a soldier appeared at the entrance to the building, gesturing at Khal Hassan to get out. The soldier spoke to him. Khal Hassan nodded silently, then returned to the car to inform Aisha and Fadhila, "He wants money."

"So that he releases them both?" Fadhila inquired.

"So that they allow us to visit them tomorrow afternoon."

Your uncle counted his Iraqi dinars. "Not enough!" Fadhila lamented. Aisha bit her lower lip as she looked out into space. Fadhila slipped her hand inside her clothes and took out a necklace and some gold bracelets. "This is all I have."

Khal Hassan refused to take the risk of bribing the soldier with gold. He turned on the engine and headed down Kuwait Street. The forbidden name of your country caught your eye. You knew Kuwait as a country. You came to know it in Iraq as a street. Khal Hassan parked the car in a nearby square. You continued on your way toward the jewelry market in

Al Ashar at the end of the Al Maghaiz souk, passing by the spice stalls in the Indian market. The atmosphere was similar to that of Al Gharbally Street in the Al Mubarakiya souk back home, if it hadn't been for the difference in dialect: traditional shops on either side of the road selling watches, clothes, shoes, carpets, and pots, plus a pharmacy and an ice-cream store. What struck you was that the Iraqis here were nothing like those in your country. The military uniform had nothing to do with it. Something you couldn't put your finger on distinguished them.

You entered the gold store with Sadiq, Hawraa, and Fadhila. A small store with a low ceiling and dim lighting. Fadhila placed her necklace and bracelets on the glass counter in front of the seller, an old, bald man with a bushy mustache.

"Deposit?" he asked her in a husky voice. She shook her head. "Sale." The man fixed his glasses on the tip of his nose, his lips forming into an O as he examined the necklace. His gaze jumped between the necklace and all of you, searching your faces. Before weighing it, he asked, "From Kuwait?" Fadhila nodded. It was strange to your ears to hear the name "Kuwait" being mentioned so brazenly in Iraq since it was forbidden in your own country, now known as the Al Nida province. He cleared his throat and then said, "Forgive me for asking." He looked at the door before asking why she needed the money. Fadhila covered her face with a piece of her abaya, hiding her sobs. He asked her to have a seat. He then disappeared into a side room through a small door, the bracelets and necklace in hand. He returned carrying an envelope and a glass of water, giving both to Sadiq's mother. She got up and made a gesture of thanks before heading outside without counting the notes in the envelope. "May God help you all," he said.

In the car, Fadhila gave Khal Hassan the envelope. He ripped the corner. He took out the notes and counted them. He turned to her, perplexed. "That's it?" He looked again in the envelope. He stuck his hand in. His eyes widened as he looked at her, fishing out the necklace and gold bracelets. "What's this?"

THE SECOND MOUSE: BLAZE
THE INHERITANCE OF FIRE

THE NOVEL

Chapter 12

Your visit to Saleh and Abbas meant you had to spend the night in Basra. One night, because of what was required, became two. You all met Abbas and Saleh on the third day, when they were paraded out, handcuffed, among dozens of young and old Kuwaiti men. This was only after having spent two depressing nights in a Hamadan hotel room overlooking the Al Ashar River, during which you had to sleep with the light on because Dhari was afraid of the dark. Khal Hassan, however, spent his two nights tossing and turning on the back seat of his car instead of renting a room, in order to save money to grease the necessary palms when you went over to visit the detainees. The visit on that third day barely lasted half an hour; the only thing you remember was the women sobbing: the mix of tears, sweat, and sheer terror on the faces of your two neighbors in the small dusty square, their heads shaven and blindfolds removed. The soldiers didn't respond to your collective plea to extend the visiting time. "When will they be released?" No one answered.

"Nothing's for certain until the trial," a soldier finally said. *Trial.* The word weighed down heavily on all of you, and despite having seen them, you returned to Kuwait more worried than ever.

As soon as you approached your street, you noticed a lot of cars out in front of the zalamat house. They were receiving mourners for Abu Taha's funeral; he'd breathed his last in the hospital after a two-week-long coma. You remember how disappointed he was at Saleh's lackluster reception at his front door a few weeks ago. "Will you go to give condolences?" Khal Hassan asked.

Fahd responded on your behalf and also for Sadiq: "My father wouldn't be happy about that." Khal Hassan didn't respond.

"Let's ask Mama Hissa," you whispered in Fahd's ear. You knew that she'd encourage you all to give condolences to those you'd played soccer with for years in the neighborhood.

You never got the chance to ask her. It never crossed your mind that being away for two nights in Iraq would transform Mama Hissa into a human lump, a heap of threadbare clothes on a sickbed. She had fallen down during your absence, worn-out, fatigued. She ordered that her brass bed be put in the living room, facing the hallway, so that when Saleh came back, she could see him as soon as he entered. She was unable to move, yet still hopeful that her son would return with you. She'd been burning incense the whole time you were gone in anticipation of Saleh's arrival. But you and Fahd didn't know any of this as you sped up to enter before everyone else. Mama Hissa's face shocked you, her eyes closed and her mouth wide open in a sad, toothless smile. She was like another woman altogether, older than the one you had known for so many years.

Mama Zaynab read Quranic verses over her head. Fawzia wiped the sweat from her brow. On the ground, next to her bed, Tina massaged Mama Hissa's legs. You ran toward her. "Did you bring them back?" Mama Zaynab asked. You didn't answer. Fahd simply shook his head, standing off to the right side of the brass bed to take in his grandmother's new face. You brought your face closer to Mama Hissa's, craning your neck under the feeding tubes hanging in the metal holder on the side of her bed. The intravenous needle might as well have been plunged into your own heart.

It pierced the skin of her hand, going deep into one of her raised veins. It drew dark-blue splotches. You could hear your own heart beating in your ears and felt the gushing of blood in your temples. You fought back the tears that had defeated Fahd. You kissed her forehead and asked, "Mama Hissa, how are you?" No response. Only the wheezing of her slow breaths.

You started to reassure her. "'Am Saleh is well." The sound of her son's name sparked life into her seemingly dead body. She raised a trembling arm, opened her palm, and scattered nothing into the air. She moved her lips noiselessly for quite a while before she let out a quivering, barely audible "Ta'! Ta'!" Come, come. Your gaze wandered to those around you, seeking an answer to what was wrong with her. Mama Zaynab closed her Quran as soon as Aisha and Fadhila came in.

"Where are they?" Mama Zaynab asked. Aisha shook her head. She was trying to be reassuring. "They're both fine . . . They'll be released soon." Mama Zaynab looked at Mama Hissa's aged face. "Come, come," she kept repeating. Mama Zaynab stared at Aisha. "You should have at least come back with Saleh for now, at least him . . ." Her body quaked, suppressing a wail.

Three heavy days dragged by. During that time a Palestinian doctor who worked in the Hadi Hospital in Jabriya dropped by. He was the one who discovered the old lady's aversion to taking her pills. He replaced the nutrient-laden IV bags. "Her condition is unstable," he stated plainly. Since the first week of the occupation, the ambulances and all the critical medical equipment had headed north, on the road of no return. You began to see the soldiers you heard so much about on a daily basis. All of you could distinguish the Republican Guard from the Armed Forces by the color of their caps. They stormed the Al Bin Ya'qub household and their next-door neighbors', asking for Ibrahim Mansour, who had vanished into thin air. They trampled the rug with their military boots and kicked down the bedroom doors. They interrogated everyone: even Tina and the old woman, who sometimes responded with "Tet! Tet!" or "Kish! Kish!" as if shooing away a fly.

"Crazy old bat!" they muttered as they left.

On the fourth day after your return from Basra, Mama Hissa's condition took a turn for the worse. Everyone hemmed her in: Aisha, Fawzia, Fahd, Tina, and Mama Zaynab. Her lips were pulled back from her hole of a mouth; they kept moving and yet not a single word was audible. Hot air gushed forth from her toothless orifice. You brought your ear closer to her silent words; maybe you'd catch a sentence. Her mouth smelled strange. Aisha sat next to Mama Hissa's twin, her elbows propped on her knees. She cradled her face between her palms and stared at the living room floor, glassy-eyed. The replica, bare without its holey abaya, caught your attention. It lay neglected on the ground below the tripod. The small circle on top of the Hitachi camera lens blinked red. You knew very well what that meant. No one took notice of your astonishment except for Tina, who was also looking at the camera. She glanced at Aisha, then jabbed you, whispering in her broken Arabic, "Crazy woman."

Mama Hissa stopped moving her lips. She opened her eyes as wide as they would go and stared at the living room ceiling, as if spelling out the alphabet in the air. You gently clasped her hand, fearful that the intravenous needle would hurt her. She was cold. Fawzia was perplexed. "Mom . . . Mom," she called out. Mama Hissa's mouth was still open.

The movement of her pupils sped up, combing the ceiling, then fell on the hallway, looking at you all. "Tet, tet." The protruding veins in her neck throbbed. She squeezed your palm. Her left eye shut, but her right one remained open, its pupil fixed on the hallway. She relaxed her grip, and you freed your palm.

Harmonious farewell sobs burst forth. "Mom, Mom . . . Um Saleh . . . Mom, the apple of my eye . . . Auntie . . . Big Mama . . . Mama Hissa!" You withdrew your steps toward her double in the corner, your moves robot-like.

You knew that Mama Hissa never moved, turning into stone, whenever the camera lens focused on her. "I'll wake her up." No one listened to you when you said that. You stood behind Mama Hissa's twin in its corner, not knowing what you were doing. You turned the face of the camera to the wall, far away from the old lady's face, whose open right eye was trained on the hallway. You yelled at the top of your voice, warning her, ignoring the wailing in the living room. "Are you camera-shy, Mama Hissa?" She remained silent. A hush fell over the room, and everyone turned to look at you. Mama Zaynab bent over and picked up the abaya lying on the ground. She cast it like a fishing net over the body of her neighbor. She hugged you. You buried your face between her neck and face. She smelled like Mama Hissa. You tried to steel yourself, not give in to sobbing. "Bibi Zaynab . . . What's with you all?"

Her voice came to you, weak, groaning in your ear:

> "The beloved of my heart, Um Saleh
> The beloved of my heart, Hissa
> Closed one eye, reassured about her family at
>   home,
> And left the other open, seeking Saleh's return!"

THE SECOND MOUSE: BLAZE
THE INHERITANCE OF FIRE

THE NOVEL

Chapter 13

You don't cry over your loved ones' deaths; you cry for yourselves, the ones who have been left behind. You cry for what they took when they died. They left you all without a wall to lean on. Mama Hissa was a wall that, in spite of its cracks, everyone relied on for support. Her absence left a lump in your throats that you couldn't spit out or swallow. She was gone. You felt as if the Al Bin Ya'qub house no longer had a roof to protect it. She took along with her what was most beautiful in her house: her vibrant voice; her scent—a mix of Pompeia cologne, the red soap, naphthalene, *oud* oil, and henna; the hum of her sewing machine; Tina's laughter; Aisha's subdued voice; and Fawzia's sight. Those around you sobbed uncontrollably. Whenever you got ahold of yourself, someone in front of you would burst out crying, triggering your tears all over again. You fled to Aisha to get a dose of her stoicism. It was a longer day than any of your long days during the time of the occupation.

Your bewilderment reached the point where you couldn't even cry anymore. Fahd was in the same boat. You both sat in the corner of the living room, close to Mama Hissa's twin, trying to take in everything going on. Death had never come this close to you before. Even with Abdellatif Al Munir being martyred and Abu Taha's death, the impact of both was short-lived.

***

Fawzia is in her mother's room with the door locked. You don't understand, or you don't want to understand, why Mama Hissa is in the bathroom being washed with sidra soap by Mama Zaynab and some strange woman. Soap of her sidra tree, sidra of lovers—the jinn's safe haven. Everything is unfamiliar. The feelings of loss and the uncertainty of what follows. She is still in the house. Even the words being spoken are unfamiliar; you can't make sense of any of them.

***

Mama Zaynab came out of the bathroom, dripping water, her sleeves rolled up. She spoke to Aisha . . . shroud, camphor, sidra soap, cotton, and nylon. *Bibi Zaynab! What are you doing to Mama Hissa?* You didn't dare ask. You couldn't believe that the shrouded woman laid out on the stretcher was your Mama Hissa. You clung to her twin even more. You closed your hands around the edge of the abaya. "Her face is radiant, praise be to God, but her right eye; my God, it's open!" the corpse-washer announced. Two men entered, carrying a casket. You knew that once she disappeared through the hallway outside, you would never see her again.

The people of the household escorted her, along with female neighbors and women from their families whom you'd never met before. Fawzia howled, tormented. Tina, Fahd, Aisha, Mama Zaynab, Fadhila, and Hawraa were all shrouded in black. They cried as they walked behind her corpse, which was tied up with string like a folded-up tent, neglected in a shed. You got up and ran when the wailing of the women in the courtyard intensified. You weren't able to join everyone else as they walked over to the body spread out on the stretcher. You stuck to the sidra, your gaze pouring out your final respects to her. No one besides you took notice of the chickens in the nearby cage, their heads raised to the sky, eyes closed, gargling. No one paid attention to the pigeons cooing in the sidra: a musical ensemble behind the intertwining branches and leaves, in the jinn's home, the sidra of lovers.

The women and Fahd crowded the courtyard entrance when the door of the car transporting the body slammed shut. They stretched out their necks, their gazes lingering on the car's back as it transported the corpse, disappearing at the end of the street on its way to the Sulaibikhat Cemetery, tailed by Khal Hassan's car and another vehicle owned by a relative of the old lady's.

You discovered that when sorrows showed up, one came tugging the hand of the next. To some degree, you weren't sure what you were crying about. You stayed in Fahd's room for the night. Fawzia was left to sleep in her mother's room, hugging her pillow as she did. Sorrow drained her, she who was the only one who used to call her mother "O apple of my eye." Fawzia didn't attend the 'aza, the mourning ceremony for her mother; neither did Aisha or Fahd, who ended up staying with Fawzia, who had been checked into the Mubarak Hospital in Jabriya— or if one went by their newly coined names, the Al Fida' Hospital in Al Ahrar—for three days while the Al Bin Ya'qub household thronged with mourners.

You were in the diwaniya most of the time with Sadiq. Through the window overlooking the street you kept an eye on the soldiers lingering outside. They parked their vehicles opposite your house. The soldiers watched the Al Bin Ya'qub house on the pretext that gatherings were forbidden. Aisha would come back at night, leaving her son in the hospital at his aunt's bedside. You couldn't comprehend what she relayed about Fawzia's condition. Diabetes. Lack of treatment. Ripped blood vessels. Folding up of the retina. All that you got was Fawzia had gone blind. You remembered how Mama Hissa called her daughter "unlucky." You didn't think about how Fawzia would carry on with her life in the dark. All that came to mind were the Ihsan Abdel Quddous novels in her room. How would she read them? You remembered Saleh's promise: "You'll go to college when Kuwait is free." When would Saleh return? When would Kuwait be free? And how could Fawzia enroll in college now? Your questions, which you knew would surely annoy everyone, took root in your head. No one would be able to answer, and you couldn't ask them in any case. Almost as soon as the three days of the 'aza came to an end, taking with it the blackness that had enveloped the house, news spread throughout all of Surra: Jasim Al Mutawwa had been released. He had been to his house. A bullet had pierced his head in front of his family. He had crumpled and fallen at his doorstep. Just as Surra was getting over the loss of Abdellatif, its sadness was renewed by the loss of Jasim.

One morning, in the second week of November, forty days after Mama Hissa's passing, Aisha was at Abbas's house. Mama Zaynab had organized a Shiite mourning ceremony for Mama Hissa's Arba'eeniya. The word was no longer foreign to you. *Arba'eeniya*. You remembered Saleh's bristling at the Arba'eeniya that was held a few months before at the Imam Hussein Mosque for those Saudi Arabia had executed for the Mecca bombings.

Abbas's house was crowded with mourners, and your street was teeming with soldiers who were ostensibly there to monitor the gathering. Perhaps no one was interested in the Arba'eeniya as much as Fawzia. "Take me to Abbas's house," she asked Fahd, Dhari, and you, wanting to attend the 'aza, especially as she wasn't able to go to the initial one forty days before. You felt sorry for how she looked. Fahd assisted her in choosing her clothes and a hijab for her head, which had started sprouting some hair. She didn't own an abaya, though, a prerequisite for attending the 'aza.

"The twin's abaya," Fahd suggested.

"Don't you dare undress my mother by taking her abaya!" she scolded him. Fahd choked on his tears. You weren't surprised by her words. You felt, like her, that Mama Hissa was the one who stood there in the corner of the living room, watching over the members of the household, assuring you that nothing would change with her passing. Fahd brought an abaya from his mother's closet. "You swear it's not my mother's abaya?" Fawzia demanded before putting it on. Fahd promised her that he hadn't gone near the tripod. She threatened him. "By God, if I see that camera without the abaya . . ." She didn't finish. She covered her face with her palms. She cried. Since that day you became her sight.

You both clasped her forearms, leading her to the neighbor's house, your cousin trailing behind. She walked with unsure steps atop the parched grass between Sa'marana and Barhiya. The absence of soldiers on the street caught your attention. You both left Fawzia there in the living room among the black sea of women: some on chairs, others cross-legged on the ground, spellbound as they listened to the recitation of the *mullaya*. Mama Zaynab was frowning, worrying her prayer beads between her fingers, mumbling.

You and Fahd found Sadiq at the door to the house. "There are soldiers inside," he let you know, gesturing with his chin to your house. He clarified, perplexed by your silence. "One of them scaled the wall and opened the door for the others. They stayed on for a bit before some of them left, but I'm sure the others are still in there."

You took off your sandals and climbed up Ikhlasa, which overlooked your house. You turned to Fahd and called out, "Hey, flip my sandals over!" Fahd bent down to your sandals and flipped them right side up, soles facing the ground, his lips resembling an upside-down crescent moon. He straightened up and looked at you, his eyes red. You hung on to the middle of the palm tree's trunk, looking down at your courtyard. There were no soldiers in sight. Nothing, except marble, its dust encrusted with footprints; it looked like there were more of them than before. You swallowed your fear and the sense of duty you felt toward your parents' bedroom, recalling Hassan's advice to not go into your house under any circumstances.

After the afternoon call to prayer, the garbage truck honked, announcing its arrival. You, Fahd, Sadiq, and Dhari were in the living room. Tina called out to you, asking for help. You dropped the bags of garbage at the front door, following the havoc unfolding in front of you. Heads poked out of the neighborhood windows. Military vehicles fenced in the truck. Ten soldiers—or maybe a few more—surrounded the truck. Others came out of your house, carrying wooden pallets. On top of them were automatic weapons and Molotov cocktails. Four of the soldiers aimed their rifles at the masked driver. One of them— seemingly the highest ranking, who was dressed differently and had a long, hooked mustache, Hulk Hogan–style—hollered, "Get out, Ibrahim, and surrender!"

Fahd turned to you, his face pallid. "Ibrahim Mansour," he mouthed. Dhari scampered inside, leaving a trail of his wet fear on the ground behind him. The driver got out, his arms raised above his head. Two soldiers surrounded him and handcuffed his hands behind his back. One of them roughly yanked Ibrahim's ghutra off, revealing a heavily bearded face. He was looking at you the whole time while they dragged him to the military jeep, before they blindfolded him and drove him away to an undisclosed location. Sadiq and Fahd scrutinized your face in silence. You didn't understand the expressions of pity on their faces. You were far away. You turned to them as soon as the military vehicles disappeared at the end of the street, behind the zalamat house.

"Did you both see the guy's face?" They nodded. "Didn't he look like Khal Hassan?" you asked, your eyes fixed on the end of the street.

THE SECOND MOUSE: BLAZE
THE INHERITANCE OF FIRE

THE NOVEL

Chapter 14

"The coalition forces": the most repeated phrase in the final month of the occupation. America, which you had only glimpsed as children in action movies or wrestling shows, became your salvation. America warned . . . gave a chance . . . deployed soldiers and prepared. America led the coalition forces to liberate Kuwait: many soldiers from the world over; Arab countries; many nations . . . many, many nations . . . but not one of the countries that had opposed your liberation. You had conjured up in your mind what you expected the American army to look like, its greatest asset being its soldiers: Rambo, James Bond, Rocky, Hulk Hogan, Ultimate Warrior, Mr. T, Superman, Batman, Spider-Man, the Terminator, and, leading them all, Captain America!

We started paying attention to the news of the ongoing war. You, who had never known what war was really like, except for what you had seen on TV, movies, news, or Atari games. No one left the house unless it was absolutely necessary—except to throw out garbage, the little there was, in the dusty plot attached to Abu Sami's house. You listened together to the news on the radio. Final deadline. Machines and ammunition. New vocabulary and ways of living: ghost aircraft, Scud and Patriot missiles. Leaflets left at all houses. Safety instructions. A generator. First aid. Hoarding foodstuffs that were easy to store. Rationing of food and drink. Candles instead of lights. Pieces of tape to hold your windows together in expectation of a blast. Sealing off any air passages out of fear that the occupier would use chemical weapons. Towels, charcoal, and kitchen utensils to craft masks. The war that you had taken as your salvation proved to be just that, but did not occur with the ease or speed that you had expected. The neck of the bottle that the enemy was stuck in, as the media put it, was long. An air war broke out on January 17, 1991. Desert Storm, as America called it; "the mother of all battles" is what the Iraqi president deemed it. Whatever it was called, it was a drawn-out affair. News came in the first week that the Iraqi forces had opened up the oil wells and spilled their contents into the waters of the Gulf. Fahd didn't appear to be joking when he asked how the fish in the sea were holding up. People who lived on the coast confirmed black waves. It was said that French planes bombed the oil wells with the intention of burying them to prevent an environmental disaster. There were tidbits galore that the neighbors passed on, each piece contradicting the next.

We would fall asleep to the sound of missiles and the smell of extinguished candles. The earth quaked beneath us. The windows cracked from the intensity of the bombing. During the first strike you gathered, you and whoever was left of Saleh's and Abbas's families, under the staircase, where you had prepared a shelter according to guidelines. Tina yelped with every explosion, covering her face with her palms. Aisha hugged her. Fadhila cried. Mama Zaynab flitted between praying and reading verses from the Quran. Fahd took an exaggerated interest in looking out for Hawraa, trying to calm her down with a bottle of water. Sadiq jammed his two index fingers into each of his red ears.

Fawzia clutched your arm, asking if you could see anything. You had no choice but to man up. You reassured her that there was nothing to see except for the sounds that she heard. The saluki's howling after each blast sounded like someone crying. Fahd couldn't control himself. He went outside, although Aisha pled, "Don't leave!" He came back with the saluki. You stiffened. The dog secluded itself in the tight space, hiding its tail between its legs. He no longer annoyed you. You got used to him being among you.

The floor below the staircase was furnished with mattresses and pillows. Cans of food and bottles of water surrounded you. You all slept packed like sardines. The radio continued to broadcast the news; none of you believed the reportage, yet didn't dismiss it altogether. You filtered what you heard, only taking in what you hoped was the truth. The power was cut. We didn't know if it was just our street, or if it extended to the rest of Surra, or if the whole country had been plunged into darkness. If we went by the news, the electricity and water plants had been blown up. It was said that the Iraqi army had decided to retreat. It was said that they had set fire to oil wells, blowing up tons of TNT exacting their revenge, or to camouflage their withdrawal from the prying eyes of the coalition planes above.

None of you caught more than a few minutes of sleep between the boom of one blast and the next. You were all under the stairwell: Mama Zaynab, Fadhila, Hawraa, Aisha, Tina, Fawzia, you, your two friends, and the dog. Fawzia woke up everyone at sunrise a few days before the liberation. The rumbling of the planes and the blasts of the explosions had stopped. The war, it seemed, was catching its breath. "Do you hear what I hear?"

You grabbed her palm, reassuring her. "It's just the growl of the generator in the courtyard."

She shook her head. "No." She placed her index finger in front of her lips and ordered, "Listen!" You all listened.

You went out to the courtyard, looking up at the sky, still drowsy. Utter astonishment left you speechless, each of you looking at the other. Dozens of seagulls, wings spread out, hovered in the sky. The din of their squawking overpowered the growl of the generator. Some of them landed on the courtyard wall, their fatigue apparent. None of you could find a reason for their presence, what with the coast being miles away from Surra. Sadiq bent down to grasp the feet of one of the birds and lifted it up. He held it upside down and examined it. On its feathers were black oil stains. "Dead," he remarked.

"Look over there!" Fahd called out as soon as he opened the courtyard door. You piled up at the door to get a look. Some of the neighbors were outside. Some were peering out of their windows. Hundreds of seagulls and coastal dunlins jostled with the cats, flies, and mice, competing with them as they foraged in the mountain of garbage on the dusty plot of land adjacent to Abu Sami's house.

"What's there?" Fawzia asked. You were her eyes. You described to her all that you saw, leaving the shrieks of the seagulls to complete the picture. The scene consumed all of you for several minutes before it transformed. But then, as the sun continued to rise, the sky suddenly turned black. The seagulls fell silent. Night fell when it shouldn't have.

Mama Zaynab started muttering, chanting, "There is no God but God, and Muhammad is His Prophet." Our world plunged into darkness. She raised her voice, urging everyone: "Profess your faith . . . profess your faith . . . Now's the time!"

Fawzia gripped your arm and asked, "What's happening?" You didn't have an explanation for her; in fact, you and everyone else were like her, hands outstretched in front of you, groping your way around in the inexplicable darkness. As if it were a bad dream. Fadhila grabbed Mama Zaynab, pushing her back inside.

***

She feels her way around. She leans on the wall. The old lady trembles. Hysteria overcomes her. "It's the end of time! It's here!" she proclaims. Fadhila quiets her down. You want to ask her about the signs that would signify the coming of Judgment Day. How would it be before . . . ?

You calm her down instead. "Bibi Zaynab . . . don't be scared." But you are just as scared as your cousin Dhari would be in a dark room. Thick black smoke blocks your view. You tell Fawzia about it.

Mama Zaynab screams as if she has just remembered her son. "Abbas! Abbas!" Fawzia lets go of your arm.

You start yelling like a panicked father looking for his lost daughter. "Fawzia!" No response.

The annex overlooking the courtyard lights up. Light shines out of the kitchen's two windows, the diwaniya, and the open door to the bathroom.

"Hey, is the light back on?" inquires Fawzia's voice from within.

***

THE SECOND MOUSE: BLAZE
THE INHERITANCE OF FIRE

THE NOVEL

Chapter 15

Seven months dragged on for an eternity. The word *rumor* that you'd all gotten used to in the days past was no longer uttered on February 26, 1991, the day on which it was declared, "Kuwait is free!" We poured out onto the street in front of your houses, despite the severely polluted air and the flickering between darkness and light a dozen times in one day alone, attributed to the smoke from the blazing oil wells. Neighbors carried flags and pictures of your emir and the crown prince that the flames hadn't lapped up when it had been a crime to keep them. You didn't go far. You were on the doorstep, clasping Fawzia's arm, describing what was happening. Flags. Photos. The neighborhood kids and teenagers singing. Clapping. The neighbors, some of them grabbing one another in what seemed an improvised traditional dance. The women's shrill, trilling cries of joy floating out of windows and merging with the voices of the seagulls up above. Fahd, despite the smallness of his body, carried Sadiq on his shoulders in a cartoonlike manner. Sadiq raised his fists up high and waved them. The honking of the cars got louder, the incessant tooting melding into improvised street song.

***

"My country Kuwait is free, its glory restored." "Beep, beep!" The national anthem continues to blare: "May you, Kuwait, always have good fortune, may good fortune always grace your head." You aren't the only joyful ones. The Egyptian workers—Jaber is among them—draped in their loose Upper Egyptian clothes, partake in your shared joy, exclaiming, "Saddam's got to hit the road!"

Fawzia smiles, crying, and excitedly claps along with the images that the voices conjure up in her imagination. Everyone's bodies shudder with the passing of the armored vehicles on your street, each one carrying a flag of the coalition countries. Fawzia listens to you as you call out, "America . . . Britain . . . France . . . Egypt.

"Sadiq is picking up the Saudi Arabian flag tossed to him by one of the soldiers. He's holding it up high. One of the neighbors is waving a giant American flag on top of his roof . . . The kids are holding up flags of the Gulf countries and other Arab and foreign nations . . . The soldiers are handing out fruit, sweets, and cookies."

Fawzia nods her head, absorbing your running commentary. She doesn't hide the tears falling from her static eyes. Fahd gets close to one of the armored vehicles, raising his shoulders to bring Sadiq closer to the American soldier atop it. Sadiq cups his palms around his mouth like a trumpet, and shouts, "My dad and his dad are in Iraq . . . Help them, please!" The soldier smiles back and hands him some bananas.

***

Abbas and Saleh didn't need the help of the American soldiers to be freed. God predestined their return, though it wasn't meant to be for the other hundreds of prisoners. Abbas's and Saleh's captivity in the Basra prison camps worked in their favor the day the uprising in southern Iraq broke out. Chaos spread within Iraq after the war and the retreat of the Iraqi army from Kuwait. Soldiers, who had been beaten down by war after war, rebelled against their leader. On his return, Saleh told you that the revolt had not been limited to the soldiers alone, according to what he had heard and experienced there. Families had come out onto the main roads of the Al Najaf governorate, making their way toward Imam 'Ali's shrine. Loud calls from megaphones urged the Iraqi people to rise up against the regime. The prisons were opened. Detainees and criminals went scot-free. The two neighbors were among the Kuwaiti prisoners who used this to flee to Kuwait on foot, just before aircraft dropping bombs quashed the revolts, making a mockery of the air embargo that America had imposed on Iraq.

Fahd jumped up and clung to his father as soon as he entered, head shaven, reed-thin body, tanned face, his chin jutting out. "Dad!" he yelped, alerting everyone. You heard the ecstatic *zaghareed* from Mama Zaynab's house at the same moment.

Aisha, whose feelings of loss for Saleh had been multiplied by the liberation, burst into tears over anything and everything. She cried for joy when the occupying forces withdrew. For the return of the long-lost prisoner. She cried, retroactively, out of sadness over losing Mama Hissa. Aisha came out of her bedroom in her pajamas, hair disheveled. Scarcely believing her eyes, she rushed to her husband. She broke up Saleh and Fahd's embrace. She was rooted to the spot before him, her lips twitching. He opened up his arms to her, smiling, fighting back his tears. She shoved him, beating his chest.

She yelled at him, "I thought you were dead . . . I would have killed you if you were!" She crumpled to her knees, hugging his legs, moaning openly, her lips closed.

Saleh's shaking body bent down and kissed her head.

No more than an hour had passed after the two prisoners' return when Khal Hassan's wife came over in her abaya, her face dull. She held Dhari by his hand. She looked at Saleh's face, driven by a hope that died as soon as he told her that he hadn't seen her husband or heard anything about him over there.

The doorbell rang a day after the two prisoners had returned. Tina entered and announced, "Baba Abbas."

Saleh ordered her to seat the neighbor in the diwaniya. "She's crazy! How can she just let him stand around in the street?" he wondered aloud. Saleh was in a foul mood, as any man would be who had lost his mother and was helpless before the calamity that had befallen his sister. Fahd and you followed Saleh to the lounge, where Abbas awaited him. The courtyard walls and its floor were coated in soot. The sky was still black. You entered the diwaniya. You found Sadiq's dad standing in the company of two men from the neighborhood. Gesturing toward the seats, Fahd's dad took the initiative and said, "Have a seat, have a seat."

Abbas shook his hand. "We'll rest afterward."

"Is everything okay?" Saleh inquired.

"Everything will be fine once the Palestinians leave our street," Abbas responded as he wagged a finger.

And leave they did. It was the last time you heard their familiar dialect, that very afternoon. Their language was no longer among the mix on your street. The zalamat house was no longer there at the head of the street, bordering Alameen the Punjabi's store, and there was no longer a family soccer team to play against on the dusty plots of Surra.

Abbas had pressed on their doorbell. He pounded on their door with both hands.

Abu Naiel had opened the door and looked at the surly faces of his neighbors.

"Listen here . . . ," Saleh had started.

He hadn't listened. "*You* listen here . . . after Abu Taha's death, there's nothing left here for us."

That's what Abu Naiel said before the existence of his household was erased from your street for good. He went on to establish a new life in Jordan. Everything faded away, everything except for his crestfallen face in your damned memory.

THE SECOND MOUSE: BLAZE
THE INHERITANCE OF FIRE

THE NOVEL

Chapter 16

My homeland . . . the home of daylight . . .
O my homeland . . . reborn again . . .
You ring the earth, the waves of the sea . . .
My homeland of daylight . . .

In those days, the love for Abdulkareem Abdulqader was no longer limited to that coming from Fahd Al Bin Ya'qub. "The wounded voice," as his fans called him, was the voice of all of Kuwait when he sang "Homeland of Daylight" and made you all cry, despite the dearth of daylight under a sky that the oil well fires blanketed with unending night, blinding the eye of the sun at the peak of its rise. You all listened to the song at a time when other areas in Kuwait were listening to the exploding of mines planted by the Iraqis before they withdrew. Fahd searched for the song's color. He wasn't able to. "It's every color," he concluded.

With the resurrection of Kuwait, your parents came back from Saudi Arabia by land. Your mother hugged you for so long that your body took root between her arms, locked in her embrace. You hardly recognized her, weak with yellow eyes ringed by dark circles. You returned to your family house. In this nation reborn, many things went back to how they had been. But this new incarnation of Kuwait could only coexist with the newness of things: accept them as they were and as they weren't.

Adnan the Syrian returned and opened up the butcher shop in an extension to the Al Awaidel house that overlooked the street. Alameen the Punjabi wiped away the dust that had accumulated on his washing and ironing business. He coated the steps at his storefront with the brown spittle that you had missed seeing for months. Life returned to Al Anbaiie Mall, which had been closed since the first week of August 1990. Shakir the Indian unveiled the glass front of his restaurant, displaying foods dripping in oil. Behind Shakir was a photo on the wall with both your emir and the sultan of Al Buhara. Above the door of his store Haydar the Iranian grocer hung up colored rubber balls, water guns, and plastic swords. Out of joy, he distributed gum, pistachios, and sunflower seeds to all the kids. Jaber the Egyptian resumed tending to the shawarma spit—one day lamb, one day chicken. He decorated the restaurant's ceiling with Kuwaiti flags and some Egyptian ones, too. Abu Fawaz mounted large photos of the emir, the crown prince, and the Kuwait Towers on his storefront. The entrance of his bookstore was packed with books; how or when they were printed, you had no clue. Their covers had images that became widespread afterward: the map of Kuwait oozing blood, a drawing of the Iraqi president riding an elephant toward the Kaaba, and another drawing of his head on a snake's body. Images that chased you in your sleep for years to come. Salim the tailor immersed himself in swathes of fabric, cutting out children's clothes in the colors of the Kuwaiti flag. Mushtaq the Pakistani barber dusted off his store sign, which read , not understanding why so many men were growing out their beards and steering clear of his razor blade. Even Abdulkareem took Fahd by surprise with his appearance on a cassette cover with a thick, impressive beard. It was said that it was his final recording before his retirement, because music was haram and because God had finally guided him to repent—although his beard had actually been a disguise meant to mislead the occupying soldiers.

"If Abdulkareem becomes religious . . . he won't sing then, right?" asked Fahd. You nodded. "Hopefully, he won't find God, then!"

Your motley street returned to how it used to be, except . . . You started to take stock of what was no longer around. You considered what the occupying forces had taken away with them when they left: Mama Hissa's spirit, Fawzia's eyesight, Tina's presence and the scent of coconut oil in her hair after Mama Hissa left, Khal Hassan, Dhari's clear speech, the "Ice cream! Ice cream!" of Abu Sameh the Palestinian, the "Khaaam! Khaaam!" of the Yemeni fabric seller, the zalamat house and its soccer team, and your Palestinian and Jordanian teachers at school. Hundreds of thousands of Palestinians left, leaving behind some family members, giving them the opportunity—or burden—to live on in this new reality, where their safety was guaranteed only by saying, "We're from Lebanon."

The Nazem Al Ghazali songs disappeared from Mama Zaynab's courtyard; her grandchildren claimed she was originally from Al Ahsa in Saudi Arabia. She was no longer Bibi Zaynab. She became "my Mama Zaynab from Al Ahsa"—as Sadiq would confirm, denying his grand-mother's tongue, which had become a disgrace after the liberation—lest she embarrass her two grandkids in front of their friends, attracting the unwanted gibe of "Your grandma's Iraqi?" She lived in hope of the day when the northern borders would open up and she'd visit her family, and when her hour came, she'd leave to die there, buried with her ances-tors in Al Najaf, next to the shrine of Imam 'Ali. The Iraqi president no longer had a presence in the Al Bin Ya'qub household, and those who had loved Iraq became pure Saudi supporters. Abu Sameh the

Palestinian's voice was replaced by that of a Syrian man. Despite the delighted response of the children to the "Ice cream! Ice cream!" calls of this new voice, it didn't sound like your street. The calls of the fabric seller turned into the ringing of your doorbells. The Yemenis became Indian salesmen; working out of bags, they filled up your street, selling incense, *oud* oil, kohl eyeliner pens, and cheap knockoff watches. The national TV station stopped airing shows that cast Iraqi actors accused of supporting their regime. Your favorite series, *Peace to the World*, teetered on the brink of suffering the same fate. It was broadcast with some scenes cut out.

Many years later, you'd remember Abdulkareem chanting a colorful song that took on the status of an anthem: "Homeland of daylight, in spite of pains, the homeland returns anew." You asked yourself if, after the occupation, the nation had returned or if they returned it to you. You rejected the idea, certain that they hadn't brought the real Kuwait back, just something that looked like it.

Missing prisoners tinged Kuwait yellow. Although the retreating occupiers had plundered much, they left behind a lot as well. Ads melding images of destruction with the caption *So we never forget* popped up all over. Boards, banners, and yellow posters inscribed with the slogan *Don't forget our prisoners* were found in the streets, on house walls, and on TV screens. The new insult among the teenagers on the street was "You Iraqi!" Abdellatif Al Munir and Jasim Al Mutawwa became a memorial statue of mute marble at the central market, erected on the sidewalk in front of Mahzouza and Mabrouka's house. Fahd stuck up photos of Abdellatif and Jasim next to a giant one of Sheikh Fahad Al Ahmad on his bedroom wall, between photos of Muayyad Al Haddad; Saleh removed them all. "Don't put up photos!" he ordered. The reason? Because they were haram and chased angels away from the house. You asked him about Fahd's photos that Aisha stuck up on the TV console and the pictures of the crucified messiah that were on Tina's bedroom wall, and the photos of martyrs: Didn't they chase away the angels, too?

The way he looked at you made you retract your question, apologizing, "Okay, okay, I won't ask again!" The photos of the martyrs and prisoners in Saleh's house, before they were removed, didn't look at all like the ones in Abbas's house. Hassan's wife and Dhari, searching for Hassan in Iraq's prisons, were batted back and forth between the National Committee for Prisoner Affairs and the Martyrs Office. No news. Some new expressions emerged to differentiate between the once uniform Arab countries: the "opposing countries"—Iraq and those other Arab countries in the same boat. Kuwait became, as Abdulkareem Abdulqader said, "the ring of the earth and the wave of the seas." In time, you all came to be stuck on a small island, not looking beyond the confines of your boundaries. All concepts were turned upside down. Florence, who in Mama Hissa's time was a reason for people to curse Abu Sami, was now the very reason for his high status and importance, as he was now the husband of an American. You continued to refer to him as "the American's hubby," not to belittle him as you used to do, but rather to acknowledge his superiority and that of his children: their link to an American woman was now a source of prestige.

It was your first day of school after the liberation. The end of 1991. It was morning assembly at Al Najah Middle School. You stood among hundreds of students, the Kuwaiti flag raised high in front of you all in the school courtyard. You all yelled for the first time in a long time, "Long live Kuwait . . . Long live the emir . . . Long live the Arab nations," before enthusiastically repeating the national anthem that you'd missed for months, observing its impact on the faces of the Kuwaiti and other Arab teachers. We trickled to classes soon after the bell announcing the beginning of the first period. While students competed at the front to get a chair, you three fought at the back, up to your old tricks, trying to get a chair in the last row as far as possible from your teacher's reach. You drew the magical button on the tops of your desks. Your class hadn't changed. You returned to it just as you had left it, Sadiq, Fahd, and you—leaning your chairs back against the wall. Your classmates in front were as they had been, except for some new nicknames: "prisoner's son" or "martyr's boy." Before you had been thirty-eight students; then you became thirty-four after losing Awad the Yemeni, Abdl Fadhil the Sudanese, and the two Palestinians Samir and Hazim.

You'd barely put your books down on the desks in front of you when the first teacher entered—Mr. Murhif. On a quick visit, it seemed. "Flip your books over," he ordered. You flipped them over on the table. On the back cover of each book was the circular logo of the Gulf Cooperation Council, containing the flags of the six Gulf nations, in addition to Iraq, which had joined some of the council's institutions, including the ones for education and sports. Mr. Murhif grabbed one of the textbooks and, pointing to the Iraqi flag, relayed what the school's administration had instructed: "Color over this flag with Wite-Out."

You started to conceal the Iraqi flag on the back of your textbooks. He ordered you to open the rest of your books. He stipulated which pages you wouldn't need anymore, certain ones with flags and maps: canceled, deleted, crossed out, outside of the curriculum, front and back of one page. "Cut it out!" Your joy at shortening your school curriculum didn't stop your old habit.

You raised your hand up high. "Mr. . . . Murhif . . . I've got a question!"

He glared at you, his eyes widening, confirming who you were. "I hope you go blind, you grumbler! You're still asking questions? Look at you after only an hour on the first day!"

You didn't just make up questions for the fun of it. You didn't understand why they made him so angry.

You straightened up and stood, following the creaking of your chair with your questioning. "Mr. Murhif . . . just a little while ago, in the courtyard, we were saying 'Long live the Arab nations,' and now we're crossing out maps and flags?"

His eyes bulged. He looked at your face, his arms outstretched. "Okay, so what? What am I to do with you?"

You grew bolder: "It's either one or the other: either we stop saying 'Long live the Arab nations,' or we don't cross out certain Arab flags and maps!"

He didn't pay attention to either of the options that you suggested. He suggested a third option, more like an order. "Or you eat shit!"

THE THIRD MOUSE: EMBERS

Sand will become embers . . .
And the sea will become fire.

—Su'ad Al Sabah

4:56 p.m.

Present Day

Whenever the details of those seven months surface, they take me back, isolating me from everything, except for that time, and that time alone. They make me confront the person I used to be, whom I no longer know. They reacquaint me with people who have been preserved in name only.

Now I'm here. Only one hundred yards separate me from Fuada's Kids headquarters. I can see the building, but I'm stuck in traffic, wedged between the crowds, police cars, ambulances, and fire trucks. All the turns to my right are blocked with burning tires and sandbags. Picking up my phone, I call my cousin. He doesn't answer; his voice is still repeating the poem on the radio. His voice climbs at times, then drops at others.

> "Explode
> The house s-snake is coming out
> From the cracks and the s-stones of your walls,

From the holes in your straw hut
The fabric of your w-worn blanket is
Spitting her fire on your garden flowers
Drying out your g-green plants."

What are you doing, for God's sake, Dhari! I call back. *Pick up, pick up, pick up!* It wouldn't be an issue if someone else ignored my call. No answer.

Ayub calls me. I mute the radio. His voice is loud, overpowering the sound of the radio in his car. "Have you guys lost it?"

I reassure him, despite my emotion. "I'm on my way to Dhari; the headquarters isn't far. I'll make all of this right."

"You'll make what right? Listen, listen to this . . ." He pumps up the radio volume in his car, which he doesn't need to do. The shouting of the person speaking is loud enough. "Those Nawasib who have adopted their slogan from the mice instead of God's religion are slipping poison into honey . . . Imam 'Ali, peace be upon him, said, 'When the people of truth say nothing about falsehood, then the people of falsehood are deluded into thinking they are in the right,' and God, praised and exalted, said in His book, 'And say: truth has come and falsehood has died, indeed falsehood was always bound to die.' O you, who claim that the mice are coming . . . you are yourselves the mice, even if you're disguised as—"

"Which station is that?" I ask, agitated.

He responds as usual, caustically, "The guy is saying we're Nawasib. It's obvious they're Shia. It's the House of Prophet Muhammad's—"

"Ayub!"

My interruption went unnoticed.

"Listen, listen, now it's your group!"

"Ayub!"

He turns the dial to the Lions of Truth radio station. They are broadcasting Dhari's voice reciting the poem while a coarse voice comments on it. It's as if the commentator has grabbed Ayub's phone and is yelling in my ear, *This is what the mice are saying, with the atheists' blessing.* Dhari's voice rises, the Islamic hymn still playing in the background:

> "Explode
> You've been s-slaughtered now
> Time after time
> The black wolves accost you
> Stealing from you the p-pulse of your spirit
> Brushing against your squandered flesh."

The thick voice rudely yells with all of its might, "May the tongues of the *Rawafid* be paralyzed. Who are the black wolves? Who? And if we are the wolves, well, wolves are better than the mice that attacked those telling the truth. Listen, you who've made the mice your symbol, Muhammad—peace be upon him—said, 'Five kinds of animals are harmful, and their killing is allowed in the sanctuary. These are the mouse, the scorpion, the crow, the kite, and the rabid dog.'"

Ayub's voice gets louder on the phone; laughing, he says, "They're all the same. Crazy is what they are!"

The speaker repeats the Prophet's words, to fit his agenda, "Five wrongdoers can be killed in the sacred mosque . . . five wrongdoers, and the mouse is at the top of the list. O you who glorify the mouse and call out to the people to protect themselves from the plague!"

Ayub asks me about Sadiq and Fahd. No news. He begs me to tell him what happened earlier. I end the call by urging him to find them both and ask them what happened at dawn prayer earlier today. I turn up the radio. Dhari is finishing his poem.

> "Swarms of predators . . . the ant
> Drink your spilled b-blood

The butcher has an intense d-desire to slaughter
The knife, a s-starving blade roaring."

The broadcast shifts to a religious hymn. I get a text message from
Beirut. "My friend, forget the novel, the hell with the novel . . . Answer
me, let me know how you are!"

THE THIRD MOUSE: EMBERS THE INHERITANCE OF FIRE

THE NOVEL

(Chapter 1 removed by the publisher)

Chapter 2

Seven dark months, and then a new state of being. It wasn't necessarily bright. It seemed better than what we had been before the occupation, but it wasn't really—something that took me many years to realize. If only I had a faulty memory like those around me! We were getting ready to attend the satire *Sword of the Arabs* near the end of summer in 1992. This was to be the first adult play we would attend. Adults were always a different matter. That year I had turned fourteen; thankfully, Saleh didn't get wound up by me being at their house most of the time.

I was in Fawzia's room. It didn't look like a blind person's room. Her walls were still crammed with flags, photos, pamphlets, and scholastic medals—hung between them was her pink dress, the one that she had worn at National Day celebrations years before. Whenever she sent me to the Al Budur Bookstore to buy her a novel, I would read it aloud to her; this had become our routine ever since the light in her eyes had gone out. We would sit facing each other. She would direct her expressionless eyes to the ceiling, listening to me. Whenever I finished a chapter, I'd get ready to leave with Sadiq and Fahd for the Al Anbaiie Mall, but she'd call out to me, "Hang on a minute!" She stretched out her arms in front of her, wiggling her fingers in the air. I brought my face close to her palms. She felt my face, lightly tracing her fingers between my nose and lips, confirming the smoothness of my mustache. "Katkout! Don't grow up," she'd plead, scared that her brother would ban me from entering their house; meanwhile, all I'd be thinking about was the softness of her palms and her fragrance on my face.

When Fawzia said she preferred to stay at home and listen to my reading instead of going to the play, Saleh offered that I go with them and make use of Fawzia's ticket. I was eager to go to the play only because of Hayat Al Fahad, who had played Mahzouza. I thought of leaving Fawzia behind. She didn't make me feel guilty about it. I asked Fahd about Suad Abdullah. "Is Mabrouka going to be in the play, too?" He shook his head, listing off the actors' names.

A momentary spat erupted between Sadiq and Fahd when Sadiq protested, "His name is Abdulhussain Abdulredha!" Fahd insisted on the actor's more common name: Hussain Abdul Redha, the star of the show and its playwright. Their back-and-forth went on, each desperately trying to convince the other. "Hussain." "No. Abdulhussain, meaning servant of Hussain." Fahd insisted that we worship God alone and that tagging on the word *Abdul*, or worshiper, to someone other than God was haram and the height of being a nonbeliever. Agitated, Sadiq shot back, "No, *Abdul* means servant . . . and *Abdulhussain* means *his* servant . . . you ass!"

"Don't you swear at me . . . You're the ass!"

"No . . . you!"

Accusations flew back and forth. "You're a *kafir*." "You're Iraqi." They both fell silent, then looked at me, waiting for me to jump in, but I hated this tug-of-war, despite the issue of names no longer worrying me as it used to four years ago: Omariya versus Umairiya. I looked at Sadiq. "Call him Abdulhussain, and you"—I gestured to Fahd—"just call him Hussain."

They retorted in unison, "It doesn't work like that!"

We went to the play. Neither spoke to the other.

I went in Saleh's car to the Dasma Theater, while Abbas followed us in his car. I remember Fahd's father seemingly content with the election campaign billboards filling the streets, for the reinstatement of parliament in 1992 after what had been a hiatus of six years. His good mood didn't last long. When we passed the Second Ring Road between Dasma and Da'iya, one of the billboards came into view with the picture of a candidate clad in a black turban, a Shia cleric. "Over my dead body!" He shook his head before adding, "If only the emir would dissolve the parliament again."

We watched the play from the second row. *If only they had chosen a different name,* I said to myself as I recollected the words sung during the opening ceremony of the Tenth Gulf Cup more than two years ago, "Hail the Arab sword . . . in my right hand I hold you!"

The memories of he who remembers everything will always be dark; how I'm cursed with my memory. If only I could forget like everyone else! I remember them hooting with laughter, widemouthed from the beginning of the first scene. Like them, I was laughing. Except Mama Zaynab wasn't. By the glow of the stage lighting, I could make out her face: silent, unsmiling. She brought her watch to her face in the dark. She groaned. I remember Fahd at the intermission, curling his two fingers under his tongue. He let out a whistle before applauding warmly, not for the touching scene where the protagonist was martyred by an Iraqi soldier's shot, but because an Abdulkareem soundtrack surprised us all, a ballad in which his voice was crying out in a manner that didn't seem to fit with the rest of the sarcastic play. "O brother . . . don't cry over who died and was martyred," he warbled. I hated to come across as vulnerable in front of others, but the darkness of the theater granted me the freedom to be myself in that moment of sudden, profound sadness. "Whoever died for the sake of this country must be the happiest!" I remembered Abdellatif Al Munir and Jasim Al Mutawwa and their marble monument. I remembered Hassan the day the mask was removed from his face. What I wanted for him was the happiness that Abdulkareem Abdulqader was singing about in his melancholy ballad: whoever died was the happiest. Did I see him dead? Happy? I wished he would just return to his house and correct his son's stammer, stop his involuntary peeing, and put an end to his chronic phobia of dark places. Come back home just as he used to. The happiest.

The laughter that rang out from the audience in the second part of the play struck me as absurd compared to Mama Zaynab's frowning. Saleh was doubled up laughing and even started coughing after Abdulhussain Abdulredha appeared in military garb, pretending to be the Iraqi president, strutting around barefoot farmers dressed in shabby clothing, making fun of Iraqis to the hilt. Mama Zaynab got up and declared, "This is ridiculous!" The darkness didn't allow me to see Sadiq's and Hawraa's faces very well. I knew their grandma's accent embarrassed them. She was angry. Livid, really. She pushed Abbas's shoulder, urging him to leave. "Iraqis aren't like this; they're not wild animals." I had just about recovered from the appalling death scene in the first part. Mama Zaynab's words hit me square in the face. I regretted not staying back with Fawzia, reading to her the novels penned by her saint Quddous. Adult plays weren't for me.

I held on to Mama Zaynab's abaya and said, "I'm coming with you!" We left, the audience's twittering bidding us farewell; I made out among them the loudest: Saleh's laughter. I left the Dasma Theater in Abbas's car.

I remember myself at the end of summer vacation in 1993, in the living room of Sadiq's father's house. His house became our meeting spot instead of the Al Bin Ya'qub house. The room had gone back to what it was like when I had first set eyes on it, its walls covered with pictures of imams, horses, and swords, as well as tableaus that Sadiq had drawn, whose symbols I was unable to decipher. Hawraa led us to where her brother was sitting. Taking a seat next to Fahd and Sadiq on the ground in front of the TV, I folded my legs one over the other. Fahd and I had just walked back from the Al Hashash video store in Jabriya. Our heads were hot to the touch, our bodies dripping sweat. Fahd could no longer keep quiet about the announcement he had read in the paper. He had called me at home that noon. "Hey! Are you still pissed off at my dad?" He knew that I was carrying a bitter grudge. What he didn't know was that my grudge wasn't against Saleh, but rather against my budding manhood, which had precluded me from entering his house. Saleh struck a compromise, telling his sister that if my reading to her was so necessary, let it be over the phone. Fawzia refused. Our reading sessions were no more.

Because I still hadn't responded to him, he asked me, "Will you come with me to Jabriya?"

There was no need to guess. "Abdulkareem's new cassette?"

He sidestepped my question. "Get changed now!" My mood brightened, almost instantaneously. I forgot the grudge that I carried against the Al Bin Ya'qub household. Who else except for Abdulkareem could push Fahd to walk from Surra, crossing over the bridge, to Jabriya at noon in the middle of summer? And who else but Abdulkareem could convince my friend to force me to accompany him to the Al Hashash video store on foot, to celebrate the yearly occasion that Fahd anticipated more than Eid itself? He quickened his pace as soon as he saw the poster of the new cassette plastered on the glass front of the store. Two cassettes of the same album and he insisted that the Indian salesman give him a promotional poster of the new album, just as big as the one that was hung on the storefront. The salesman said, "More, you pay half a dinar more." Fahd gave him a dinar. He unrolled the poster on the shop counter, on top of the cassettes and movie catalogs, admiring Abdulkareem in his gray dishdasha and sloping egal, gawking like someone beholding something remarkable.

"Why do you like Abdulkareem so much?" I asked him.

"Because he sings to my soul." His gaze remained locked on the poster.

"But . . . ," I said hesitantly. He left Abdulkareem's face on the desk. He looked at me to finish. "His voice is so . . . mature!" I said. He knitted his brows and pulled at his lips. I started to explain to him what I couldn't describe. I opened my mouth as wide as it would go and exhaled an "Aaaaaaaaaaah!"

"You animal!" came his peeved response.

I overlooked his insult and asked, "Is the second copy for me?"

"One for me and one for Aunt Fawzia," he responded, his mind elsewhere.

"How is she?"

His features softened as he replied, "Asking about you."

"Why did Saleh ban me?"

While staring at the photo of Abdulkareem, he said that I had become a man.

"I know, but Fawzia's blind!"

"Yes, but *you* can see."

We were crossing the bridge on our way back to Surra. On both sides of the road, at the beginning of the bridge, stood signboards: terrifying, dust-covered images of the occupation, each labeled   . I asked Fahd what he wouldn't forget from that seven-month period. The evil Iraqis; the opposing countries; the martyrs and the prisoners; the fires and the destroyed buildings; the minefields; the oil wells and their smoke that shielded the sun for several months following the day of liberation. He remembered everything in numbers:

seven months of occupation; five countries that supported Iraq; 605 prisoners; 570 martyrs; 727 oil wells spitting out fire, burning day in, day out for nine months; and more than one million land and sea mines planted. I remember him doing the math, adding it all up while I kept on walking in silence.

"What's wrong?" he asked me.

I told him that my mom wanted me to forget all that had happened. He asked me what *did* Ms. Principal want me to remember. It was the first time he referred to my mom the way Mama Hissa used to. It was the first time the moniker didn't get under my skin. Whenever my mom saw a photo or a report on TV with the slogan *So we never forget*, she turned it off. She'd stroke my head as she enumerated all the things that she didn't want me to forget. "Don't forget that Kuwaitis worked as trash collectors after having been kings in their own country." "Don't forget that we became refugees overnight and the next morning were scattered all over the globe." "Don't forget that some of us, despite the government aid we received in exile, survived on donations during the months of occupation." "Don't forget that some sacrificed their lives for the sake of the country." "Don't forget that we brushed aside all our internal conflicts and differences for our country's sake." "Don't forget that you are worthless without your country." Then finally, and most important, "Don't forget that the world keeps on turning."

"What about the torture, the oil wells, the mines, and . . . ," Fahd asked.

"My mom said, 'Forget about it, all of it.'"

He stared at my face. "And have you?" I stayed quiet, turned around, and looked at the board: "And your father?" he asked, interrupting my reflection. I don't remember my father saying anything about what happened to us except for two phrases he kept on repeating. The first: "Isn't it a shame that all this oil was wasted?" And the second: "God bless the emir who dropped all the debts and loans of his citizens."

We finished crossing the bridge, continuing onto Tariq Bin Ziyad Road in Surra. Fahd insisted on visiting Abbas's house as soon as we approached our own street. I asked him when he'd listen to the new cassette. "Later," he responded. He'd never said that before. Usually, whenever a new album by Abdulkareem was released, he'd disappear into his room for the entire day, only to come out the next, having memorized all the songs.

We sat down on the floor in Abbas's house. Sadiq sat between us, absorbed in the Desert Storm video game. He deftly controlled a Sega game pad, piloting an American helicopter to strafe a detachment of Iraqi soldiers. Blazing through rounds of ammo, his chortling grew louder as he took electronic revenge, louder than the explosions on the TV in front of him. Abbas was sitting on the couch behind us, observing our enthusiasm while tallying the dead bodies. "There! Behind the shed," Hawraa directed her brother. Sadiq blew up the shed and whatever was behind it. The counter at the top of the screen kept on changing, tracking the number of dead.

Fahd and I waited for the game pad to come our way so that we, too, could have a go at the remaining Iraqi soldiers entrenched behind a ramshackle wall. We aimed our rockets at the ditches in case some of them were hiding there. We broke the record-high scores that Sadiq had set.

"Hawraa! Look, look at this move!" Fahd called out. He exchanged one of his grenades for their gunshots and doubled the body count on the screen.

I turned to Abbas and asked him about the victims of our shots and rockets. "Are they considered martyrs?"

"Of course not!" he answered.

I went back to watching the screen, reassured. Fahd left with the rising sound of the sunset call to prayer. I caught sight of the Al Hashash bag on the floor next to me. I picked it up and headed for the door.

"Where to?" Hawraa asked me.

"Fahd forgot Abdulkareem," I answered as I ran off. I caught up to him before he reached his house, which was now off-limits to me. "Fahd!" I called out from our gate as I waved the bag at him. He had just reached the door to their courtyard.

"Leave it there. I'll get it tomorrow," he shouted back.

I couldn't understand how after our grueling trip he was willing to leave the cassette behind that easily. I looked inside the bag—inside was one of the Abdulkareem Abdulqader cassettes he'd bought. Its title? *You're My Thirst, 1993.*

***

5:02 p.m.

Present Day

There are no police to break up the traffic that I see no end to. I feel bad for the cops, paramedics, and firemen, both the paid employees and the volunteers—all of them combined are still not enough to cover the disaster-stricken areas. They look aghast. What if a loved one happens to be among the victims? I look around me; maybe there is a way to pass between the cars and get to where I need to be. On the walls of some houses I notice the Fuada's Kids' tag crossed out: *The mice are coming . . . protect yourselves from the plague!*

I grab my phone and scroll through the Twitter feed. The picture of Dhari's ID continues to make the rounds among users. Each retweets it with a comment directed at Dhari. "Knowing where the Fuada's Kids radio station is based, it's no surprise that you're an atheist, Rafidi." It seems that our headquarters is no longer a secret as Ayub said. Another comment responds to the first: "If you read his name before you spoke, you'd know that he's a terrorist Nasibi." I look at Dhari's face in the ID photo making the rounds. He has Hassan's features: his calm smile;

shiny teeth; and tidy, dark beard. Nothing in the comments resembles my cousin. Nothing. The picture disappears behind the publisher's name as my phone rings.

"Hello?"

"Hey, man, damn the novel . . . Just tell me you're all right!"

At a time when I fear for others, his worry for me is a comfort. My voice contradicts my answer. "I'm fine."

"Really?"

I don't respond. He asks me how things are. He urges me to leave. There's no point in . . . and things are going from bad to . . . "I know this isn't the best time, but what do you say? Should we print the novel?" he asks without skipping a beat at the end of the call.

I gaze at the green flags and outsize images of turbaned men above the buildings. They resemble, in their content, black flags and pictures above some houses and schools in Surra. "Print all of it," I tell him, provoked by what I see.

"What you have to say is important, no doubt. But please, for God's sake, it would be a shame to see it banned just because of these four chapters!"

It runs through my mind as I survey the traffic around me. "Cutting it out won't change anything! You don't know. The censorship situation is the worst it has ever been. Haven't you heard of the massacre of books we have over here?" I respond, angered by the traffic or maybe his words. Or both.

"Hey, calm down, calm down."

My hesitation gives him a chance to put on more pressure.

"It isn't me saying this . . . This is the editor's view . . . We get rid of four chapters and I promise you, your novel will be . . ."

We end the call with what seems to be a bet. If we get rid of the four chapters, the censors will let it pass, or won't they? I turn, come out of the traffic, go onto the sidewalk, and cross to the next street. Our building disappears behind a huge one. The hymn on our station is still playing when Dhari's voice surfaces. "We resume broadcasting our program, dear listeners . . ."

Not much longer now, cousin! The sun has nearly gone down. I look at my watch, five minutes past five: just a couple of minutes to go. I know you're waiting for the sunset call to prayer so you can break your fast, but you won't hear it when you expect it, as you're now in a Shia-dominated Jabriya. There's no harm if it comes late by ten minutes, according to "your" time. "God is great," as the call to prayer says, which is no longer only a call, but an exclamation that precedes every slit of a knife, gunshot wound, and explosion. I yearn to arrive, to relieve you of this burden. I'll reach the HQ soon, just in time for the six o'clock bulletin based on the brief that Ayub emailed. I myself will take charge of Sadiq's show, *I'm History in Its Entirety*. Maybe Sadiq has finally turned on his phone and Fahd will now answer my call instead of Abdulkareem. At nine o'clock I'll devote myself to my show, *Nostalgia*. In such moments I try to flee from the present to the past to forget scenes like from earlier today.

Cars suddenly stop in front of me at the red light, and I notice that our station has gone silent. I turn up the volume as loud as it will go. To my right, people are gesticulating frantically at what's behind the huge building. Others just continue to look straight ahead. My ears prick up at the radio, at the sound of what seems like repeated knocks. Or calls for help. I'm not sure. Maybe it's a weak transmitter. Maybe it's interference from another radio station. The sound gets closer, only to grow distant again. It's still not clear, but I pick up a few words: "Oh God, oh God." I feel sick. I look up at the sunroof, seeking some relief in the spaciousness of the sky. "And rain comes from God"—the song echoes in my head. Why does the earth reject me? Why does it spit me out? I remember what Dhari says whenever things get tough: "God will bring the rain." Mama Hissa's voice stirs from its sleep and swallows Dhari's voice, yelling, "The sky's going to fall on us!" I need a magic button like Sadiq's. I'd press it and everything would disappear, or at least I would.

The beeping of the cars behind me alerts me to the green light. "Oh God, oh God." Something is happening to Dhari. My heart is aching, cousin. I speed through the lights. Our building comes into view. The station's windows are spitting out thick smoke. The sunset call to prayer rises up, "Allahu akbar . . ." God is great. Dhari's voice suddenly explodes on the radio. He gets closer. He moves away. "Almighty God, please make the darkness of the grave easy on us. O God, make my grave spacious and illuminate it. Almighty God, make the darkness of the grave easy on us . . ."

The tragedy of what's probably going to happen to you, Dhari, doesn't prey on my mind, but rather your clear voice ringing in my ears, neither stuttering nor stammering.

"God will bring the rain, Dhari . . . God will bring the rain."

THE THIRD MOUSE: EMBERS
THE INHERITANCE OF FIRE

THE NOVEL

Chapter 3

One afternoon in the spring of 1994, Fahd grabbed a tin panel near the sidra. It was part of Mama Hissa's chicken coop. He raised it to reveal the moist sand left behind by the rains of the departed winter. The perfect breeding ground for mealworms. Sadiq and I started digging our fingernails into the sand, searching for a lively worm plump enough to attract the spring birds that appeared in the *al habal* season, one juicy worm that would mature into a dung beetle, unlike the small worms that at best would grow into insignificant beetles. No other hobby made us feel as exhilarated as al habal, bird catching, other than al qumbar. I hated al qumbar, though, ever since that last time I went six years ago, because of Abbas and his toxic words. I kept this hobby of mine, the unique pleasure that it was, far and safe from our neighbors' toxic conflict. A dead starling lying next to the tin panel distracted me. Its belly was full of small, wriggling, nausea-inducing worms. "What's with you?" Sadiq's words jolted me. Mama Hissa's words were still fresh in my memory.

"Just like how maggots crawl out of a man's stomach . . . ," I said aloud. He didn't mind me. I stretched out my hand to the moist sand. There were a lot of worms in the spot that had been hidden by the panel. Sadiq started to pick them up with his fingertips to squeeze each in the middle, assessing its condition.

"Give me your hand!" he said. I had already removed my hands from the soil and dusted them off, having seen burrows that no worm would be able to dig, and some dark-brown pellets. I sniffed the air, a foul smell that I knew only too well. I thought the mice had disappeared. Mama Hissa's words buzzed in my ears—you didn't have to see them to know they were there. Sadiq and Fahd thought I was exaggerating when I started to describe the stench. No one believed me. "Delusional," they said.

Our worm harvest was plentiful. At the bottom of the empty cola bottle, they wriggled animatedly. We folded the edges of our dark winter dishdashas around our waists. Carrying the green net traps and bottle of worms, we hastened to Mishref, the deserted area at the end of Damascus Street, an area that less than ten years later would be solely residential.

After half an hour spent walking, carrying our traps and bottle of worms, we were on the deserted tract of land. A safe haven before it splintered off into five residential areas: Salam, Hiteen, Al Shuhada, Al Siddeeq, and Al Zahra'a. Sunny yet chilly weather, beneath a clear blue sky. The *nuwair* spread out as far as the eye could see, an endless yellow carpet of wildflowers. We kept walking, moving away from the hustle and bustle of the streets. I was happily soaking up the spring atmosphere until I spotted a stray dog nearby. *"Hsh! Hsh!"* Sadiq chased him away by throwing a stone. "Stray dogs are cowards, you know," he said.

"There, there . . . a *hamami arabi*!" Fahd whispered excitedly, pointing to a gray shrike not so far away. We stopped at a distance from the songbird. It appeared to be hovering around a dried-out sidra tree. Landing atop it, the bird slipped its beak into its white chest, ruffling its feathers before flying off once more. Beneath the branches, a few steps away, lay a small mound of neglected stones. We didn't pay attention to how far away the bird was, confident it would swoop down and return to its familiar surroundings. Fahd scooped up a handful of sand, letting it strain through his fingers in midair to determine the direction of the wind. Grains of sand drifted with the wind to their destination. Moving the stones from their place, I made a mound in the direction of the wind blowing toward the sidra. I propped the trap against the stones, showing it off so it would attract the shrike when it returned to its perch among the branches. We knew it would face the wind with its white chest. I covered part of the trap with soil. Sadiq shook out a mealworm from the soda bottle. He held it between his fingers, removing the grains of sand plastered to its sticky, sallow body. He fastened it to the middle of the trap with a rubber band, wrapping it around the worm's body. The worm started to wriggle and stretch out. We distanced ourselves by a hundred feet, observing the dry sidra, far away from the nuwair flowers.

The shrike approached, flying low, majestically hovering around the sidra. It landed on a dry branch, its white chest facing the wind. It looked around. The black line around its eyes made the bird seem like a robber from a black-and-white movie. It grew aware of the worm's movement above the pile of stones. A stray dog caught my eye through the nuwair flowers, its head poking out, tongue lolling, watching the bird as intently as we were. The shrike descended onto the pile of stones and carefully took in its surroundings, head moving to and fro in what could have been one of our traditional dances. It approached the trap. The dog steeled itself. The bird cautiously brought its head closer to the worm, investigating. The dog withdrew momentarily. The shrike shifted even closer, attempting to maneuver the worm free. My eyes darted between the dog and the bird. My heart beat wildly. The dog set off, running toward the bird, whipping up a long trail of dust in its wake. It wasn't like Abu Sami's saluki, even if they shared a resemblance. It was covered in filth. Menacing. Stray dogs forget their cowardice when they're starving.

The bird opened its black beak. We didn't move. We held our breaths. We watched the dog in what seemed like a scene from one of those wildlife documentaries. Something fell from my memory when the blast of a violent explosion left a whistling in my ears as a cloud of dust fell from the sky. It took us a while to realize that the dog had stepped on a mine. Fragments of his body were strewn everywhere. Though we were still sitting down, we gasped as we tried to catch our breath. We shuddered. We feared any movement from us would result in a similar fate. We started to study the ground under each of our steps. At first, we didn't make a run for it. We were on autopilot. Fahd turned around, looking for the shrike. "Seems like it got away." Sadiq freed the worms from beneath the pile of stones. He released the juicy worm from its rubber band in the trap.

To this day, I don't know why our legs didn't take off like the wind, leaving the scene right after the explosion. Or why we started looking for the shrike, as if it had some hidden power to protect us. We knew it had been close to the ground, but in spite of that, it had vanished. Cars had crowded together at the end of Damascus Street, at the beginning of the sandy path, where the asphalt met the sand. A car took us home. I vaguely remember the driver yelling at us, giving us a mouthful about how stupid we were. I forgot details as easily as one does a dream. However, I remember what Sadiq said about the entire episode. I'll never forget it: "One dies . . . so that the other can survive!"

The month of Muharram coincided with the beginning of summer vacation in 1994. I was in my room, planning to go out, when the doorbell rang on the evening of the tenth of the month, according to the Islamic calendar. I slipped a bottle of cologne into my dishdasha pocket, heading off to the Al Anbaiie Mall, where Fahd was waiting for me. I found Sadiq standing behind the courtyard door, carrying two pots of food that Mama Zaynab prepared every year on the anniversary of the murder of Hussein, son of Imam 'Ali. Sadiq handed me the food. "Here, take it quick."

"This is too much," I responded. He looked in the direction of the Al Bin Ya'qub household, explaining that Mama Zaynab had sent him with this food: one pot for us and another for Saleh's household. But Abbas told him before setting off that it was enough to get the food to our house, skipping his neighbor's house altogether. I asked him what Mama Zaynab wanted.

He cut me off. "You're questioning my dad?" He then went on to suggest that Fahd's dad wouldn't eat their food anyway. The relationship between my two neighbors had gone from bad to worse. I placed the two pots of food on the table in the living room. Sadiq left me to go with Abbas to the hussainiya. I set off for the Al Anbaiie Mall.

"*Tafaddal!* Come on in!" yelled Jaber as he turned the shawarma spit when I passed by his restaurant. "Want a shawarma? Or a ketchup macaroni sandwich?" I waved at him and shook my head. "Jaber's place is no longer cool, and McDonald's is now the place to be, eh?" he quipped. The famous American chain had just opened up its first branch a few weeks earlier. They said it was the biggest branch in the world. That cars formed long lines in front of it. That it used part of its profits to support Israel. Many things were said, but don't look for truth on the lips of liars.

I went past Jaber, passing in front of Al Budur Bookstore, where Abu Fawaz was perched on a chair by the door. "It's been a while!" I smiled in response. "Who's reading to the Al Bin Ya'qub girl now?" he asked. I pulled at my lips and shrugged, shaking my head. As I went past him, he grumbled, "Cat got your tongue?" I ignored his cat comment and turned to face another cat, sitting on a stack of empty Coke crates in front of Haydar's store, the edges of his dishdasha up to his knees, and sucking a cigarette. The owner of the store wasn't there. Both he and his son were missing from his store, as they were every Ashura, the anniversary of Imam Hussein's death.

"How are you, Fahd?" I asked him before entering the grocer's store. I found Ibn Shakir Al Buhri standing in for Haydar and his son. He sat behind the gum and sunflower seed counter. I gave him half a dinar for a pack of cigarettes before joining Fahd and sitting on a Coke crate next to him.

I had barely taken a drag, staring at its glowing embers, intoxicated, when he warned me, "Cover it! Cover it!"

I hid my cigarette, holding its butt between my index finger and thumb, keeping the embers out of sight behind my palm. I held the smoke in my chest. Fahd did the same while Abbas's car passed by on the road in front of the mall and then disappeared at the end of the street. On the back windshield was one of those small stickers that had started appearing on some cars, openly indicating the sect of the driver in a way we were unaccustomed to before the occupation: a sword, like that of Ali Bin Abi Talib's, and a ship with the names of the imams on the sails.

I released the stale air from my chest. I asked Fahd since when had he started caring if Sadiq's dad saw him smoking. He didn't answer. I ground out my unfinished cigarette with my foot. I splashed some cologne on my palms, cheeks, and clothes. I gestured with my chin toward the letters *H* and *F* on the wall of the generator building in front of us. Above them were the lyrics of a song, "Between you and me a whole world, long and dark as the night," stamped with Abdulkareem Abdulqader's nickname, "the wounded voice." I told him he could be offending Sadiq by doing that. He looked out into space, issuing thick smoke from his nostrils before saying, "Sadiq's my brother."

"And Hawraa?"

No response. Abu Fawaz yelled out to him, "Hey you, son of Mulawwah! Majnun Layla!" We turned to face him. He cautioned Fahd, "No good will come of it!" Both Fahd and I looked at each other

in confusion. How did he know about Hawraa? "If your families knew
. . . they'd die from grief!" the man went on. Fahd's face went red; he
didn't know how to respond. Abu Fawaz's voice grew soft. "Leave it, my
son, leave it!" He got out of his seat, looked in our direction, extended
his two fingers like a peace sign, and brought them close to his lips,
saying, "It's bigger than you!" He snatched the cigarette out of Fahd's
fingers. He threw it away. "Leave it, my son!"

***

6:52 p.m.

Present Day

During scheduled power outages, the roar of house generators fills the night—at a time when darkness is sovereign. The pack of candles Dhari had brought that evening melted before he could even light them. He left before confronting the darkness that scared him. Pure darkness, if it hadn't been for the flashing red from the fire engines, green from the ambulances, their colors alternating, revealing the soot on our building and the terrified faces of its residents on the tenth floor. Some of them are sitting on the sidewalk, getting first aid, breathing through masks. It's only me who needs a mask to block out the stench that everyone, except for Ayub and me, has gotten used to.

One of the residents claims the fire was caused by an electrical fault. Another blames it on the stove. A third cuts them off. "The forensics team found an empty canister and a lot of mice that had run out of the burnt-up apartment, in the hallway of the tenth floor. The apartment door was locked from the outside, and the key was in the hole on the outside." "Murder," one of the residents suggests, and asks his friend

exactly where the key was. The wailing of the fire engines and ambulances drowns their voices. An old voice repeats in my head, unsuitable
at a time like this, yo-yoing between the beginning and the end of a
familiar song. "The key's with the blacksmith . . . And rain comes from
God." The main door opens to reveal two rescue workers in white garb
walking briskly toward the ambulance, its doors open, waiting for the
arrival of a small piece on a stretcher. I don't understand the rush. I drag
my crippled leg toward them. They push the stretcher into the vehicle.

"Hold on. Wait!" I grab the arm of one of the medics as he shuts
the ambulance doors. He extends his arms, forbidding me to get any
closer. His face is stern. "You can't."

I beg him. "Please, brother . . . don't turn me away." He looks at
me quizzically. "Your relative?"

"My cousin" escapes from my lips.

His features soften. He looks at his colleague. They both shake their
heads as they reopen the doors. I approach what's left of Dhari under
the white blanket inside the ambulance. The man grabs my shoulder.
"Are you going to be okay?"

I nod my head in affirmation. His palm is still squeezing my
shoulder.

"You sure?"

I pass my finger under my nose and wipe away snot mixed with
tears. "Yes."

I kneel by the stretcher in the ambulance. I grab a corner of the
blanket and slowly peel it back. The blanket had created a mask I
thought looked like Hassan's, and now I see someone who doesn't look
like his son. Something resembling a body was sweating the smell of
roasted meat after having been doused in *oud* cologne. O you sheikh,
you promised me rain. Dhari, is this how you'll bow out, son of Fuada,
without rain? You're disappearing, my cousin, and if your father returns
to ask about you, what do I say? Do I tell him about the remains of his
son and how he's nothing more than a charred body the length of an

arm? By the time the firemen had handed you over to the medics, it was too late. You left as a charred piece. Ashes that an old fire had passed down. You left me behind. You left me with your stammering words in my ears, the interrupted words that I will now miss. A pot of food and handful of dates are waiting for you on your right. Your sun was blotted out before sunset; the sky embraced its darkness and . . . it didn't rain. I put the blanket back over the charred body. I look at the protrusions of the body under it. What if it was someone else?

"Stay strong."

I turn to the voice behind me. I find Ayub. Soot has consumed his clothes, his face, and his palms. I turn to him as if he has the power to change something that is inevitable. Or to come with news that makes what happened untrue. Maybe whatever that was on the stretcher is from someone else and not my cousin after all.

"Ayub! Thank God you're here." I rush to him, saying, "Don't worry, it's not confirmed, not a hundred percent." He smiles. Tears draw tracks in the soot on his face. I smile back. I shake my head. "I didn't see his face . . . maybe it's not Dhari . . . he even smelled different, you know?"

He looks at my face in surprise. I run my finger over my teeth. I remember my missing tooth. I ask him why he's looking at me like that. He hugs me. He's trembling.

THE THIRD MOUSE: EMBERS
THE INHERITANCE OF FIRE

THE NOVEL

Chapter 4

Alone at home. It was the start of summer vacation in 1995. Ever since it became impossible for me to enter the Al Bin Ya'qub household and my father had purchased a large piece of land on the Abu Hayyan Al Tawhidi Street in Rawda to build a new house, my love for our house was greater than ever before. Rawda wasn't more than a few minutes away from Surra by car, but I loathed being somewhere that wasn't my own. Mom was at the market, getting her stuff together, like every year, before our trip to London. It didn't even occur to me to try convincing her to allow me to stay in Kuwait, and there was no point trying to persuade my dad that I could be left behind . . . with whom? Two years before, I had asked her if I could stay behind. "By God, who raised the heavens, you can't sit for a minute on your own!" she had answered. I gave in, even though the heavens had nothing to do with it. My dad was more preoccupied than ever building our new home. He was neither present nor important in my life anymore. It wasn't because he was always away from the house, between the company and keeping an eye on the construction, but because he just couldn't grasp what it meant for me to be uprooted from Surra. He would talk to me of the large diwaniya overlooking the courtyard and of the swimming pool, jacuzzi, sauna, and ceramic steam room in the basement of our dream house. My indifference toward the blueprints of the new house that he would spread out in front of me bothered him. "Where do you want your room?"

"Anywhere . . . does it matter?"

His eyes flashed, his fury dammed by his two lips.

That evening the house line rang. Aisha greeted me before she said, "Here, have a word with Fawzia." My heart leapt upon hearing her name. It was the first time she had asked to speak with me since I'd been banned from their house, the reason being that I was now of legal age.

Her voice came over the line with clear reproach. "Is that it, Katkout? You've outgrown us?" Despite the position that Fawzia held in my heart, the nickname "Katkout" irked me.

I responded, remembering a claim that I was proud of, "I'm a man!"

She let out a sigh before continuing, "You're not *a* man—"

"What?" I cut her off, wide-eyed.

"You're the king of all men."

I couldn't control how much I pined for her and how I longed to read Ihsan 'Abdel Quddous's novels in her room. "Fawzia, I miss you so much." She didn't let me finish what I wanted to say.

She dove in. "You know what? If my eyesight came back for even one minute . . . I'd only want to see you." She woke me up from the muteness that had struck me. "Katkout!"

A loud laugh slipped out in spite of myself.

"Has your mustache come in?"

I felt the bristles of my mustache without answering.

"Never mind Saleh. I spoke to him . . . It's okay for you to come on back and read to me." I asked her how she got him to agree. "He's a lion when it comes to me," she said, just as she always did. She chuckled, telling me that Aisha was the one who got him to change his mind because Fahd's reading was absolutely atrocious and because Aisha read in a loud voice like a schoolteacher, and because I was seventeen and she was twenty-three. Changing the subject, she said, "My mother, God rest her soul, really loved you a lot."

I choked on my tears. "Me too." I was tongue-tied. A wave of emotion washed over me.

"Yallah, come over then," she beckoned.

I asked her to give me some time to get my plastic sword ready first. Her memory let her down. She asked me why the sword. I recalled an old scene. "So that we can parry. Me with my sword and you with your nose."

She restrained her laughter, coming across as angry as she exclaimed, "Katkout!"

"I'm sorry, Fawzia."

"What?" Her voice grew louder.

I caught myself. "I'm sorry, Auntie Fawzia."

***

7:15 p.m.

Present Day

The racket of fire engines, ambulances, and rescue cars falls away, leaving a silence in their wake and wisps of smoke mingling with the smoldering air and pools of water around the building. People disappear into their houses, fearful of the security men's bullets that have now become legal after the sudden announcement of a curfew starting at seven o'clock. The darkness outside the building doesn't look like the darkness inside. We stretch our hands out in front of us, as if we have been plunged into ink. We grope the walls, walking up the stairs to the tenth floor. Ayub notices my slow pace. "Are you limping?"

"It's nothing."

The whop-whop of helicopters sails through the area. The caw of the corpse-catcher sounds too close; its echo fills the place. Bullets pierce the silence outside. Ayub is in front of me, his phone's screen light dissipating the darkness of the stairwell. I keep my phone in my pocket in case his battery dies before either Fahd or Sadiq calls. Ayub halts, sticks his hand in his pocket, and pulls out a bottle of cologne. He pours it in his palm. Bringing it up to his nose, he inhales it like an addict. He puts his hand out to me. I refuel on the scent before we keep going up. I fumble with the buttons on my phone and call Dhari. The phone is off.

"Watch out," Ayub whispers.

I look on as the light from his phone reveals a body on the stairs that was hidden by the darkness. I bend over the body, searching for a possible ID, but there isn't one. It's the corpse of a man who appears to be in his early thirties, with thick-rimmed glasses. His arms are hugging papers to his chest. I grab one of them and ask Ayub to bring his phone closer. The letters read: *Religion is a blindfold!*

"No wonder the medics let him be," Ayub muttered. I shake the body; maybe he's still alive.

"Dead!" says Ayub.

I bring my ear close to the man's chest.

"Dead," Ayub repeats.

He turns his phone light to the top of the stairs. I can just make out a body larger than an arm in height on the banister. We keep moving. It's the huge corpse-catcher. I look at it up close for the first time. It's just as people say: an eagle body, an owl head, and it's crow-colored. It stares at the corpse behind us. Loud banging reaches our ears, its echoes suppressed. Ayub turns to me, pointing to the source of the sound. The elevator. My face lights up. Maybe it's Dhari. I urge Ayub to hurry up before the darkness kills Dhari. Ayub doesn't answer. We're between the second and third floors. We go up to the door leading to the hallway between the flats. I run in the darkness toward the suspended elevator, the banging still going on.

"Who's there?" I yell.

The voice of a girl responds from the upper floor, asking for help. Disappointment floods me. I turn my back on Ayub in the hallway. "It's not Dhari," I say to him as I return to the stairs.

His calm voice behind me objects, "And the girl?"

"It's okay . . . The power will come back in the morning. She won't die!"

He grabs my arm. I turn to him and look at his face, visible in the light of his phone. I'm surprised by the confusion in his features. We're unable to help ourselves. Why is it that he's still endowed with chivalry? I ask him why he's looking at me like I'm a criminal. I grab his hand, urging him to follow me up to the tenth floor. He pulls his hand away. "Have you lost it?" he yells at me.

"You're the one who has lost it!"

I don't give him a chance to say a word. I explode in his face. Maybe he'll come to his senses. "Is she your sister? Your daughter? Your relative?" His eyebrows furrow, criticizing my words. I, too, scrunch up my eyebrows disapprovingly. What have we got to do with the person stuck in the elevator? We are all still stuck in this place they call a nation! I yell in his face, "Wake up! Wake up!" The screen light dies in his hand. We plunge once more into the ink, the silence. A sudden pain on my left cheek is followed by a sound like a thunderclap that throws me to the floor. The young girl in the elevator is still crying out for help. Ayub runs to where the elevator is stuck. I rub my cheek with my hand to soothe the stinging pain. A whistling in my left ear pierces the silence of the place. Like a terrified mouse, I crawl toward the corner to find refuge. I'm shivering. I imagine Dhari's final moments. The fire devouring him. Screaming in pain. Screaming in horror. Screaming, begging God to bring the rain or ease the darkness of the grave.

The young girl bangs on the elevator door. Dhari, in my head, is pounding the locked apartment door as the flames lap up his dishdasha. His palms leave black marks on the door. He yells, "Rain! Rain!" The flames crackle. The girl in the elevator yells. Fuada yells, "Protect yourselves from the plague!" And as for me, I am the plague. I'm the one who brought all these disasters. *Fahd and Sadiq, if only you two hadn't followed me to the dusty plot. Dhari, if only I hadn't asked you to come. You came because of me. You died because of me. Your voice plays back to me, I hear it garbled on the radio. Oh God, oh God.* I cover my face with my hands. I moan. I weep. Ayub leans over me. I don't know how long I've been rambling and hallucinating. He clasps my hands and removes them from my face. He carries a flashlight in one hand. The other is wrapped around the slim, black-robed girl from the elevator. A young girl. She looks about nine. Ten at most. Hair unruly. She looks at me while pushing away the locks covering her wide eyes. "Uncle," she says before parting her pink lips to ask, "are you guys all Fuada's Kids?"

I look at Ayub. I can just about make out his smile. The girl starts telling her story. Three days before, masked men in black stormed her house. They dragged her father across the floor before thrashing him in front of his daughters because of his involvement with a group violating the emergency laws. It happened one day after his release from the Tahrir detention center. She is the oldest daughter of three, whose mother died in the Avenues Mall bombing three years earlier. "*Ummi* went to God . . . but my father . . ." She says neighbors were looking after her sisters during the three days she spent on the banks of the Bayn River, calling out for her father. She heard that all those who'd disappeared since the start of the war had settled at the bottom of the river. "But my father never answered." A policeman had carried her to our headquarters so we could broadcast news of her missing father; maybe someone had seen him somewhere other than on the bottom of the Bayn River. My face blanches as I look at Ayub. He shakes his head, confirming what he has always feared. Our headquarters aren't secret anymore. The girl says the policeman warned her not to leave the building or go out at night. She ends her tale with the same question, "Uncle . . . are you both Fuada's Kids?"

We're sons of bitches, I say to myself. Which face should I show her, when I only possess a weak one? It doesn't correspond to the young girl's expectation of what Fuada's Kids should look like. I skip her question with a question of my own.

"Hissa," she answers.

How can the smell of *oud* accompany a name like this, wafting here despite the stench of burning and decay? "Yes, honey . . . we're Fuada's Kids." I choke on my words.

"Which one are you?"

"This here is the writer," Ayub responds, smiling. She comes closer to me. She turns to Ayub and takes the flashlight from him. She flashes the light onto the palm of her hand, showing me the drawing of a crossed-out mouse. "I really love you all so much."

I kiss her small palm. "And we love you . . . Hissa."

THE THIRD MOUSE: EMBERS
THE INHERITANCE OF FIRE

THE NOVEL

Chapter 5

"Leave her door open," Saleh said. I climbed the stairs with Fahd to Fawzia's room. I was unusually nervous in the Al Bin Ya'qub household. I felt like a stranger, not as if I was in the home of my sweetest memories. Even Mama Hissa's twin, in its tatty abaya in the corner of the living room, didn't help me overcome these feelings. Nothing in me moved, except for the lump that I thought I had swallowed over the past five years since our old neighbor's passing. I had just crossed the bedroom threshold onto the floral carpet when I saw Fawzia sitting bolt upright in her chair. Even Fahd's gaze started darting between us both, while he was moving his hands as if he were playing the oud. He fluttered his eyelids dramatically. He sang a song that for him resembled the colors of the rainbow: "I saw you; I saw you. My heart trembled; my patience wavered." Fawzia's eyes were fixed on the ceiling, lacking in sight but full of tears.

She smiled, chastising her nephew for his song selection. "You could only think of 'I *saw* you'?"

Fahd responded that the song wasn't for her. He threw a lingering glance my way. "It's your turn."

Fawzia responded instead with the words of another Abdulkareem song without singing it. "Even my eyes, what good are they, if they can't see you?" She said Fahd wasn't the only one who memorized Abdulkareem's songs. Her nephew applauded her, his lips stretched by a wide smile. She extended her palms in another direction from where I was standing.

I rushed toward her with my hand ready to greet her. "How are you, Fawzia?"

"Welcome, my brother; welcome, sight of my eyes."

Fahd kept on singing mockingly all the while, moving his hands, strumming the air. "I've seen you . . . My mind's yearning . . . My color changed and my pulse stopped."

As I held her palm in mine, I saw my reflection in a now-meaningless mirror in Fawzia's room. The description in Fahd's song matched me completely. I heard within me an Abdulkareem song other than the ones that Fawzia and Fahd had already sung. "She was with me, all life long, as close as an eye and its eyelashes . . . She was with me since childhood, a love that was written."

"Abdulkareem sings for me alone," Fahd used to say. In that moment I discovered that Abdulkareem sang for all of us. His voice was no longer too grown-up. He had become more my age, or maybe it was I who'd grown up like him.

The presence of four chairs, instead of two, caught my attention. It wasn't long before Hawraa joined us, on the pretext of visiting Fawzia, and occupied the fourth chair. Her father was traveling, accompanying her grandmother to Jordan, a land conspiring between two lands, each one forbidden to the other, where relatives arrived from Kuwait and Iraq to see one another. Each time, Mama Zaynab would return with less desire to see her family but a stronger longing for the soil that she hadn't set foot on for more than five years. I didn't express surprise at Mama Zaynab's journey to meet her family in Jordan, even though Sadiq claimed that his grandmother had traveled to see her family in Al Ahsa. Hawraa occupied the chair in front of Fahd. "We're missing Sadiq," I said, despite my certainty that there was no way to get him here, he who wasn't interested in entering an Al Bin Ya'qub household when it was no longer open to all of us; even for me, it was only by sleight of hand. I had made a pit stop at Al Budur Bookstore before coming here, carrying the novel that Abu Fawaz had recommended, *Holes in the Black Robe* by Ihsan Abdel Quddous.

Fahd didn't miss a beat when he saw the novel in my hands. "Like the holes in Mama Hissa's twin's abaya!"

Fawzia furrowed her eyebrows and sighed deeply. "God rest her soul." She asked what we missed most about her. Many things, we all said. "Like what?"

Hawraa responded that she didn't actually miss her that much, because ever since she was a child she felt that Mama Hissa and Bibi Zaynab were one and the same. She stammered before repeating the end of her sentence, replacing "Bibi" with "Mama." To her, it seemed as if Mama Hissa were still alive. Fahd smiled as he stuck out his fingers like claws. He said that he craved her tasty achar with mutabbaq samak. Fawzia drew a deep breath. She said that she missed the *oud* cologne fragrance in her mother's milfah. The three of them looked at me, seeking an answer. I missed her stories of the sidra's jinn, animals, talking trees, the Kayfan girls, the Canopus star, and the four mice.

"The four mice?" Fahd interjected. He asked me if his grandmother had ever told me that story. I don't know why I nodded. I bestowed upon myself a privilege that time hadn't actually allowed Mama Hissa to give to anyone. Fahd's interest piqued, he begged me to tell him what his grandmother had never told him.

"Later!" I responded.

Fawzia got involved, asking me to tell them some of Mama Hissa's tales.

"And what about Ihsan Abdel Quddous?" I asked her.

"We'll get to that later."

Their curiosity wasn't satiated with the names of stories that we had all memorized. They took an interest, though, when I looked at Fawzia's face and told them that I had memorized the second part of Shail's story. The story of Canopus was the story of the most beautiful celestial body in the Milky Way. Irritation flashed across Fahd's face, his gaze suspiciously flitting back and forth between his aunt's face and mine.

"Are you sure that my mother really knew about the Milky Way?" she asked.

"She said that the teacher from the literacy course had taught it to them," I answered quickly. I leaned on the back of my chair. I set the stage for my story: "Zur Ibn Al Zarzur, illi 'umro ma kadhab wa la halaf zur . . ." Fawzia's face lit up.

"When Shail, the Canopus star, disappeared into the southern sky, weighed down by his great sin, and Shuhab set off searching for him, carrying his lamp out in front, the moon heard their tale. It became a full moon, lighting for Shuhab the dark paths of the sky. Shuhab's line of vision extended farther, enabled by the lamp he held. Days went by when Shuhab could be seen in the sky, in the form of a shooting star calling out to his friend. Whenever Shail appeared, Shuhab would rush after him, crossing the distance of months without rest, but every time it seemed he had finally reached his friend—after the course of many long months—his friend vanished. Shuhab visited the moon, and it was completely full and radiant, the most resplendent body in the whole of the Milky Way."

The tears in Fawzia's eyes, triggered by my description of the moon, forced me to go quiet. Fahd grumbled. I continued. "Shuhab complained to the moon about not being able to catch Shail, and asked the moon, the largest body, the one that inevitably sees everything, to show him to his friend instead of simply lighting the paths of the sky. The moon sobbed. An enormous tear fell from the sky onto the earth that the mice had ruined. Crops grew in it once more: rice, wheat, maize, and barley. The moon asked Shuhab to return to plow his land instead of wasting his time. Shuhab didn't understand. 'But you see everything!' he said to the full moon, begging him to show him where his friend was. The moon answered that he couldn't see anything in spite of the light that he cast in every place, because he was actually blind. Shuhab went pale, not believing that the beautiful celestial body, all the light that he reflected around him notwithstanding, couldn't see a thing. But because he was blind, he found himself illuminating the way for others. Shuhab then picked up his lamp, bidding the moon farewell, and no one knows which way he went, whether he went searching for his friend or returned to his land."

Fawzia passed her finger under her eyes as soon as the tale was over. She smiled and said that I was good at making up stories. "I didn't make it up!" I insisted.

She was content to smile while Fahd jumped in, insisting, "Mama Hissa never told boring stories like that."

"Boring stories? Come up with one like it if you can!"

Hawraa burst out laughing. Fawzia's face was serious as she encouraged me to write stories for kids. Maybe one day I'd be a famous writer.

"I'm confident that you will be."

I didn't read Abdel Quddous that day. Before I went home, Fawzia said, "You're the sight of my eyes . . . and the best brother in the world . . . Write for me." At the door to the courtyard, Fahd grabbed my arm as I made for home.

"You love my aunt like a sister . . . right?"

I nodded. He pulled me closer and squeezed my arm. "Swear to God!"

I couldn't look him in the eye with Mama Hissa's voice in my head warning, "The sky'll fall on us!" I freed my arm from his viselike grip. "Just leave God out of it, please."

***

8:00 p.m.

Present Day

I'm sitting on the ground of what remains of Fuada's Kids' headquarters. I lean back against the wall amid the blackness that tinges everything. The blackness caused by the absence of light and the soot caked on the ground, walls, ceiling, transmitter, the computer, and printers. Hissa, in her black robe, is in the corner, hugging her knees to her chest. She plays around with Ayub's phone, searching for a game to kill time with until the curfew is lifted at sunrise. Ayub cuts yellow pieces of tape that the criminal investigators used to cordon off portions of the apartment. He feels something with the tip of his toe. "Weird!" he exclaims as he directs his flashlight to a charred mouse. He disappears inside the rooms, flashing his light, searching for anything left intact after the fire.

Hissa comes forward to sit down beside me and clasps my arm. "I hate the dark; the dark took my father. I was going to die in that elevator in the dark." She pays no attention to my silence. She looks at my face and says, "I love Mama Hissa."

From where did she come up with Mama Hissa's name? I don't have the chance to ask. She rummages through her bag, takes out three small books, and hands them to me. I don't mask my smile as I clutch the three books. The first in a series of children's stories: the Ibn Al Zarzur stories. How this little girl is able to make me forget all that is going on! She says that she loved Mama Hissa the storyteller. She hands me a pen and asks me to sign one of the books. I give her a choice: Shail's story, the sidra jinn story, or the story of the three palm trees.

"I like the Kayfan girls."

"I like them, too . . . and their friend," I whisper.

"I have two sisters." She grins. "I'm Ikhlasa, and my two sisters are Barhiya and Sa'marana." She giggles. She vows then that when they grow up, if things don't change, she'll start an organization like ours and call it the Kayfan Girls. Who said that writing is useless? I open the cover to an illustration that Sadiq created using watercolors. An image of Mama Hissa seated in her black abaya between three boys wearing dishdashas and a girl with long black hair in a poofy pink dress is on the first page of each of the stories in the series. The old woman sets the stage for her story, "Zur Ibn Al Zarzur . . . illi 'umro ma kadhab . . ." I write in the blank space above the illustration: *To little Hissa, a.k.a. Ikhlasa . . . for you, the best story ever told by Mama Hissa.* She puts her books back in her bag. She kisses my cheek. Ayub's phone rings in her hands. "Uncle! Your phone is ringing."

He yells back, asking who's calling. She reads out the number to him. The Al Bin Ya'qub household number on the screen pushes me to take the phone from her hands. "Hello!" Hawraa is still with Fawzia in Surra. She asks me about how her stomach and her back—Sadiq and Fahd—are doing.

I don't have any new answer. "All will be well, God willing."

She says that Saleh is still in Mubarak Hospital. It's confirmed that his condition is critical. "I'm scared that 'Am Saleh will die with one eye closed and . . . one eye open."

I recall his face this afternoon at the door to his house. I remember how disparaging he was. "This is your group's doing, you sower of fruitless earth." Now, which one of us sowed the other, Saleh?

I ignore what Hawraa is saying and ask about Fawzia. She says that she's been silent since that afternoon. I remember the last time I saw her, eighteen years before in the Diamond Hall of the Sheraton Hotel. What does she look like now? Hawraa tells me she is fine, as are her two boys, then ends the call. She advised us not to go out until the curfew is lifted. I notice Hissa fishing for something in her bag. She grabs it and brings it close to her mouth. She holds it out to me. I shake my head, letting her know that I'm not hungry. She laughs. She puts whatever was in her hand back in her bag. She takes back Ayub's phone. Directing the lit-up screen toward the barricade tape, she rips off a small piece, and ties back her hair with it. Next thing I know, she's seated beside me, shining the light in my face. "Uncle . . . can I ask something?" I nod encouragingly. She asks me how old I am.

"Forty-two. And you?"

"Eleven." She fidgets. She seems weighed down by a question.

"You want to say something, Hissa?" It pains me to say her name. She nods. She says she wants to share a secret with me, only if I answer her question first.

"Don't you smell it?"

"What?"

She pouts. "Nothing. Forget it."

Ayub watches us from the door of one of the rooms. I beg her to go on. She does. She's embarrassed to be disgusted at the decaying air, because no one else takes notice except for her, her father, and the policeman who brought her to our headquarters a few hours before. I assure her that Ayub and I smell what she smells. She beams. She asks me what's behind the smell. Because I'm older than her father, or so she thinks, I must have a more convincing answer than what he had said. I ask her what he said. She hesitates before answering. "He says that the smell won't go away unless the Bayn River dries up and the corpse-catcher dies. And both of those won't happen until . . ."

Hissa falls silent. Ayub comes closer and hugs her, encouraging her to go on. She shakes her head. He asks her what her father's name is. She shakes her head again. He asks her what he does. She shakes her head. I run out of patience. "We've got to know who he is so we can help you, Hissa!" I shove aside the pain of her name as I try to get a straight answer out of her. She ends up describing him. He's thirty-five. Tall and thin. Thick black glasses. The masked men took him three days ago.

Ayub and I exchange glances while she asks, "Uncle, are you sure you can smell it?" I describe to her the stages of the smell. At first it's bitter, burns the eyes. She nods in agreement. Then rancid like rotten eggs. She raises her eyebrows, absorbed.

She shoves her hand in her bag and hands me a perfume bottle. "Here, take this."

Ayub's phone beeps with a text message. His eyes widen as he reads it. Holding out his phone, he brings the screen close to my face. Hawraa's text reads: "Someone's beating down the door!"

THE THIRD MOUSE: EMBERS
THE INHERITANCE OF FIRE

THE NOVEL

Chapter 6

Two years of writing stories and changing others. I would retire to my room to write on pieces of paper in preparation for my visits to Fawzia. I became her Ihsan. I peppered my stories with Mama Hissa's anecdotes and the national songs that Fawzia loved. I annoyed Fahd with the excessive romance in what I wrote, despite the love that bound him to his Hawraa, who no longer attended our get-togethers in Fawzia's bedroom. Fahd ended up dropping out as well, obviously. Their relationship was clear, an ebb and flow, push and pull.

Fahd installed a new phone line in his room; each day, his voice mail would play a different, usually solemn, melody. One could tell from the song of the day which stage their love was in. "We didn't plan to meet . . . and if we did, it would be in hardship." Such songs would sadden me when I heard them on his phone. Fawzia clued me in. "Fahd spoke to his mom about Hawraa."

Aisha didn't tell her husband. She simply warned her son. "Her father is Abbas, and yours is Saleh . . . Are you crazy?" Hawraa spoke frankly with Fadhila. Her answer didn't differ much from Fahd's mother's. I felt their bitterness, which was reminiscent of my bitterness toward whom? Deep bitterness and feelings of loss when I was made to leave Surra in September 1997. We didn't travel that summer because we were moving from Surra to Rawda. I was in my car that night, parked across from our old house when Fahd and Sadiq came to see me off. My parents had moved to the new house a week before, whereas I stayed back, stretching out my time before Surra spit me out. I made room in my house for the new owners, scarcely believing that a stranger would now live in my room, becoming a neighbor to my old neighbors.

"My aunt is waiting for you in the courtyard; she wants to say bye to you," Fahd said.

"Tell her I said bye."

"She's waiting for you!"

"Tell her I said bye," I repeated. I turned on the engine, my finger pointing into the distance. "I'm going to Rawda . . . not another country." But I was well aware that I was on a journey, never to return. I drove off. I reached the end of the street at a house that had been owned by the zalamat seven years earlier, next to Alameen the Punjabi's store. The image of Abu Naiel's grief-stricken face on his last day appeared. Comparing the distance between Amman and Surra, and between Rawda and Surra, didn't ease my bitterness at having to leave my old street. Rawda is close by, and Amman is far away. In my case, distance had nothing to do with my emotions. Unwarranted feelings pushed me to turn my car around. I didn't stop at our house or Abbas's house. I stopped in the courtyard in front of the house between them. I looked over at the Kayfan girls: Ikhlasa, Barhiya, and Sa'marana. The black iron door. The sidra behind the wall. I opened the window on my left. A chorus of the night suweer among the grasses in front of Sadiq's and Fahd's houses chirped, singing my farewell song. Most of the cars on their street were dusty, wrapped in fabric covers. Their owners were abroad. I hated traveling. "You've come back, have you?" Sadiq's yell surprised me from his doorstep.

I made up a reason. "I came back to tell you to let Mama Zaynab know that I said I'll miss her . . . take care."

"It's not like you're moving abroad!" he joked, staring at my face.

I gunned my engine and set off, looking at the butcher's shop in the Al Awaidel house and the stores in the Al Anbaiie Mall, despite the haze in my eyes. They all were bursting with life, except for Al Budur Bookstore, its facade plastered with Abu Fawaz's name and his phone number, announcing *For Sale*. At the bend in Abu Hayyan Al Tawhidi Street in Rawda, I glided by Shehrayar's, a restaurant whose shawarma looked nothing like Jaber's in Al Anbaiie Mall, and which didn't sell macaroni sandwiches with ketchup. I was struggling to breathe in my car with all the cigarette smoke. All the windows were closed so that Abdulkareem's voice couldn't slip out: "Farewell to our final night together." I doused myself in cologne before entering the house. My mom knew what leaving our old street really meant. That night she stayed very close to me. She opened up her arms as wide as they could go, hugging me for a long time when I entered the new house for the first time; my arms didn't reciprocate. She breathed me in.

"Your cologne's nice," she whispered in my ear, "but your breath stinks." She squeezed me in her arms, reprimanding me for smoking. I didn't say a word. I was restless in her embrace. She knew exactly the depth of my loneliness in the new house. "If you're not at ease in the new diwaniya, go to Surra and see your friends whenever you want." I untangled my body from her hug.

"Mom." She gazed at my features, anticipating what I was going to say. I stared into her eyes. "Say, by God Almighty, who raised the heavens, that I won't ever go back to Surra."

She rested her palm on my shoulder and worriedly asked, "Why?"

I couldn't look at her face any longer. I insisted that she say it. She evaded me. She gave me a sidelong glance. "What's gotten into you?"

She kept asking, and I kept responding with "Swear, Mom."

"Why all these oaths? Why don't *you* swear? Should be easy, seeing as you don't seem to want to go back!"

My voice jumped a few octaves. "I can't . . . I can't, Mom . . ."

She embraced me in her arms once more. I knew that I wasn't good at what she was used to doing, sticking to her oaths, making God a boundary between what she said and did. I couldn't stretch my finger to the sky and invoke it to bear witness, believing it would fall on my head if I broke my oath, because a promise like that would be no small thing, and because I wasn't like the sparrow's son, Ibn Al Zarzur, who never lied in his life. My mother's eyes twinkled. "Honey, you're blowing this all way out of proportion!" She took my face in her hands. "Has someone upset you?" I pursed my lips so nothing would come out.

"Honey, what's eating you? Will you breathe easier if I swear?"

I nodded my head like a petulant child. She nestled my face between her neck and shoulder, stroking the back of my head. "Damn Surra . . . By God who raised the heavens, you won't go back there while I'm still around!" I raised an arm and hugged her fiercely.

"But why?" she asked.

***

8:34 p.m.

Present Day

Both Ayub and I call Hawraa. No answer. The Al Bin Ya'qub house. No answer there either. Hissa clings to my dishdasha. "I'm going with you!" Ayub begs us to stay put while he goes to his cousin in Surra.

I get up from the floor, dusting the soot from my dishdasha. "I'll go with you."

"It's Surra," he reminds me.

I nod my head. "I'm still coming with you."

He assumes that I still haven't been back to Surra. He sets his surprise aside and looks at the girl. She looks back at him. He looks at me and inquires, "And the curfew?" As if the curfew only applies to me and her.

"God is our protector," I answer.

We rush downstairs. I carry Hissa. Ayub leads us with his flashlight. The corpse between the third and second floors is still there, its features deformed in the dark, the corpse-catcher perched with its claws on the man's chest, slipping its hooked black beak in, tearing the flesh apart.

"Corpse-catcher!" Hissa shrieks. I shield her eyes with my palms so she won't catch sight of the body under the bird. The open main door reveals flickering lights outside. Ayub turns off his flashlight. From behind the door, he peeks out to look at the street. He raises his head to ensure that there isn't a sniper on top of the surrounding buildings. He looks to the left.

He goes out the door, mumbling, "Sons of bitches!" I follow him, holding Hissa's hand, wondering why the colorful language. I find him standing at a distance from his car. It's on fire.

"My car is over there." I hobble toward it as much as my limp allows me. Ayub trails me. He becomes aware of my pile of scrap on wheels.

"Your car's a piece of junk. Does it even run?" I nod. He points to its front, the missing windshield. "Accident?" he asks.

"I'll tell you later." He almost says something. I tell him not to worry. I drive my car with no lights. Ayub searches for the radio dial. "And this is the result of the thirty-five booby-trapped cars exploding in four minutes. The cabinet has announced that the Kayfan area has been struck and urges all citizens everywhere to stay in their homes." For once Kuwait National Radio doesn't bury the truth.

"Not true!" Ayub yells.

"Al Mansuriya is in flames."

"Rumors," he dismisses.

"Hostages are being detained in a hussainiya in Bnied Al Gar."

"Pack of lies!"

"The Ministry of Interior Affairs encourages snipers not to target the black birds; they alone guarantee the recovery of corpses."

"What a load of . . ."

"People wounded in clashes in Rawda today at dawn."

I turn off the radio.

"It's all bullshit," Ayub reassures me. I don't answer. Houses on the right are in flames. A mountain of car frames burns at the exit of the Fourth Ring Road. Ayub grumbles, urging me to turn around. "Quickly!"

I head for another exit. Hissa stretches out her little finger and whispers, "Uncle, look up!" I look at the low-hanging moon, nearly full, allowing us to make out things in the dark.

"Yikes!" Ayub says. I follow Hissa's finger; where it's pointing has nothing to do with the moon, then. The fires cast trembling light on the dozens of corpse-catchers perched atop dark lampposts.

At the roundabout I ask Ayub, "Where to now?" I follow his directions to the Fifth Ring Road, driving my car with zero memory of this area. He calls Hawraa. No answer. Another fiery mountain blocks the exit, belching a thick, dark plume of smoke. And another like it blocks the way leading to Tunisia Street. Another's flames can be seen from afar, decreasing our odds of reaching Al Fahaheel Road, opposite the Hadi Hospital. Jabriya is surrounded by mountains of fire that are closing in from every direction.

"Where now?" I ask Ayub.

"The bridge!"

I remember the bridge with its barricades and masked men. I hesitate.

"Do we have any other choice?" a resigned Ayub asks me. I stay silent. He guesses the reason for my hesitation.

"Don't tell me it's because you don't want to go back to Surra!" he bellows. I keep driving toward the bridge.

"I went there this afternoon." I see him do a double take. I haven't gone anywhere near Surra for twenty-three years.

"You went to Surra?"

"I went to Fahd's house to look for him."

His eyebrows bunch up as if I reminded him of something he forgot. He grabs his phone and makes a call. He looks at me before drawing the phone away from his ear. His face blanches.

"Abdulkareem Abdulqader again," he says. He makes another call and lets out a heavy sigh. "The phone's off!" He looks at his watch. "It's 9:10. Where on earth are they?"

THE THIRD MOUSE: EMBERS THE INHERITANCE OF FIRE

THE NOVEL

Chapter 7

I secluded myself even further when I first moved to Rawda. In a bubble of my own making: worrying my parents. When it was time to go to the mosque, I felt alone, not knowing the others there. The imam's voice was unfamiliar, his words no longer understandable. The carpets smelled different from those of our old mosque. None of the mosque's many columns recognized me when I leaned into one. Dad was taken aback by my observations during our return to the house.

"Are you coming here to pray or to smell the carpets and sit against the columns?" He didn't wait for my answer. He went on to say that the God we used to pray to in Maryam Al Ghanem Mosque was the same God in Rawda Mosque; He was the same God everywhere. "You're blowing things out of proportion. It's not that different."

I became familiar with the area as Abu Hayyan Al Tawhidi became more than the name of the street I lived on. Soon after my move, I got to know him more. I was making up for the loss of my old street.

I kindled a new relationship. My days were spent in the Al Faiha pub-lic library searching for Al Tawhidi among the books. I wolfed down the pages. I had never read anything like it in my life. I halted at his confidence in his relationship with his God, as well as his trust in His pardon and absolution even in his final hours. At that age, because of my mother and Mama Hissa, fear was the primary determinant of my relationship with God. I wrote a story that evening as soon as I got back to my room, struck by what I had read in the library about Al Tawhidi when he responded to his companions about their warnings and reminders of being fearful when meeting God at the time of death: "As if I'm coming before a soldier or a police officer! When in fact, I'm coming before a forgiving God." I had almost finished my story when I was overcome by trembling. Mumbling calls for forgiveness, I ripped up the papers and burned them on the sidewalk outside our house. My eyes followed the smoke billowing from my pages into the sky.

I raised my head, looking up. I considered the roiling smoke of my story as atonement for the sin of writing it; perhaps God would forgive me and perhaps the sky would actually stay where it was. I knew now that it wouldn't fall as our old neighbor had kept asserting years before. But I used to believe that something would happen. I felt my heart-beat slow down at Mama Hissa's voice in my head: "May He forgive you, my boy." I didn't regret burning my papers, for even Al Tawhidi himself burned his books before he died. I would say this to justify my actions every time I wrote a story and let it go up in flames. When I was in Surra, there was someone I wrote for, who liberated me from it, who understood what I meant. I would see the effect on her face; she was my inspiration when writing, helping me choose the words she'd understand. The writing I did in Rawda became a sanctuary, albeit dis-turbing. I would pour all my questions into it, crossing the boundaries set by Mama Hissa and my mother. I reread them; I shuddered, then turned them into ashes.

My relationship with Abu Hayyan became one of ebb and flow. I understood him, but then I didn't, shouldering my religious upbringing and Arab cultural beliefs that prevented me from wandering too far and deep within my thoughts.

***

It's odd that the only person who understands me died nearly one thousand years ago. I slow down and read his words about the stranger: the one who has no name to be mentioned, the one with no drawing to distinguish him, who has no writings to be published, who has no excuse to be excused, who has no sin to be pardoned, and who has no fault to conceal. The strangest of strangers is he who becomes a stranger in his own country. He who is most distant is the most alienated at home.

***

When Dhari saw my car, opposite Al Faiha public library, near Khal Hassan's house, he joined me. I caught a whiff of his *oud* cologne before he whispered in my ear, "Assalamu alaikum." He shared with me, still in hushed tones, my mother's concern. "She's worried about you." Poring over the titles of the books on the table in front of me, he asked me what I was reading. I grabbed a book that was open to the page of the concise biography of my new street's namesake. "No need to read anything," he lovingly warned me. He patted my shoulder, saying that he understood me. "You're lost." I was afraid he'd rattle off one of his cookie-cutter religious sermons. But instead he looked at me and smiled, avoiding the look of disapproval on my face. "Haven't you missed Surra?" The scent of fresh buckthorn came to me.

"I can't go."

"More like, you don't want to go," he corrected me. I nodded my head meekly. He shut the books on the table in front of me and said,

"I'm just like you . . . since the day my dad disappeared, I've hated the place." He gazed at my face as if he were reading what was within. "But you, you love it so much, you can't bear to visit it as a guest." He straightened up. His smile widened. "What if I bring Surra to you here in Rawda?"

***

9:16 p.m.

Present Day

On my right is Jabriya gas station. "The car needs—"

"Later!" Ayub cuts me off.

I gesture to the fuel gauge. "It's empty!"

Hissa warns me about the masked men at the gas station on our right. Ayub yells, urging me to speed up toward the turn of the final street leading to the bridge. A police car behind us cuts through the darkness with its lights flashing red and blue. I slow down, running parallel to the sidewalk on the right. The police car speeds past and blocks our way at the upcoming turn. A young policeman gets out, his eyes peeking out from behind a mask. Hissa crouches down in the back seat. One of the policeman's hands is on his holstered gun, while his other carries a flashlight. He approaches us, examining my wrecked car as his walkie-talkie crackles on his belt. I step out of the car, pulling my lame leg. I hand him my ID. He passes his flashlight between my face and the face on my ID. He bends down in front of the window, looking at Ayub, demanding his ID. Ayub hands it to him. He requests that the officer let us cross the bridge for the sake of . . . The officer cuts him off and explains that if he's lenient with us for being out past curfew, the army's bullets won't be as lenient, and even if we were to escape those . . . He doesn't finish, gesturing toward the bridge. "They'll butcher you!"

I turn to where he's pointing. Two masked men, atop the bridge, holding a body, toss it in the Bayn River. Others shoot their guns in the air. I nod at the officer, understanding. I beg him to find a way for us to pass. I explain to him the meaning of the message we got from our family in Surra. "If we don't cross . . . they'll die!"

"If you do cross . . . then *you* will all die." Perhaps my face expresses what I can't verbalize. I choke on pleading words. He steps back, bringing his walkie-talkie to his mouth. He asks for a way through. The answer comes back to him garbled. A ring of fire surrounds Jabriya. The voice advises him to return to the police station. The officer raises his palms and shakes his head. He orders us to go back to where we came from; otherwise, we'll be ambushed and killed. "The country is burning," he says in a strangled voice. Neither the ambulance men nor the civil defense forces nor the volunteers are able to recover the thousands of bodies. Only the corpse-catcher is playing this role. I think back to the corpse in the building stairwell. Ayub gets out of the car, begging the police officer to do something.

"Nothing doing," he says. He inspects Ayub's ID and says that his name will guarantee him safe passage through the first barrier. But he'll end up floating on the Bayn River if he gets to the second barricade. Ayub lets out a long sigh before turning around. He controls his voice, fearful of attracting the attention of the men on the bridge. He gnashes his teeth. With a mix of pleading and anger he asks the officer to do something, anything. The officer raises his head and combs the tops of the visible buildings. He reminds Ayub of what the sniper might do if we stay here for too long. Ayub throws his phone and wallet on the car seat. He turns his back to us, running toward the bridge.

I want to follow him. The officer grabs my arm. "Ayub!"

He turns to me, having already reached the opposite sidewalk leading to the bridge. He brings his finger to his lips. "Shhh!" He then steals away between the dry bushes. He ducks down into the shrubbery and disappears.

The officer pushes me toward my car. "Your pal's nuts!"

Hissa presses her palms up against the glass window and yells, "Where's Ayub, Uncle?" The masked officer notices her in the back seat. He flashes his light on her. His eyebrows jump. "Hissa?"

She nods her head from behind the glass, confirming her identity. "I told you not to leave the building at night!" he reprimands her in a low voice. Her shoulders touch her reddening ears. His voice grows soft, asking her, "Did you find your dad?" Sadness washes over her face. He looks at her, his brow furrowed. He leans closer to the window, staring at the young girl's palm pressed up against the glass. He opens the door. Grabbing her hand, he looks at me bug-eyed, asking who we are. I look in the direction of Ayub's disappearance and don't answer. He shakes Hissa's palm and shows me what's on it. He repeats his question impatiently. I'm overcome by muteness. He shoves his finger at me.

"You are . . . ?" He hands me the IDs, Ayub's and mine. He orders me to tailgate him so the snipers know we are with him. The caw of the corpse-catcher rises, terrifying like the warning sirens wailing in the distance. I stretch my hand toward the bridge, begging him to wait for my friend to come back. His eyes widen. "Your friend?"

He cautiously pushes me with his arm toward the opposite sidewalk. We stand among the bushes where Ayub vanished. I mask my face with my palms. He gestures with his arm toward the bottom of the bridge. I know that Ayub is the most driven of all of us. I know that he's the most committed to what we do. But the idea of swimming across the Bayn River? Even if he somehow overlooked the rancid smell, what if he swallowed some of the water? I follow him with my eyes, tracking him as he reaches the middle of the river, swimming slowly. Dozens of expectant corpse-catchers land on the opposite bank. The light of the full moon and the burning barrels on the bridge reveal their contours. They stand like old hunchbacked women, swaying in their shabby black abayas. Singing a caw from their depths, infusing the atmosphere with even more horror. They leap over one another, approaching closer to where the water meets the dry land. As if they were awaiting a ship returning from afar. But the ship . . . but Ayub . . .

Where's Ayub?

THE THIRD MOUSE: EMBERS
THE INHERITANCE OF FIRE

THE NOVEL

Chapter 8

There, in the diwaniya of the Rawda house, Fahd, Dhari, Sadiq, and I were gathered. Sadiq introduced us to his cousin Ayub—a nice guy I used to see in passing on the special occasions when he'd visit his grandmother Zaynab. He quickly became part of the gang. Our ages ranged from twenty to twenty-two. My cousin really did what he said he would. He convened a spirit of togetherness that I didn't imagine I would ever experience in any other place than Surra. It wasn't completely like Surra, though. But he did what he could. It took me years to realize that his supporting me, in those days, was out of worry; it was also meant to motivate me to give up the books I was reading. He wasn't able to convince me to give up smoking, which consumed my health, but he was able to distance me from the books that corrupted my mind. That's what he said years later anyway. Abu Hayyan Al Tawhidi had completely disappeared, except for his name on the signboard at the head of our street. Just as my cousin had completely disappeared after

Fahd introduced the oud to the diwaniya. He hid it from his father, who swore to God, "If that oud enters my house, I'll break it over your head!" This had been the same man who had used his hairbrush as a microphone while singing along to Abdel Halim. But as Mama Hissa would say, "Only dead people stay the same."

Sidestepping Fahd's grumbling about his father, I asked him, "How's Fawzia?"

"My aunt's fine" is all he said. He didn't go on to say, which would have frankly pleased me, *She's asking about you.* While Sadiq turned his back to us, facing the PlayStation game on the TV, I reclined on my back, puffing my cigarette smoke toward the main ventilation shaft in the ceiling. The quietness of the diwaniya annoyed me. My father never should have replaced the old air conditioner. I missed its roar, its vibrations, and the dusty smell when you turned it on.

On the marble floor Fahd sat, hugging his oud, treating its pegs and tuning its strings. It surprised me that in just a few months he had been able to learn to play so successfully. He was able to become Abdulkareem for whoever wanted it, whereas I struggled to become Abdel Quddous for the one I so wanted to do that for. He started to read poetry; he who, except for schoolbooks, never cracked open a book. In one corner of the lounge, he left the oud and a poetry collection. He would search for eloquent words, befitting the colors, tastes, smells, and seasons in Abdulkareem's voice, in case he ever met the man in person. He was absorbed in his favorite corner, searching through stanzas of poetry. "Ohhh!" he yelled in agitation, scattering the books in front of him. We turned to him to ask what had happened.

"These are more like newspaper bulletins than poetry," he lamented. He started to list the themes of the poetry: Syria's Golan Heights, the Sabra and Shatila massacre, the killing of the children in Balat Al Shuhada School in Iraq, the Lebanese Civil War, the Iran-Iraq War, the hijacking of the *Jabriya* plane, the café bombings, the American air strikes on Libya, and the plight of Palestinian children! In a newscaster voice he boomed, "That was the news bulletin, and now on to you folks for the details!" We were in stitches at his blotchy red face.

"And what about love? There's no love?" Ayub asked.

"There is love . . . but who's in the mood to read about love in the middle of a war?"

"All of these collections were published before the nineties," Ayub observed.

Fahd picked up his oud and started singing a song, for which he chose a color. I never once asked him about Hawraa, content to follow their developments through his playing and singing in the diwaniya, like the night suweer who never wearied of singing, intent on getting an answer from its partner. The automated answering machine in his room responded, "Adorn yourself with patience, and I'll adorn myself . . . my heart for the sake of your eye has endured much . . . and be patient: perhaps one day it will be solved." I never wished for anything in those days as much as I did for those two to have their hearts' desires granted. Maybe one day it would be solved. But one day in 2000, at an hour that Saleh at first considered blessed, the time when his son let him know he wanted to get married, he responded with a "Damn you!" He cursed the hour that his son decided to get married, his desire knotted to his neighbor's daughter's name.

When his wife told him about their daughter's wishes, Abbas said he'd rather marry his daughter to a dog than to Saleh's boy. I—and I alone—was tormented by what reached me from Saleh's and Abbas's words. I could no longer respect such men. Fahd and Hawraa's shared catchphrase—"If only they weren't freed by the Iraqis!"—wounded me deeply. What pained me even more was my response to that phrase: "If only." What if they'd never returned, and their children kept on singing, "Where did my daddy go? To Basra he's gone!" Although I'd witnessed the neighborly clashes of Abbas and Saleh, it was difficult for me to listen to their words. Words that in the years to come would become more commonplace: words broadcast by radios, televisions, Internet sites, and written with spray paint on the sides of houses, burdening Fuada's Kids and their followers with what was beyond their capacity to conceal, after failing to treat it outright. So much hatred was revealed to us in those days. I wished they were just two school kids, Saleh and Abbas, standing in front of my mother in their school uniforms, and that she could silence them forever by smacking them across their lips. My wish seemed a laughable one because it grew to encompass many who appeared in the following years, with no one capable of silencing them. One of them would die striving to silence the other and confiscate the key to heaven, even though "The key is with the blacksmith, and the blacksmith wants money, and the money's with the bride, and the bride wants kids, and the kids want milk, and the milk is with the cow, and the cow wants grass, and the grass wants rain, and rain comes from . . . God!"

Sadiq, who I thought wasn't paying attention, busy with his video game, actually was. He told me frankly that he wasn't invested in the back-and-forth of the star-crossed lovers, but was still optimistic about the desired outcome because he trusted his sister. "And because Fahd is my brother and I know him," he added. After his father's refusal, however, he didn't hesitate to enlist me as an intermediary to advise Fahd to stop chasing his sister, because this was their fate, and there was a better ending in what God had chosen for them. Insults upon insults were hurled at me because of the message I passed on to Fahd. He was livid. Hawraa no less than him. They agreed to end my role as an intermediary because no good would come of what Abbas and Saleh had chosen.

"Destiny is what we choose it to be!" they kept insisting.

Skinny is what I had always known Fahd as. But there's a difference between skinny and gaunt. He was being eaten alive from the inside out. This was clear from his sallow face. His voice. His sandbag eyes. My friend was drying up. He grabbed his oud. He sang what seemed to be a capitulation to fate, a yellow song, "If I were the tree who had the fate to live in the coolness of your shade, even the heat of the sun wouldn't have burned my eyes." Sadiq had disappeared from the diwaniya, making himself scarce. He couldn't take his friend's songs, which droned on about the departure of Hawraa. Fahd, Ayub, and I barely met up anymore. In the end, I completely lost hope for a happy ending to the love story that I had watched blossom since childhood. I called Sadiq, pleading with him to return after he had achieved what he wanted—forbidding his sister from communicating with Fahd. He stipulated one condition. "He's got to stop his ridiculous oud playing and singing about my sister!" Giving in to my pleading, Fahd neglected his oud, leaving it in its leather bag in the corner. Sadiq came back to the Rawda diwaniya, and so did Dhari, after the reason for his absence was no longer being played. The PlayStation was back in action. And so returned the heady smell of *oud* cologne, which I had missed on two occasions—the first after Mama Hissa's death and the second when Dhari left the lounge. But the diwaniya that I had loved became a loathsome place and source of worry, thanks to Fahd and Hawraa, and the complications I thought I had left behind in Surra.

It wasn't until 9/11 that we had something else to preoccupy our minds. As the world's eyes turned to New York, the attacks became the hottest topic of discussion in the diwaniya. Dhari defended. He justified. He would have risked his life to prove that the whole thing was just a game to sully Islam. Sadiq countered, cursing Al Qaeda and those in their ranks, while Ayub just let them both get agitated only to make fun of them. Their debate dragged on that night, going as far as insulting the religious symbols of both sects. Each reminded the other of past events attributed to the opposing sect. They delved deeply to establish the truth, quoting God's words from the Quran, one challenging the other, going back in history to the time of the Prophet and what came afterward. I didn't make any effort to shut them up, taken in by each retelling of history according to the cumbersome religious legacies passed down to each of them by their fathers. Sometimes I was with one, sometimes with the other. Fahd whispered to Ayub to pass him the oud from the corner when the din of their voices became unbearable. He balanced the oud against his lap, singing with his eyes closed, his face tilted to the ceiling. "If you treat me with stubbornness, I will turn to the sky for mercy!" Both of them came to their senses, looking at me as if their reconciliation had been undone. Dhari left, followed by Sadiq.

Fahd opened his eyes, looking at the door. "Good riddance."

Khal Hassan's wife called me incessantly, asking about Dhari. Who were his friends? Where did he go? Why did he cut himself off from the diwaniya? I didn't know much.

Five months passed like this before Fahd's face regained its color, and he plunged the diwaniya into a cerulean haze the day he sang "Hour of Joy." Sadiq returned after a long absence. I understood that something was going on in Surra. Mama Zaynab's stance was clear-cut as day, the moment she swore on everything holy: God in His sky, by the Prophet Muhammad, Imam 'Ali, the milk of Mama Hasiba, and the breasts that fed her son. When Abbas insisted that the marriage was unequal, she reminded him of her mother, Hasiba, and how nothing impeded her marriage to her father, Kazim. "They got married and lived together for many years . . . Everything was fine!" she said, making the whole thing seem easy.

Sadiq shared with me what his grandmother had divulged to him. If my mom hadn't taken that oath about Surra, I would have been there in a heartbeat, knocking on Mama Zaynab's door and kissing her forehead. Hawraa was right when she said that, by having Mama Zaynab around, Mama Hissa hadn't really died after all. Her neighbor's ill treatment didn't deter her from doing what had to be done. Despite her poor health, she put on her abaya, clutched her cane, and dragged her feet to Saleh's door. She knocked on it, repeatedly. He turned her away. Once. Twice. She went a third time. She remained in the courtyard, refusing to enter a house that didn't afford her respect. She shook her head. "Hissa's eye is still open!" she told him, unable to hold back her tears. "Hissa's eye is watching you." Fahd's dad turned pale. She told him that she wanted to die with her eyes closed for her own household, and that the last thing she would see would be her granddaughter's son by Fahd. "What's between me and your mother is greater than the games between you and Abbas!" she said, turned around, and started shuffling away while pointing her finger toward the small garden in the courtyard. "I take Hissa's sidra as a witness against you!" she declared with finality, leaving Aisha and Fadhila to do as much as they could to resolve the matter.

As for me, I stayed far away, being kept abreast of developments by Fahd and Sadiq. Hawraa and Fahd's affair was a complex one. Two steps forward, five steps back. Sadiq's dad imposed the condition that if they had to get married, then they had to observe Shia rites; Fahd's dad opposed, warning his son that if he gave in so soon, "Tomorrow they'll have you wearing a turban!"

Spurred on by Mama Zaynab, the four of us—Sadiq, Fahd, Hawraa, and I—all agreed to reach a consensus. "Go on, you all," she urged. Fahd and Hawraa got married in March 2002. They never disclosed whether it was done according to "his" sect or "her" sect. Sadiq and I, after standing as witnesses at their marriage, committed to not divulging the matter of sect to anyone. I remember how Dhari, Sadiq, Ayub, and I were preparing Fahd on his wedding day as if it were a group wedding. We organized everything while Saleh went on pilgrimage to Mecca and Abbas withdrew to the confines of his home, avoiding the wedding altogether. Sadiq and I waited while Fahd finished his Moroccan bath in Salmiya, while Dhari and Ayub went to get his wedding attire: the dishdasha, ghutra, and bisht from Alameen the Punjabi's shop. Sadiq and I spied on Fahd from behind the glass door of the barber's, but the steam prevented us from seeing what was happening. "How's our groom?" I asked, laughing.

"Guys! I'm dripping in oil!" My laughter became a sad smile. If only the woman who had originally said that could have seen her grandson at that moment!

After we had gathered in the Rawda diwaniya, we decided to set off to the Sheikhan Al Farsi wedding hall in Surra, where the men's festivities would take place. Afterward, we'd continue our celebration of Fahd, leading him in a procession to his wife in the Diamond Hall at the Sheraton Hotel in the old city, where the women's party was already in full swing. How cheerful Fahd was that evening! He beamed at everything in the diwaniya. He looked different with his shaven chin and his long mustache, low at the corners of his lips, which he had stubbornly kept—going against the popular trend of removing it entirely. His egal was tilted just like Abdulkareem's. He sat very still on the couch in the lounge, so as not to wrinkle his dishdasha. He stopped us from smoking so that the smoke wouldn't pollute the fragrance of incense and *oud* cologne in his clothes. He didn't budge from his perch, except to go to the corner of the diwaniya to drench himself further in the scented cloud spewing from the censer and the Arab colognes that my mother had put there for this occasion. Even when the time for evening prayers came, he remained still, worried about his dishdasha. "I'll pray later." His mother called him and joked that the dinner buffet at the Sheraton had mutabbaq samak, so he had better hurry up. "Meoowww!" he responded in delight.

Soon after we finished our evening prayers, led by Dhari, Fahd straightened up, carrying his bisht and posing in front of the mirror to make sure that he was looking sharp before we departed. He jabbed Ayub, then pointed to the corner of the diwaniya. "Bring the oud." Dhari's eyebrows arched in surprise. Fahd winked at him. "I mean the *oud* cologne, man!"

My cousin slipped his hand into his pocket and handed Fahd a small bottle. "*Oud* cologne from Mecca . . . Never in your dreams would you get something like it!" Fahd laughed as he spread the cologne on the back of his hands and his neck. He held out the bottle to Dhari, who refused to take it back, insisting it was a wedding gift.

We left the diwaniya. I was even more nervous because Fahd had insisted that Sadiq and I ride with him. "I want you with me." I waved to him with my camera, letting him know that I'd be following them instead so that I could take photos of the mini procession that we were going to have on the street. He said there was no need for photos because his mother was already waiting with photographers at the hotel. "Or he should take the photos," he said, gesturing at Dhari. Dhari looked at me but said nothing. I opened my car door. Fahd repeated, his face pallid, "You and Sadiq, come with *me*!"

I shut the door and turned on the engine. I gestured to my watch. I knew why he was acting this way. I mean, who wouldn't if his father had insisted on going on *umrah* on the day of his son's wedding? Sadiq took off in his car with Fahd as his passenger, while Dhari and Ayub followed them in Dhari's car. I trailed the two cars, my camera forgotten on the seat behind me. Damascus Street was alive with the honks of our cars and the flashing of our lights as we led Fahd's procession. Dhari showed off by driving doughnuts. Soon enough, our celebratory mood was shared by the rest of the cars on the street, at the intersection between Rawda and Adailiya. We passed by the entrance to Surra: Tariq Bin Ziyad Road, or Mahzouza and Mabrouka's street. Sadiq's car turned right toward the Sheikhan Al Farsi wedding hall. Dhari's car followed, skidding on the asphalt, half a disheveled Ayub appearing through the window, masked by his ghutra. I followed Damascus Street, heading back to Rawda.

***

9:27 p.m.

Present Day

The officer runs to his car. He turns on the lights. I follow him, asking him to wait until I confirm that Ayub has reached the Surra bank. He looks at his watch. He refuses. Three minutes later the helicopters start combing the area.

"But . . ."

"No exceptions."

"I'm begging you."

"Not happening."

I make a dash for my car, following him. Images of Ayub in the river envelop me. Has the fire consumed Dhari and the river swallowed Ayub? Some houses on the street are burning. Fire laps them up, with no fire trucks nearby. For a while now, I've been familiar with how fear feels. What overcomes me now is more than fear. I turn to Hissa in the seat behind me. There's a smile on her lips but worry in her eyes. Her presence pushes me to play the father figure, gathering all my strength.

I open the lid of the compartment under my elbow to grab a bottle of cologne. Hissa sticks her head out between the front seats.

"Um Bint cologne?" she asks excitedly. She stretches out an open palm, then pulls it back. She gives me her other palm instead, the one without the mouse drawing. I pour a little of the golden liquid into it. I don't ask how she knows about this old-fashioned perfume. She inhales the scent in one deep breath. "My father loves this cologne!" She then cuts through my silence in a low voice. "And I love my father." The rumble of the search-and-rescue helicopters approaches from afar. I drive even closer to the officer's car. I turn the radio dial. Kuwait National Radio seems to regret having not buried the truth a little while earlier, broadcasting "Long live Kuwait, long live the motherland."

"I know this song . . . Abdulkareem . . . my father loves him."

I swallow my answer: *And you love your father. It seems that you and your father love each other very much, Hissa.* An old face comes back to me, accompanying the voice on the radio, and I don't tell Hissa that Fahd loves Abdulkareem, too. I look around. My eyes take in the destruction. My ears hear the "long live." I turn the radio dial, shame eating me alive. It's the same thing with Fuada's Kids. At the peak of everything's downfall, we sang, "This Country Demands Glory." We lied. Don't look for truth on the lips of liars. We only hoped that we were telling the truth just this once.

The police car crosses the roundabout. I follow him. Another station broadcasts a Quranic verse about how when the day of resurrection arrives, it cannot be denied. My ears are with the radio. My eyes roam the vicinity. The thunder of a great explosion pierces the calmness of the night. The street shudders under the car wheels. The voice on the radio continues, "Some will be brought to their knees, and others will be exalted. When the earth will tremble terribly and the mountains will be ground to dust." Hissa's scream as she cowers in the back seat mirrors the explosion. The gas station behind us bursts into flames as tall as a building. "And they will be floating like particles of dust," the radio ends. The distance grows between my car and the policeman's. I speed up to follow him. We cross the streets in Jabriya toward the highway. At a final turn near the Tareq Rajab Museum, the officer parks his car in front of some trees shading a metal fence that overlooks the main road. He flicks off his headlights. A voice comes through the static of his walkie-talkie as he approaches. I can't make out what it says, except the area names of Qurtuba and Adailiya. The officer points toward a dark pedestrian tunnel leading to Rumaithiya. I white-knuckle the steering wheel.

"And my car?"

"It's too risky," he warns.

"God is my protector."

He pauses before pointing me to what's behind the woods, next to the tunnel. There's a gap in the metal fence wide enough for a car to pass through, leading to the outside of Jabriya. He asks me to hold on. He makes for his car and returns with a pair of bolt cutters that he hands to me. "Piles of burning tires might be blocking the Surra entrance." I stare into his eyes. I ask him to come with us. Jabriya is on fire. "Gas stations in Jabriya, Qurtuba, Rawda, and Adailiya . . . everywhere has been eaten up by flames. Where can I possibly go now?" he says, seemingly resigned to his fate.

He gestures to the road with his chin. His eyes crease from behind his mask. He puts out his hand to shake mine.

"Protect yourselves from the plague . . ."

THE THIRD MOUSE: EMBERS
THE INHERITANCE OF FIRE

THE NOVEL

Chapter 9

Fahd didn't reproach me for not going to the male wedding festivities; he understood my unspoken excuse. He forgave me with a hug when he found me at the Sheraton entrance before midnight, waiting to hurriedly usher him to his bride. Dhari was content to simply shake Fahd's hand at the hotel entrance, congratulating him before leaving with the claim that he had another engagement. We didn't try to force him to stay, understanding his aversion to the band that awaited our entrance. I don't know which of our two hearts was beating faster, mine or the groom's, while we cut across the hallway to the wedding hall on our way to the bride and groom's stage.

The closer we got, the louder the beating of the drums grew. We reached Aisha at the end of the hallway, her face full of makeup. She clutched the edge of her hijab under her chin, smelling like a cocktail of perfumes, while the rest of her hijab was loose, hardly covering her bushy hair. She quickly explained to us how to enter and at what pace we should approach the stage. All at once the ululations erupted as soon as we entered behind Fahd. He walked ahead with slow, deliberate steps to the beat of the drums. The entire wedding hall was dark except for the spotlight on him, leading us slowly toward our destination; the women could see us, although we couldn't see them. Fatouma's voice boomed on the microphone. "Bride and groom, may God watch over you, the moon and the stars walk behind you." My head tilted back involuntarily and I scrutinized the ceiling, trying to find . . . I'm not sure what.

Against Aisha's advice, Fahd turned and moved out of the spotlight, confusing us, and made his way in the dark to the audience on the side. The whole hall lit up. Fahd bent over Bibi Zaynab's head and kissed it. He kissed her hand. The cries of joy swelled. Sadiq, Ayub, and I all followed suit. Bibi Zaynab was resting her hand on her cane, unable to hold back her tears of happiness. She had come dressed in her best despite the visible fatigue on her face. She entrusted Fahd with her granddaughter, warning him, "God is watching you!"

Sadiq brought his face close to his grandmother's. "Get up and dance, Mama Zaynab!"

She laughed, gesturing to him to bring his ear closer: "There's no Iraqi music!" she replied. Sadiq's ears went red. He looked around and then plastered a smile on his face, at a time when melancholy mingled with my laughter.

Relatives circled around the bride and groom, taking photos. Aisha orchestrated the photographers like a seasoned director. All I saw of Hawraa was the train of her dress. She was ensconced in a pearly garment reaching from her head to her shoulders. I forgot the tension of the past months as soon as Fahd planted a kiss on his wife's forehead. She was as still as a statue, not responding to the chorus of well-wishers. Her black eyes were radiating joy, however, and her cheeks were flushed behind her veil.

I carried on, leaving Sadiq and Ayub to congratulate Fadhila. At that moment, Fatouma took a break, passing the microphone to the DJ to congratulate the groom with an Abdulkareem song chosen by Hawraa. I became aware of Fawzia and her jet-black hair, sitting motionless in her seat. Her eyes were on me. I looked to the door, perplexed. I turned back to her. Her eyes were cold, fixed on the ground. I secretly cursed her for just how enchanting she looked in her pink robe. Here was the child who once danced in the national operetta. A pink butterfly fluttering in gardens of songs. In spite of the music, there was no joy on her face. It was the same expression. The same foil-like nose. The same hair that went past the middle of her back, wiping out the memory of Saleh's razor, and the same toffee skin that I adored. She was as she had always been. Except for her body, touched by the years. I averted my gaze, hoping to temper my fantasies. But something awoke within me; Abdulkareem's voice faded away and the drums in my head fell silent. I started to hear her old song pulsing from my depths: "We're telling you, we've got a story for you . . . and for all the listeners . . . the best story ever." I left the wedding hall, turning my back on Fawzia, Bibi Zaynab, the married couple, and the best story of all.

After an outlandish rivalry between the fathers over where the couple should live, Hawraa moved to the new wing in the household of her husband's family. Each father thrust himself into the married couple's life, offending the other. At first it was funny, and fodder for joking in the Rawda diwaniya. There were superficial fights, or what seemed as such, for example when the couple's living quarters were being furnished.

"Her dad says Al Baghli mattresses are better, and mine says Al Jraiwy is better!"

"Long live the American mattress!" Ayub cheered.

Fahd didn't laugh along with us. "My dad says LG appliances, and hers says Panasonic," he went on. I noticed the seriousness on his face.

"Why?" I asked him.

"To keep it in the family!" he responded, with the conviction of both men involved. I recalled the names of the companies he had just mentioned. I linked one of them to a sect, understanding how far this age-old rift had reached. Fahd started talking about his father and his father-in-law choosing their preferred names for the baby yet to be born. He ended up making light of the whole thing. "Thank your lucky stars that your father and mother don't have these issues!"

He finished furnishing their new living quarters. He made sure to appease both sides, knowing neither one would ever be completely pleased.

Seven months after Fahd's marriage, Hassan's wife phoned me as I sat in the diwaniya. Between her panting and yelling, I couldn't make head or tail of what she was saying. And I couldn't absorb what was being broadcast on TV: breaking news about Kuwaiti youth attacking infantry soldiers on an American base on Failaka Island. Two of the perpetrators were killed. A number of suspects were arrested, their names not made public. My aunt confirmed that Dhari was among them. We were on tenterhooks in the diwaniya. The public prosecutor, after two weeks, released twelve of the accused, including Dhari, who remained silent. He didn't share anything with us, except his sadness at having missed the chance to be among the scores of mourners who saw the two fighters off to their final resting place. He had known one of them. He spoke of him with reverence, a man of his word who had been loyal. We would listen to him as he agonized: "God rest his soul, he committed himself to taking revenge when Kuwait TV showed scenes of those massacred by Israelis in Khan Yunis in Gaza. He kept his word and took revenge."

"Who said that Khan Yunis is in Failaka?" Sadiq asked incredulously. Dhari got up, his eyes red and his face stern. Sadiq faced him, his chest puffed out. Their noses were a hair's breadth apart.

"Jew!" Dhari said.

"More honorable than your guys!" Sadiq responded.

Fahd, Ayub, and I diffused the tension before they came to blows.

The competition between the sworn enemy fathers-in-law was revived in Hawraa's final month of pregnancy, February 2003, after they both found out it was going to be a boy. Both fathers then started confirming the names they each had chosen for the coming grandson. Each warned Fahd and Hawraa against choosing certain names at a time when Mama Zaynab was away in the cardiac surgery wing at Mubarak Hospital. She squinted her eyes in the hope of reading the ticker at the bottom of the small TV, worry eating her alive over the news of American forces preparing to invade Iraq. "If they open the borders, take me there dead or alive," she advised her son.

Fadhila shuddered, then said, "After a long life, God willing."

Mama Zaynab turned to Hawraa. She signaled for her to come closer and then cupped her granddaughter's bump. "And you! When are you due?" Hawraa smiled. "Don't be late," her grandmother added.

Fahd kept me abreast of everything happening there, far away from me. He described Hawraa's anxiety. When I reassured him that they were natural feelings for any woman rushing into her first birth, he shook his head. "Hawraa's worried about Mama Zaynab. Me too." *Me too*, I said to myself.

Fahd smiled as he stretched out his arms to me in the hospital hallway, his baby boy in his hands. "Hassan . . . named after your khal Hassan." As I held the baby, I remembered my uncle's face on the day his mask had been removed. I looked at the baby sleeping in my arms and mirrored Fahd's smile. "And after the optician Hassan," I reminded him. He pretended to be baffled. "Shhh! We were just kids!" I looked at his face and our lives flashed before me in mere seconds. The kitchen cat now had a kitten who looked just like him. After standing in the hallway for a while, I asked him about Hawraa. "The family's well," he answered. I nodded my head in understanding before proceeding out of the hospital. We were no longer children, so I wouldn't be allowed to go in and congratulate her.

After the baby made it through his second day, Fahd carried him to the ICU at Mubarak Hospital. Mama Zaynab, connected to feeding tubes and cords to measure her pulse and blood pressure, was strong enough to hold the baby in her arms. She couldn't speak. Her eyes scarcely smiled at the sight of little Hassan before she slowly closed them in peace.

The next day I read her obituary in the newspaper. Abdul Nabi Abbas Mohammed's widow. They didn't tag on her family name, though it was a noble one, because by mentioning her name openly, her true origins would be revealed. She died without a name. Her final leaf fell at a time when her dear Iraq fell completely.

*****

9:42 p.m.

Present Day

"Uncle . . . can you see?"

Hissa gets her voice back after her shrieking at the explosion of the Jabriya station. I slowly drive my car without headlights. Deliberately, as if the car has arms, groping its way down the road. I answer the young girl's question, certain. Except that I . . . am not. The darkness here is thicker than elsewhere. As if I left the full moon behind me in Jabriya. Something resembling clouds or dust floats in the sky, making the night even darker. I remember Mama Hissa warning Fahd: "I can see in the dark." She was able to do many things, things that only she could do. I am afraid that if I turn on the headlights the bullets will find us. With the road ascending, I turn right toward Damascus Street. In the darkness, I avoid a familiar ugliness: gray hills opposite the sidewalk, and stones, blockades, and dirt on both sides of the street. I don't see anything here. The smell itself makes it seem like I'm close to the bridge. I listen to the sound of my tires plunging into the water that swamps Damascus Street. Such feelings take me back to the road under the bridge, at the time when it started to overflow with sewage a few years ago. Are we seeing the beginnings of a new Bayn River?

"Can I ask something?" Hissa whispers. She hasn't stopped asking questions since Ayub freed her from the elevator. Oh, Ayub. This girl mistakes my silence for approval. "Uncle . . . can humans breathe underwater?" The motivation behind her question forces me to stay silent. She knows the answer. She is thinking of her father. I'm thinking of Ayub. The sound of the water dies out under the tires. It disappears when we reach Tariq Bin Ziyad Road. The name of the street usually pulls me back to my memories of growing up. This time, I wouldn't be thinking of anything had Hissa not shown off her knowledge of *Rest in Peace, World*, a series that aired many years before her birth. Mahzouza and Mabrouka's street. The psychiatric ward. Fuada and the mice closing in. Because of our radio station, Hissa learned about the show. She watched episodes on YouTube and she likes it, as she says, except for the ending. She asks me why in the final episode Mahzouza and Mabrouka flee to the hospital for crazy people. Why didn't they confront the mice? The series ended with a scene I will never forget, the two of them running scared witless on this street. I don't tell her that years later their fleeing was a motivation for Fuada's Kids.

My silence prompts another question. "Uncle, is the house far?"

I point out in front of me in some direction I don't see. "Ali Bin Abi Talib Street."

The name pushes her to ask, "May God be pleased with him, or peace be upon him?"

Who are you trying to play, Hissa? Me? I was just like you, always wondering, Sunni or Shia? It's taken me a long time to get here, the point that Mama Hissa had reached, faced with a question that irritated her about whether the zoo was in Omariya or Umairiya. In this darkness I can't find any refuge from her question. No pigeon landing on the nearby wall to distract her. No coop on my right to turn to and preoccupy her with a "Look over there!" I could then point to the chickens looking up at the sky, confiding in God. And no fabric seller spreading out his goods on the ground and yelling at full throttle, "Khaaam! Khaaam!" Instead, I'm now facing this girl's questions. She is trying to figure out who I am, and I myself don't even know. I go past the Surra roundabout. I proceed straight ahead, driving between Humoud Barghash Al Sa'adoun School and Jaber Al Mubarak High School. Some houses on the street are lit up. The rumble of generators behind their high walls injects a sense of life in a silence that resembles death. The girl asks me about the house we're headed to. If I were someone else, I'd reprimand her for the endless questions.

"Mama Hissa's house," I reply. She gasps. She asks me if it's the house of the old lady who narrates the stories in my books. I nod.

"Swear!" she yells. I don't.

Here's Surra's third residential block and Ali Bin Abi Talib Street. The area seems in a better state than Jabriya, but who knows for how long? The windows of some of the houses on the street, including the Al Bin Ya'qub house, reveal light inside. I park next to the sidewalk. The Al Bin Ya'qub household's cars, along with Hawraa's car, all have punctured tires. I get out, clutching Hissa's hand, approaching the door. She pulls her hand away and goes right for the three palm trees to examine them, her features frustrated. I press the doorbell. A minute passes. No answer. I crouch down and reach below the metal door. The girl joins me and whispers in my ear, "Is this Mama Hissa's house?" I look at the long-standing dryness that has struck Barhiya and Sa'marana, and at the timid greenness in Ikhlasa's fronds, and I don't answer. I stuff my hand into the gap under the door. There isn't enough space. I can barely pass my fingers through. The feel of the rusty latch doesn't resemble the old touch that I know. I try to get the bolt out of the hole in the tile, but it's no use. Hissa kneels down. She squeezes her two small palms under to deal with the bolt. She succeeds in lifting it. She straightens up and pushes open the door, striding before me into the courtyard.

THE THIRD MOUSE: EMBERS
THE INHERITANCE OF FIRE

THE NOVEL

Chapter 10

The sequelae of war were evident: left-behind weapons weren't the worst of it. Panic would cripple Mother whenever the sirens went off, warning of missiles slipping through from the bombed Iraqi side, screeching over school buildings. A corner of the house had been transformed into a shelter from any possible danger. She never tired of phoning my dad and her brothers, imploring them to stay safe. Sleep evaded my father because once more his heart was in his mouth: there was a chance that the stock market would collapse. While Baghdad was getting bombed, "instability" permeated Kuwait. My mother called me every hour to confirm my whereabouts. "Wallah, by God, if you leave the diwaniya when the sirens are going . . ." If only she knew how dangerous the goings-on in the diwaniya were! I distanced myself from the others, phone in hand, and reproached her. With this mania of hers, she was making me look like a mama's boy in front of my friends. She had her usual answer at the ready. "The cowards stay safe."

On TV were live scenes of the Baghdad bombings. Fires, smoke, bombs, and the roar of fighter jets. We watched in silence. I don't know what was running through each of our minds during this bout of muteness. I focused my eyes on the screen, but I couldn't maintain my attention. I remembered Fahd and me as children, throwing ourselves into the roles of Iraqi soldiers, yelling, dancing the hosa, promising the nation imminent victory from God. I remembered collecting stones in a pile in the Al Bin Ya'qub courtyard, hoping to be like the Palestinian kids, the stone-throwers. I remembered Fawzia and "Our country demands glory." I remembered Saleh and the Iraqi president's photo. I remembered Abbas and Khomeini's photo. I remembered Mama Hissa venerating Fahad Al Ahmad, the martyred prince, the man who had fought the Jews. I remembered her night chatter about her husband listening to speeches of the leader Gamal Abdel Nasser. With my eyes fixed on the screen, I remembered everything. I remembered and realized how we were mere lab mice in someone else's real-life experiment. But whose?

The thunder of the explosion on the TV left behind ashes that colored the screen. Dhari was the most affected. His serious countenance didn't hide his red eyes and his agitation. Shaking his head, he quoted one of the Prophet's sayings: "Chase out the infidels from the Arabian Peninsula." He was on edge. Ayub grabbed the remote control and muted the TV. Dhari and Sadiq started a war of words: the invasion of Iraq or its liberation. I don't know how every discussion dragged us here in the end. The American military base on Failaka Island. The foreign fleets in the Gulf's waters, sometimes called the Arabian Gulf, other times the Persian Gulf. It started as a joke that one would use to harass the other. The joke soon took a sinister turn. They argued. Their voices grew louder. Its name was. It then became. Before—after. In centuries-old maps. Truth. Allegation. Made-up history. I chipped in, trying to make light of the situation. I told each of them to call the

Gulf according to what they thought it should be, and close the case. They said in unison, "It doesn't work that way!"

"Will you guys cut it out, or should I get my oud?" Fahd interjected.

Dhari yelled when the patch of fire on the mute screen ballooned. His usual stuttering dissipated on his tongue. "Haram!"

Fahd asked him what was so unlawful about his father's killer being murdered. "I mean, you're the son of a martyr!" My cousin's face turned pale, his lips trembling. He, who had hoped for his father's return, or if nothing else a document stating his fate. He had spent years not knowing the whereabouts of his missing father, in limbo between two labels, neither of which was realized: prisoner or martyr. The deceitful label slapped him, flinging fate's doors of possibility wide open. Sadiq intervened, trying to convince Dhari of the necessity of what was going on. "One of them has to die for you to survive!" Scenes of the deserted Mishref plot came back to me, before it was divided up, at the time when the excavators had come in: terror-stricken jerboas, homeless lizards, and the dog that fell victim to the mines.

I started thinking about what had happened to the gray shrike. I turned away from those old scenes, distracted, nothing about Iraq concerned me except that Bibi Zaynab had closed her eyes before she witnessed these fires and the legacy of ashes. Unexpectedly, worry washed over me at the thought of Hassan stuck in one of the prison camps, a target for the bombs. *And the people there?* I asked myself. I found my heartstrings being pulled only by those I knew were linked to the old woman who had died a few days ago. I recalled the faces of Abdellatif Al Munir, Jasim Al Mutawwa, my uncle Hassan, and those of the soldiers who had wreaked havoc on my country—burning oil wells, planting mines—and   those   huge   billboards   emblazoned   with
. But these were all excuses, and not a single one convinced me that we were watching the meting out of justice on TV. Silent images on the screen. The wailing of the sirens that the glass windows couldn't block out, harmonious with Dhari's sobbing, for he had begun crying like a

child. Our tongues were paralyzed, each of us looking at the others. We all had questions for Dhari that none of us dared utter. *What are you crying for? For what has been reduced to ash on the screen in front of you, or over the abrupt realization that your father is dead?*

With the doubts about Uncle Hassan's fate came the sealed fate of Fahd and Hawraa's son. Little Hassan died. But his great-aunt's digital camera kept him from vanishing completely. Twenty-eight photos, one for each day he was alive before death stole him away in his mother's embrace. She had bent over him, feeding him her breast. She had leaned farther still, dozing off. He had dozed off, too. She then woke up to find him in her arms, blue-faced. Her screams didn't stir any sympathy from the angel of death that had taken off with her son's soul. The dispute of the two fathers-in-law started up again, despite each one's grief: In which cemetery would the body be buried? Our cemetery. No, *our* cemetery. As if one of the graveyards led to hell and the other to heaven. Fahd disappeared with his son's corpse. He came back, his face stony, answering whoever asked about where he'd buried his son: "In the ground."

There were two mourning ceremonies for little Hassan. One of them was in a hussainiya and the other in the Al Bin Ya'qub house. Fahd stood, receiving condolences in the morning at the house and in the afternoon in the hussainiya. He then disappeared from the diwaniya. He rarely visited. He stayed by Hawraa's side, taking her from one psych clinic to the next. He was weak, but his wife's fragility forced him to be somewhat strong. Hawraa's condition grew worse. She no longer let her husband get close.

"God will compensate us with another child," he would reassure her.

She exploded in his face, crying. She clawed at her right breast till it bled. "I don't want another!" she shouted. Fahd was forced to commit her to a mental hospital, resigning himself to her doctor's orders, fearful of her self-harm. Sadiq informed me: no improvements in his sister's condition. She spent her waking hours in the hospital room, frowning and staring out the window. She would yell suddenly and clamp her hand on her breast, squeezing it hard while grinding her teeth. "I don't want another!" Doctors and nurses swarmed around her, injected her with tranquilizers, and restrained her wrists to the sides of the bed. She spent a year in the hospital. During that time, Abbas and his family moved to a new house in Rumaithiya. Sadiq said that they moved there because it was difficult to stay in their old house after Mama Zaynab's passing. Fahd attributed the move to his father-in-law's misery in a neighborhood that he could no longer tolerate. "Frankly, it's better this way," he didn't hesitate to add.

When Fahd and I were alone in the diwaniya, he'd speak to me sorrowfully about his wife. She would call him, saying, "I really miss you." He'd go running to the hospital. Once there, she'd yell, "Get out!" Dark circles ringed her eyes. In spite of her doctor's assurances, he'd almost given up on her.

"It's just a temporary thing," I'd say. Time went by. He abandoned their new wing in the house since his wife had moved to the hospital. Without her, the place became deserted. He went back to sleeping in his old room opposite Fawzia's. I would call him every night and Abdulkareem would respond, "How long the night is without you, how long the night . . . How long time is without you . . . it's never-ending." The song was followed by his recorded voice. "I'm not here right now. Please leave a message." I knew he could hear me. "Fahd . . . pick up." He wouldn't pick up.

This time, before I ended my message, I added, "I know you can hear me . . . I'm waiting for you in the diwaniya." On that occasion, I didn't have to wait for more than fifteen minutes before hearing the slam of his car door. He entered, his face pallid. I poured tea in a glass cup. I handed it to him. He held the teacup, examining its sugar content. "My father said, 'There's no more kids between you two now; divorce her.'" He went on that Fadhila was accusing Aisha of bewitching her daughter. A laugh escaped me.

"This is serious," he protested, upset. He explained how Fadhila blindly believed some hoax fortune-teller about there being an amulet buried under Mama Hissa's sidra and that its power was renewed whenever Hawraa passed by it. Staring at the ground, he said, "I've spent two days digging under the sidra . . . I didn't find anything." He corrected himself as he forced a smile. "Actually, I found your old passport." The surprise of finding a passport we had buried fourteen years earlier didn't stick because I was so caught up with circumstances other than my own. The words crowded up on my tongue, but not a single one escaped. He felt that curses chased him because of his family, as if Mama Zaynab's passing had left him and his wife bereft of blessings. He pointed to the corner of the diwaniya as soon as he finished drinking his tea. I handed him the oud. He was content to play a familiar tune without singing. I started to search for the words from one of Abdulkareem's songs: "How hard you make it . . . every day you're in a different state . . . sometimes near . . . sometimes far."

One afternoon, he looked me in the eye and asked me if they had made the right choice in getting married. I shook his shoulders. "Fahd!"

He turned his gaze away. "I'm tired." Between losing his son, his wife being on the verge of losing her mind and refusing to have more kids, and his family meddling in everything, he wasn't capable of doing anything except cradling his face in his hands. His body shook. "She doesn't want me," he said in a stifled voice.

I asked him to take me to the hospital. I knew he'd be annoyed. "Can't I visit my sister?"

He wiped his face with his palms and answered, embarrassed, "Sure, you can."

He drove without talking, just listening to the songs issuing from the CD player. We had reached the age of twenty-six that year, 2004, and he was still just as I had known him as a boy. I recall his words about his favorite singer: "He sings to my soul." I looked over at him in the seat next to me, silent and listening. I asked myself whether he had been more faithful to Abdulkareem, or vice versa.

"Our fate was written down, to live apart, my love; we walked in the paths of time, the nights of sadness taking over us." I stretched out my hand and turned down the volume.

"How's Fawzia?" I asked. He moved my hand away from the stereo and turned the volume back up.

"We've grown tired of this hope, waiting for dreams to come true." I pressed the power button to silence it. I turned to him. "Your dreams aren't lost . . . trust me!" He forced a smile.

It was the first time I visited the psychiatric hospital in the Al Sabah health district. An oppressive place that resembled the hospitals in old Egyptian movies, with antique tiles like the ones in Mama Hissa's courtyard. Faded, yellowing white walls. I examined the hallways and the faces of the nurses. Nothing like the place that I knew as a child in the TV show that portrayed a hospital that to us, despite the misery of its stories, was one bursting with love, laughter, and jokes. Fahd went ahead of me to his wife's room, and then I heard his voice calling me in. I opened the door. Sadiq sat next to Ayub, who was visiting his cousin, while Fahd went to fix Hawraa's hijab to cover her hair. He whispered in her ear, "Darling . . . see who has come to see you." She looked at me in silence. Her coal eyes summoned faraway memories in mere seconds. She went back to looking out the window.

Sadiq left the room, cradling his ringing phone. "Hi, Dad," he answered before disappearing behind the door. I tried to get Hawraa to talk. "How are you?" Silence. Her face remained fixed on the window. Her arms were free despite the metal cuffs encircling her wrists. She seemed in a decent enough state. Sadiq returned holding his phone and informed Fahd, "My dad's asking about yours and if he was here or not." Each of the fathers would call ahead to avoid bumping into the other. One of them visited the hospital on a seemingly hourly schedule. Saleh rarely dropped by. And if he did, it was only for Fahd's sake. Ayub piped up that they both needed treatment here, especially if it involved electrotherapy sessions to wipe out their twisted memories.

"Like Mahzouza and Mabrouka," Sadiq chortled. Fahd laughed despite the evident sadness on his face. A sigh from Hawraa attracted my attention. A half smile was drawn on her face. This encouraged Ayub to tell one of his jokes. He looked at her, inviting her to guess who he saw in the hallway before entering her room. She didn't answer.

"Dr. Sharqan and Abu Aqeel running, chased by Fuada with her mousetrap!" The half smile on her face became a full one. The full smile opened into a laugh. The laugh breathed some color into Fahd's bilious face.

I felt at peace. "Thanks be to God."

It wasn't long before Abbas arrived. "How is she?" he asked before sitting next to his daughter. She had taken her medication half an hour before we arrived. Her father picked up a newspaper that was on the coffee table. He fixed his glasses on the edge of his nose. Shaking his head, his eyebrows knotted at the headlines on the front page. Newspapers were full of news about the killings happening in Iraq and how one sect was wiping out the other, after the fall of a regime that had been suppressing one sect for decades. And in reaction, some gathered here to demonstrate, carrying signs with the slogan *In Solidarity with Our Brothers in Iraq, Against the Assailing Sect Supporting Iran*, clearly naming the two sects. At the forefront of the protests were parliamentarians of one Islamist bloc. "Asses!" said Sadiq's dad, describing the demonstrators, spreading out the newspaper before me and pointing to a photo at the heart of the page. "This here is your ass of a cousin with them!"

Sadiq interjected, reproaching his father, "Dad!"

His father's finger still pointed to Dhari's face in the photo, among the crowds that the government had issued an order to disband. He turned to Fahd and asked, "Is your father Saleh with them?" He then started to curse *them*, without naming them outright. Sadiq's ears went red. Fahd stayed silent.

Without turning away from the window, a frowning Hawraa exploded, "The mice are coming!"

***

9:53 p.m.

Present Day

A huge generator occupies the heart of the small garden. Exactly where the old chicken coop used to be. Its roar bothers those living in Mama Hissa's sidra. The tree appears to be in good health. Towering and very leafy. I close my hand around the young girl's and rush her inside as quickly as my limp lets me. I try to avoid looking at what has become of the courtyard. It seems small, unlike the one we used to run wild in years ago. Here we played anbar. There I stood in front of the old camcorder recording a message for my mom. And at this black door, we clung to Mama Hissa's abaya, begging her to take us. She didn't do so, and God didn't respond to her prayer that day when she laughed and said, "May God take you all!" The little girl asks me to wait, pulling at my hand. She looks at the tree, dumbstruck, as if she's in an abandoned museum.

"The jinn live here?"

"Later," I respond, my chest tight.

I tread carefully in the old hallway. Everything seems in place in a house I don't know anymore. The cerulean Persian carpet has become cold marble. The AC has disappeared from the wall. There are central AC vents in the ceiling that flap, a ceiling without carvings or any crystal chandeliers. Spotlights have taken their place, spread out like reachable stars. I wouldn't recognize this house if not for the wall in front crowded with photos. Fahd as a baby. A kid. A teenager. A groom. And other pictures of everyone who passed by here: Mama Hissa, Tina, Saleh, Fawzia, Hawraa, little Hassan, and . . . The liquid haze in my eyes prevents me from seeing any more. Hawraa's phone is on the table in the middle of the living room. I pick it up and jam it in my pocket.

"There's no one here, Uncle."

She squeezes my palm. I proceed to knock on the doors of the rooms. I open one after the other. A stranger in a strange house. I climb the stairs, seeking support from the banister for the pain in my knee. Fawzia's room first. I knock on her door. No answer. I push the door, entering with my right foot. As soon as I step on the pink carpet, I'm jolted, electrocuted almost. Everything in here is just as I left it last time. Medals on the wall. Old photos of the emir, the crown prince, and Kuwaiti flags. The poofy pink dress. Videotapes and yellow dog-eared Ihsan Abdel Quddous novels. The two reading chairs in their place. I turn my gaze to the corner behind me. Mama Hissa's twin is upright by the bed, in its heavy abaya. I have to be the adult here. Hissa hands me a tissue from her bag. She has taken notice of the abundant tears I didn't feel streaming down my face.

"Uncle . . . are you crying?"

I shake my head. I blame my tears on the rancid smell burning my eyes. She takes a deep breath. She puffs out her chest. She looks around. "But . . . there's no smell like that here." She approaches the pink dress hanging on the wall. She raises her head to appraise it. She says it looks like the dress of the girl drawn on the first page of the Ibn Al Zarzur story collection. I nod my head without saying that if she saw the owner of the dress when she was young, it would be clear that it is the same girl. Hawraa's phone rings in my dishdasha pocket, lighting up with a message. It's from Sadiq: "If Fahd comes back . . . I'll come back." I throw my weight onto Fawzia's bed. I call him immediately. Once. Thrice. Ten times. The phone's off. Half my worry slides off my shoulder. The other half weighs down my other shoulder. I play around with the phone, searching for more messages. Nothing, except a three-day-old message from Abdulkareem . . . I mean Fahd, responding to Hawraa's message asking him to consider divorce. He wrote in his response: "I say farewell, O tortuous night . . . farewell to you as I travel on the clouds . . . and you see me like a mist . . . like an illusion . . . a mirage."

"That's God's choice and not yours." The words slip out from between my lips, reflecting the images crowding my head.

"Uncle, what's the matter?" Hissa asks.

"Nothing."

The lights go out suddenly. Hissa bristles and sticks to me. She trembles like a wet pigeon. "I don't like the dark!" I try to comfort her. There's no doubt that the generator is out of diesel. We catch a sound in the living room below.

She squeezes my arm, pulling it to her. "Someone's downstairs."

I place my finger on my lips. "Shhh." I take off three of the medals from the wall with the help of the light from the phone. Wrapping the ribbons of the medals around my fist, I secure the metal medallions on the back of my hand.

Hissa follows me. She rambles. Images of her house being stormed flood back. She raises her voice. "The masked men. Uncle, Uncle . . . the masked men. They're here."

I grab her by the shoulders and shake her. "Don't be scared!" Her fear makes me confront what's really bothering me, and I can't bear that right now, in this moment. I drag my steps approaching the stairs.

One of the voices downstairs says, "The courtyard door is open!" I look down into the living room below. An old man with a long beard, a flashlight in hand, and a woman in a *niqab*, and . . .

THE THIRD MOUSE: EMBERS THE INHERITANCE OF FIRE

THE NOVEL

Chapter 11

The beginning of 2005: we seemed to be stuck in a bottleneck, having been trapped at the bottom of the bottle for a while, not knowing where the opening led. Everything around me was strange. I was noticing this, two years on, and no one else seemed to, or maybe they did and just didn't say anything. While stopped at a traffic light, with Iraqi songs blaring from the cars around me, my mind wandered. The first thing that came out of Iraq, when its regime fell, was its songs, the crappy ones and the good ones. I didn't know if the people had stopped singing during the years of the sanctions, or if their songs simply weren't crossing our northern border. I summoned Mama Zaynab from my memory. If she had lived longer, would she still be Bibi Zaynab, blasting Nazem Al Ghazali's song in her courtyard, not forced to mask her dialect, dancing at Sadiq's wedding to an Iraqi song, then dying with her noble Iraqi name declared, proud? The songs in the street grew distant. Cars started honking, alerting me to the green light.

The atmosphere was toxic. Without noticing it, we inhaled the rotten air. We were responsible for it. Our phones took on a new role, serving as constant reminders of how infected people's minds had become. Photos and video clips of religious men issuing sermons, fatwas, and fake miracles. Laughter at the turbaned men. Debates between the Sunni sheikh and the Shia sayyid. So-and-so's foul language. See how ignorant the Nawasib are. Rafida conspiracies. We were inhaling our hatred like air. It was impossible to escape. Frankly, everything came down to "us" and "them." Even when you browsed YouTube, searching for a song or a comedy sketch, inevitably the comments below would take you off track. Which sect was the actor or singer from? *Rafidi* or *Nasibi*. The vomit that was spread throughout the Internet leaked to the television channels. Dedicated channels. Controversies followed by thousands. Between the sayyid and the sheikh, who brushed off whom. And I, every time, would turn off the television, shut the laptop or phone, damning Abbas and Saleh as if they were the ones responsible for all this. I didn't know that in every neighborhood there were several replicas of them. I imagined a tomorrow, not a tomorrow that gathered us in a turbulent land, like Mama Hissa's courtyard, which brought us together at times and tore us apart at others.

After Ayub got a job there, I started writing stories for the *Al Rai* newspaper. I was given a weekly column, saying whatever I liked under the cloak of metaphor, as if I were washing my hands of a collective sin we were committing. Every time I wrote, Fawzia would be my hidden reader. I'd derive a blind love from her, for the land and the people. My stories took place on our old street. Pieces I wrote myself without having to use my imagination, except when it came to the names. I adopted pseudonyms for us and for Surra. Stories of the three friends became five: Turki, Mehdi, Mish'al, Jaber, and Abdullah!

Mom wasn't exactly happy about what I wrote until my column became well read. Her friends praised my work. My dad had nothing to do with me except to repeat his question about what good was writing. As long as there was no money to be made, he wasn't enthusiastic about what I wrote. His wealth had grown exponentially, and he intended to buy a new house. He was taking me away again from the house that had, after eight years, almost become my home. The diwaniya played a part, despite everything, in making Rawda a beloved place. My mom convinced him that the new house should be bought abroad, because foreign houses are assets for when something happens. She lost her peace of mind at the time of the bombings in 1985, and in 1990 she lost faith in Kuwait altogether. Because it was what she wanted, the house ended up being in London. At that time, my father amassed a fortune—his balance in the banks doubled, benefiting from the American presence in Iraq. He owned a fleet of trucks that lumbered back and forth on the northern road whose borders had been shut for years. He delivered food and medical supplies under contracts made with the American army.

During those days, we spent most of the time in the diwaniya, playing cards, using a deck that had reached Kuwait from Iraq. These cards, which fetched exorbitant prices, had become popular after the fall of the Iraqi regime. Each card featured a prominent figure in Saddam's regime. My cousin had boycotted the gathering space because of my father. "Your dad's working with them!" My silence made me just as culpable. He bellowed in my face when I told him that my father had nothing to do with me. "Your father's money is covered in blood!" He disappeared. The blood then appeared in my food, drink, and everything in the house.

When I asked my dad, he said I didn't understand. I didn't understand what? I asked. "A smart man grabs opportunity with both hands!" My father grabs . . . and . . .

News of Dhari reached me soon after, from my mother. He spent most of his time hosted by state security, subject to endless interrogations surrounding the clashes that had erupted in the Um Al Hayman area between the security forces and an armed group affiliated with Al

Qaeda, members of which were known on the street as valiant mujahideen by some extremist Sunnis and terrorists by others. Kuwait was on a loathsome security alert. And because Dhari already had a file with the Ministry of Interior, accusatory fingers were pointed at him every time such an incident occurred.

Their investigation eventually took an interest in us because of Dhari's connection to our diwaniya, which people were suspicious of. I was taken aback by the investigator's questions regarding the reason for our get-togethers, our relationships with those we didn't know personally, and the places that Dhari frequented. "Cigarettes, oud, PlayStation, and cards! That's our diwaniya for you," I told the officer before he released me. He said that my stories in the paper didn't suggest that I had any hostile inclinations like my cousin. I didn't know that they read my stories in the state security bureau! Dhari, who had brought Surra to Rawda, whose idea it had been for us to get together in the diwaniya, became the reason for its shutdown and the splintering of its pioneers.

Sadiq and Ayub boycotted our space in the beginning, immediately after the discussions around the battle of the two sects in Iraq. "God damn whoever brought Dhari into the diwaniya!" they both said. Our diwaniya that had brought us together over video games and cards started to bring us together over rumors that each would tell from his point of view: the historical dispute between the Prophet's companions and his relatives; if not for the stance of so-and-so, there wouldn't be . . . the fall of the Abbasid caliphate in Baghdad because . . . And when I stepped in to end the dispute, I became a reactionary restricting their freedom of speech, and my diwaniya a suffocating place.

Mom begged for me to stay out of trouble. "No diwaniya, no headache." She said my friends were like sacks of coal, always leaving a stain on the dishdasha of the one carrying them. I wanted to embarrass her by reminding her that one of my friends was her nephew. She didn't care. "All of them are the same!"

Only Fahd remained, hesitating now and again whenever his desire to play the oud, forbidden in his house, dragged him over to the diwaniya. Hawraa had overcome her ordeal completely, except for her non-negotiable stance on not getting pregnant again. Every time Fahd tried to cajole her, she would request that he forget the whole thing. She settled into her parents' home in Rumaithiya for some weeks, Fadhila fortifying her with Quranic verses to undo any black magic. She washed Hawraa with lote water before Hawraa returned to Saleh's house. The master of the house didn't stop pressuring his son. "Divorce her!" Our diwaniya disintegrated into several café meet-ups. We'd gather from time to time, conditional meetings guaranteed by—at Sadiq's and Fahd's request—Dhari's absence. When Dhari did come, our meetings became just Fahd, him, and me. In a building his father owned in Jabriya, Ayub set aside an apartment for entertainment as a replacement for the Rawda diwaniya. We would get together, far from Dhari—Fahd, Sadiq, Ayub, and me . . . the one who hated this tug-of-war. I, who'd become the rope.

***

10:05 p.m.

Present Day

I toss the medals at my feet. Between Fawzia's room and the stairs. I observe those entering below, carrying flashlights. The little girl hugs me from behind. Lines of light stream forth from the flashlights, overlapping and growing distant in the dark. Hawraa searches for her phone on the table in the middle of the living room. "It was here; I'm sure of it!" Her two boys hold the lady's hands. Is it Fawzia? Who else would raise her head to the ceiling like someone pondering how one star gave life to the next? The woman in the niqab and the bearded man make me think twice before heading downstairs. Ever since the niqab and the beard have become a source of fear, we've been counting the steps between us and them. The woman stands next to the old man. He grabs his phone and pushes some buttons. He reassures Hawraa that she'll find her phone. Hawraa seems anxious about the smashed-up car by the door. The phone rings in my pocket. Everyone looks, with the exception of Fawzia, to the top of the stairs. I come down the steps, Hissa in tow. Beams of light converge on my face. The phone in my hand flashes with Abu Sami's name. I shake the hand of the man who doesn't look like the man whose saluki scared me when I was a child. He doesn't recognize me until Hawraa greets me. And I wouldn't have placed him if not for his name appearing on the screen of Hawraa's phone. The two boys lunge at me, hugging me. "Uncle! Uncle! Where did our daddy go?" they ask.

I kneel down and hug them each in turn. I look into the eyes of their mother, her gaze transmitting a silent question: *Where did my brother go?* The woman in the niqab lights a candle on the table in the middle of the living room. She turns to me and nods her head in what seems like a greeting. Hawraa points to her, saying, "Um Sami . . . Florence."

I say hello. Fawzia, in the commotion of questions, looks up to the ceiling in silence. She looks like someone else. Chunky in an unhealthy kind of way. Extinguished, with gray hair and skin closer to ash than old coffee. Wrinkles travel her forehead and cheeks, drawing what resembles continents of an unknown world. She squints, her eyes devoid of light, morphing into a giant ear fixed on my voice. Her lips take on the shape of a smile that I can't read. I approach her, holding out my hand. "Fawzia, how are you?"

Her smile widens. She nods her head and a childlike spirit floods her face, aged before its time. "I'm well." Even her voice doesn't sound like it used to.

Hawraa alerts her to my outstretched hand. "Give your hand, Fawzia." She hesitates. She stretches out her arms in front of her, wriggling her fingers in the air. The whiteness of her eyes disappears behind a radiant blush. I hesitate. I bring my face closer, between her plump palms. She clutches my ears. My cheeks. She traces her trembling fingers between my nose and lips.

Tears pour down her face. "Katkout . . . is it really you?"

I nod my head between her hands. She turns her face. She tilts her head, bringing an ear in my direction, waiting for an answer. "It's me."

I don't say that Katkout has become a rooster, feathers plucked out, good for nothing except for yelling, "The mice are coming." And that the mice aren't scared of cocks that only scream among broken eggs. Hawraa invites us to sit down while nervously cracking her knuckles. Abu Sami and his wife excuse themselves. To avoid attracting attention, he says he won't turn on the generator. He leaves.

Hawraa starts telling me of a call she received two hours ago. "A stranger advised me to be careful after the HQ was burned down. Now it's everyone else's turn." It's possible their intention is to storm the homes of Fuada's Kids to kill them one by one. The phone call didn't last long, she says. "Someone knocked on the door. I was paralyzed. I sent Ayub a text to let him know. I left with the boys and Fawzia from the back door to Abu Sami's house. I was so scared that I forgot my phone here."

Her voice grows soft. She asks me about Fahd and Sadiq, her face full of anguish. "Neither of them was at the HQ during the fire . . . Isn't that right?"

In a voice that sounds like my own I answer, "Just Dhari."

She clamps her hands over her mouth. "Dhari?"

I nod my head meekly. "Dhari." She stares at my face. She asks how he is. I'm unable to say. Her face turns sallow. She cries for him. Or maybe she's crying for me. I remember Sadiq's message on her phone. I look past my tragedy. I tell her about the message. She reads it. Her reassurance regarding her brother's safety compounds her worry for her husband.

"And Fahd?" she asks me. I remember his last message to her: "Farewell, O tortuous night . . . farewell . . . I travel on the clouds."

"He's well, God willing . . . well," I respond. Heavy knocks on the door can only mean something grim.

Hawraa gasps, hugging her boys. Hissa leans in closer. She confirms it's the masked men. This is how they banged on the door before kidnapping her father. "They'll come inside. They won't stay outside for long." Her stifled cries become fierce groans. The sofa soaks up a warm liquid under my thighs. I get closer to the table and blow out the candle. I carry Hissa in my arms. I tell everyone to lay low upstairs. Fawzia is the first to run toward the stairs. We follow her, she being the only one who can see in our darkness.

THE THIRD MOUSE: EMBERS
THE INHERITANCE OF FIRE

THE NOVEL

Chapter 12

We had stopped looking outside, only peering within; isolating our-selves as a nation. Ever since we had taken down the photos from the walls. Ever since we'd cut every possible thread tying us to the past. However, the July war of 2006, between Hezbollah and the Israeli army in Lebanon, revealed another face of Kuwait—one that had been absent for many years. Something similar had happened six years earlier when the Israeli forces pulled out from the south of Lebanon. Images of Hezbollah's yellow flag proliferated rapidly, stuck to car windows, prais-ing the statements of Nasrallah, whose photo came to occupy the walls of many diwaniyas. Even Ayub, who wasn't troubled by any religious concern or preoccupied by any political stance, put up the yellow flag in the Jabriya apartment for some days. The joy wasn't restricted to one particular sect. It wasn't a victory solely for *them*. Both sects considered the end of the war a victory large enough to encompass them all. Except for a few, such as Dhari, who reminded us how Hezbollah had been involved in hijacking the Kuwaiti plane at the end of the '80s. My father was also not enthused; he only saw the destruction of Lebanon, and how its tourism was taking a hit. If Mama Hissa had still been alive, she would have included the name of Nasrallah, the general secretary of Hezbollah, among the names of the "real men" on her list: her husband, Gamal Abdel Nasser, Sheikh Fahad Al Ahmad. I was observing what was going on around me with no opinion of my own.

"Mama's boy," Sadiq pestered me. He knew that my mother didn't have an opinion on anything because everything invoked fear in her. And because "All cowards stay safe!" Maybe he was right. I thought about retorting with *I'm my father's son!* But I didn't. Not out of love for my mom, though.

In the middle of 2007, my phone rang late one night, flashing Fahd's name. I was fighting off sleep while editing a story before filing it for the newspaper. *This call must be trouble,* I predicted. "I've been in the hospital since noon," he told me.

"I'm getting dressed. I'll be right there," I answered him, half-awake. I didn't ask why he was at the hospital. I didn't even know which hospital he was in. I took off my pajamas and pulled on my dishdasha. I got in the car. I had scarcely lit my cigarette when he sent me a text message: "Hussain Makki Juma Hospital." I stubbed my cigarette out in the ashtray before starting the engine. My phone trembled between my hands as I reread the text. Hussain . . . Makki . . . Juma. The hospital whose name people were too superstitious to pronounce. They would point to it as a symbol just as they would only allude to the disease that caused people to go there, fearful that this very disease would hear its name on their tongues and be spoken into existence. People would replace the inauspicious name with another one, such as "the wicked disease," "the bad thing," "the sickness that God spared us of," or use English, as their word had a nicer ring to it: cancer.

The doctor reassured us that tumors usually struck women well past their fifties. Hawraa wasn't even thirty yet. "Let's hope for the best," her doctor said. The panic on Fahd's face was as if he were the one being diagnosed. There was peace on Hawraa's face, as if the infected part of her body were of no consequence to her. Fadhila kept on chanting Quranic verses to break the black magic spell afflicting her daughter. The days passed by slowly until the examination results arrived. We were hopeful that the tumor, which had taken up residence in her right breast, was a benign one. But it wasn't.

"My sister's crazy," Sadiq said a few days later in one of the Hussain Makki Juma Hospital's hallways. Her doctor had a good bedside manner and had put Hawraa at ease. The discovery of the malignant tumor wasn't very late, and yet it wasn't exactly early either. He explained to her the available treatment options. Sadiq said that his sister skipped over all other possible treatments to the last resort. She asked her doctor about the likelihood of a mastectomy. "Quite high," the doctor responded apologetically.

She cut him off before he could go on, not giving him the chance to add anything positive. She clasped her hands under her chin. She nodded and smiled, expressing a joy that was incongruous with his response. "Thank you . . . thank you, Doctor."

If only the removal of all tumors were as easily done as Hawraa's— by having the affected breast removed eight months after diagnosis. Fahd was caught smack in the middle between Saleh's desire to separate the couple and Fadhila's absolute unwavering conviction of a magic charm buried somewhere by Aisha. Hawraa's recovery didn't change the situation much. "Some tumors only stop growing when the body dies. If only they'd all die so we'd bury one of them in the cemetery of the other, just to spite them all, and we'd all live together in peace," Fahd said.

"Come on!" I responded, understanding the intense pressure he was under.

"We just want to live in peace," he answered me. I changed the topic and asked him about his wife. "Hawraa's happy," he said. After inspecting her chest post-mastectomy, Hawraa informed Fahd in a worn-out voice that she was ready to get pregnant again. But it wouldn't be easy going forward. Not for another five years, or at least three, the doctor told her.

"Five years without a pregnancy and the woman has lost her mind, her religion, and . . . a breast!" Saleh said to Fahd before urging him again, "Divorce her!"

Some days later, Fahd and I sat in the diwaniya. We were alone when his father called him, asking, "Is Abbas with them?" I wouldn't have known any better if Fahd hadn't told me about a memorial service being held at the Imam Hussein Mosque for one of the members of Hezbollah. Twenty years before, the newspapers had pinpointed him as one of those involved in the hijacking of the *Jabriya* plane. He, according to which side you spoke to, had either "died" or was "martyred" in Syria a few days earlier. Fahd refused to answer his dad and hung up on him. That's when I asked. Fahd let out a heavy sigh. "'Am Abbas and Sadiq." I braced my forehead against my hand, damning this tasteless piece of theater: all of us had lead roles. A very poor director was orchestrating it, or maybe a very smart one, seeing as we weren't aware of his presence. Our sectarian clot had reached the point of no return. At a time when the person being eulogized was in the land of the dead, we split up into two, preoccupying ourselves with his fate—in heaven; no, in hell—when in fact we were the ones in hell after living out our lives hiding this hatred that was within us, yet openly discussed in newspaper articles or in the heated arguments between parliament members, which people hungrily followed while I was still naively writing my symbolic stories of warning!

After the memorial service, Ayub called me from his office at *Al Rai*, letting me know of some political movement's decision to hold a national unity rally that, due to its name, had attracted interest from prominent political and religious personalities of both sects. "We've got to meet there." Ayub seemed serious like I'd never known him to be, and this pleased me; it pleased me a lot, in fact, as I was being eaten alive by worry over our damned future. I didn't have to bear it all alone. We were in dire need of someone to point out the wound clearly, even if it was necessary to cut through it and drain it of its putrid pus. My hopes were bolstered by this imminent rally; maybe it would do something, or at least say something worthwhile. Ayub contacted Fahd, Sadiq, and Dhari, telling us all the same thing: "Seven thirty, Tuesday evening."

Dhari called me afterward, surprised by Ayub's call and his interest. "This event isn't as well intentioned as it sounds to you." I pleaded with him to delay his judgment until after Tuesday evening.

The four of us sat in the last row; our fifth member carried his camera and his recording equipment, preparing to cover the event. The open venue was packed to the rafters. The young organizers started running the sound and light checks. It ended up being a free satirical play. It openly made fun of us, the audience, shamelessly. The rally speakers stood in a line: previous ministers, clerics, and members of parliament, all behind the platform, each waiting his turn with the microphone. One of them started his speech with a prayer for Prophet Muhammad, his family, and companions. Another started with the same prayer, but stopped with the Prophet's family, excluding his companions. Half the audience responded to the first, and the other half to the second. They spoke at length as I grew restless in my seat. I drew patience from the hope on Ayub's face while he altered his filming angles. He was preparing sanitized news that he would publish in a soiled tomorrow. I turned to Fahd, Sadiq, and Dhari in surprise over the men onstage and their disregard for the audience as they applauded wildly, their chanting getting louder: "Unity, unity, national unity!"

Sadiq stifled his laughter at the empty slogans. He looked at me, pretending to grab a pen and drawing a small circle on his palm. He pushed down on it with his finger repeatedly. I shook my head. "If only!"

One of the guests, all of whom were well known for their financial corruption, stood up and spoke. His picture appeared behind him on the big screen. He waved his arms with theatrical flair and exaggerated expressions. He yelled, spittle gathering at the corners of his mouth, "Despite the storm . . . we've come together with love . . . Sectarianism won't cleave us . . . and . . ."

"Just look at that son of a bitch—what is he babbling on about?" slipped out of my mouth into Fahd's ear. My language took Fahd aback. It also caught me off guard. He squeezed my knee. "It's just the usual . . . Let's see who's next."

The microphone moved from one hand to another. The voices were different, but the words were the same. The turban, beard, and bisht agreed; politics and religion—all of them singing from the same hymn sheet, "Everything is fine and we're fine." A member of parliament concluded that what united the sects was greater than the lies being spread about discord by those seeking to ambush state security. Our country was apparently a paradise, and all the happenings were nothing more than lies, slander, a fiction concocted by sick souls. And as it should be, he had to quote the Prophet's saying about sedition and God's damnation of those who awoke it. I was beyond disappointed. I, who had to shut down my diwaniya and almost lost my friends because of the poison they had injected into our homes as children. I, who embraced my muteness ever since my mom had raised her hand threatening to slap my mouth if I uttered a word. I remembered my first fight at school like it was yesterday. The blood on Sadiq's shirt. The humiliation on Fahd's face, crying, caught between two boys preventing him from saving his friend. Me out cold on the cool sidewalk, my tooth knocked out. I shivered. My mouth felt dry. I listened to the drumming in my chest, as if someone had shaken Mama Hissa's sidra within me and released the jinn. I stood up and raised my arm once the Q&A began. I paid no mind to Fahd and Sadiq, who were urging that we leave.

"You love drama," Sadiq said, poking fun at my irritation.

Fahd became aware of my state. "Why are you so worked up?" he asked. All the questions from the audience were from the VIPs seated in the front row; it seemed like everything had been rehearsed.

I raised my voice as I extended my hand as high as it could go. "Mic! Mic!" I don't know what had come over me all of a sudden. A perplexed Dhari got up from his chair and patted me on the shoulder. The scent of *oud* cologne on his hand wafted up to me.

"Calm down!"

"This is a joke," I snapped. I remembered Mama Zaynab's words: "We're not wild animals that they can make fun of!"

Either Dhari or I was on another planet. He was simplifying the matter, and I didn't see it as simple. It pushed me to release all that I had kept trapped inside of me since childhood; to talk about a hatred that had only grown as the days passed by. The audience craned their necks in our direction. Embarrassment crept onto my cousin's face, while Fahd and Sadiq were strapped down to their chairs like they didn't know us. Dhari grabbed my arm and squeezed it. He whispered, "Easy does it . . . God will bring the r-r-r-rain."

I didn't intend to make fun of his stutter, but I did. I answered him, yelling in my outburst, "I don't want the r-r-r-rain, I want the damn microphone!"

He let go of my arm and sat next to Sadiq and Fahd. I spat one question in the faces of the puppets onstage: "If sedition is asleep, if this thing staring at us and lying in wait for us is in fact nothing, if we're such angels and our country is a paradise, and if we have nothing to worry about under the guidance of our wise government, then what has brought you all here today for this rally?"

I pulled a ghutra off one of the organizer's heads when he force-fully yanked the microphone from my hand. Like schoolboys. He faced me, chest puffed out. I did the same. He pushed me, so I pushed back. He cursed my mother; I cursed his ancestors. He hit me; I hit him. I only remember voices spouting profanity at us. Ghutras on the ground, sandals flying. Fahd whipping someone with his egal. Sadiq stamping on someone's stomach. Ayub crashing the camera down on the back of a guy holding Dhari in a choke hold. "Calm down!" everyone else entreated.

We calmed down in the police station while we signed bonds of good behavior, promising never to do that again. It turned out to be a great night for national unity after all!

Without it, the Rawda diwaniya wouldn't have opened its doors once more. We got together, the five of us, without reservation. We circled around the newspapers the following day, reading the headlines: *Intruders wreck national unity rally*. Ayub guffawed at the description. He raised his fist high, his voice booming, "Long live the wreckers!" Fahd pumped his fist, Sadiq and Dhari following suit, all laughing. "Hear! Hear!"

Ayub turned to me and asked, "What are you thinking?"

***

10:28 p.m.

Present Day

I don't think of anything except being in the company of two women and three children in possible imminent danger. We walk up the stairs single file, Fawzia at the front and me at the back. I carry Hissa, her robe wet, in my arms. The generator in the courtyard suddenly roars to life. The spotlight awakes from its sleep, revealing the naked fear on our faces. Hissa is in my arms, semiconscious. One of us fears the dark, and the other, when trying to hide, fears the light. Hawraa's phone rings. The caller: Abu Sami. He says a black car is parked by the gate of the Al Bin Ya'qub house. One of its passengers gets out. He climbs the boundary wall and jumps inside. Hawraa grows weak. She sits on the steps, hugging her two boys. "We're going to die!" I beg her to go higher up. Her legs fail her. "We want to live," she mumbles deliriously. The sound of someone opening the hallway door travels up the stairs. He slams the door open against the wall. At this point, the sound of any voice would reduce us to wraiths. Unless it's a familiar one.

"Hawraa . . . Hawraa . . . where are you all?" we hear Ayub call out.

The two boys, followed by their mother, run downstairs. A worn-out Ayub falls on his knees at the base of the stairs. Naked, except for white underwear soaked in blood and on his body something resembling seaweed. He looks up to me and Hissa, fighting back a smile. "I saw your pile of scrap parked outside . . . and knew that you guys were here." I sit on the stairs, catching my breath. I set the girl down. I stare into Ayub's eyes and don't respond. He knows I'm angry about the way he acted at the bridge. He lies down on his back, laughing with a sad face or crying with a face of joy, about escaping death. "I was going to die." I look at my watch, calculating the time that has passed since his disappearance into the river. He sits up and justifies his tardiness. "Forget about the bullets from the men on the bridge, the corpse-catchers have started attacking live bodies!" If the volunteer patrol hadn't found him and transported him here, he wouldn't have arrived in this state. He says this while pointing to the bleeding wounds on his body. It's as if he's only just become aware of his nakedness. He bends. "I'm sorry." Hawraa goes upstairs. She comes back with one of Fahd's dishdashas. Ayub puts it on after washing himself.

Hissa sits on the ground. She draws mice on the boys' hands; they have completely surrendered to her. Hawraa turns on the TV and flips through the channels. The national TV station urges families to avoid the militias by staying away from threatened areas, to keep off the seven main roads, and to stay at home. Names of the areas appear on-screen while the anchorman reads out the news. Damascus Street is overflowing with sewage. Peaceful protests on Cairo Street, despite the curfew. Residents of Hawally put out burning fires at the entrance of Tunisia Street. Khaldiya: clashes on Tripoli Street between armed men and security forces. Salmiya: Baghdad Street under the control of rebels and families demanding the end of the curfew to make it easier for them to reach safety. Abdullah Al Salim: an IED explosion between Fatima Mosque and the gas station on Sana'a Street. The closure of Al Aqsa Mosque Street without any reason given. The news moves on, after broadcasting the names of the seven closed roads, to Kayfan: images of civil defense workers extricating corpses from under the rubble of houses overlooking Fahad Barrak Al Sabeeh Street. I look at Fawzia and the name of the area on the screen. I stretch out my hand to Hawraa and grab the remote control. I mute the TV, worried that Fawzia will pick up on what's happening in Kayfan. Everyone has been doing their best for a while now to shield her from any bad news about her beloved area. I follow the figures on-screen, thinking of Fawzia. She doesn't need all this coddling. Nothing on the radio or the television points to a place she loves. She doesn't know that Andalus Park has now become Kayfan Oasis and that Abdul Wahab Al Faris Mosque, which was burned down last week, is the same mosque that people long ago used to call Bin Abidan Mosque. She doesn't know that Al Mas'ud Theater has become Al Tahrir Theater, and that Al Tahrir Theater became a prison camp when the prisons were overcrowded with militants and suspects. If only she hadn't lost her sight, she would have still been able to read the newspapers; she would read of the municipal council's decision to change the name of Ishbiliya Street to Fahad Barrak Al Sabeeh Street. She's confident that no harm has come to the locations of her cherished memories and that the corpses in the news are in a street far from hers. If only she had heard the news broadcast on the radio a little while ago, when I was searching for a safe route to get out of Jabriya: "Kayfan has been struck!"

Ayub breaks my train of thought by snatching the remote control from my hand. He turns off the television. He looks at me and asks about what happened to us at dawn today . . . Sadiq, Fahd, and me. I shift my gaze to Hissa, who has almost finished her artwork on the boys' palms. She's drawing X's that go through the mice. Ayub persists, "Where are they?"

Hawraa repeats his question like an echo. "Where are they?"

I know exactly what happened. But I . . . "I don't know where they are . . ."

THE THIRD MOUSE: EMBERS
THE INHERITANCE OF FIRE

THE NOVEL

Chapter 13

I spent months using everything I could think of to try to convince them. We should be a patriotic group, a genuine one at that, including members from all religious and political leanings. We would sound the alarm and call a spade a spade. The country was in a deplorable condition.

"It doesn't call for all this," Sadiq said after he laughed, claiming I was going to extremes. "You're making a mountain out of a molehill." He didn't give me a chance to explain that the molehill had actually become a malignant tumor. "What, a group with only five members?" he scoffed.

While Dhari exercised restraint, Fahd remained neutral. "I'm up for whatever you all agree to." Ayub was as enthusiastic as I was, maybe even more so. He said that the group's headquarters, if we agreed, could be in his apartment in his father's building in Jabriya.

Dhari was opposed to this. "Get rid of the b-booze you've got lying around in there first." Ayub ignored his words.

Ayub and I did all that we could to achieve our aim. After a few days, Fahd said that he was wholly convinced of the importance of the project, after Hawraa and Fawzia had expressed interest as well. He said that they would be the first members to join the group. "We've become seven!"

Dhari threw up his hands in what looked like surrender. He directed his words at Fahd. "May God grant you all success, but I'm against m-men and women mixing. It's either me, or your wife and your aunt!"

Fahd stayed calm. "Keep cool and say peace upon the Prophet, man!"

Dhari said, "Peace be upon the Prophet, his family, and his companions."

"The best of them," Sadiq added, specifying.

Dhari knitted his eyebrows. "All the companions of the Prophet are good . . ."

"They're good for *you* guys," Sadiq thoughtlessly answered.

The disappointment that had come over me during that farce of a rally was the very same I felt now in the diwaniya. In each of us was an Abbas or Saleh rearing his head just as we were about to agree. We had spent months without getting one step closer to establishing the group. I was afraid to utter a word and have everything come crashing down. I knew that if I didn't succeed in this endeavor, it would be equivalent to undoing everything that I'd done in the hope of keeping us together as friends. It was my last hope for us, the five of us, who had become seven, to do something. My gaze wandered between them, listening to their opinions, searching for anything that would prove my mom wrong when she said my friends were sacks of coal. Coal, whose harm didn't stop at staining my clothes black. Coal that blazed one day, then became ashes; the ashes that are all you get from fire, just as Mama Hissa had warned all those years ago.

Fahd convinced my cousin that Hawraa's role would be at home, restricted to managing the group blog and website. "Where's the mixing in that?" Sadiq jumped in, frustrated by Fahd's justification. "I as her brother and Fahd as her husband don't have a problem."

Dhari glossed over Sadiq's words. He asked Fahd, "And your aunt? May God ease her condition, b-blind as she is . . . What's her role?"

"My aunt—thank you for your well wishes—my aunt's memory is important. She has stories, a store of national songs richer than the Ministry of Information's, and we need—"

"Songs? God grant you success, but I'm against m-music . . . It's either me or your aunt!" Dhari cut in.

Voices rose in debate, each one trying to convince the other, whereas Sadiq remained silent. Fahd asked him what he thought. He responded, his ears flushed with blood, "God grant you success . . . but either I'm with you all . . . or Dhari is!"

Many days of deadlock ensued. I begged them to listen to me. It was easier than all their complications. A blog, Facebook page, radio station, and my weekly column in the newspaper. This is what we'd start with, then we'd expand our activities, and each of us would express his opinion as long as it didn't go against our mission. Ayub's face was my main motivation to keep on talking despite their interruptions. I didn't get annoyed. Their discussions, despite their conflicting views, reassured me that they believed in the importance of the idea.

We wouldn't have reached a consensus if the newspapers hadn't published, during those days, images of offensive slogans about the Prophet's companions that had been scrawled on the walls of a mosque and now shattered glass windows of a hussainiya. "Where are we headed?" Dhari said, as if he had only just then perceived the gravity of the situation. Ayub answered him that we, we were the ones who would determine where we were going.

"But . . ." Dhari hesitated.

Ayub jumped to kiss his forehead. "Please, for God's sake, without any 'buts.' We've got to get to work."

Dhari smiled like I'd never seen him smile before and said, "God will bring the r-rain."

Ayub started to weave his way through the diwaniya, dancing and clapping. He wiggled his shoulders as he walked around, his steps deliberate, singing an old ditty: "Drip, raindrop, drip . . . our house is new . . . our drainpipes are now iron." His infectious clapping moved me, then Fahd and Sadiq, resulting in the four of us circling around Dhari, who was trying but miserably failing to keep from smiling. Our clapping became delirious, and Ayub's dancing soared to a zenith that made it like a *zar*, an exorcism party, only missing the traditional drumming and the incense. I listened to the drops of rain splattering on the street's asphalt. I smelled the aroma of moist soil. In my head, the sky was showering down indulgently.

We agreed that our group wouldn't be backed by any authority, political movement, religious group, or government—so that only we could represent ourselves. Deciding what to call the group was all that remained. They started to select names: Ayub suggested "the Alarm Bell"; Dhari proposed "the Anti-Sedition League"; Sadiq and Fahd didn't pay attention to him as they had already agreed on the name "Like Before." I shook my head, rejecting all their suggestions. We needed a name that commanded attention. A name that would strike terror into people's hearts, to make them aware of the danger of staying on the same path. Sadiq turned to me. "Fine then . . . you choose a name."

I looked everyone in the eye before saying, "Fuada's Kids."

Dhari gaped at me. "Who's this F-Fuada?"

Fahd sprawled out on his back, laughing uproariously.

I told Dhari that it was the Fuada from the *Rest in Peace, World* television series, the crazy hoarse-voiced history teacher Fuada, who said that the mice were coming, carrying the mousetrap, calling out, "Protect yourselves from the plague!"

Fahd could barely bring his laughter to heel. "Fuada? Scary? Only you're afraid of her! She doesn't scare people," he said as he gawked at me.

He got up from the floor and, taking on a serious air, said, "Okay, enough with the jokes . . . seriously, you're the one who thought of the group, so now you'll choose the name."

I stood my ground. "Fuada's Kids. With the slogan, *The mice are coming . . . protect yourselves from the plague!*"

"But that name is a joke!"

"This whole situation is a joke!" I shot back.

THE FOURTH MOUSE:
ASHES

All of them are villains,
the murdered and the murderers
They claim . . . that they . . . are carrying
the cross to Golgotha
when they . . . are burning the roots
if . . . they bloom . . . with buds

—Ali Al Sabti

11:05 p.m.

Present Day

"I don't know where they are!"

I stay silent. I hate how I'm choking on my tears like a child. I remember myself with both of them at dawn today. I feign a cough that tightens my vocal cords. Ayub and Hawraa are still staring at me, demanding an answer.

Fawzia tilts her head. She turns one ear to me, sensing my voice. She repeats their question: "Where are they?"

"What I do know is that we were together. The three of us. We were celebrating in our own way the successful completion of the first day of the truce. We finished broadcasting the last of the programs after midnight. We chose the song 'This Country Demands Glory,' Fawzia. We filled the silence of the airwaves with it during the night hours until the broadcast resumed with your morning news bulletin, Ayub. We left the HQ for Rawda. 'Should we go home?' I asked Fahd and Sadiq, thinking that on an occasion like this, my day should not end just like any other. 'Of course not,' Sadiq said to me. He was the one who made the suggestion, 'Gamal Abdel Nasser Park, let's have dinner there.' I laughed. Where did he get that idea? The park's been dead for so long. He said he needed a place far away from people. He said he was missing a place that felt familiar.

"Actually, I felt just the same. I'm always nostalgic for old places. We parked our cars in the plot opposite the park, carrying bags of food. Fahd wouldn't have agreed to go anywhere if it hadn't been for his dread of returning to the house you had left, Hawraa. He was missing his sons. And there's no need for me to add that he was missing you, too. Not a single hour went by without him grabbing his phone and checking for a message from you. I won't keep talking if you keep crying. Here, take this. Dry your eyes. Okay. So we spent three hours together. Hours deeply rooted in the past. Oh, if only you had been with us, Fawzia! Our memories brought back to life the old park, which even the McDonald's there now hasn't been able to revive. There were boxes from Happy Meals and plastic toys scattered on the ground at the entrance opposite the deserted restaurant. Sadiq bent down to pick up a small rubber ball, with the golden arches on it. He looked around him as if afraid that someone would see him. You know your cousin, Ayub. Crazy. But even you can't imagine what his craziness drove him to just before dawn today. He looked at us, juggling the ball back and forth in his hands, and asked us if we were game. We exchanged looks, Fahd and I, each waiting for the other to cave.

"We took off our sandals. We folded up our dishdashas, wrapped the hems around our waists. None of us said a word. Our eyes were laughing, somewhat embarrassed. Sadiq started searching, beneath an ancient sidra, for flat stones of different sizes while holding the rubber ball. Fahd joined in immediately. I don't know how, but I felt myself shrinking. My dishdasha became wide, loose, the sleeves baggy. I looked at Fahd's and Sadiq's faces: now neither had a thick mustache or a beard. Fahd's face was smooth and dark with wide eyes, and his hair was jet-black. Sadiq's face had regained its old redness, pimples sprinkled across his cheeks. I rolled up my sleeves and then joined them collecting stones. We crossed the park. Nothing looked like it used to, except for the giant trees running parallel to the wall, braving the dryness, and the rusty, neglected swings on the spongy black floor. We built a small pyramid of seven stones for anbar. We formed two teams, one of them a man down. We took turns throwing the McDonald's ball at the seven-stone pyramid. It crashed to the ground like a bombed building. Each of us pushed the others out of the way to pick up the ball. We rolled in the soil and dry grass like street cats. One of us threw the ball at the other's head, definitely against the rules. Fahd ran, laughing. Sadiq followed him, laughing. I caught up with them, drenched in sweat and shaking with laughter myself. The ball moved from our hands to our feet. Fahd kicked it far away. The two of them ran toward it. I became Khalid Al Harban and started commentating loudly on Fahd's technique: 'Muayyad Al Haddad's with the ball . . . He crosses . . . He goes . . .' He kicked it powerfully. He nutmegged Sadiq. 'GooOOOOal! Allah, Allah, Allah! Muayyad Al Haddaaaaad . . . *ya salaaam*!' We flopped on the ground, catching our breath, coughing, laughing, coughing. Fahd straightened up, holding his lower back in pain. An old image of his father sitting cross-legged on the ground came to me. The words fell out of my mouth, telling him not to shower at night. Mama Hissa's joke to his father years ago didn't make his son laugh today. His face turned pale. Sadiq looked concerned. It prompted Fahd to check his phone. Your voice wasn't there in his in-box, Hawraa. Your husband broke into a smile. 'The chest has a key!' Sadness tinged the happiness on your brother's face. He said, 'Ohhh!' before asking Fahd, 'What reminded you of the song?'

"Fahd looked around him and replied, 'Same thing that reminded you of the park.' Sadiq continued to repeat the song. He belted out, 'The key's with the blacksmith.' Fahd joined in, looking serious like Abdulkareem, 'And the blacksmith wants money.' As soon as they finished singing, 'And rain comes from God,' Sadiq opened the bags of food. We started to eat like ravenous little boys. The three of us hadn't gotten together like this, liberated from everything, our diwaniya, our headquarters, our houses—since I left Surra in 1997, twenty-three years ago. Each of us started to test the others' memory. 'Do you remember Abu Sameh and his song "Fill the Jug Up for Me"?'

"'Of course.'

"'And you, do you remember Mama Zaynab pushing the supermarket cart on the asphalt?' Our first fight. Al Najah Middle School. Mr. Desouky with his bulging eyes. Mr. Murhif. Al Anbaiie Mall, Al Budur Bookstore, and *Al Riyadi* magazine. Mama Hissa's stories and us sitting in the courtyard; when the power got cut in September 1990; Shail, the star of Canopus up in the sky at a time just like this thirty years ago. The Peace and Friendship Cup. The zalamat house. Al habal and al qumbar, our favorite pastimes, and the gold souk in Basra. Fawzia, her chocolate, and how she'd retire to her room to read Ihsan novels—"

"Me?" Fawzia interrupts, as her name has caught her attention. Ayub and Hawraa turn to her.

"Yes, you," I say. She squints her lackluster eyes, saying that she only remembers what I read to her. "Fawzia! Ihsan Abdel Quddous novels. You used to read them. You used to be able to see," I remind her.

Her eyes widen. She is trying to remember. "I've never been able to see in my life." I look at her, finding no words to respond. She points to her ear. "Finish the story."

"Which story?" I ask her, perplexed.

"Fahd and Sadiq's story."

I finish their story while looking at Fawzia's face. "Fahd asked me about the draft of *Inheritance of Fire*, my novel, when we were talking about you and Ihsan's novels. I didn't answer him since I'd kept quiet about it ever since I started writing. Ever since I decided to write us as we are: Fahd, Sadiq, Ayub, Dhari, and me. Without the masks of Turki, Mehdi, Mish'al, Abdullah, and Jaber—the masks I had gotten used to hiding behind. Sadiq sensed that I was holding back. He smiled at me while grabbing a sandwich and asked if we both knew what he was craving. He didn't wait for us to guess and said, 'Jaber's Egyptian sandwiches, macaroni and ketchup.' Fahd laughed, but I kept my lips shut as I remembered how delicious they had been. With a frown on his face, Fahd said that he was missing Mama Hissa's food and her sour achar. His phone rang; it was Khala Aisha. She was worried about him. We had been out all night. He reassured her, as he got up from the ground and dusted the grass off his dishdasha, that he'd be heading home right then. Before hanging up, he told his mother that he was craving mutabbaq samak. He hung up, looked at us, and announced with a flourish, 'For lunch today, we'll have mutabbaq samak!' He clawed the air with his nails and let out an excited *'Meeeeow!'*"

THE FOURTH MOUSE: ASHES
THE INHERITANCE OF FIRE

THE NOVEL

Chapter 1

More than three years had passed since the surgery that Hawraa had warmly welcomed. Her doctor informed her to prepare herself for pregnancy. And in accordance with a treatment plan administered under his supervision, she gave birth to twin boys in 2012. These twins cemented Fahd's conviction that Fuada's Kids was important, even though it had already been in existence for four years. "It's all for my kids," he'd say. The goal of our activities in the first few years, each via our own radio show or blog, was to get closer to people by stirring up their nostalgia. Granted, the past wasn't perfect, but we didn't need to be reminded of that, because it was better than where we had ended up. I worked on preparing and presenting my show, *Nostalgia*. Sadiq called his show *I'm History in Its Entirety*. It was the most controversial because of the issues he covered, and because he was trying to revisit history from another perspective, and that's exactly what people refused to do. *What's New*

Today was a variety show, mostly artistic in nature, hosted by Fahd, which relied on Fawzia's archives.

While Dhari worked on a comprehensive religious program, Ayub specialized in broadcasting news programs, making use of his work at the newspaper. The old-world character of our radio station and the reliance on people's distant memories stoked a great wave of optimism. The larger communication companies and banks started to compete to advertise on our online radio stream and website. Our way of doing things spread like wildfire. Companies adopted the very same approach—whipping up shared memories—to reach the general public through their ads on TV, radio, and newspapers. They marketed their services by exploiting people's nostalgia for "back then" or "the good old times," which became popular terms, more proof of how everyone had lost these memories.

While we reminded listeners and visitors to our website of what they had loved, we were simultaneously telling them what they had blinded themselves to out of hatred. In the beginning, our group had a good amount of exposure. A lot of people gave us a warm welcome, though some were suspicious about our reluctance to reveal our names, share our location, and be present at press events. Some tried hard to figure out who our group supported. Those loyal to the government named us the opposition. The opposition accused us of supporting the government. The religious groups saw us as a rebellious entity, outsiders. The anti-religious groups classified us as a religious movement.

I had stopped publishing my column, but Ayub had convinced the editorial board to allocate me a weekly column separate from the old one. I started to publish articles under the pen name "Fuada's Son." In the beginning there was an onslaught of vitriolic attacks, which put the newspaper in a difficult position, even though I was only writing about what was going on around me. I didn't understand how the reader was engaging with the writer. The reader had become a deadlier censor than the censors themselves. People were doing wrong, I was writing about it, and others were blaming me for writing about it! My consolation was in Ayub and the people who started to support us. I don't know how the seven of us became seventeen, then seventy . . . Our numbers kept multiplying: dedicated university students, activists. They all organized symposiums, concerts, and theater performances in the markets and public spaces. They would champion our slogan, *Protect yourselves from the plague!* And we'd be among the onlookers. The five of us spent most of our time working at the radio station, our headquarters. We became closer than ever before. I would observe my cousin. He had changed a lot. "And what about your jihad, sheikh?" Fahd teased Dhari. Dhari answered him, saying that, first, he wasn't a religious cleric. Then he gestured to the transmitter and the microphone and pronounced, "*This* is my j-jihad." Only Ayub shared his sentiment. He approached Dhari and kissed his forehead. Both of us knew the extent to which Dhari was torn between the heavy religious legacy he'd shouldered ever since he was a teenager and his skeptical mind that took a second look at everything. Dhari was only engaged in jihad with himself. Sadly, as much as our group was able to make progress, the problems between the two sects grew, bubbling before bursting forth, uncontrollable lava. Revolutions in neighboring countries inflamed the souls at home.

One afternoon, we sat in front of the TV in the diwaniya, like mourners attending a funeral. We listened to the statement issued by the government. It blamed the people for having abused their freedoms. Freedom of expression was an original right, but . . . the people, on the pretext of exercising this freedom, had abused it. They transformed it into sectarian sedition, in the newspapers, at public rallies, and inside the parliamentary dome. The sect became the authority instead of the state. The statement ended with "We are greatly saddened by the events that are storming the country today, and unfortunately are forced to implement a new system, in accordance with the current climate, rather than the 1962 constitution, because Kuwait's security is above all else . . . We are asking God the Great and Almighty to pour out blessings of safety and security on our dear country . . . Peace be upon you and mercy . . ." We witnessed demonstrations we'd never seen the likes of before. In front of the mosques, the hussainiyas, in diwaniyas, and on the streets. And because disaster, as usual, was too embarrassed to come alone, it dragged along its friends. The price of oil collapsed. Belts were tightened and taxes imposed. Gas prices went up. Food aid stopped. Public sector employees had their salaries cut in half. The value of the Kuwaiti dinar dropped for the first time.

While we were awaiting a government response to the naked chaos that gripped the country, frustration reigned everywhere after the GCC suspended most of its agreements. Two of the member countries were forced to impose visa restrictions on Kuwaiti citizens to stem their sudden mass migration, which resembled a refugee crisis as thousands of people sought a safe place that wasn't too far from Kuwait. Even when two more countries withdrew after disputes over oil production quotas, the media still broadcast the old song, "Our Gulf Is One and Our People Are One!" When Fahd made fun of this on his show *What's New Today*, because the song didn't reflect our current reality, he was called out by the Ministry of Information: "Final warning . . . or your website will be blocked and your activities suspended!" The "final" warning came out of the blue without a first or second one before it. It was a painful blow to Fuada's Kids and its supporters. We were slowly suffocating, ever since the government had imposed pre-censorship on newspapers after parliament had been dissolved once and for all, in an even worse way than it had been in the mid-1980s.

Days flew by, and the twins, or Fuada's grandkids as Fahd and Hawraa called them, grew up quickly. They attended most of our get-togethers in the diwaniya. Bright-eyed, they'd listen to us talking about the old courtyard. Their questions about their parents' grandmas, Hissa and Zaynab, were never-ending. With the twins in mind, I wrote the Ibn Al Zarzur series. And for their sake, Sadiq drew the illustrations for the stories just as the old woman had described them years ago. Fahd started reading them these stories every night at bedtime. He would replace some of the Arabic words with English ones that his two boys could understand.

I started to take the boys to the seaside every week, when they both turned five, on the condition that they didn't speak to me in English. Their parents worried about their sons' attachment to electronic devices, but didn't seem concerned that their boys spoke a broken Arabic that resembled code. I found the twins' company pure joy. I don't know why. My relationship with them pushed Fahd to ask me, "When will we see your kids?" It was the very same question that my mom kept repeating. I'd never respond, thinking, *How can I when tomorrow isn't promised to any of us?*

Fahd's silence seemed to say, *We won't ever see your kids.*

One afternoon, I was with the twins on one of the beaches in Salwa. Between the sea and the swings, I think I tempered their addiction to devices. In their company, I escaped the suffocating atmosphere strangling the country. I liked their many questions. I tried to decode them when they sprinkled in English words I didn't know. And I liked that I couldn't tell the twins apart. Each one resembled the other like his reflection in the mirror. Two boys created in one placenta. They suckled at one breast. They had the same face, voice, movements, and questions. They were full of mischief. Whenever I asked one of them who he was, he answered with his brother's name. They allowed me to finish what I was saying to one when it was meant for the other. They then would explode in peals of crazy laughter. "I'm not him! I'm meee!"

"Uncle, what are we?" One of them blurted out this question while running toward me, shaking the sand off his swimming trunks. I asked him what he meant.

His brother hesitated before saying, "Are we like Mom or like Dad?"

What would Mama Hissa have said? I looked at the sky. "Darling! *Habibi!* You're Muslim and that's all there is to it . . . The Prophet says—"

His brother cut in. He begged for an answer to a final question. "The Prophet . . . Is he like Dad or like Mom?"

I sought refuge in my watch. I got up. "It's time to go now."

His brother grabbed my arm, on his face a look pleading for my answer, swearing it was his last, last question. He pointed his little finger up above. "God, *subhanahu wa ta'ala* . . . Shia or Sunni?" I imagined the sky falling. I saw my mother's hand poised, ready to strike. I felt compassion for myself and for her, for a situation that happened a very long time ago.

"Ask God for forgiveness, *habibi*. You said 'God glorified and exalted,' meaning God is above both and above all such things."

"God forgive me."

"May He forgive you, my boy."

I threw two towels on their bodies and pushed them out in front of me to the car. I was on my way back to Rawda, Salwa on my right and the sea on my left. The twins were in the back seat. A somber voice on the radio talked about the different groups and sects of jinn. This sect is better. The other sect is corrupt. I silenced the radio, not knowing any jinn other than the purehearted ones living in the sidra. One of the boys stretched his arm between the two front seats. He pointed at a sign with an arrow toward Al Masjid Al Aqsa Street on the right. He knew I was annoyed. He promised that it was the last, last, last question. "Uncle . . . is the Al Aqsa Mosque in Salwa?"

"No, darling, it's in Jerusalem."

His brother poked his head between the seats. He brought his face close to mine, his eyebrows raised, staring with his wide eyes, like his father's were as a kid. He asked me the last, last, last, last question.

"Jerusalem? Where's that?"

***

11:30 p.m.

Present Day

"You're sure that he told Khala Aisha that he was craving mutabbaq samak?" Hawraa asks, staring as if there is something catastrophic in that detail. I nod my head. I continue where I left off.

"Sadiq told him to hold on, saying, 'We're just getting started!' Fahd apologized, using Aisha's worry as an excuse. And so that his mother could finally go to bed. As soon as we had crossed the road, we became aware of two groups of young men on the dusty plot where we had left our cars. Seven. Eight. Maybe ten. I don't remember. When leaving the park, I felt like I was ten years old again, and that these guys had gathered to set off fireworks to celebrate the successful first day of the cease-fire. Most of them were adolescents and the rest in their mid-twenties. Older maybe, by a bit. I tried to make out their faces. The weapons in their hands could only mean bad news. Sadiq and Fahd headed for their cars, while I stood watching what was going on.

"An argument broke out between two of the young men. 'You unbeliever.' 'Damn you. You Rafidi.' 'You Nasibi. You all . . .' We . . .

it quickly escalated to clubs, daggers, and empty bottles. I turned to Fahd and Sadiq, urging them to do something. Anything. Was I wrong, Ayub? Fahd was in his car. After he turned on the engine, he put down the window and said, 'They're idiots!' Sadiq opened his car door, too, intending to get in. I yelled out to him. He turned to me and said, 'You mean we should die because of a few mice?' I damned both of them silently. I ran toward the group. I plunged into the dust. I yelled, 'The truce, guys, the truce!' You understand my motivation, Ayub. Only you understand. Tell me I was right.

"Fahd's and Sadiq's calls to me, telling me to stop, telling me I was crazy, got louder behind me. I advanced farther into the madness. I pushed one body away from another. I stood between this one and that one. I wiped my face with the back of my hand, getting rid of someone else's spit. 'You Nasibi.' 'I'm not Nasibi.' 'You Rafidi.' 'I'm not Rafidi.' The yells increased. 'Umar. Umar, Umar, Umar.' 'We'll never be humiliated.' 'We'll never be defeated.' Even now I can hear their screams. Don't look at my trembling hands. If you were with me, you'd understand. What happened at dawn today was horrible. Horrible. I was scared. I was scared for . . . for . . . I don't know, but I wasn't scared for myself. You believe me, Ayub, don't you? Hawraa, I . . . I didn't mean to be the reason for the loss of your loved ones. I never thought that things would . . . would . . . one of them smashed my knee with his club. I fell to the ground. He punched me above my left eye. I found myself between Sadiq and Fahd as they dragged me away on the ground. They propped me up against my car. Running, they started back to the crowd. I yelled at them both, understanding the extent of the imminent danger. 'Come back here, you lunatics!' I screamed at them. A young boy ran up to me, screwdriver in hand, with blood gushing from his shoulder. He looked terrified. I felt sorry for him. I steadied my hands on the ground and pushed my body to get up. 'Don't worry. Show me where you're hurt,' I said to him.

"He raised the screwdriver up high. I tried to dodge his blow, but he brought the screwdriver down hard on my lips. The ground shook and I felt dizzy. I remember myself spitting up blood. I coughed, like I was hacking up a rock. The boy jumped into a car. Gunning the engine, he took a sharp turn, and made for my car. He rammed into it before taking off. I could barely stand. My head was spinning. I looked for my friends. I strained, following their voices, with my ears, into a ring of dust. There was no sound other than 'You bastards, you *Kharijites*, you Wahhabis, you Iranians, you pigs!' It was tragic. Religious men, who claimed holiness, were cursing with the vilest words. But the feeling of disaster that paralyzed me had nothing to do with the conflict. The yelling and accusations in Sadiq's and Fahd's voices were why I felt so sickened. One of them was yelling in the face of the other. I leaned my body against my car. I started to slap myself like this. Like this. No, no, harder than that. Like this! Maybe I could wake myself up from the pain that kept me down. Maybe what I was hearing wasn't actually their two voices after all. My body remained heavy, my head spinning. The two of them slipped away from the crowd and kept on fighting. They clashed with their fists. 'Screw your dad!' 'Screw *your* mom!' 'You little shit.' 'You pig.'

"I fought the pain in my knee and dragged my injured leg toward them. My strangled yell tore my throat; my tooth was dangling. 'You bitch, you're with them. You son of a bitch.' 'Enough. Enough, that's it. Fahd! Sadiq!' I heard my voice muffled in my ears, accompanied by a whistle, distancing the voices of the dusty plot. Fahd turned to look at the ground around him. He searched for . . . for a rock. He leaned down and picked up one about this big. No, no. A little bigger.

"Sadiq pummeled Fahd in the back with his fists. I yelled, 'No, no!' Fahd raised his hands up in the air. I was . . . I was running, and jumped over one man. My sandal flew off. It fell onto the ground, with the sole facing upward.

"Ayub. Hawraa. Don't look at me like that. You understand me, Fawzia. I'm . . . I'm an ass, I confess. I stopped to flip over the sandal. I don't know what pushed me to do so. Loyalty to Mama Hissa or fear of the sky falling. I don't know. Then I kept on running but . . . but . . . Fahd had already brought the rock down on Sadiq's head. Maybe his shoulders, I'm not sure. He fell to the ground, his blood drawing a line in the sand. If only I hadn't stopped for the sandal, maybe . . . I remember Fahd, with his arms up high. Then . . . then he took his palms from his head, and he leaned over Sadiq, shaking him. 'Don't you dare die, you bastard . . . Sadiq, Sadiq!' he yelled. I was on my knees, helpless, crying like a child. I cried like I am now. Fahd headed for the street, cursing himself. One of those behind me yelled, 'You son of a whore.' He hit me with something on the back of my head. I don't know what. I remember voices fading out to the sound of car wheels grinding across asphalt outside the park. And the last thing I remember seeing is Sadiq crawling on the dirt toward his car. And a man in a dishdasha in the middle of the road flying in the air. I'm not sure. Maybe it was someone other than Fahd."

"Khala Aisha was in Mubarak Hospital with 'Am Saleh," Hawraa says as tears drown her face. My gaze shifts between her and Ayub, seeking clarification. Hawraa adds in the middle of her weeping, "A car accident in Rawda . . ."

"The closest hospital to Rawda . . . Mubarak Hospital . . . Jabriya," Ayub adds.

Hawraa stands up and, thinking aloud, says, "Khala Aisha came back from the hospital where 'Am Saleh is. She went out a second time with the pot of mutabbaq samak." She yells at the top of her voice, startling her two young ones, "All this and you still don't get it?"

The twins cling to their mother. "Mom . . . where did Dad go? Where did Dad go?"

"What are you all waiting for? Fahd's in Mubarak Hospital!" Hawraa screeches.

THE FOURTH MOUSE: ASHES
THE INHERITANCE OF FIRE

THE NOVEL

The Final Chapter

We were in Rawda, in my diwaniya, looking out on Shahab Ahmad Al Bahar Street. The Abu Hayyan Al Tawhidi sign had been taken down years ago; it had become a new street like so many others. No memory of who we were or had been. I remember that on the day the sign was removed, I recalled the words of Abu Hayyan, which I had memorized in my teenage years: *The stranger who has no name to be mentioned.*

While the twins played on the sidewalk in front of the house, we were preparing for our second peaceful sit-in, "Second Coming," one in a series of sit-ins we had organized in the square opposite the closed parliament building. We were still on a high from the first sit-in the day before, "First Coming." All the news outlets had covered it, making it the talk of the town. Thousands came out despite the cold winter evening, denouncing the statements made by religious extremists online, which led to conflicts in several areas, resulting in the deaths of youths blinded by extremism. After sunset, people gathered in the square. They crowded together like pilgrims on Hajj. Their grumbling rose and fell like the roar of the sea. Women and men. Religious figures, old people, children. On the front lines: the religious figures, poets, actors, singers, and sportsmen that we had idolized as children. The pure zeal of some made them seem young. Others, who had long been out of the public eye or whose health was frail, surprised people by taking part at all. The poor condition we were in as a country motivated them all.

Khalifa Al Waqayan was on his feet in his winter bisht, his arms crossed across his chest, deep in silence. Perhaps some people didn't recognize him, just those who repeated his poetry verses, like us in our radio broadcasts. Not far from him stood Abdulkareem Abdulqader. He was leaning on his son's arm, a fury like no other on his face. People gathered around him chanting his hit song, "Today's Nation." Although Abdulhussain Abdulredha had made us laugh his whole life, he made us cry that day. He seemed tired, sporting a white mustache that we weren't familiar with. His ghutra was an unruly mess on his head. His features were serious, downcast. He leaned against a palm tree, calling out in agony, the timbre of his voice no longer recognizable, "We want to live!" A young man approached him. He kissed his head. He pleaded with him not to be so emotional. Abdulhussain Abdulredha seemed to have thrown himself into a role more tragic than any we had ever seen onstage or on TV. Muayyad Al Haddad sat on the sidewalk nearby, Khalid Al Harban next to him, hands folded under his chin, frowning as he watched the crowds, fear for our future in his eyes. Shortly before our sit-in ended, Mahzouza and Mabrouka showed up, Hayat Al Fahad and Suad Abdullah, in black clothes, each one clasping the hand of the other. They echoed the calls of their friend, the psychiatric ward patient: "The mice are coming . . . protect yourselves from the plague!" And us in the middle of the crowds, each looking at the others, crying. Fahd, Sadiq, Ayub, Dhari, and Hawraa, who called Fawzia on her phone so she could hear the people yelling.

We were recalling the scenes of our first sit-in, while in the diwaniya, as Ayub posted online announcements for the second one. The twins, racing each other, burst into the lounge, their faces ashen. They asked their father about the black bird that had landed on the house's boundary wall. Black feathers, black beak, black legs. Fahd responded, laughing, that it was a *ghurab*. They furrowed their brows. He clarified for them in English: "crow." They shook their heads, no-no. They said that the bird had two round eyes in the middle of its face, a big head, on top of which were two ears like a cat's.

Sadiq couldn't control himself and chuckled at the cat's description, looking pointedly at Fahd. "Children of international schools! At their age, we knew all the birds, those that stay in one place and those that migrate." He smiled and informed the twins that what they had seen was a *boom*. He added, rounding his lips, saying it in English, "Owl."

They shook their heads, stretching out their arms taut in front of them, saying, "It's this tall!"

I found myself laughing. "Then it's an *u-qab*. Too bad for you, I don't know how to say that in English."

Ayub's phone rang with a call from the newspaper, while we disagreed on the nature of the black bird. He nodded his head, bug-eyed, and said nothing other than, "You're sure?" His face said that the news was confirmed. He ended the call. "Avenues Mall . . . gone!" He didn't finish what he was saying about the massive bombings that had demolished the sprawling mall, at the height of its popularity. He cut himself off. "It has begun!"

"Rumors! Just rumors!" a livid Fahd yelled at him.

***

Midnight

Present Day

Hawraa mutters prayers, hugging her boys in the back seat. Fawzia is silent. Hissa peers out of the window, fearing the appearance of masked men obstructing our path. The gas indicator flashes behind the steering wheel, letting me know the tank is empty. I ignore it, images of gas stations in flames flash in my mind. I slow down next to a metal fence. "The entrance to Tunisia Street," Ayub reminds me. Smoke still billows from the mountains of rubble, but they are no longer burning. Women and men stand at the entrance, carrying flashlights. Some illuminate the way with their car headlights, while others remove the stacked tires, clearing a path for the cars to pass to Jabriya despite the curfew.

The faint light from Mubarak Hospital reveals unprecedented numbers of corpse-catchers. The area around the hospital is choked with cars. We all get out except for Hawraa, whose legs can't carry her. "I'm scared." Ayub supports her as the twins guide Fawzia. I hold Hissa's hand, and all of us proceed to the gate. Young men block the big black birds from entering. They carry spears like those we would carry when out for al qumbar. We have barely passed through the hospital gate, protected by the young men, when Hissa slips her hand out from mine. She dashes into the chaos. I call out to her as she walks past the wounded individuals splayed out on the floor. I follow her with my eyes. She disappears. The waiting room around the reception desk has become an emergency operation theater. I search for the young girl. I find her hugging a young man with a swollen face. His leg is wrapped in a cast. Two men prop him up.

She yells out, "Dad! Dad!" The man's face lights up. He bends down to hug the girl. He takes off his glasses, wiping away tears. He grabs her shoulders, examining her. Returning her hug, he asks about her two sisters. She reassures him, "They're fine . . . with the neighbors." Hawraa looks at her two children and joins in the bout of crying. Ayub calms her down, saying that the two boys should get to see their father. I advance toward a man in a Red Crescent uniform at the reception desk. I ask him about the patient Saleh Al Bin Ya'qub. Hawraa raises her voice behind me. "Fahd! Fahd Saleh Al Bin Ya'qub." The man shifts his gaze between us.

"Saleh or Fahd?" he asks.

"Both," I answer.

He taps on his computer keys. "Saleh is in the basement, observation unit, general room 4." Hawraa rests her hands on the counter, her ears pricked up. The man continues his search. "Fahd . . . sixth floor, private room 12." Hawraa bends over and grips her knees. She doesn't say a word. Her body tilts. Ayub rushes to steady her. Yelling at the nurses, he demands a wheelchair.

"Fahd's on the sixth floor," I tell him. He nods his head.

I run, climbing the stairs, ignoring the throbbing in my knee. The first floor. Third. Fourth. My run returns to heavy limping in the hallway of the sixth floor. An old kitchen smell, combined with that of disinfectants. I pause at the door of room 12, preparing myself for certain pain. I fill my chest with breath as if it were my last. I slowly push the

door open. Aisha is in her abaya, sitting on a chair facing the bed. She
holds her phone in one hand, directed at Fahd. She might as well be
a statue. The man spread out on the bed isn't the Fahd that I know. A
dark-blue stain rings his eye. His lips are swollen, his mouth toothless.
Parts of his head are shaven, interrupted by stitches of surgical thread.
His chest is exposed, covered with medical sensors. A yellow tube comes
out of his body, its liquid collecting in a bag hanging behind the bed.
A red tube goes into one of his veins, replacing what had flowed out
onto the Rawda asphalt. And because I have prepared myself for worse,
I readily accept this picture of Fahd. Aisha is stiff, mute. She observes
her phone screen, her features tight.

"Assalamu alaikum," I whisper.

Nothing moves, except her lips. "Shhh. Fahd's sleeping."

I get closer to the bed. I'm reassured by the rise and fall of his
chest and his slow breathing. His finger is hooked up to the wire of the
upright device next to him, which produces an intermittent beep, color-
less. Its screen shows wavy lines that I'm unable to decode, but they're
reassuring nonetheless.

Fahd mumbles in a feeble voice, his eyes closed, "Dear listeners . . .
I welcome you to a new episode of the *What's New Today* show . . . traa
. . . raa . . . traa . . ." He murmurs the tune to one of Abdulkareem's
songs, green music that he usually finds refuge in during the breaks
of his show. Then he goes silent, descending into sleep, snoring. The
intermittent beep of the machine becomes a continuous tone. Its red
sound unnerves me. The wavy lines become one long horizontal line.
I shake his body.

His mother rebukes me. "The boy's sleeping!" She indicates with
her eyes the wire that has come undone from his finger. She puts her
phone to one side. She grabs her son's finger and fastens it once more
to the wire. The red tune is silenced. The machine resumes its intermittent beeping, and the wavy lines come back on-screen, measuring
heartbeats and things I don't understand. Aisha resumes taking photos

with her phone. I ask her what the doctor said. She answers without shifting her eyes from the phone screen. "Shhh . . . the boy's asleep." I look around me. A pot of food covered with foil sits on top of the small fridge in the corner of the room. I stand behind her, peering down at her phone. Fahd appears on the screen. I shift my gaze between Fahd on the bed and Fahd on the phone screen, its button flashing red. Her actions unsettle me.

"Khala Aisha," I call out to her.

"Shhh!" She cuts me off. My friend opens his eyes slowly. In disbelief, looking at his mother, he asks her what she is doing. She answers, the phone in front of her face: "For when you get well. You'll see for yourself and know where the path you've chosen has brought you!"

He lets out a sigh, followed by a smile. A tear flows from his eye. "Are you lying, *yummah*?" He looks at me, his lips as usual in a broken smile. He controls the tone of his voice but can't suppress the gasps chopping up his sentence. "That's it? Sadiq's gone?"

I shake my head. "Sadiq's fine."

His eyes widen. "Where is he? I don't see him with you."

I pat his shoulder. "He's around . . . asking about you."

His toothless smile turns him into an old man. "And Hawraa . . . where's she? I don't see her here with you."

I gesture toward the door. "She's on the way."

He furrows his eyebrows. "Swear."

I point my finger to the sky. "Wallah, by God who raised the heavens."

He closes his eyes and says, "I believe you." His mother is still absent, her phone in front of her as if she's watching a film. "Water," Fahd mumbles in a weak voice. I pour some into a plastic cup. I bring it close to his lips with my other hand behind his head. He barely swallows the first sip. A second sip, and then a vein in his neck quivers. He opens his eyes, with droopy eyelids, and gazes at the door. The intermittent beep of the machine becomes a continuous tone once more. The third sip goes unfinished. A stream of water dribbles from his smiling mouth into my palm. Aisha takes notice. She leaves her phone on the bed. She grabs Fahd's finger, ensuring that the wire is attached properly. The device continues its long tone. The screen shows a fixed horizontal line. The numbers become zeros. She removes the wire and reattaches it, watching the screen. The tone and the screen don't change. She removes the wire again, throwing it on the floor. She clasps her son's wrist. She hits the back of his hand like someone scolding a child. Then she kisses the palm of his hand before resting it on his chest. "Sleep, my darling, sleep," she says and then turns her back to him.

She leaves the room, her pace deliberate, not hurried. My eyes are on the screen, on his finger, on the sensors on his chest, on his eyes fixed to the door. Aisha returns, accompanied by a nurse. The latter doesn't stay long. On seeing the screen and hearing the continuous tone, she runs out immediately. She comes back, a doctor striding ahead of her. She gives Fahd a shot. She plants the needle deep in his vein. She hands the doctor a pair of defibrillators. The doctor removes the sensors from Fahd's chest. He fastens the defibrillators. Fahd's smile is as it was. His eyes remain on the door, despite the electric shocks. "He's with God now," the doctor says.

Fahd's mother disappears into her thoughts before she shakes her head. "You don't understand!" It seems all too familiar to the doctor. He doesn't say a word. Fahd's mother gnashes her teeth. She stares at him. "You're a doctor? I wouldn't trust you with sheep!" She gestures to the door. "Get out!"

He turns to me. "Stay strong," he says, before he turns and follows the nurse out.

Fahd's mother goes to the door to shut it. She removes her abaya and balls it up. She throws it carelessly onto the chair and rolls up her sleeves, determined. She carries the pot of food from atop the fridge and rests it on Fahd's chest, carefully removing the foil. She hands me the pot cover. "Hold this." I hold it and the smell of Tina's old kitchen fills the room. Aisha brings her lips close to her son's ear, whispering, "Fahd . . . darling . . . get up . . . The mutabbaq samak is ready." She dips her hand into the rice in the pot. She tears off a carefully chosen piece of fish. She laughs. She repeats his refrain, *"Meeeeow!"* She brings her hand next to his lips. "Yallah, come on now . . . bismillah." He doesn't move.

My words slip out, contrary to what I know to be true. "Khala . . . Fahd's sleeping."

She nods her head. "I know . . . but he just has to wake up . . . The food's gotten cold, and he likes it hot." She shakes her head, and her eyes are bloodshot. "Hot . . . like my heart," she adds, her voice hoarse. I distance myself from them both. I lean my back on the door to the room. Fahd's eyes are fixed on the door. On me. His mother slips her fingers into his mouth. She raises her voice. "Cat!" She yells at an even higher pitch, *"You* said that you were craving mutabbaq samak!" She shrieks banshee-like, her fingers between his lips. "Eat! Eat! Eat!" She raises her hand, in it the remnant of the rice and oil. She brings it down on his face, slapping him. "You think you can die whenever you feel like it? I'll kill you, I swear to God, I'll kill you if you die and leave me!" She shoves both hands in the pot of rice. She stuffs his mouth. She slaps him. She passes her fingers between the tufts of his hair and pulls at them. His eyes remain fixed on the door. She pushes the pot from his body, and it clangs on the floor. Grabbing him by the neck, she shakes him. She beats his chest with her fists. Resting her head on him, she releases a never-ending groan. A long groan that sends me off to the end of the hall. "My heart is burning!"

I go down the stairs quickly. I fall, faltering with my limp. I curse my leg. I reach the ground floor. Hissa holds my hand. She drags me to her father. I yield to her without realizing it. He extends his hand, introducing himself. "My name is Ibrahim Mansour. Are you Fuada's Kids?" he asks me, his face beaming. I ignore him, proceeding to . . . I don't know what.

"We're sons of bitches," I say audibly. His name reminds me of how my uncle couldn't protect himself from his fate all those years ago.

The twins scamper over to me, clinging to my dishdasha. One of them asks a question. The second repeats the first's question. "Uncle, Uncle! Where did Dad go? Where did Dad go?" Ayub yells out to me, calling me to the entrance of the emergency room. He sits beside Fawzia. I don't look at him. He gets up and follows me.

"How's Fahd?"

"He's eating mutabbaq samak," I answer as we pass the hospital gate. I point my finger upward and say, "Above . . ."

He tilts his head up. "Really?" he asks me, skeptical.

"I swear," I respond as I keep walking. My phone beeps, alerting me to a text: "By God who raised the heavens, if you don't leave Kuwait . . . you're not my son and I don't know you!" I mean to throw the phone far away, but don't when I remember a voice that I miss, a voice whose owner I left behind me, upstairs in the hospital room. My fingers work of their own accord on the phone's buttons. I bring the phone close to my ear. *I'm not available at the moment. Please leave a message.* I hear Abdulkareem's voice as I make my way to my car. *Go with forgetfulness . . . and I'll go with Canopus.*

I fling the phone on the ground. Ayub picks it up. He follows me. He closes my car door for me. He pokes his head through the window, asking, "Where to?" I turn on the engine, my lips taut. He turns around, jogging to open the passenger side door. He sits next to me. I step on the gas as I imagine the heads of people I hate. I drive at top speed, my headlights off.

Ayub knows. Ayub understands. "The bridge?" he asks as if he's answering himself.

There isn't anyone at the green-flagged barrier at the start of the bridge in Jabriya. I continue, driving slower. Hundreds of corpse-catchers circle around in our Stygian sky. Their collective cawing eggs me on to violently extinguish their desire. To satiate their hunger. I open the compartment under my elbow. I hand Ayub an Um Bint cologne bottle. He dabs some on his finger. He passes it between his nose and lips, taking in a deep breath. I hold out my palm to him. He pours some of the golden liquid in it. I rub it on my face. Weapons lie strewn on the ground, like the remains of a battlefield. Screams get louder and closer. I continue driving at a snail's pace. I make out, before the middle of the bridge, what the fires of the burning barrels reveal. I flick on the headlights. A conflict between "them" and "them." With swords, Molotov cocktails, and stones. I continue driving, accelerating.

Ayub spurs me on. "Faster! Faster!" he yells. I crash into the monsters. I put an end to their fighting. Bodies scatter on both sides of the bridge. Others raise their swords and stones, running after us. Ayub turns and glances behind. "Quickly! Quickly!" he yells. At the end of the bridge, at the black-flagged roadblocks in Surra, the roar of the engine fades to a sputter, then dies out. It gives up. The engine is running on fumes. Ayub opens the door. He turns to the beings on the bridge, sheer terror written on his face. "Get out! Run!" I get out, hobbling on my wounded leg to the head of Tariq Bin Ziyad Road. I get rid of my sandals. I don't turn to look at them. I run. Ayub is in front of me. They're chasing us, the black birds watching them, their caws melodious. Ayub slows down. He grabs my hand. We run together. Each of us yells to the other, "Run! Run! Run!"

He runs, I run, under a sky I wish for once would fall. Drops on my face compel me to look up. I see, among the scattered clouds, Shail's star breaking forth in the distance, and Shuhab's cutting across the horizon . . .

It starts to rain.

About the Author

Saud Alsanousi is a Kuwaiti novelist and journalist born in 1981. He won the International Prize for Arabic Fiction for *The Bamboo Stalk* in 2013, and *Mama Hissa's Mice* was nominated for the 2016/17 Sheikh Zayed Book Award. His first novel, *The Prisoner of Mirrors*, was published in 2010 and won the fourth Laila al-Othman Prize, a prestigious award for novels and short stories by young writers. He also won first prize for his story "The Bonsai and the Old Man" in the July 2011 Stories on the Air competition organized by *Al-Arabi* magazine with BBC Arabic. In October 2016, the Gulf Cooperation Council presented Alsanousi with the Contribution to Literature Award in Riyadh. His work has appeared in a number of Kuwaiti publications, including *Al-Watan* newspaper and *Al-Arabi*, *Al-Kuwait*, and *Al-Abwab* magazines. He currently writes for *Al-Qabas* newspaper.

About the Translator

Sawad Hussain is an Arabic translator and litterateur who is passionate about all things related to Arab culture, history, and literature. She has regularly critiqued Arabic literature in translation for ArabLit and Asymptote, among others; reviewed Arabic literature and language textbooks for *Al-'Arabiyya Journal* (Georgetown University Press); and assessed Arabic works for English PEN Translation grants. She was coeditor of the Arabic-English portion of the seminal, award-winning *Oxford Arabic Dictionary* (2014). Her translations include a Palestinian resistance classic by Sahar Khalifeh for Seagull Books and a Lebanese young adult novel for University of Texas Press. She holds an MA in Modern Arabic Literature from the School of Oriental and African Studies.